SOUND OF MADNESS

MARIA LUIS

He is my ruin.
My complete and utter devastation.
Loyalty or death.

I make my choice in a palace of flames,
and wake to total darkness . . .

And at his mercy.

Calloused hands bring hell to my door and
his velvet voice spews only poison.

"A traitor to the queen," he calls me, and though I don't know his
name, it's clear that he's no Prince Charming.

Monster.
Villain.
A man who demands that I take it all—and submit.

But no one will ever mistake me for a damsel in distress.

He wants me on my knees, but it won't be me who breaks.

Only, falling for the most hated man in
England was not the plan.

If war is hell, then love is carnage,
and the blood that's spilled belongs to us both.

PLAYLIST

"Born Alone Die Alone" — Madalen Duke

"That's Just Life' — Memphis May Fire

"Popular Monster" — Falling In Reverse

"Go To War" — Nothing More

"Vultures" — Asking Alexandria

"Blackheart" — Thomas Bergersen (Two Steps From Hell)

"Lady of the Dawn" — Peter Gundry

"Firestorm" — Audiomachine

"Dark Rider" — Audiomachine

"Till Death Do Us Part" — Audiomachine

"Between Good and Evil" — Audiomachine

"See What I've Become" — Zack Hemsey

"Light of the Seven" — Ramin Djawadi

"Destiny of the Chosen" — Immediate

"Lívstræðrir" — John Lunn & Eiør

Sound of Madness (Broken Crown, Book 2)
Maria Luis

Cover Photographer: Wander Book Club Photography
Cover Model: Zach B.
Cover Designer: Najla Qamber, Najla Qamber Designs
Interior Formatting: Nada Qamber, Najla Qamber Designs
Editing: Kathy Bosman, Indie Editing Chick
Proofreading: Horus Proofreading

To those who live in the dark,
I see you.

And to Liane,
knowing you was a gift.

Good job, honey.

CHAPTER 1

Flames nip at my heels and smoke incinerates my lungs.

I should flee.

Should run as far away as my feet can carry me—but I'm a fool. A loyal fool who values a twenty-year-old friendship over my own life, no matter the fact that Buckingham Palace is on *fire*.

"*Margaret!*"

I barely manage five steps down the corridor when the window to my left shatters. Shatters and splinters, shards of glass exploding, and I hurl myself to the ground, arms shielding my head, back rounded to take the brunt of the pain should it come.

And it does.

Like wrathful raindrops of hell that shred my flesh.

A cry wrenches from my throat, and my vision shimmers with unshed tears. It would be so easy to remain as I am. To become one of the dead, like the scores of others who won't escape the palace tonight.

But I'm . . . I'm—

Crawling.

Crawling on my hands and knees, crawling through a sea of broken glass, crawling toward the queen. My best friend. The only person I call family.

Get up, Rowan. Get up!

I grit my teeth and push to my feet.

It hurts to breathe, hurts even more to move, and still I sprint toward Margaret's rooms. Up the narrow stairwell, where dark, billowing smoke twines like vine around my legs. Down the next corridor, where I pass empty room after empty room, the doors swung open, the occupants having already fled. No one returned for Margaret.

No one except for me.

A quick glance to my left reveals fire licking at the windows. Those flames flicker, climbing higher and higher, until the night sky disappears behind a terrorizing swarm of orange and red and yellow. One wrong step, one wrong move, and the last memory I'll have is the scent of burning flesh.

I cut around the next corner—and grind to a halt.

A hard body sits slumped outside Margaret's door, legs splayed crookedly, head drooped forward. I know him instantly. That mop of messy blond hair. Those familiar military-style trousers.

"Clarke?" His name is a strangled sound on my tongue. "*Clarke!*"

Demolishing the distance between us, I collapse to my knees beside him. Grab him fiercely by the shoulders and shake. Blood thrums in my temple and my chest cleaves in two when his hand drops from his thigh to the floor.

Palm up. Fingers loosely curled.

Utterly and completely lifeless.

"No. Clarke, *no.*"

With trembling hands, I grasp his face, lifting gently, and meet unblinking hazel eyes.

Horror slithers through my veins, slow and lethal, until the suffocating sweat drenching my skin becomes only ice. Ice that splinters, ice that cracks, because it's not the bodyguard's blank stare that snares my attention, but the ring-sized hole marking the center of his forehead.

Nausea swirls as I stagger backward and land unceremoniously on my arse. *Look away!* But there's no wrenching my gaze away from the blood trickling into one blond brow and smearing the bent bridge of his nose.

Buckingham Palace is caught up in an inferno and someone *murdered him*. And Margaret—

"Oh, God."

Someone knew only Clarke stood in the way of reaching Margaret, and if a man like Clarke can fall . . . I don't stand a chance.

I'm defenseless. Weaponless.

He isn't.

Reluctantly, my gaze sweeps over Clarke's limp frame. *Just do it.* Remorse burns in my lungs as I inch up his shirt and snag the pistol from the holster at his hip—the gun that I've never seen him without, in all the time that I've known him.

"I'm so sorry," I whisper raggedly, hastily tucking his shirt back down before reaching for his hand. Head bowed, I fold one atop the other over his stomach. He didn't deserve this.

No one deserves this.

Fighting back despair, I cut my stare to the floor, only to spy blood staining the rug, leading opposite the way I had come.

Either Clarke managed to wound his attacker or . . .

Don't go there. Don't you dare go there.

With Clarke's pistol clamped between my hands,

I follow that trail of red down the hall, around the next corner, until, finally, I stop before a darkened stairwell.

My finger finds the trigger.

The sole of my shoe hits the first rung, and I grimace when the wood whines beneath me.

I glance down, over the smooth banister, and debate how long I have until the flames reach this floor. Even now, I can hear windows shattering. *Crack! Crack! Crack!* Each one louder, closer, until the implosions match the frenetic stutter of my heartbeat.

One step down, then another.

"Margaret?"

Then, so faint I nearly miss it: "Rowan . . . I-I'm here!"

My feet move of their own accord, the gun steady in my grip. And then I see her, the woman who's always felt more like a sister than a friend—and my worst fear is confirmed.

"You've been shot," I breathe.

Half-slouched on the stair rung above her, with her hands pressed to her bloodied abdomen, Margaret offers a weak laugh. "Tell me something I don't know."

"Clarke—"

"That I know," she whispers, jerking her face away before I can see emotion ripple across her features. But I know her too well—just as she knows me—and her grief is palpable. Absolute. "I know."

I'm so sorry.

The words beg to be free, but now isn't the time to give them life. Instead, I dart forward and snake my arm under hers. Despite the heat enveloping the palace, her skin is frigid. I swallow tightly. "We need to get you to a hospital."

"No." She plants a feeble hand on the curved wall. "The palace . . . take me to the palace."

"Mags," I mutter, biting back a pained hiss when she

loops an arm around my back and catches the particles of glass still lodged in my skin, "if we stay, we'll be dead. Now please just—"

She slides out of my grasp, her body pitching forward. "—*Margaret!*"

My fingers grasp the back of her shirt, but it's not enough to defy gravity.

We tumble forward together.

Elbows crashing against stone, knees dragging and rolling over my shoulder. Clarke's handgun slips from my grip, clattering somewhere out of sight. And then my head bashes against the wall, and I roll once more, landing on my back with a *thud* that drives the air from my lungs.

Fuck me, everything *hurts*.

Arching my spine to relieve the stinging pressure, I claw onto all fours and get no farther than my elbows and shins. My forehead greets the wooden stair rung as I drag in deep gulps of air. The grain of the wood is slick with something that smells suspiciously like blood. No doubt my own.

Focus. I need to *focus*.

"Mags?" On trembling limbs, I drag myself over to the balustrade and peer down the stairwell. "*Mags!*"

She's face-down, her white-blond hair a near ash-brown in the dim light, her arms splayed wide.

My heart lurches.

We need to flee. We need to *run*. But when I finally reach her side and ease her onto her back, her face is devoid of color and her lips part on jagged, uneven breaths. Dazed blue eyes find mine.

"The palace," she whispers again.

I choke back a wretched laugh. "We're here!" I wave my arm at the empty stairwell, frustration sharpening my tone. "We're already bloody here, and we're going to die here if we don't move. So please just let me—"

"In Sevenoaks," she utters on a battered breath, her fingers circling my wrist, "the Palace. Take me . . . take me to the home with the drawbridge and t-the moat."

A . . . *moat?*

I tip my head back and stare at the ceiling, two stories above us. Hopelessness sits like a shroud upon on my shoulders. Margaret is delirious and in no shape to walk anywhere, and I'll never leave her to suffer alone. Sisters, always, no matter our lack of shared blood. Which means . . . this is it.

This is the end.

I don't know what it says about me that instead of blind panic, all I feel is the sting of relief.

God knows my father won't mourn the loss of me, and Mum—well, I suppose this is a rather fitting end.

Like mother, like daughter.

Both Carrigan women swept away in a blaze hot enough to smother our screams forever.

"Holyrood."

"What?" Startled, my gaze snaps to Margaret's ashen face. "You want to go to *Edinburgh?*"

Offering a weak shake of her head, her blue eyes slide shut. "Not Scotland. Bring me to Holyrood," she breathes, panic prompting the words from her faster, more urgently, "bring me to the Godw—"

"We won't make it."

"I saved you. I saved you—remember? S-Sevenoaks," she repeats with a desperate squeeze of her fingers around my wrist, "the house with the . . . moat. Take me there."

My throat goes dry. "We're going to die. You know that, right?"

She answers, softly, "I know."

We both know.

She's bleeding out and I'm five steps away from losing consciousness, and still I shove myself to my feet and pull her up until she's half-balanced against me. Debilitating pain erupts across my body, like sharp-edged knives dancing over the pearls of my spine.

Stay strong. Do not *fall.*

I glance over the banister—at the two remaining flights of stairs that I'll need to haul Margaret down. She may be a queen, but she's as mortal as I am.

We won't leave Buckingham Palace alive, that I know deep in my soul.

But twenty years after Margaret saved me from my childhood home going up in flames, I finally repay my debt. I carry her, I stumble with her, and as we face down a wall of fire that reminds me of the nightmares that plague me, even now, I curse her, too.

She and I both know that I would have rather died in that stairwell.

CHAPTER 2

DAMIEN

"Where do you think you're going?"

My stride slows, then stops altogether.

Seven months. Seven fucking *months* of hearing that voice ask me the same damn question, over and over and over again. My fingers itch to pummel his face, to rip out his tongue. Rendering him mute really shouldn't spark as much joy as it does.

Then again, my mum always said that I was born with war in my blood.

She wasn't wrong.

Turning away from the Palace's front door, I raise my gaze until I spot Jude Calvin on the upper gallery of the great hall.

"Didn't hear me the first time?" he asks, leaning casually against the centuries-old banister. He drops his elbows to the dark, glossy wood. "I said, where the bloody hell do you think you're going?"

The weight of the holstered gun at my lower back is pure temptation.

I could have Jude swinging from that banister in seconds. Chest oozing blood, eyes forever sightless. He wouldn't stand a chance and I wouldn't mind the cleanup. Hell, I'd welcome it.

Sweet, fucking *temptation*.

I angle my chin, keeping him in my direct line of sight. "You ever get tired of hearing the sound of your own voice?"

"Do you ever get tired of trying to *run*?"

Running would imply that I'm scared—and that couldn't be further from the truth. I stay because it keeps Holyrood unnoticed, the way it's been for over a century. The way it'll stay long after I'm dead, when my ashes are scattered over the ruins of Holyrood Abbey in Edinburgh like all who've come before me.

In the interim, I remain a traitor to the queen.

The man who infiltrated Parliament. The snake slithering within Britain's midst.

If I weren't on the verge of losing the last threads of my sanity—of becoming the wild beast the world thinks me to be—I might feel honored by all the attention. Flattered, even.

Or maybe you feel that way because you've already descended into madness.

"Nothing to say?" Jude drawls, smirking. "The Priest brother most likely to share his opinion—*silenced*. Never thought that I'd see the day."

My lips spread in a thinly provoking smile. "Nothing to say when I don't see anything worth commenting on."

Jude doesn't miss the insult.

The smirk evaporates as he jabs a finger in my direction. "You better not be thinking about going to London or I'll—"

"We've been over this, Calvin. I don't answer to you."

"According to your brother, you do. And Guy told me not to let you leave the Palace—dead queen or not."

My nostrils flare.

As a spy for the Crown, Jude should have been first in line to rescue Queen Margaret from Buckingham Palace. Instead he'd hovered by my side while Guy had rattled off assignments, inspecting his nails before murmuring, "Looks like yet another day will pass before you get to play the hero again. How does it feel being universally despised?"

Like I've waited my entire life to fulfill a destiny my mother predicted from birth.

Fucking prick.

"Instead of worrying about me, you should have gone to London."

Jude raises a brow. "Matthews is here, too. So is Paul."

"Matthews is a surgeon," I growl tightly, "and he needs to prep the OR. As for Paul—"

"The thing about keeping an eye on you, Priest," he cuts in with mock gravity, pushing away from the railing to move toward the spiral staircase, "is that it's a two-person job. You rarely do what you're told."

Like a dog, I'm expected to piss, shit, and sleep where directed.

I may stay out of obligation but I don't do it eagerly. In Guy's attempt to save me, he's only managed to trade one prison cell for another. My bars are the Palace's sixteenth-century walls, my chains a metaphorical collar that no one—especially not my oldest brother—intends to remove anytime soon.

I've become the king of the damned.

"We both know how this works," Jude murmurs, stepping down from the stairwell. "I tell you to heel, you sit. I tell you to run, and you bloody sprint. And if I tell you that you won't be going to Buckingham Palace to save the queen, who's more than likely already dead, anyway, then you'll fucking *stay*."

Irritation festers beneath my skin.

Seven months.

Jude's shoes clip against the ancient tiles.

One step.

Two.

"Don't tell me that the cat's got your tongue." His mouth twists with anticipation, like there's nothing he enjoys more than seeing a Priest—a *Godwin*—backed into the proverbial corner. "And here Paul thought we were going to have a big problem on our hands tonight. You know, considering that you've been kept here against your will and all."

My feet remain rooted in place.

"But"—that sneer hardens—"I told him that the fight's gone out of you, that we have nothing to worry—"

The words stutter into silence the second my gun kisses his forehead.

His eyes go wide.

Mine only narrow.

"Pulling the trigger," I murmur coolly, "would be the highlight of my year."

"You wouldn't."

I fit my finger over the polymer lever. "There's really not much I wouldn't do."

"If you kill me, your brother—"

"Won't give you a bloody thing. No other reason you'd be crawling up my ass unless he promised you something." I stroke the trigger, a gentle, loving caress that turns Jude's gaze cross-eyed. "So?" I prompt, voice low. "How much are we talking?"

His hands flex down by his sides as though there's nothing he'd like more than to stab me in the gut. Not that he can when he's clearly unarmed.

His mistake.

There's no one here to stop me. He knows it as well as I do. Matthews is on the other side of the Palace, prepping the operating room, and Paul is no doubt squirreled away somewhere, still nursing his wounded shoulder from when I stabbed him three weeks ago.

"Cat got your tongue, Calvin?"

His dark eyes narrow into slits. "*Don't* mock me."

My finger never wavers, and the muzzle never retreats from his pale skin. If he were smart, he'd swing out a leg and kick me in the knees. Turn the tables around so that I'm the one begging for life. He won't though. Jude Calvin should never have been allowed to take Holyrood's oath, and I'd be doing us all a favor by ending his contract here and now.

"Damien . . ." Warily, Jude's gaze darts from my face to the gun. "You can't *actually* shoot me. You know that, don't you? It's against the—"

"Get the hell out of my sight," I clip out, then turn away.

I anticipate the counterattack as soon as I hear the air sing.

Balancing on the balls of my feet, I evade his swinging fist with a sharp twist of the waist. My fingers snag the material of his shirt, and then he's flying forward, stumbling over his feet, and crashing down onto his hands and knees. The sole of my heavy boot lands on the center of his spine, and—*crack!* his chin collides with the tiled floor.

"Jesus," he groans, hands splayed out on either side of his head. "Get the *fuck* off me."

Without remorse, I dig my heel into the bones of his back as I holster my gun.

"I'll tell him." Jude's lungs wheeze with a harshly drawn inhale. "I'll tell Guy that you've tried to kill me twice now.

D'you hear me?"

Dark laughter reverberates in my chest. "You go ahead and do that."

Lifting my foot, I wait for Jude to rise before ruthlessly driving him back down. No mercy. Wasn't that what Mum whispered to me minutes before she died? *You are a weapon*, she'd said, *and you will be shown no mercy when they come to destroy you.* If the last number of months has proven anything, it's that. I've been hunted by the Met—by its bastard police commissioner Marcus Guthram—and even here, in my own home, I'm hunted.

Chained.

Collared.

No fucking mercy.

Fisting the back of Jude's hair, I snap his head up, so that he has no choice but to look at me. "Stop me from leaving one more time," I mutter, jerking him closer with my foot propped on his spine to stretch his neck, "and you'll be lucky if you ever piss again without a catheter."

Fury bleeds from his gaze.

Too bad that I don't give a damn.

I leave him sprawled on the floor.

Holyrood has bigger problems than Jude Calvin, starting with the fact that no one ought to have been able to breach Buckingham Palace's security. Cameras positioned in every hallway. Fingerprint-activated sensors on every doorknob leading into the queen's apartments. If an unlicensed hand so much as brushed one, they'd receive the shock of a lifetime. The wiring was dialed with enough voltage to initiate instant cardiac arrest—and someone bypassed *all* of it.

I wrench open the heavy oak door, its hinges squealing with age and regret. Guy told me to remain at the Palace, but if Saxon were here, he'd understand. We were raised to put the Crown above all else.

If war is in my blood, then Holyrood is embedded in my bones.

The wooden planks of the drawbridge groan beneath my feet. Heavy fog conceals the moat, just as it shelters the surrounding forest and swallows the stars. The first time Pa brought me and my brothers here, to the Palace, he convinced us all that ghosts haunt the property.

Nowadays, I know better.

The living are the monsters that the dead could never be.

Shadows tunnel my vision, but the crunch of gravel snaps my attention to the darkness enveloping the front drive—unmistakably footsteps, but none that are familiar. If it were anyone from Holyrood, they'd be running—either because they had the queen, and she was injured, or because she was dead, and we'd all failed her.

I reach for my firearm.

Cock my head when I hear another rustle of gravel.

The hairs on the back of my forearms stand tall, but my heart doesn't hammer with fear. Seven months of being locked away hasn't erased the familiarity of dancing with the devil. A dance that I once welcomed with reckless abandon.

Weapon raised, I prowl across the drawbridge on silent feet.

Come out, I ache to purr, *come out, wherever you are.*

A snapping twig draws me forward.

A smothered hiss strokes adrenaline down the length of my spine.

Let me see you.

My eyes adjust to the night, tracking the curve of a tall bush and then, finally, a figure emerging from the fog.

No, not emerging but *dragging*.

Doubled in half, a hand clutched at its middle, it creeps forward with a distinct limp that renders me momentarily motionless. A hand shoots out to grasp the bush as though praying for stability, but the branch doesn't hold. It yields with a *snap!* just as the figure teeters.

"Don't move."

Labored footsteps inch closer.

"One more step," I say, my tone thick with warning, "and I'll put a bullet in your head."

"Please." That voice—feminine, raspy, *pained.* "P-please. Are you—"

"Your name."

"Holyrood," she says instead, the second syllable breaking on a fragile gasp, "I'm l-looking for Holyrood. *Please.*"

If there was moonlight, I'd demand that she reveal herself. But she's nothing but shadow, nothing but a strange woman appearing on our front lawn in the middle of the night, all while asking about a secret agency that she should know nothing about.

"Give me," I growl, "your name."

"Rowan." The name teases forth a memory, but I barely have time to grasp it with both hands before she exhales on a shattered breath, "Rowena Carrigan . . . and I have the queen."

And then she falls, hands meeting gravel on a broken cry, and the fog—and the moat—swallow her whole.

CHAPTER 3

ROWENA

'm being flayed alive.

Razors scour my flesh, digging, prodding, *scraping*. My back bows.

Lips part on a strangled cry.

And then a calloused hand fits against my bare shoulder and lowers me back down with a firmness that speaks to a lifetime of being obeyed.

"Don't move."

A command I may have heeded, if not for those razors hacking away at my spine, until there's nothing left but the sensation of being butchered. *Stop. Please, stop.* Temples pounding furiously, I fling out an arm and strike something sharp.

Metal crashes to the floor.

"Jesus. She needs—"

"She doesn't need a damned thing, Matthews."

"You bloody well may be a genius, but you're not the doctor here. I am." Metal meets metal with a startling clang. "And I'm telling you, she needs to be sedated."

"No," I gasp, slicking my tongue along the dry roof of my mouth. "No more."

Matthews curses under his breath. "She shouldn't be awake. Not yet. Give it here, Godwin, before I string you up by your bollocks."

"I'd like to see you try."

Steel cloaked in velvet. That voice belongs to the sort of man who baits you to the edge of a cliff with nothing but a husky purr and a curve of his lips before hurling you into the swirling waters below. Even now, I feel the crash of the waves threatening to pull me under, to drag me so deep where no hope exists.

Godwin, Matthews called him.

The irony isn't lost on me.

In this moment, with my naked back exposed to a pair of strangers, my fate is in the hand of God.

"The sedative," Matthews persists, "give me the blasted sedative before she realizes what she's lost."

Lost?

I lift my head from the thin pillow cushioning my cheek and open my eyes.

A blanket of night greets me. No shadows. No stream of sunlight pouring into the room. There's nothing but the uneven hitch of my breathing and the faint beeping of a machine off to my right and the startling realization that something is very, very wrong.

My pulse skips.

"Hold her down." *Godwin.*

My lungs shatter as I draw in great gulps of air.

"Didn't I tell you?" *Matthews.* "She's not read—"

"I can't see." Panic crawls under my skin as I pitch forward, evading grasping hands. My legs tangle with the sheets. Arms flail outward, reaching, reaching, *reaching.* But there's nothing, no one, but the blanket of night that dredges terror from the depths of my soul. "*I can't see!*"

"Miss Carrigan—"

A gentle hand finds my arm but not my flesh. There's something there, something between me and the surgeon. Overwhelmed, I push away. Twist my body around until my knee accidentally slips from the table and I'm teetering into oblivion.

Darkness descends and gravity wins.

I fall, hurtling toward the unseen ground.

Calloused hands catch me, roughened fingers digging into the bare skin of my aching back. The razors—the *glass*. From Buckingham Palace and the shattered windows. Heat flares everywhere Godwin touches, and I grit my teeth to keep from screaming. They must have been removing the shards of glass from my skin, and the fire . . . the *fire*—

Those fingers move south, leaving a trail of agony in their wake, before clutching my waist.

My feet graze the floor for barely a second before I'm effortlessly lifted onto the table, legs dangling over the edge, fingers finding the outside of my thighs, like a child about to be scolded or, worse, like an invalid who can't be expected to do anything on her own.

I can't see.

Godwin hovers just out of reach, and even though he no longer touches me, I can *feel* the disdain physically vibrating from his body. It clenches like chains wrapped around my throat, suffocating the air from my lungs as I desperately try to gather my bearings. He expects me to crack, to shatter like ancient glass. And bloody hell, I want to do just that. I want to claw at my eyes and crawl out of my skin. I want to tear out of this room, only to fall to my knees and let the tears spill free.

I spent years dying under the thumb of my father, only to become *this*.

Imprisoned by my own body.

Fighting the urge to laugh hysterically, it takes all my strength to turn in the direction where I think Godwin stands and pull myself together. *No weakness here,* I want to hurl in his face, even as bleakness grips my heart. *I will not break—not for you, not for anyone.*

"The queen," I rasp. "Is she—"

"Alive." It's Godwin who responds. There's no audible relief in his voice, though my ears catch a certain lilt in his vowels that I can't quite place. A hint of an accent buried so deep that it's nearly undetectable. "She's lucky."

I swallow, roughly. "She was shot."

"And came out of surgery quite well, all things considered," Matthews says from my left. "It's you we've had to worry about, Miss Carrigan."

Me.

The glass entrenched in my back.

The fire that ravaged my skin.

The wooden beam that fell, seconds before I ushered Margaret from the palace, and took me down with it. I remember heaviness clamped across my middle, flames dancing so close that their fiery breath teased my hair and face, before I somehow managed to shove myself free.

Charred flesh. Bubbling blisters.

So much *pain.*

I peel my fingers away from my legs and whisper them across my stomach. The roughened texture of medical bandages greets me, proficiently wrapped and revealing nothing about what lies beneath.

But I know.

The same as I know that if I lift my hands to graze my face, I'll find more of those same dressings tucked around my head, over my eyes.

Luck doesn't come twice in a single lifetime, and I've already escaped once unscathed. To hope for a second chance . . . I curl my fingers into a tight fist and lower them to my lap. "Am I blind?"

Silence greets me, as if the two men have stopped to exchange a look.

Dr. Matthews, if he really is a surgeon, clearly thinks the same as Godwin—that I'll break under the weight of the truth. But I've been broken enough times in my life to know that while this pain is unbearable, I've survived worse.

So much worse.

"It's a yes or no question. Yes, I'm blind or no, I'm not."

"Actually, it's more of a wait-and-see." There's a tiny pause, and then Dr. Matthews adds, "You've transient post-traumatic cortical blindness. Most likely from blunt-force trauma, based on the scarring on your skull."

My mouth grows dry. "I don't know what that means."

"There was a case, not that long ago, where a woman fell from a six-story building. She suffered a break in her tibia, as well as calcaneal fractures. Doctors found she had no external injury to the head. Two hours after she was brought to the hospital, she had a complete bilateral loss of vision."

I clutch the table, trying to stave off the swirling nausea. "What does any of this have to do with me?"

"Your eyes were unresponsive when Godwin carried you in. To cut a very long story short, Miss Carrigan, your MRI matches the woman's case study."

"I don't—" Clearing my throat, I angle my face toward Dr. Matthews. "I don't understand. If I've lost my sight, shouldn't it hurt? Shouldn't I feel *something*?"

"The woman experienced no other symptoms, not even headaches. You may, however, see dark streaks across your vision or even floaters. No, no, don't—" He stills my attempt to jump down from the exam table with a hand on my shoulder. "It's alarming, yeah? It will be. It'll be disorienting and require adjustment on your part, but things should clear up."

"Things *should* clear up?" It takes every bit of self-control not to snatch the bandage from my face and throw it to the ground. "Don't you mean that things *will* clear up?"

"That's where the wait and see element comes in. The woman's vision returned to her completely on its own within a matter of days, and I imagine yours will do the same. What's truly a miracle is how you managed to find yourself here at all," Dr. Matthews hums, as if the entirety of my diagnosis is nothing but medical curiosity for him. "With the impacted infarcts in the Broadmann area 17, you shouldn't have been able to—"

"Clarke's car drove on autopilot," Godwin interjects, and I can almost visualize him crossing his arms while he coolly assesses me. "The queen was under firm instruction to come here if anything ever happened to Clarke. There wasn't a damn thing Miss Carrigan had to do besides sit in the driver's seat."

He says *here* as though it's a place of known notoriety.

Last night, I saw nothing of this so-called *palace.* Leaving Margaret in the passenger seat, I'd stumbled from the car in search of the owners. Holyrood, Margaret called them. While she never divulged anything else, it's becoming abundantly clear that these people—these people who also knew Clarke—are in some way tied to the Crown.

Guardians, maybe.

And, if not guardians, then at least allies in a war ripe to explode at any second. Someone killed Clarke, and someone shot Margaret, and someone set Buckingham Palace on fire.

If that's not an act of war, then I don't know what is.

I tilt my head, listening.

Guardian or not, Godwin's voice is a match for the man that I already met. The man who promised to shoot me if I failed to give him my name. And here I am . . . without my sight, without any knowledge of where I am, completely at his mercy.

"Bring me to Margaret."

The air around me thickens at the sound of a single footstep. Heavy, commanding. Deadly. "No."

"You have no right to keep me here."

Another step, and this time Godwin doesn't stop until I feel the texture of soft fabric against my bare knees. Beyond the material lies a land of hard flesh that doesn't so much as twitch when I angle my leg to keep him at a firm distance.

"I have every right," comes his husky, velvet baritone. I feel the grip of the sea at my feet, a tempting seduction to let the current drag me under. And then I'm drowning, those waves sucking me so far deep beneath the surface that I can barely breathe when Godwin's calloused fingers find the table beside mine. "Matthews, leave us."

The surgeon hesitates. "She needs the rest of the glass removed."

"I'll take care of it."

It, not *her*.

No, this man—*Godwin*—has no concept of compassion. Which is only fitting because I've already spent a lifetime of going without. Father taught me that particular lesson the hard way. And if Godwin is anything like Edward Carrigan, then at least I have personal experience on my side.

I'm no pawn to be moved at a whim across a chessboard.

Godwin will learn that soon enough.

"I'll be fine, Dr. Matthews." Ignoring the irrational desire to seek him out, I keep my gaze trained forward. Do I face a window? Medical equipment? Godwin alone? From the way his hands bracket mine, and the alluring scent of cloves that I catch on every inhale, there's no doubt in my mind that I'm face to face with Godwin, for better or worse. "No need to worry."

"Your burns—"

"Have been dressed. Right?"

The surgeon's disgruntled "yes" reveals nothing about their severity. Not bad enough to need a skin graft, yet bad enough to make me wish that I could strip out of my skin. So much for silver linings.

"I'll be back at half past to discuss your next steps," Matthews mutters gruffly. "Godwin, use the sedative if she—"

"Out."

Godwin utters the word with such authority that the surgeon doesn't argue. His harried stride echoes like a death knell as he flees the room, the door clicking shut behind him.

Immediately the fingers resting beside my own disappear.

Godwin brushes past me, and I twist my head to follow the sound of his footsteps. *One, two, three.* He moves so far to the right that rotating my body to such an angle has agony rupturing down my spine. And my ribs . . . bloody *hell.*

Swallowing a whimper, I barely stop myself from pressing a hand to my diaphragm. "I want to see the queen."

"The queen isn't taking visitors."

My heart plummets with a burst of dread. "Dr. Matthews said that she came out of surgery."

"Let me rephrase—she won't be seeing *you*."

The clear-as-day hostility in his voice straightens my spine. "Why in the world wouldn't she see me?"

His answering silence reveals more than a thousand words ever could. Judgment. Disdain. *Suspicion*. Each second that passes, where he leaves me to draw my own conclusions, feels like a lash snapping against bare skin, striking deeper and deeper until I'm raw and floundering. Dr. Matthews may have tended to my injuries, but it's obvious that further kindness won't be coming my way. Not from this man—this *Godwin*.

At the hard clip of his stride, I draw my fingers into a fist. "You told the doctor not to sedate me."

"I need you lucid."

"Why?"

"Interrogations don't work when the guilty party is too drugged up to participate."

Shock has my mouth falling open. "Guilty? There's no way . . . You think that *I'm* the one who shot Margaret?"

"It's up for debate."

"It's ridiculous!"

"Is it?"

That velvet voice comes from behind me now, raising the tiny hairs on my nape. I can't see him, but I *imagine* him—large and ruthless, with broad, heartless features that speak to a lifetime of brute resilience. Dark hair. Cold, dark eyes. Clarke's polar opposite in every single way.

While the good die young, beasts live on forever.

As if he's dived straight into my head to pluck out every one of my thoughts, the beast at my back demands, "How did Clarke die?"

The bold question strikes true, and the visual that follows is nothing less than a nightmare. Clarke's unseeing hazel eyes, the droplets of blood that carved their way down the slope of his nose. The weapon that I took to use as my own, now lost to the flames and to the chaos and to the all-out destruction.

"He was . . ." I swallow past the growing lump in my throat. "He was—"

"He was *what*?"

"Shot," I manage. "He was shot."

"Where?"

Increasingly familiar hands fall upon my shoulders, angling me forward. I can't bear to think about what lies beneath the bandages so tightly wound around me, so I dig my fingers into the table to keep from tipping forward. "The forehead. But I wasn't the one who killed him, so your *interrogation* is completely unwarranted. The queen will tell you exactly what happened. All I know is that I—"

"You weren't on the list."

My lips part. "What list?"

The razor comes again, and though I'm prepared for its sharp edges, a broken moan still escapes. My grip on the table grows desperate, and I link my ankles together to keep them from swinging like a child's.

"What list?" I repeat thickly. *Do not flinch, do not show weakness.* I bite down so furiously on my bottom lip that blood beads on my tongue. "If there's some list I should know about, then tell me."

"Of people allowed access to the queen." Another pluck of glass from my skin. With a hiss, I feel its jagged edges tear free, just as Godwin's thumb smooths over the curve of my shoulder. "She didn't have you listed, but you were at the palace anyway—and on the night that all hell broke loose."

"You can't be serious." I whip around, intending to say

my piece, only to be held immobile when his palm moves to the back of my neck. Unable to shake him off, I gnash my teeth together. "Margaret is my friend."

"And yet she never gave us your name." The razor rakes down my spine, Godwin's hand still damn-near collaring me like a dog. "An alleged best mate decides to spend some quality time and the fucking place goes up in flames. A bodyguard is dead. The queen has been shot. A mysterious killer is out causing havoc, and you—"

A scream rips from my throat, and it has nothing to do with Godwin's ridiculous assumptions and everything to do with the agony enveloping my left shoulder blade. Nausea looms, and though my world remains elusively dark, I slam my eyes shut anyway.

"Stop," I breathe, fingers spasming, "please *stop*."

I'm covered in bandages, and crystallized shards of hell penetrate my back, and my eyes see absolutely nothing, all the while this man—this blasted *bastard*—twines my weaknesses to his advantage and bends my body to his will.

My nails carve indents into the thinly padded table beneath my thighs. "I did not shoot the queen."

"Someone gave you access to her," Godwin says, "and it wasn't me."

"And who are *you*?" Agonizing pain or not, inevitable death or not, I won't let this man do to me what so many others before him have done—run me to the ground, use me for their own gain, steal my light and fortitude.

Never again.

"I don't know you," I hiss from between clenched teeth, "and yet I'm not accusing you of anything. I'll only say this once more: I didn't shoot Margaret. I definitely did *not* kill Clarke. And, in case you're busy coming up with more absurd conspiracy theories, I can promise you that it wasn't

Clarke who tried to take out Margaret either."

Those calloused hands briefly pause on my back before peeling away completely.

"Clarke was her bodyguard."

For the first time since unofficially meeting him, there's hesitation in Godwin's voice. It's subtle, maybe even a bout of wishful thinking on my part. But there's no mistaking the thread of disquiet when he stiffly adds, "*Only* her bodyguard."

Turning my head, I plant my chin on the curve of my right shoulder.

Though I can't see him, I take strange delight in knowing something that the Almighty Godwin doesn't. Only, the delight is extremely short-lived when I think of Margaret in the car as we made our way to Sevenoaks—of the sobs that racked her body. Tears that she didn't shed for herself, or even for me, but for the man I left slumped outside her door.

The man who took his very last breath protecting her.

Quietly, I confess, "She was with Clarke."

"What the hell do you mean she was *with* him?"

"They were together—in every meaning of the word."

Godwin rises, the air between us straining with tension that feels suffocating. *Menacing.* A chill strokes down my spine when he growls, "You're lying."

Ten years ago, I would have trembled before all that anger.

Rowena Carrigan at twenty-three had no courage, no self-respect. A *whore*, my father's friends whispered behind his back—but they could have said it to his face, and he only would have laughed. Because it was through me that Edward Carrigan scaled the ladder of ambition. The charm I wielded like a weapon, the tears I hid, the inner confidence that never lasted more than a handful of hours. Each rung he climbed was on the back of his daughter's defeat.

I've tasted dirt, I've drowned in self-loathing, and though it's clear that I've hit rock bottom all over again, I turn toward Godwin, desperately wishing that I could see the smug look wiped clean from his face, and throw down the metaphorical gauntlet:

"From where I'm sitting, it looks like *you* know nothing at all."

CHAPTER 4

DAMIEN

Clarke and the queen—together.

Bloody fucking *hell*.

I pride myself on knowing every detail about a person—their triumphs, their failures, the secrets they'd move Heaven and Earth to keep under lock and key. No one is off-limits. Not our enemies, not even our allies.

But this . . . *Jesus*.

Clarke never let on, and the damned bastard knew *me* well enough to keep all PDA with the queen hidden away from the security cameras. Cameras which, in the last seven months, have become my only lifeline into Buckingham Palace.

Over a hundred years of serving the royal family, and the lines between Holyrood and the Crown have finally blurred.

Unless Rowena Carrigan is lying.

With my hands planted firmly on the exam table, I piece together my limited memory of her—the smooth, porcelain skin, and the vivid violet eyes, and the hair so deep a shade of black that it encompassed all color— with the woman seated before me now.

That thick mane of hair is gone.

The striking eyes are concealed behind white bandages wrapped around her head.

And her skin, once so perfect, is mottled with blisters from the fire.

Still, she manages to glare down her nose at me like I'm nothing but the grime beneath her shoes.

I'd expect nothing less from the prime minister's only child.

"Does your father know where you were last night?" I ask, keeping my voice purposefully low in a smooth taunt that I know, deep in my gut, will shred that prim composure. *Give me your secrets, Miss Carrigan.* And if she doesn't hand them over, I'll take them, each and every one, until she has nothing left to give. "Or do you spend your days pretending that your old man doesn't want your friend stripped of her crown?"

"Stripped of her . . .?" The muscles in Rowena's upper back flicker as she jerks her head to the side. "Why would you say that?"

"Maybe we both know things that the other doesn't."

"You're wrong," she utters tightly, twisting her broken body around to face mine. "There's no *pretending*. My father has always supported the royal family, and that didn't stop with the king's death. He's loyal to Margaret."

Edward Carrigan is loyal to no one but himself.

It may have been Marcus Guthram who put out the warrant for my arrest, sealing my fate to a life on the run, but it was Rowena's father who appeared from the shadowed wings of the House of Commons to cut me a deal.

Take out the king, he'd said, *and no one will ever know what you've done here tonight.*

And when I told him to shove the offer up his ass,

Carrigan ensured that I would be forever remembered.

The Mad Priest.

The terrorist who stormed Westminster and struck the match of rebellion.

My fingers twine around the thin sheet in a pitiful attempt to ease the rage battering down my veins.

Since that night, I've lived for nothing but vengeance. Against Guthram, who turned on us all and served my head on a platter to the Metropolitan Police. Against Edward Carrigan, who dealt his power like a king, though I could crush his throat with a twist of my fist—if only the chains were cut from my wrists and I could leave this godforsaken house.

And here I've been gifted his daughter.

Now blind. Now ruined. Now *mine*.

A good man would ignore temptation.

A better man would turn Rowena Carrigan over to her father—or to someone, at least, who cares to keep her alive—and wash his hands clean.

But I'm not a good man—not a better man either.

Not anymore.

"My father was best mates with the king," Rowena adds, as though uncomfortable with the lingering silence. "It wouldn't be in his best interest to see Margaret deposed."

"Wouldn't it?" I stare at her, at those bandages that reveal nothing of her expression but the fullness of her mouth and the hollows of her cheeks. I drag my fingers over the sheet, crumpling the fabric within my grip, because it's either that or strike her down. Now, while she suspects nothing. "No king," I say, barely leashing the bite in my voice, "no queen—who'd be left to lead the country?"

That full mouth of hers pulls sharply to one side. "You're speaking *treason*."

"Or just stating the facts."

"You can't just . . . just *imply* that my father wants the throne!"

"I'm not implying a damned thing. Ask yourself what the PM has to gain with the queen dead. There's no other heir, no one to stand in the way of taking what he wants for himself. Maybe some random cousin, further down the line, but who's to say that he wouldn't take them out, too?"

"*Stop.*"

Her hand flies out, and it takes two attempts for her to make contact with the back of mine. Instead of letting go, her slim fingers glide north, linking around my wrist to squeeze tight.

A warning, a silent threat.

I lower my head. Brush my mouth over the shell of her ear. "If you're looking to do permanent damage, you'll have to try harder than that." A dark, victorious smile curves my mouth when she audibly swallows. "I don't bruise easily."

Her nails carve unapologetic half-moons into my flesh. "I don't know what sort of . . . *organization* Holyrood is, but if Margaret catches wind of you claiming that the prime minister wants—"

"What makes you think that she doesn't already know?" Not giving Rowena the opportunity to retreat, I pin her fingers to the table. A shocked gasp breaks from her cracked lips, and then I lean forward and close the gap between us until my breath ghosts over her mouth. "For being the queen's best friend," I murmur, purposely baiting her, "it seems you know nothing at all."

"Don't you *dare* throw my words back in my face."

"Or what? You'll strike me down? Call for backup?" My gaze tracks the thick bandages wrapped around her from breastbone to hip. Between a strained rib and the second-degree burns littered across almost every trace of exposed flesh on her upper body, Rowena Carrigan is the very manifestation of misery—and I don't feel an ounce of pity. "No one is coming to help you, and you've nowhere to run."

"I'm not going to run like a . . . like a *coward*."

"Probably wise," I drawl, "because you wouldn't get very far."

A feminine growl reverberates in her throat.

Too bad she can't see that I'm not even remotely close to shaking in my boots.

It's painfully obvious that Rowena is alone—physically, emotionally. She may claim to be the queen's best mate, and hell, she may have saved the queen's life tonight, but their "friendship" is clearly a one-way street.

Queen Margaret had multiple opportunities to add Rowena to the list that I had her write up, not even a month ago. "*Tell me every person who might need access to you,*" I'd told her, "*and think hard on it.*"

Via Clarke, the queen sent over sixteen names, not a single one of them belonging to the woman seated before me. The same woman whose own father so desperately wanted the king dead that he was willing to enlist a Priest to get the job done.

Fact is, the queen kept this friendship a secret for a reason. If she were her father—ruthless, cunning, albeit a bloody tyrant—I'd say that Queen Margaret concocted a plan to take out her opponent's daughter without ever lifting a finger to do the dirty work herself.

But while she may soon be wishing that she were dead, Rowena Carrigan is still wholly alive. Shattered, maybe. Broken, absolutely. And definitely breathing fire when she snaps, "I may not be able to see you, Godwin, but I know exactly what kind of man you are."

"Enlighten me." Beneath my palm, her hand flexes, her

fingernails turning into claws once again. "What kind of man is that?"

She barely takes a breath before she strikes: "A snake."

The Mad Priest is a snake.

Damien Priest is a snake.

I'm . . . I'm—

Flattening her hand against the table and dragging her close, familiar fury clamping tight around my lungs. "Pretty words for a woman who won't admit that her father would gladly slit her queen's throat."

"A snake," she reiterates swiftly, spitting out the words like she hopes they'll draw blood, "who doesn't like to be left in the dark."

"It's my job to know a person's move before they even think to make it."

"And did you know that Clarke planned to fuck Margaret before he ever dropped his trousers?"

The word *fuck* coming from that mouth of hers should be illegal.

The Rowena Carrigan I remember from researching her father, back before he was elected Prime Minister, was a woman prone to obnoxious giggling and endless bouts of stroking a man's ego. *This* Rowena, however, seems more likely to tear off a man's cock with her teeth—then smile, those same teeth bloodied from her spoils.

She's a goddamn she-wolf.

"It's currency, you know," she says, pulling again on her hand.

Like before, I don't relinquish my grip.

And, like before, I don't rise to her obvious taunt. Maybe she was right to call me a snake. I bait people to my side, then take them out before they can even consider escape. The weapons I've designed, the technology I've created, the lives I've ended with absolutely no remorse—all were done in the name of Holyrood, and the queen and the king who came before her, despite the fact that John tore my family apart.

But Guthram and Carrigan . . . I want them dead for *me*.

It's for that reason alone that I'm willing to bide my time, to play the game most likely to satisfy my end goal. And that game is entertaining the prime minister's daughter, no matter the fact that I'd enjoy nothing more than to finish what the fire started and drop her dead body on Edward Carrigan's front steps.

Sweet, fucking *temptation*.

I tilt my head to the side, faking curiosity. "What currency?"

"The space between a woman's legs."

Lip curling, I drag my gaze down over her ruined body. "Is that so?"

"It is." That stubborn chin of hers goes up a notch. "And I learned a long time ago how to become very wealthy while opening my legs to no one."

"Is that a warning?"

"It's a reminder," she replies, a razored edge to her voice, "that I know your games because I've bested them before. So, whatever you think that you're planning with this *interrogation*, I suggest going back to the drawing board. I'm not easily swayed."

If she expects applause for that little performance, she's come to the wrong audience.

I don't clap my hands and I don't offer praise.

Instead, I move—my fingers to her shoulder, still bare from the post-op with Matthews, and my other hand to the tweezers left abandoned on the rolling station set up next to the exam table.

The rise and fall of her shoulders freeze. "What are you doing?"

"Following the good doctor's orders," I return softly, lethally, "and removing the rest of the glass from your back."

"*No*—"

The glittering shard disappears between the tweezers' twin metal teeth, and I pull it free from her bruised flesh.

A sob bursts from her lips.

I lower my head, my mouth finding her ear, and utter a warning that'll stay with her long after I've left this room: "This snake leaves his mark, Miss Carrigan, and trust me when I say—my bite is always fatal."

CHAPTER 5

DAMIEN

"Clarke fucked her."

It's the only thing out of my mouth when Guy finally strides into the library at half past six, his face covered in soot, one sleeve burnt to shit and hanging from his elbow.

I expected shock. I expected his infamous temper to splinter the hard-fought control he wears like a second skin. I expected too fucking much, apparently, because Guy stops only long enough to tear the frayed material from his arm and throw it on the floor. Without sparing me a glance, he unholsters the gun from his waistband and sets it down on the closest side table, a seventeenth-century piece with ruby-encrusted edges that looks delicate enough to snap in half.

My eyes narrow on his lean frame. "You're not surprised."

"No," he answers, easing his weight forward as he plants his hands on the table, "I'm not."

Age-old frustration eases into my blood, a low, simmering fury that's stayed with me longer than any dream, any woman, any tangible scrap of hope. I unwind from the armchair and come to my feet. "You knew."

The admission is there, written all over the harsh grooves of his face and embedded in the rigid set to his shoulders. He *knew* Clarke and the queen were together, and he never uttered a bloody word. Not to me, not to Saxon either. If he had, I'd know.

"How long?"

Fisting a hand on the table, he blows out a heavy breath. "Damien, it's not—"

"How. *Long*."

A muscle flickers in his jaw. "I put Clarke with her for a reason. Is that what you want to hear?"

"You assigned him to her over a year ago." Disbelief creeps in on the heels of frustration. When my brother resolutely keeps his silence, I . . . "Fucking *hell*."

Swinging his head in my direction, Guy pins me with a glare meant to intimidate. Twenty years ago, that pointed stare might have been enough to shut me up. Hell, it probably would've been enough to have me retreating to the computer he stole from a Parisian university. Numbers were my safety zone, code my haven. And with almost seven years separating us, Guy became more of a father figure to me than Henry Godwin ever was.

Guy gave an order, and I did it to perfection.

He barked at me to get in line, and I crept back with my tail limp and dragging behind me.

But I won't bend to his will, not on this.

Like every other member of the royal family to come before her, Queen Margaret is off-limits. Forbidden. Instead of thinking with his prick, Clarke should have considered the ramifications for all of us if things went south and the queen kicked him to the curb. One angry snap of her fingers and it would all be over—the oath, what four generations of Godwins have sold their souls to see live for yet another day. No fuck is worth risking the survival of Holyrood. No fuck is worth risking the *people* of Holyrood.

The simmering heat in my blood flares and, having closed the distance to my brother, I drop my hands to the table and shove my face close to his. "You knew he was fucking her," I growl, my voice so low that it emerges as a thunderous rumble, "and you never stopped him?"

"I planned for it."

"Planned for *what*?"

"The queen's predictability." His blue eyes fix unerringly on my face. "She didn't let me down."

"Explain."

"Blond. Boyish good looks." The corner of my brother's mouth hitches humorlessly. "Every man the queen has ever dated matches Clarke's description. It didn't take a lot of guesswork to assume that she'd be attracted to him."

"You put Holyrood at risk." Disgust curdles in my stomach. "Jesus Christ, you put *all* of us at risk, and for what? Because you wanted to interfere with someone else's life? Clarke's life? The queen's?"

"This is nothing like your—"

"We both know you're not some matchmaker, which means that you sent Clarke because you *wanted* him to fuck her."

"I told him to put a leash on her—however he saw fit."

A leash.

Like the one he clipped to my proverbial collar the minute he demanded that I stay trapped within these walls.

Seven months.

Seven bloody *months*.

"She's a liability," Guy continues, pushing away from the table. I don't miss the way he takes his pistol with him, re-holstering it in a single move as he heads for the side-board—and the alcohol. "She was a liability as John's heir and she's even more of one now. We need her compliant."

"No, you want her meek while you play puppeteer."

Expression stony, my brother uncaps a bottle of Glenfiddich. "If we want her alive, then we need her to do what she's told. Compliant. Meek. Whatever the hell you want to call it, it's all the same."

"She doesn't want to die," I snarl, "which means she'll *do* whatever she's told. No lying. No subterfuge. You shouldn't have jumped straight to the mind games."

"Those mind games gave us information we wouldn't have had otherwise." He pauses. "Clarke was our emissary."

"And now your emissary is fucking dead."

Instead of answering, Guy pours three fingers' worth of whisky into two tumblers. One he downs immediately; the other he shoves to the side in a silent offer for me to drink with him.

I don't move.

My thumbs dig into the antique wood, and the sharpened edges of the rubies pinch my calloused palms. I welcome the sting with an in-drawn breath, and I more than welcome the burn of flesh ceding as my grip reflexively tightens.

Better to feel pain than to give in to the rage.

There's no code I can rewrite to turn this night around. No amount of surgery I can do with my untrained hands to resurrect Clarke from his palatial grave.

He died in that fire, and for what?

On orders, not from the Crown but from my oldest brother. Because, as in all aspects of his life, Guy Godwin isn't content until everyone in his path kneels in deference to his great, unparalleled wisdom.

Rightly assuming that I won't be taking that shot of

whisky, Guy wraps a hand around the second tumbler and tosses back the Glenfiddich in one pass. He hasn't even swallowed before he's reaching for the bottle to pour himself another pairing.

"Is the guilt already eating you alive? Or are you celebrating another life that you've managed to ruin while playing King of Holyrood?"

He pauses with the tumbler halfway to his mouth. "I did what was necessary."

"Life is fragile, and you shat all over it."

One second he's holding the glass and, in the next, it's shattering against the closest wall. He whirls around, his face a mask of the same fury that's swirling in my gut. "There are casualties in war, brother. Pa was a casualty. Mum was a casualty. Clarke—"

"Mum was weak," I grit. "If she was a casualty, then she has only herself to blame."

Guy's fingers grab the front of my shirt and maybe, if we weren't the same height, he'd have better luck dragging me forward. As it is, he drives his face centimeters from mine and hisses, "You have no bloody idea what you're talking about."

But I do.

I remember everything: the whispers that she hurled my way whenever my brothers fled our tiny, pitiful flat. The anger she reserved for me alone when I begged for more food or turned our cheaply made furniture into toys—fortresses that I hid behind; tabled shelters from which I watched her wither away, each day with battered hope inside my chest that she would just *die*. The pain she wielded with her words in my ear and her palm across my face and her constant talk of "no mercy."

The world would show me none, and it was best I

learned early.

Her lesson.

Her prophecy.

My own fucking reality.

I circle Guy's wrist with my fingers. Yank him away before I give in to the undiluted anger unfurling in my veins—that constant, humming mantra of *no mercy* that never, ever quiets—and purposely add two, then three steps between us.

I don't agree with Guy assigning Clarke to the queen with any motive beyond the obvious: keeping her safe. It's counterproductive to play underhanded moves when you're a team working toward a common goal.

And since Holyrood's inception, our mission has remained unchanged.

Protect the Crown.

Die for the Crown.

Do not *fuck* the Crown.

Not for the first time do I wish Saxon were here instead of holed up in Oxford. He may be sleeping with the king killer, but there was no mistaking the fear in his voice when he rang earlier tonight. Fear for the worst—that the family he's spent a lifetime protecting was gone for good. For now, I'll let him stay in that house he thinks is a secret. For now, I'll let him think that he can walk away from Holyrood.

No one walks away, least of all a Godwin.

He's shoved that lesson down my throat so many times that I've choked on the words.

As if we've come to some unspoken truce, Guy scrubs a hand over his soot-covered jaw. "Where is she?"

She.

Otherwise known as the queen.

"She came out of surgery a few hours ago."

"And?" Guy's blue eyes, a shade identical to my own, shift from me to the Glenfiddich soaking the pale blue rug. "Is she breathing?"

"According to Matthews, she's a miracle."

He rakes his fingers through his dark hair, visibly tugging on the strands, before nodding once. "I'll shower, then head over to talk to her."

I wait until he's stepping out of the library. Then, "I'll go with you."

Guy's stride grinds to a stop, and he looks back at me over his shoulder. "I think I can handle her on my own."

"And I think I'll go with you anyway."

"What?" A rough, cynical bark breaks from his mouth. "I keep one secret and suddenly you can't trust me?"

"Maybe I just think that those of us who are leashed should stick together."

"You aren't bloody *leashed*," he bites off.

"Feel free to let Jude know that."

As if his shoes are weighted with anvils, Guy turns all the way around. Slowly. With dread etched into his features. "What did you do?"

"Your confidence in me is really something else."

"Damien, what did you *do?*"

"We had a discussion," I offer, keeping the vibration of my tone noncommittal, "and we came to an agreement." The memory of digging my boot into Jude's back brings a small, satisfied smile to my lips. "The queen isn't the only one who's predictable, brother."

Holding Guy's gaze, I tuck my fingers into the front pockets of my trousers when we're shoulder-to-shoulder. "One of these days," I murmur, "your need to always have the upper hand will bite you in the ass."

A vein in his forehead strums to life. "I'm keeping you *safe*."

"No, brother, you're killing me."

"Damien—"

"I'll wait for you outside the queen's room."

When I make a move to pass him, Guy locks a tight, unrelenting hand around my arm. "If you leave this estate, they'll kill you. Guthram. Fucking Carrigan." His gaze hardens to steel. "You can keep your name off the internet, and you can lie to Saxon all you want about what went down that night, but the facts don't change—you're a dead man walking."

Probably.

But even if I am, I'm taking them both down with me.

And unlike both Guthram and Carrigan, I have a newfound ace up my sleeve: a woman stranded in enemy territory, who'll no doubt be desperate to save her own neck once she realizes that the queen intended for her to die.

Rowena Carrigan is my Trojan horse.

CHAPTER 6

ROWENA

"I need to see the queen."

Behind me, Dr. Matthews huffs out an aggravated breath. "You've mentioned," he mutters, smoothing the last of the ointment over my burns before stepping away, "and like I've already said, I don't hold that sort of sway."

Liar.

From what I've gathered, Nathaniel Matthews is the only doctor here at the "Palace," which means he holds more power than he's willing to admit.

With the astringent scent of the antimicrobial cream permeating the room and my nose, I press my case: "You keep the lot of them alive. What more sway could you possibly need?"

"Around here? Being Godwin would be a good start."

At *his* name, my heart hardens to stone.

Godwin may have left hours ago, but I can still feel his hot breath on the back of my neck and his unsympathetic fingers grazing my spine. Each tug of glass from my flesh sharpened my hatred while each demeaning insult hurled my way . . . Well, those made me *ache*—to return the favor tenfold, to treat him with the same callous ambivalence that he so easily bestowed upon me.

Sticks and stones may break my bones, but words can never hurt me.

Clearly, Godwin has failed to master even the most rudimentary basics of humanity.

"He's vile."

A sink turns on nearby, the water flowing at a trickle. "He's . . . troubled."

"Troubled implies he's redeemable, and I think it's safe to say that Godwin is long past being saved." My lips press flat. "Only a monster takes advantage of the indefensible."

Dr. Matthews clears his throat. "He wasn't—"

"And you're defending him."

"Hold on now, I'm not *defending* him."

I keep my hands firmly planted on my thighs and my face turned forward—heedless of the fact that Matthews' voice, and the rush of water from the faucet, comes from beyond my right shoulder. "Aren't you?"

"Of course not!"

"He made me bleed."

"Between the glass and the fire, your skin was—*is*— quite raw."

"And that excuses him for manhandling me?"

I tilt my head, hold my breath, and *wait.*

The sink turns off, followed by the distinct sound of a towel rubbing briskly against skin, as if the good surgeon is determined to buy himself time. But his hesitation stretches on, and on, until he's left with no choice but to ditch the rag. It lands with a wet *thwack* on a counter. Even then, he says nothing.

You cannot beat the best, Dr. Matthews.

"I suppose . . ." Ducking my head, I draw my shoulders

inward and drop my voice to a husky murmur. "I suppose working for Holyrood takes precedence over your care for a patient."

"I don't . . . I'm not one for . . . That is to say—*fuck*."

Smothering a victorious grin, I layer on another dose of self-pity for good measure. "I barely escaped with my life."

"Except you lived!" Agitated footsteps shuffle past before returning a second later. "You're *alive*."

"Without my sight," I whisper in a painstakingly aching voice, dialed all the way to ten to pull on every one of his heartstrings. "I'm alone, Dr. Matthews, totally and completely *alone*. I don't even know what this place is, never mind how I'll—"

"Ightham Mote."

The hospital gown crinkles beneath my fingertips. "Sorry?"

"You're at Ightham Mote," he says, "but we call it the Palace. You won't find it anywhere on a map. Or rather, you would. Everyone thinks we're an insane asylum."

I nearly laugh at the irony.

Godwin, the snake, absolutely deserves to be locked away.

Gritting my teeth at the visceral memory of his impersonal, cruel touch, I dip my chin to my chest and ignore the aching pull of flesh stretching across my nape and shoulders. Dr. Matthews was all too kind to point out that he'd removed ninety-seven shards of glass from my back—all of which I heard drop into a metal basin.

Ping. Ping. Ping.

I'll hear that sound for the rest of my life—nestled beside the long-ago memories of my mother's screams, minutes before Margaret dragged me from my bedroom window.

I was born in fire and nearly died in its fiery embrace, too.

Resolve stiffens my spine. "You'll take me to the queen."

A rush of air bursts from Dr. Matthews' lips. "Godwin gave me strict orders to keep you here."

"I'll scream."

"Miss Carrigan, this is out of my—"

"I'll scream until you're forced to sedate me, and when the medicine wears off, I'll wake screaming again." If expression had sound, then his jaw just came unhinged. Before he can protest, I add, "I'm about to become your worst nightmare, Doctor. Don't think I won't."

A beat passes, and then yet another.

My stomach twists with anxiety and frustration, a cocktail of panic that I remember all too well from years spent talking to men who'd rather stick their hands down my knickers than pretend, for even a second, that I was anything more than a quick shag that put them on the path to bigger and better things.

I shove my former self deep down, internally silencing Young Rowena's fears and her tears and her everlasting pain. "Well?" I demand.

"I'll take you to her," the doctor says briskly, "but you'll need to . . . You can't be walking through the Palace like that."

Because I have no other option, I allow Dr. Matthews to swap out my hospital gown for new clothes. He doesn't offer information on where they came from and, to be perfectly honest, I don't ask. Not now, when the chance to see Margaret is just minutes away.

He angles my head through a hole of material, then positions my arms so that I can awkwardly slip them into a pair of sleeves. Bandaged like a mummy or not, when the cotton skims exposed sections of skin, I let out a low hiss.

"The dressings and ointment will protect you from infection," he says, not unkindly, "but there's nothing to be done about the constriction to your—"

"I'll be fine."

"Yes, of course you will."

I'm shuffled into a pair of loose joggers with a draw-string around my waist, thin-soled hospital slippers but no real shoes.

Then, and only then, does Dr. Matthews lead me from the room.

Pain accompanies my every step. It aches in my legs, from my tumble down the steps; in my abdomen and rib-cage, from the beam that nearly crushed me; in my back, which burns as hot as the flames that almost took my life.

I'm as broken as I've felt for years.

Broken, but never defeated.

I grip Dr. Matthews' arm like a lifeline. Turn my head from left to right, like a marionette puppet attached to invisible strings. In another world, I'd be given time to re-cuperate. But there's nothing easy about this life that we've all been thrust into. Britain is a land on the brink of war where death is the only constant and pain the only engine that drives us forward into another day.

And, right now, I don't know which pain is worse—the threat of bile that rears its ugly head when Dr. Matthews ushers me to the left, a little too abruptly, or the unset-tling realization that my sight might be gone for good. An entire lifetime of being locked within the bowels of Hell, forced to crawl through its embers on my hands and knees, and now I'll be stuck with Clarke dead and Marga-ret bleeding as my last visual memories.

Karma, probably, for the years that I spent at Father's beck and call.

Lungs squeezing tight, I force one foot in front of the other and do my best not to limp.

Broken.

But never defeated.

"Here," the doctor tells me, "let me get the door for you."

My weight rocks backward as soon as Dr. Matthews releases me. Toes flexing in the flimsy hospital slippers, I grip the floor with everything that I am. *Hold your ground.* I last only seconds before I start to sway, and it takes every bit of strength not to reach out and look for something to stabilize my unsteady frame.

Do. Not. Fall.

A door clicks open, its base sweeping across tile or stone.

The doctor grasps my elbow, and I follow with my head down.

A shuffle of movement catches my ear and I frown. There's no way that Margaret could be . . .? No. Of course she isn't *walking.* Bloody hell, I'm no doctor and even I know that she won't be doing much of anything over the next few weeks, let alone just hours post-surgery.

But there's no mistaking the subsequent shuffle of feet . . . or the chilling clank of chains.

My heart stampedes inside my chest. "Dr. Matthews, where are—"

"Who the bloody hell is *she*?" comes a nasally masculine voice.

"Your temporary cellmate."

What?

The comforting hand on my elbow disappears, leaving me to stumble in my newfound darkness. And, for better or worse, I *stumble,* one foot tripping over the other, my body careening so sharply to the left that I ram into a wall with jarring force. A burst of metallic warmth fills my mouth as I bite the inside of my cheek.

"You can't leave me here." Shoulder jammed against

the stone for leverage, the pads of my fingers dig deep into the grout. "Dr. Matthews, I don't understand—"

"You shouldn't have promised to scream."

And then those clipped footsteps retreat, departing the way we came, with a farewell that leaves me chilled to the bone: "Play nice, Barker. I expect to find her alive when I come back."

CHAPTER 7

DAMIEN

The queen is sprawled out on the four-poster bed.

Pillows cushion her blond head and heavy blankets shield her body.

If anyone told me that I'd finally meet Queen Margaret while she was holed up in bed, and looking like death, I would have laughed.

There's no laughter now. Not a single spark of joy anywhere to be found.

Thirty-one years of personally serving the royal family, of bending over backward to keep them all alive, and here we are in the end—Guy shored up by the bedroom door, me seated on an uncomfortable armchair by the fireplace, and the queen, tucked beneath her covers, looking like a child terrified of the ghosts lurking beneath the bed.

Or maybe it's us who terrify her. Tough to tell when she's barely said a word since we knocked on her door.

Finally, she asks, "Where's Saxon?"

Living in Oxford with the woman who assassinated your father.

I meet Guy's stare with a subtle jerk of my chin. Now isn't the time to confess that we had Isla Quinn in our grasp and let her go free. Or, hell, that we know she murdered King John in the first place.

Our tangled webs are growing bloody roots at this point.

"There were some rumblings up in Aberdeen," I lie, maintaining a neutral expression. Rumblings. Fake murder plots. So long as it keeps her from asking too many questions about why Saxon isn't at the Palace—and *won't* be here for the foreseeable future—then I have no problem blurring the truth. "He'll be back when it's all sorted."

"Right." Her mouth visibly tightens with displeasure. "Of course."

"He rang when he saw the news." That, at least, is the truth. Guy may have kicked Saxon out of Holyrood, but my middle brother hasn't put down the torch—not officially. Frustrated as I am that he chose a woman over our oath, Saxon will always have my loyalty. "I told him to stay in Scotland." Another lie. Another smooth excuse that rolls right off my tongue. I don't look at Guy when I add, "We'll take care of what happened tonight."

"What *happened?*" The displeasure spreads from the firm tilt of her mouth to her blue eyes. "What happened is that Buckingham Palace *exploded*. What happened," she grits out, "is that I'm nobody's fool. Someone tried to kill me last night. No one would have ever found my body. No one would ever know that I didn't just burn alive."

Against my will, I think of Rowena Carrigan.

The queen may have been shot, but the prime minister's daughter . . .

Burned alive is somehow fitting and still lacking in every single way. Matthews had gagged as he cut away her shirt from the ravaged skin beneath. The fabric had melded to her forearms and abdomen, her flesh an adhesive glue that took the older man over an hour to fully clean out.

I hadn't gagged. Hadn't replied to Matthews' mutterings as he worked diligently over her prone body. But I'd watched, unable to turn away from the woman who looked like she'd barely escaped the devil's lair, and I'd waited to feel something *more*. Pity. Compassion. Empathy for a fellow broken soul.

In that moment, I'd burned alive, too.

For vengeance and hate and the anticipation of seeing Edward Carrigan finally fall. Hell if it doesn't feel like the universe didn't drop Rowena into my lap with a curt, "Do your worst."

And, God help her, but I fucking plan to.

"What happened," Guy says with his arms crossed over his chest, drawing my attention back to the conversation, "is that if it weren't for Clarke, we would have found out too late."

I almost bark out a dry, humorless laugh.

After a year of pestering Clarke to come up with a code word to signal if the queen was in danger, the bastard finally picked one after the king died. He'd chosen Dunrobin, the Scottish castle where Queen Margaret lived after her sister's assassination.

Twenty-four hours ago, I'd no idea that his choice hid a sentimentality for a woman he never should have touched. And then, with one text sent after two in the bloody morning—

I pin my gaze on the queen.

One mention of Clarke and she can barely look me in the eye. By all accounts, she should have died there beside him. She definitely shouldn't have made it to Kent, let alone survived the damage done to her internal organs.

As he stitched her up, Matthews had called her a miracle.

I don't believe in miracles or fate or a monarchy anointed by God. Don't believe in much of anything beyond cold, hard facts. And the facts tell me one thing only: "You were shot first."

"How . . ." The queen blinks. "How in the world do you know that? Did you watch the security tapes?"

"The cameras were tampered with." *And now they're gone.* Just like every other bit of evidence we could have used to retrace the bastard's steps. Swallowing my frustration, I drop my elbows to my knees. "Clarke would have assumed that the assassin planned to take him out first, if only to make it easier to kill you once he was dead. And," I add grimly, thinking of what Rowena revealed, "because the shooter managed a head shot."

Guy curses beneath his breath.

All the color drains from the queen's face.

I do nothing but hold her hollow stare. "Clarke thought you were already dead, didn't he."

Her throat bobs in silent confirmation as she closes an arm over her midsection, like she's worried that her intestines might spill out after all. "I couldn't get up," she whispers, her fingers tangling with the bed covers. "I could hear them struggling. I could . . . I could *feel* the blood coating my fingers. It—it was everywhere. I was dying. I should be *dead.*"

I don't bother to deny it. Still . . . "You were allowed to live."

Two pairs of eyes swing in my direction.

"What the hell are you talking about?" Guy bites off. "She nearly bled out."

"Roughly five percent of people survive a gunshot to the head compared to the almost ninety who live after a shot to the abdomen." Between my spread knees, I link my fingers together. "The queen lived; Clarke didn't. Whoever staged tonight's attack isn't an amateur. They hacked our cameras. They bypassed every security measure we put in place to keep the queen safe. They *blindsided* us. You think they'd suddenly toss all that to the side to maybe kill her in the end? No," I mutter, shaking my head, "it was part of their plan. Had to be."

The blue of my brother's gaze turns piercing. "The fire—"

"Destroyed every shred of evidence, which is exactly what they wanted. I—*we*—have nothing but the bullet that Matthews fished out of the queen's stomach."

I squeeze my hands together, doing my best to ignore the dampness pooling in my palms. Dampness that's not from anxiety or even regret but from the constant hum of rage that threatens to spill over and wreak havoc on everything in my path.

Buckingham Palace was my domain, which means that it's my failure. Clarke's death is now on my conscience. Every single staffer death will forever be on my head. The fact that I didn't set the palace on fire, or pull the trigger, doesn't matter when the killer is still out there.

I will find you and haunt you and destroy everything that makes you you.

"Damien."

At my brother's low timbre, I force my hands apart and drag them over my trousers. Turn to the woman in the bed with a look on my face that I'm sure would send small children scrambling. "I'll do what I can. Look for leads, pull footage from nearby city cameras. Until then—"

"You'll fake your own death," Guy interjects.

A leash.

A collar.

Good idea or not, my chest grows impossibly tight at the absolute finality of my brother's words. "Sod off" is right there, begging to launch free, but some inexplicable gut response tugs my attention away to look at the queen.

She watches Guy, her stare blazing with grief and anger. Her fingers coil over the bedsheets, dragging the blankets damn near up to her chin. At this rate, she'll either suffocate or disappear altogether.

"You cold, Princess?" my brother asks from his post by the door. "Or just thinking about your own mortality?"

My chin jerks in his direction at the same time she retorts, "In case you've forgotten, I'm your *queen*."

"For now."

Jesus.

"Guy," I mutter roughly, "shut—"

The queen throws up a hand, silencing me mid-sentence, even as she hauls herself up in the bed, pushing and heaving with one palm on the mattress. Sweat beads across her upper lip and her fingers visibly tremble as she gathers the blanket again in a tight fist. "Explain yourself, Priest," she says in a tone carved from stone. "What do you mean by *for now?*"

"Just that I know all about how you fought Clarke tooth and nail when it came to every order. After what happened tonight, I hope you're prepared to do everything we tell you. No more objections."

The queen's mouth flattens into a thin, angry line. "You work for *me*—not the other way around."

Pushing away from the door, Guy closes the distance between them. One hand fists the headboard while the other lands on the mattress, scant centimeters away from her leg. He leans down, invading her space. "I've been in this world longer than you've even been alive, Princess. *I* watched your sister be gunned down while you were still playing with dolls. I—"

"Don't even *speak* Evie's name."

"—dealt with your father while you were banished to Scotland for *safekeeping*. And you know what I learned?" He removes his hand from the headboard to grip the pillow propping up her head. "I learned that while your time is finite, Holyrood is here, king after king, queen after bloody queen. So, you're my queen *for now*. And if you die—like you almost did tonight after I explicitly told Clarke to get you out of London—there'll always be another one of you to shuffle into place."

CRACK!

I watch, in startled silence, as Guy lifts a hand to cup his left cheek.

She slapped him.

Bloody fucking hell, she *slapped him*.

Mouth dry, I step forward. "Your Majesty—"

"I want him out." Her furious stare doesn't leave my brother's face, never wavering, completely honed in. "Today."

Guy's lips peel back in a snarl. "Holyrood is mine."

"Wrong," she snaps, gripping the blanket like it's the only thing keeping her from lunging forward and clawing out his eyes, "it's *mine*. My ancestor founded Holyrood and yours bent the knee. Which means that your oath belongs to me and you do as I say."

"Guy"—I throw him a hard look—"fucking *apologize*."

His shoulders heave with a sharp breath. "No."

I'm going to murder him. If the queen doesn't do him in first, I'm going to *murder* him. "Just say the damn words," I bark, my patience waning fast. "You lost your temper and the queen—"

"Is the queen."

But it's not Guy who spits this out but Queen Margaret herself.

With one hand cradling her wounded stomach, and her face red from exertion, she lifts her chin so that she never severs eye contact with my brother. "We've met twice now," she utters in a voice pitched so low that she's nearly inaudible, "and I've walked away both times with the same opinion: you are a *bully*, Guy Priest. If our lives had crossed paths while my father was still breathing, I'd have no choice but to put up with you. But he's dead and I'm not, and so the only time *we* will ever meet again is on the day of your funeral." She pauses, and an almost feral light glitters in her blue gaze. "Maybe, if you're lucky, I won't spit on your grave."

No mercy.

Guy wanted her compliant and instead she's revealed her claws.

It'd be impressive, if not for the fact that she's just gone ahead and tossed a bomb into Holyrood's very core.

"That isn't a good idea."

At the sound of my voice, the queen ends her staring contest with my brother and swiftly turns on me. "It's my decision."

"You don't understand our politics."

"It's my *final* decision, Mr. Priest."

"Holyrood is a powder keg waiting to blow." Striding forward, I snatch Guy by the shirt and shove him behind me, then square off against the woman determined to take us all down with her. "Our father was murdered, and you know what happened? His second-in-command exiled us to Paris for five goddamn years."

"Maybe he hoped to keep you all safe."

"Or maybe he wanted all of this for himself." Slashing an arm at the luxurious room, I think of that night, weeks ago, when I came across Paul, Jude, and Benji circling

Saxon. There was no loyalty in the drive of their fists on my brother's flesh, nor in the gun that Paul leveled on the back of Saxon's head. There'd been only greed even if no one else saw it but me. "Remove the leader from his pride and the vultures will swarm."

"You don't know that."

"And you don't know any of us. You've been sheltered—"

"*Sheltered?*" Disdain practically drips from her expression. "How sheltered am I when my father was murdered in front of me? Or was my innocence only tarnished the second that I watched Clarke fall? Or, I know! It was the moment when I crawled down the hallway of my home, bleeding out and almost dead, and realized that *no* one can be trusted."

I meet her gaze, allowing the answering silence to drown us both until . . . "And Rowena Carrigan?" I ask, ignoring my brother simmering behind me. "Do you trust your best mate? After all, she saved you last night."

The muscles in her neck jump as she averts her eyes.

"Answer the question." I step in her line of sight, refusing to be ignored. "Do. You. Trust. Her?"

Her chin dips with a hard swallow. "No," she whispers, squeezing her eyelids shut. "I don't trust her. I *can't* trust her."

"Why?"

"Because she knew."

Guy steps beside me. "*What* did she know?"

That hand on her stomach turns white-knuckled. "Clarke learned that Edward Carrigan plans to see me removed as Queen."

My brain latches onto the most obvious: "Parliament doesn't have the ability to do that." Not anymore, at least. Not after King John stripped them of that power five years ago—a decision that led to one of the most devastating riots this country has seen in centuries. "Your father saw to that."

"They do," she replies slowly, "if I'm removed on the grounds of being mentally unfit to rule."

Fuck. And, because it seems like the only fitting thing to say, I thread my fingers through my hair and say it again, "*Fuck.*"

The queen gives a terse nod. "Rowan knew—there's no way she didn't—and she never said a word, not even in warning. And then the fire . . . What's the likelihood of her wanting to spend the night in the same week Clarke learned that her father plans to see me deposed?"

You're speaking treason, she'd said.

A snake, she called me.

All that holier-than-thou attitude and it turns out that Rowena Carrigan is nothing but a conniving little liar.

"I'll take care of her." Jaw cinching tight, I pass a hand over the side of my face and mentally turn the situation over in my head. "There's no way we can risk pretending that you died in the fire, even while we neutralize the situation."

"I agree."

"Good."

She sits up tall. "And I think that—"

"Guy stays."

The queen stiffens at my tone. "Absolutely not. I refuse to—"

"We can handle only one war at a time," I tell her. "Who do you choose? The bully you know or the devil you don't?"

Warily, her blue eyes shift to my brother. "I don't like you," she breathes.

Guy drops to his haunches, one hand on the bed, the other poised on his knee. "The feeling is mutual, Princess. The feeling is entirely fucking mutual."

CHAPTER 8

ROWENA

The cell is a perfect square.

Ten limping steps take me from one wall to the next. Thirteen when I veer off course and accidentally stumble over Alfie Barker's outstretched legs—which happens more often than not. Unfortunately.

"Will you stop moving?" Barker snaps, yanking his foot out of the way. The near-silent *thud* that follows tells me he's either banged his fists on the floor or his head against the stone wall. "Back and forth, back and forth, all bloody day. You're driving me absolutely mad."

"Tell me about your daughters again." In my thin-soled slippers, I take another careful step. "Specifically, whether or not they know that their father is a complete arse."

"I don't give a damn if you can see or not, Carrigan. If you take one more fucking step, that doctor is going to come back and find you breathless."

"Breathless?" With careful precision, I adopt a tone soaked with saccharine sweetness. "I think you've too much confidence in your masculine prowess, Alfie."

The insult doesn't go over his head.

A heartbeat of silence passes, and then, over the sound

of rattling chains, Barker snarls, "I'm going to *kill* you."

If he wasn't restrained, I'd probably be more worried.

But he is, and I'm not, and the way I see it, the sooner I push him to the brink of insanity, the sooner someone will be forced to take me from this blasted cell and put me somewhere that isn't a prison hole. So long as Godwin thinks I'm hiding priceless information, I'm still valuable.

Valuable enough that he won't let Barker kill me.

Not yet, at least.

"How do you think it would happen?"

A sharp breath precedes an even sharper, "I have no idea what you're talking about."

"If you killed me, I mean." The only sounds in the cell belong to my shuffling stride and the faint trickle of water that I swear comes from a nearby stream. Meanwhile, Barker's silence, lengthy and resolute, proves what I knew all along. "The thing is, Alfie, I'm not sure you could do it."

"I could," he grits out. "You don't know anything about me."

I might not know *Alfie Barker*, the man sharing this cell, but I've known hundreds of men just like him. Men who don civilized masks and pretend every wrong that they commit is done in the name of protecting their child or their spouse or their home. But the mask always come off, and when it does, that shred of civility disappears right along with it.

Once upon a time, my father protected me, too.

And then he realized how much more he stood to gain when he fed me to the wolves.

"You'd strangle me?" Pretending to think on it, I hum deep in my throat. "No, not strangulation. It doesn't seem very *you*, Alfie. Too up close and personal. You're more the sort to hide behind a gun."

A small, heavy pause. "Are you saying that I'm a coward?"

"All I'm saying is that you're quite the contradiction. One minute you're sobbing, the next threatening to kill me. I don't know, maybe that's just the way you get it done. Pull the trigger; let the tears fall free." When Barker lets loose a feral growl, I shake my head. Easy. So bloody easy that it—manipulation—should be a crime. It definitely feels like one. As always, I feel the pull of regret deep in my gut.

Do what you have to do to get free.

I throw out my hands and, to my relief, they graze roughened stone. Another round completed, even if I did take a few extra steps.

"Is that what happened?" I ask with forced nonchalance, turning around to start all over again. "Were you crying when Holyrood caught you and dragged you here—"

"That mouth of yours will get you into trouble one day, Miss Carrigan."

That voice.

His voice.

I didn't even hear him enter the cell, but instinctively, I stagger backward until my arse collides with stone and my palms splay out on either side of my hips and pain rips through my entire being. Stifling a whimper, I jerk my head to the side. There's nowhere to run, no chance for escape. And even if I could somehow make it to the door, there's no doubt in my mind that *he* would catch me.

Catch me and drag me back and take—

"Don't tell me that you're nervous now," Godwin drawls, so much closer than before. Each arrogant step matches the staccato of my heart until I'm balancing on my toes, straining against stone, and the heat of him is right *there*, not even a breath away. "I so enjoyed sparring with you."

Before or after you made me bleed, you bastard?

Desperate to appear unfazed, I dig my fingertips into the wall and lift my chin. "I don't spar with snakes."

"Smart choice. You wouldn't win."

The droll comment grinds my teeth together. "And, for the record, I'm not nervous. *You* don't make me nervous."

The warmth of his body infiltrates my personal space, swallowing the stale air from the cell and all the oxygen from my lungs. And then I feel it—*him*. His hands coming to rest on either side of mine, against the wall, and his breath, then his lips, brushing the slope of my neck as though I belong to him.

"You're a liar, Miss Carrigan."

The words vibrate against my skin. Velvet. Steel. *Condescending.* A shiver skates down my spine, and I wish—God, I wish—that I could stay perfectly still. But even now my shoulders tremble with the startling realization that whatever comes next . . . there's no stopping it. Not with a madman at the helm. "I'm not lying."

"Your pulse would argue otherwise," he counters, his lips purposely grazing my throat, "but I'm not worried. We have more than enough time to get the truth out of you."

And then, before I can even process what's happening, my hands are yanked together, wrists forced to kiss by hands the size of boulders, and *clink! clink! clink!*

My heart stutters.

Palms pool with sweat.

Both are a sharp contrast to the cold metal now weighing down my arms.

The bastard . . . the bastard *cuffed* me!

"Let me go!" I thrash in place, swinging out a leg to kick him—and hit nothing but air. "I said, *let me go!*"

The chains linking the handcuffs go taut, as if Godwin fisted them in his grip, and then I'm snatched away from the wall in a single pull. The unexpected momentum throws my world off-kilter as up becomes down and left becomes right and darkness caves in completely. What little confidence I gained marching back and forth across the cell deteriorates instantly.

I can't see, and I'm going to die.

I can't see, and Godwin will take advantage of the weakness.

I can't see, and Alfie Barker is clearly enjoying himself because he exclaims, "Thank God you've shut her up," with all the palpable giddiness of a kid opening gifts on Boxing Day. And maybe it's the hopelessness of the situation or the brokenness of my body, but either way I crash to my hands and knees. Hard.

Don't give up, don't give up, don't give—

"Self-pity isn't a good look on you."

Godwin's harsh words flay me alive, more sharply than the razor he used ever could, and then muscular arms fit under my stomach and haul me off the floor. No compassion. No empathy. I swallow, tightly, when his hand lands on my shoulder, his touch careful but somehow still unbelievably arrogant.

"Walk," he commands, his voice pitched low next to my ear, "or I'll drag you."

I bundle my fear in a knot, then shove it so far deep that it'll never resurface. "That's not much of a choice."

"It's an ultimatum, Miss Carrigan. You're all out of choices."

With dread swimming in my gut, I walk.

Godwin guides me out of the cell, his hand rooted on my shoulder, and I swear Barker releases a breath of maniacal laughter when the door snicks shut behind us, locking him inside and leaving me to deal with the devil at my back.

If I were on my way to freedom, I'd ask Godwin what Barker did to deserve imprisonment. My cellmate revealed little more than what I prodded out of him—that he's a father of two and that he was caught by Holyrood over a month ago—but kept his mouth shut otherwise. And I was locked in that cell right alongside him as though I haven't spent years supporting the royal family.

Thieves and liars, brutes and murderers, all of them.

Words uttered by my father within Westminster's Jewel Tower just two months ago when asked about the escalating number of anti-loyalist uprisings. The four-teenth-century stone walls had echoed with his booming voice, and the ancient floors had trembled under the on-slaught of his expectation for *more*. More independence from the Crown, more control. All around me, members of Parliament had nodded and hollered their support, all while draining their glass tumblers completely dry. King John stripped them of their power five years ago and now my father seeks to return it to them.

But not at the expense of Margaret's life.

It isn't true. It *can't* be true.

Godwin is the brute here, the liar, not me.

The man in question tightens his grip, as if in silent warning for me to behave. Muttering "In here," he turns me at a fifteen-degree angle and nudges me through a narrow door frame. Barely a second passes before the door clangs shut; the ensuing silence is all I need to know that we're completely alone. For better or worse. *Again.*

He lets me go.

I stand in place, cuffed and straight-backed.

"Sit down," he orders in the same breath that I demand, "What do you want with me?"

The scrape of a chair is my only answer. Its wooden

feet wail against the floor, dragging closer and closer until anxiety doubles the pace of my pulse and—

A grunt escapes my lips when my knees abruptly collapse.

Unable to stabilize my weight in time, I tip backward and drop onto the chair that he so *graciously* shoved behind me.

Fury gathers in my gut.

"A gentleman," I hiss, balling my hands into fists, "would never manhandle a woman."

"There aren't any gentlemen here, Miss Carrigan. You get me. Only me."

"The world's biggest bastard. How utterly *fortuitous*."

I cock my head, hoping he'll say something that'll prove my point, but he doesn't.

No, he *laughs*.

This deep, raspy chuckle that reminds me of thorny vines just aching to puncture my skin and draw blood. He laughs like I'm the butt of the joke; he laughs like there's nothing he's anticipating more than becoming my very worst nightmare; he laughs like I'm doomed, and we both know it, and I'll be stuck here until he's good and ready to do away with my dead body.

"What," I bite off, "do you *want* with me?"

"We're going to play a little game, you and me."

The chain rattles as I clasp my fingers together. "I'm not interested."

"Didn't ask if you were," he murmurs, and I have the immediate visual of him slipping his hands into his trouser pockets as he circles me like a predator confronted with its next meal. It's all there in his tone—the way he plans to trot me along, toying with me like a cat would a mouse, until either I stumble and fall, or he personally crashes me to the ground. "But we're going to play anyway. Cooperate and I'll let you visit with the queen."

If I could see him, I'd punch him.

As it is, I sit so still that I'm surprised I don't become living, breathing stone. "Another one of your ultimatums?"

"Think of it as a gift," he counters smoothly. "Give me what I want, and I'll make sure you get the same."

"You had me thrown in a bloody cell!"

"That was all Matthews."

I shake my wrists, making the cuffs clink noisily. "Then prove you're sorry by unlocking these."

Godwin's answer is a solitary, deafening, "No."

"Take. Them. *Off.*"

His footsteps pause. "Say *please.*"

I grind my teeth. "Only a chauvinistic arse would demand that I beg—"

"Say the word, Miss Carrigan, and maybe I'll play nice with you."

How many times have I been forced to *play nice* for the sake of stroking a man's ego? How many times have I flirted when I felt sick to my stomach, and laughed when I wanted to scream, and prostrated myself before men I didn't give a damn about and who most certainly didn't give a damn about me?

And *this* man expects me to beg.

I won't do it, not even to be free.

"Sod off."

If he's at all surprised by my change of heart, he doesn't give me the satisfaction of an audible reaction. But his pacing recommences a moment later, that loose-limbed stride of his surrounding me, cornering me, until I find myself shifting in my seat, just to alleviate the mounting tension threatening to choke the air from my lungs.

"Get on with your little game, Godwin."

"When was the last time you saw your father?"

My head begins to pound. "Are we seriously back to that again?"

"Answer the question."

"For God's sake, my father is *not* trying to kill Margaret. The sooner you get that through your thick skull, the sooner—"

The chain between the handcuffs jerks forward, nearly sending me sprawling from the chair to the floor. But I hang there, in the delicate balance of neither here nor there—heart in my throat, fingers searching for purchase—fully prepared for an abrupt landing.

"This game," Godwin growls, "will only turn out well for you if you play along."

"And if I refuse?"

"There are hundreds of different ways to break you, Miss Carrigan." The handcuffs clink and clank as his fingers wrap around my wrists, binding them together. He yanks me off the chair so that my arse leaves the seat while he holds my weight in just one hand. It's a move designed to intimidate, and I hate that it does. "I'm giving you one last chance to give me information without coercion," he adds.

A soft, disbelieving laugh climbs my throat. "You don't call this coercion? You have me *bound*."

"Almost gentlemanly of me," he husks, "when all the alternatives would leave permanent damage."

Permanent damage.

As if the last twenty-four hours haven't already left me scarred in more ways than are even evident right now.

Ten years. That's how long I've spent doing everything in my power to separate myself from Edward Carrigan. But there's no denying that if Father were here, he'd find a way to spin this conversation to his advantage. He would shield the truth, butter up the lies, and do what has to be done to come out of this alive—a future that's becoming less likely with every second that I hang from Godwin's hold.

Margaret was my sister when I had no family. She was my best friend when I trusted no one and nothing, least of all the man whose blood runs through my veins. Last night, I saved her life at the risk of my own, and, injured or not, her absence now speaks louder than words ever could.

I'm on my own.

Donning the mask that I once wore so often, I push a soft, tempting smile to my lips. *Make a deal. Beat him at his own game.* The smile doesn't waver, not even when I feel the blistered skin along my jaw pull grotesquely tight. And so, with the confidence that I've faked for most of my life, I put Young Rowena on stage for her grand reentry into society:

"I'll play, Godwin, but *only* on my terms."

CHAPTER 9

"Terms," I echo, tasting the word on my tongue and finding it . . .

Intriguing.

With her dangling helplessly from my grasp, the last thing Rowena Carrigan ought to be trying on for size are negotiations. But here we are—me, standing with my legs spread shoulder width apart; her, fighting to maintain that prim composure of hers as her feet struggle to touch the ground. Composure, I note, that splinters every time the handcuffs crack together.

Still, she manages a decisive nod. "I'll answer your questions, but you'll answer mine, too."

I stroke my thumb over her pulse, just to see her flinch. "I'm not the one who's *bound.*"

The smile on her face turns lethal. "And I'm not the one so desperate for information that I'd assault an innocent woman just to have my way."

My jaw clenches at her implicit dig.

There's no double standard here.

If Holyrood has taught me anything, it's that a person's sex means nothing on the battlefield. Women are just as ruthless as men. Soft curves belie sharp, analytical minds; gentle touches underscore brutal fighting skills that would lay any man flat. I've gotten this far in life because I never underestimate my opponent.

Especially not when the opponent in question is the prime minister's daughter.

The enemy of my enemy is my friend.

Whoever came up with that blasted proverb clearly never dabbled in British politics.

"When was the last time you saw Edward Carrigan?" I ask again, acquiescing to the terms without giving her the satisfaction of saying so out loud.

That lethal smile dims, just a little. "Two months ago."

"Where?"

"*Tsk tsk*, Godwin. That sounds a whole lot like two questions."

"You don't think I know that?" I lift my arm, my core muscles tightening with her weight, and put her face even with mine. "Answer the question," I growl.

Her legs swing outward, and this time she manages to nail me in the knee. It doesn't hurt. Barely even registers. My gaze is locked on her full mouth when she snaps, "Put me down and I will."

I stare at her—at this woman hanging from my one hand. The bandages around her head have drooped to cover her nose and reveal the upper curve of her right ear. She looks ruined. She looks weak.

The fire in her voice argues otherwise.

If she were anyone else, I might even feel . . . impressed.

"Put me down." And then, with her teeth bared in what's probably meant to be a smile, she adds, "Or I'll kick you where it hurts."

I jerk her closer, putting us nose to nose. "Lie to me

and you'll hang yourself."

"I'd welcome that day," she says, her breath a hot whisper over my mouth, "with wide open arms."

Insolent. Impudent.

I wasn't lying when I said that that mouth of hers would get her in trouble.

With one last squeeze of my fingers around her wrist, I drop her onto the chair. Its feet clatter against the floor, but Rowena's weight settles it onto all four legs. With her cuffed hands in her lap, she angles her chin so that she's looking in my direction.

For a moment, it's almost possible to imagine the intensity of her glare. If she had her way, I have no doubt I'd incinerate on the spot.

Sorry to disappoint.

Grabbing another chair, I plant it down in front of hers and straddle the back.

It's a silent order to get on with it, and Rowena doesn't mistake it as anything else. Her palms press together. "We don't speak, my father and I, but I listen and I watch."

"Why?"

"My relationship with him is none of your business."

Narrowing my eyes at her obvious attempt to weasel out of answering, I opt to swap tracks and catch her off guard. "Ask your first question."

Her lips part, then clamp shut.

"Didn't let yourself get that far ahead when you were plotting terms?" When she doesn't respond right away, I drop my elbows to the back of the chair. "You have three seconds before you forfeit your round."

She jerks her head down, her thumbs working over each other in a clear attempt to settle her nerves. Then, quietly, "Has Margaret mentioned me? Since she came out of surgery, I mean. Has she . . ." Her shoulders fall forward. "Has she said anything at all?"

She said that you can't be trusted.

A good man would evade the question entirely.

A better man would lie and tell her exactly what she wants to hear.

But, at the sliver of raw vulnerability in her voice, I find myself saying, "Don't bother asking something when you already know the answer."

Not a lie. Not the truth either.

My response lives in the murky gray, and it's enough to have her inhaling a short breath through her nose. A beat passes, heavy with tension, and then she shakes her head with a low, pained chuckle. "Right."

I don't speak.

Finally, she straightens her shoulders. "I saw him at the Jewel Tower."

At Westminster? Built centuries ago, the Jewel Tower was first intended to hold King Edward III's treasures, but it's been used as nothing but storage for decades now. Which, now that I think about it, makes it the perfect place for a secret meeting.

Fuck.

"Who did he meet?"

Rowena shifts in the chair but keeps her mouth shut.

I narrow my eyes. "Miss Carrigan—"

"Don't you think that I know what you're trying to do?" she says, her voice rising sharply. "Don't you think I know that if I say one wrong thing, you'll pass judgment on him? And even if we . . . even if he and I aren't—*dammit.*"

With my elbows propped on the back of the chair, I scan her face—what little of it I can see, at any rate. If Buckingham Palace hadn't exploded last night, if Clarke hadn't been murdered, if the queen herself hadn't nearly died . . . I may have dropped the issue.

But Hell literally landed on our doorstep less than twenty-four hours ago, and, taking my hatred for the prime minister out of the equation, our leads are still slim to none. We're short on time, down one agent, and stuck with the hand that we've been dealt.

Rowena Carrigan is all we have.

Resting my wrists on the chair back, I link my fingers together. "Ask me why Alfie Barker is chained in that cell."

Her chin jerks back. "What?"

"Ask me."

"I don't . . ." Her mouth twists to the side in chaffed resignation. "Fine. Why?"

Leaning forward, I drop my voice to a husky murmur. "Because he tried to have your best mate killed. Because, in case you haven't figured it out already, that's what we do. We protect the Crown at all costs."

She huffs out a grim laugh. "So, what? You're *heroes*?"

"To some," I allow.

"And to others?"

"We're the monster in your dreams. The villain you don't ever want to meet on a dark, quiet street."

Her throat bobs with a convulsive swallow. "And to me? What are you to me?"

Your worst nightmare.

Because even if she had nothing to do with the fire at Buckingham Palace, she's still my best way to cut Edward Carrigan down at the knees. Revenge isn't pretty. There are always casualties, and I'm willing to shed blood to get what I want.

Vengeance.

The chance to leave the Palace behind and not look

over my shoulder every other step, always watching, always prepared to find a knife plunged deep in my back.

Carrigan's lackeys already managed to get me once.

"Godwin?" Rowena asks, her tone wary.

"I'm your judge, jury, and executioner," I tell her softly, without a hint of warmth. "Now tell me who your father met with."

It's not a request.

With a sigh of frustration, she collapses back in the chair. "They were all MPs. The room was packed, shoulder to shoulder."

Of course it was.

If this meeting took place two months ago, that means Carrigan started plotting the queen's removal from the throne almost immediately after King John's assassination. Definitely a quick turnaround, though . . . Does it make sense to burn your competition to the ground when you already plan to strip her of her identity?

A life taken versus a life politically ruined.

The two aren't mutually exclusive, and I'm not sure the motives align.

"What's the likelihood of you letting me walk out of here sometime soon?"

I tear my gaze away from my hands to look at Carrigan's daughter. "This room or the Palace?"

"Both." Her fingers knot the fabric of her shirt. "No, not both. The second. I've cooperated."

"Barely."

"I answered your questions," she returns sharply. "You asked and you received. And now I'm telling you that I want to leave."

"There's no end date to treason."

Her mouth falls open. "*Treason*? I'm not . . . there's

not—"

"You say that you just *happened* to visit the queen and then all hell broke loose." I pause, letting that point hit home. "Then you tell me that you don't speak to your father, but clearly you're protecting him."

"I-I—"

"You watch," I drawl, "and you listen. Isn't that what you just said?"

The handcuffs rattle as she scrambles to sit forward. "Godwin, I'm telling you right now, I don't know—"

"You do," I say, cutting her off. "You know exactly what was said in the Jewel Tower, and I don't hear you rushing to tell me a damn thing."

"Taxes!" she cries out. "They were talking about bloody *taxes.*"

She's not the only one who watches and listens, and one look at her body tells me everything I need to know. Rowena Carrigan is lying. Maybe it's a front to save her old man. Maybe it's nothing more than a last-ditch effort to save herself. Either way, I'm no fool. She's hiding something.

"Like I said, we have time to figure out if you're telling the truth."

"You can't just keep me here."

"Miss Carrigan—"

"Stop calling me that!" Her shoulders heave with fast, panicked breaths, and the sliver of exposed pale skin at the base of her throat turns a flushed pink. "I don't beg—I *won't* beg—but you have to let me go, Godwin. *Please.*"

"Just because you can't see," I say quietly, "doesn't mean you don't already know too much."

Without warning, she tears the bandages from her head and throws them to the ground at her feet. And those eyes—those striking violet eyes that I've never seen on anyone else—blink back at me.

I half expect her to lurch back in recognition.

Damien Godwin may exist within the shadows, but Damien Priest's reputation is known far and wide. And no matter how many nights I spend stalking the internet to remove every trace of myself, new articles always emerge. I'd say that everyone wants a piece of me, but the truth is far darker. I'm the devil who proved that Westminster is nothing but a fragile glass house. One snip from my hand, and the whole farce of democracy will come crumbling down. The Mad Priest is the villain society loves to hate, and he always strikes terror into the hearts of innocents.

But if Rowena is terrified, she doesn't show it.

Breathing heavily, she juts her chin forward. "Tell me what you see."

At the barely concealed anguish in her voice, my chest compresses. Not pity. Not sympathy either. But the inexplicable heaviness lingers anyway, and I hear myself rasp, "Rowena . . . don't."

"Tell me," she reiterates fiercely, "what you *see*."

I see a woman on the verge of collapse.

I see a woman on the brink of madness.

I see the shattered shards of rage that tear at my soul— only I see them in *her*.

My hold on the chair turns so violent that I'm surprised the wood doesn't splinter.

Walk away.

The words bleed from somewhere within. A threat, a command.

Self-preservation.

Wrenching my gaze from hers, I launch to my feet and immediately put distance between us that doesn't do a damned thing to release the intangible hold of her violet eyes on mine, of the unspoken knowledge that Rowena keeps secrets that could rival my own. Secrets, I think, that have nothing to do with the queen or her father, and everything to do with *her*. Broken, kindred souls.

I recognized her in an instant.

The skin across my back stretches as I clamp a hand over my shoulder, digging my fingers into the rigid muscles there that throb and ache and shriek for relief the tighter I cling. A memory of survival. A reminder that compassion has no place here in this room, in my heart.

I turn for the door. "We'll continue this tomorrow."

"You can't do it, can you?" When I don't answer, Rowena attempts to stand and I glance back just in time to see her bad leg collapse. She lands on the floor in a tangle of limbs, her hands balled into fists that she plants on the ground. Knuckles white with tension, shoulders hunched forward and emphasizing the bare slope of her neck. A broken laugh falls from her lips. "You can't even look me in the eye and tell me what you see."

Doing so would inflict unnecessary pain.

Her long hair is gone, shaved down to her skull—a job I did myself when Matthews determined that the fire had burned the soft flesh of her head. Her skin, from her collarbone to the slope of her right shoulder and the upper half of her face, already puckers with blisters. And her eyes . . . unique though the color is—well, it's obvious that she's staring into a void.

Even now, she focuses on a spot to my left, clearly confident that that's where I stand.

The difference between her reality and mine is in the space of a single meter.

I watch her silently, her hands chained together as she shifts onto her knees. And then, with her mouth pressing flat, she crumples to the side and thrusts out her right leg, like she can't bear to put weight on it.

"Godwin, did you . . ." She cocks her head to the side. "Did you leave?"

The monster in me wants to keep her locked away in the dark. To let her realize, slowly, that she's weak and defenseless and completely at my mercy.

I want to make her *beg*.

But those aren't the words that crawl from my chest and emerge gruffly: "I'm here."

"Then aren't you going to answer my—"

"I see a woman with secrets," I tell her, keeping my voice low, "a woman who almost took those secrets with her to the grave." I step backward, toward the door. "But what you don't see is a man who's honor-bound to tear each of those secrets from your soul. So, I'll be back for you tomorrow, Rowena, and when I do, there won't be any more games."

"You're *leaving*?" Something that looks like panic flickers across her face. "Godwin, think this through. I'm not—I'm not a traitor. Whatever you think that I know, I promise you that I don't."

Except that she does. "I'll see you tomorrow."

"What the hell am I supposed to do until then?"

I look back at her, at those unseeing violet eyes that are locked on a spot two paces away. And then, grabbing hold of the vengeance in my heart, I utter only one word:

"Pray."

CHAPTER 10

ROWENA

I don't pray.

But when the door cracks open early the next morning, and that maddeningly arrogant stride enters the room Dr. Matthews left me in, late last night, I wish that I took his advice to drop to my knees and get on with it.

Another round with Godwin will end in murder—whose is still up for debate.

Ignoring his heavy footfalls, I stand vigilantly by the glass-paned window, my fingers resting on the sill. One deep breath in, for fortitude, and then I expel the wretched truth: "When I was a girl, my father left me to die."

Godwin pauses.

There's no change in his breathing and not a single word falls from his lips, but he stops in his tracks—I know it deep in my soul.

Just like I know that I've captured his attention.

"We had a summer house in Golspie, this tiny village in the Highlands where nothing ever happens. But somehow . . . somehow Golspie felt more like home than London ever did. Or does, even now." I graze my forefinger over the textured wood of the windowsill. "Margaret and I met when we were eight. My father introduced us. Brought me right over to Dunrobin Castle, just a mile up the road, and told me that Mags needed a friend." I pause, curling my fingers into a loose fist before pressing them flat once more. Over my shoulder, I ask, "Did you know that when she was first sent to Scotland, they tried to pass her off as the Duke of Sutherland's niece?"

Silence fills the room, and then his voice comes, deep and raspy: "I didn't."

A small, bitter laugh pushes its way past my lips. "She blurted out the truth less than twenty-four hours later. Queen or not, Margaret is a good person. Honest to a fault. Unwaveringly loyal. And, even then, when she was just a princess hidden away in the Highlands, she knew that I needed her friendship more than she ever needed mine."

"Why are you telling me this?"

"Because you're the hero, aren't you?"

This time, there's no mistaking the aggravated sound that rumbles deep in his chest.

Victory thrums in my veins.

All night I planned for this moment. Strategized until I could barely keep my unseeing eyes open and I crashed, face down, on the soft bed I found tucked against one wall. As much as I want to battle Godwin with rancor and wit, those tactics won't work. The man fights strength with brutality and hate with malice. But yesterday, when I'd been unable to keep my walls upright, he'd softened. For a heartbeat. Maybe even less than that.

It was enough.

Enough for me to see that to attack, I have to break.

"Because," I continue, turning away from the window, "you clearly think that I'm here to stab Margaret in the back. If proving you wrong means opening Pandora's box, then I'll do it." Against my better judgment, I step forward. One foot. One risk. A shudder of relief rolls down my spine when my leg doesn't buckle. "I was thirteen when our cottage caught fire. Faulty electrical wiring, we were told—but faulty wires don't erase the memory of a bedroom door being bolted shut or my mum's screams from down the hall or the fear that gripped me when I ran to the window and saw my father on the front lawn."

I wish I could look Godwin dead in the eye and read his expression.

But I see nothing at all.

I watch, and I listen.

These days, watching has taken on an entirely new meaning.

"He saved his own arse," I say without inflection, careful to quash all emotion from my voice. Because, while I'm willing to peel back my layers to win my way out of the Palace, I won't reveal it all. Not to a man more likely to laugh in my face than cradle me close and share my pain. "If it weren't for Margaret climbing the tree outside my room, and smashing the window with a rock, I wouldn't be alive today."

Godwin draws in a deep breath, and even though I shouldn't, I can't help but visualize that inhalation expanding his broad chest. I felt him yesterday, when he dangled me from his grasp. Big, rough hands. Muscular legs that didn't so much as budge when I kicked him. A body strong enough to lift a grown woman right off the ground without breaking a sweat. I might not be tall, but curves . . . Well, those I have in spades. A fact that didn't seem to trouble Godwin one bit while he was playing caveman.

"Obviously, my father and I have a . . . complicated history. And I'll be the first to say that loving someone like him isn't"—possible—"easy. But even with all that, I don't think he's behind the attack on Buckingham Palace."

"He's putting it to Parliament that the queen is mentally unfit to rule."

I jerk back. "*What?*"

Those footsteps start again, slow and methodical, drifting closer and closer until I feel him at my side. "And he plans to do it soon, I'm sure," Godwin says as our arms brush. A single touch and I feel singed, down to my core. "Clarke told the queen, who told us."

Swallowing roughly, I shake my head. "Are you sure? There's no way he would—"

"Your father is not a good man . . . but you already know that."

For once, there's no disdain in his tone. But that doesn't mean I don't feel his words like a blow to the stomach. I've never been naïve to my father's motives—no, it was so much worse than that.

I was always so blasted *hopeful*.

Hopeful that if I did what he wanted I'd earn his love. And, if not his love, then at least his approval. Neither ever came. Not during those emotionally tense years following the fire and Mum's death; not in all the time that I spent as his "partner-in-crime" while he worked London's political circuit; not even two months ago, at the Jewel Tower, when he'd spotted me, hidden within the shadows, and turned away like I meant nothing to him.

Nearly ten years without any contact and it was like I didn't even exist.

I might not want to believe that Father would so underhandedly unseat Margaret from what's rightfully hers, but . . . I can see it. If it means returning power to him as prime minister, and power to the rest of the politicians who take their seat in Westminster every day, Edward

Carrigan will be ruthless.

The same can't be said for him trying to kill her in the fire.

"Explosions aren't his style," I say.

"Then tell me what is."

Tipping my head back at the gruff command, I concentrate on the hard pitch of Godwin's voice and turn in his direction. "Blackmail. Political sabotage." I touch my tongue to my bottom lip. Muster up the strength to give him this last sliver of truth. "Spies to weed out his enemies."

Before I can move, Godwin's wrapped a hand around my upper arm, away from the bandages. Fiercely he twists me around, growling, "Who?" His breath is hot across my temple and his proximity so close that goose bumps flare across my blistered skin. "Who the hell does he have working for him?"

"Did, past tense." I wonder if the smile I offer looks as ruined, as shattered, as it feels stretching across my face. "And you're looking at her."

The hand on my arm tightens imperceptibly. "I told you what would happen if you lie to me."

I shake him off with a sharp bite of my nails down the back of his hand, and his hiss of pain . . . It washes over me like music to my ears. I hold onto the sound, the only reminder I'm likely to get that I can still inflict damage. Knives and guns have never been my choice on the battle-field. My body is a weapon, my mind the only tool I've ever needed for destruction.

"Men are easy to break, Godwin."

He doesn't utter a single word, but I'm close . . . Close enough to drag one finger down his hard-as-steel frame. "Should I tell you all the ways I can cut a man down at the knees?" I ask softly, tilting my head.

In the ensuing silence, I imagine what my eyes don't reveal—his gaze greedy on mine and his Adam's apple bobbing with nervous anticipation. I paint an unmistakable flush on soft cheekbones and crowded teeth appearing behind a thin-lipped smirk while he debates his next move.

I picture him, for better or worse, like all the targets that I've ever hunted for the sake of politics and the future of England and Father's unrelenting ambition. It's easier than acknowledging the truth—and the truth is that Godwin could ruin me. Permanently.

But only if I let him.

"I think I will," I say, answering my own question. I drift sightless eyes over the massive body poised just centimeters away, awareness zipping down my spine. "It always starts the same, you know. A shared glance from across the room. A small smile that hints at more to come. A game that I've already won before I've even given my name."

Pressing a hand to his chest, I feel the coiled muscles jump to life beneath my palm. No matter the fact that he stands as still as stone, unmistakable heat and power radiate from beneath the confines of his thin cotton shirt. He's a predator. Death encased within flesh and bone. Each pulse of muscle a visceral reminder that unlike the wiry-framed politicians of my past, Godwin is the devil molded into the body of a god.

A god who remains perfectly inscrutable while my fingers chart the undiscovered territory of his broad chest.

Feeling unsteady, I force a light, airy chuckle past my lips. *He's just like all the others.* I repeat the words in my head like a mantra, over and over again. A man, not a god—and certainly not the devil. Godwin is no different than the men whose secrets I stole right before I slipped from their beds.

Liar.

In all those years, and in all the years since, I've never felt the lick of nerves chasing my heels like I do now.

Each graze of my palm reveals a storied tale of strength and dominance. Every sweep of my fingers tells me all I need to know: if Godwin ever did possess softness, it was destroyed long ago.

This is not a man who will melt for me.

But I'm in too deep to turn tail and run, and so I continue doggedly, "It's a brush of fingers when no one is looking and a whisper in his ear when he wavers to do the right thing. But the wrong thing . . . the devil on his shoulder, the angel dead on the floor, defeated, that's where the true wreckage happens."

Determined to shatter his resolve, I curl my fingers around his muscled forearm and tug him down, down, down. He complies—just like a man—and I press my lips to his skin. Unlike the marbled gods housed at the British Museum, though, Godwin's jaw is dusted with stubble. Masculine. Untamed. My grip on him tightens, a knee jerk reaction that I can't hide, even as I drag my mouth over his cheek to find the shell of his ear.

I linger.

I bide my time.

And then I graze my teeth over his lobe, and breathe, "Every hero has a weakness . . . even you."

I should have known better than to taunt the beast.

In the span of a second, my wrists are clamped behind my back and my feet stumble backward and then I'm turned around so abruptly that my cheek kisses chilled glass in the same moment that Godwin's massive body traps me against the window.

A harsh breath shudders over my lips.

His hold on my wrists goes ironclad tight. "Your tricks might work on every bloody member of Parliament," he growls in my ear, "but they won't on me."

I don't stop to think twice.

I shove my arse backward, right into his groin, and feel him. Long and thick and straining against his trousers. My heart pounds recklessly in my chest, its twin echo shattering all train of thought. Ears ringing, I flash him a triumphant look.

"Your cock would argue otherwise."

The sound that escapes him is nothing short of a snarl. It's vicious and angry, and bloody *hell*, my breath catches when I feel his free hand clamp down on my hip.

He doesn't shove me away.

No, he drags me into the hard cradle of his body, so that there's no mistaking the solid length of him against the base of my spine. The position flattens my cheek against the windowpane, and oh *God*. Behind my rib cage, my heart takes on an entirely new rhythm that screams *flee! Run! Save yourself!*

I don't have the chance.

Not when his velvet voice wraps like a noose around my neck, squeezing all the air from my lungs: "Don't play games that you're not willing to lose."

"That's not—"

"I'm not a man you can wind around your little finger, and I'm not your father, using his daughter to do his dirty work." He presses even closer, his chest plastered against my back. "When I come for you, you'll never know. I break the weak and I wreck the strong, and when I fuck a woman, it's not because her father told her to spread her legs for me."

Embarrassment and self-loathing flood my body, heating my face and wrenching my heart in two. It's too close to the truth. Too dirty and raw and—

"Let me go," I whisper, struggling in his arms, despite the fact that his hand remains a shackle around my wrists. "Let me *go*."

"There are no heroes here. Remember that."

I stomp on his booted foot, but the bastard doesn't even grunt out in pain. "I said, *let me go*, Godwin."

"Damien."

A startled noise emerges from deep within my throat. "What?"

"My name is Damien Godwin," he says in a tone as merciless as the waves that strike the white-chalked walls of the White Cliffs of Dover, "but you'll know me as Damien Priest."

I freeze.

Go absolutely still.

He chuckles, the sound so low and wrathful that terror sparks in my blood. And then he strokes my hip with his thumb, like he has all the time in the world to make me wish that I were already dead, even as he dips his head forward and whispers in my ear: "No one escapes the Mad Priest, Rowena . . . least of all you."

CHAPTER 11

DAMIEN

Freedom tastes like desolation.

With my back plastered against the shadowed walls of the Parliamentary Offices, and my eyes locked on Westminster's Victoria Tower, across Abingdon Street, there's no hiding the fact that seven months has forever altered London's landscape.

I may have lost my humanity, but this city has been stripped of something far worse.

The streets are empty, the people gone. Sirens wail somewhere off in the distance, the sound so bone-chilling against the utter stillness that it feels like I've stepped into a post-apocalyptic world.

This is not my home.

This is not my London.

But somehow, someway, it's come to this.

Dropping one knee to the wet grass, I peer around the corner wall of the Offices. Illuminated by only streaks of moonlight escaping a thick sweep of clouds, the Jewel Tower stands like an ancient fortress, its stone walls artfully crumbled but still holding strong after seven centuries.

Two guards congregate near the front door, identical

SA80s slung across chests dressed in combat body armor.

"Bloody taxes, my ass," I mutter under my breath.

The only reason Carrigan would assign security to the Jewel Tower, of all places, would be if he has something inside worth protecting. Which means that Rowena lied to me . . . *again*.

Gritting my teeth against the memory of imploring violet eyes, I press deeper into the shadows and prop my forearm on my bent knee. The movement activates my wristwatch, its blank face glowing red. I tap the tiny map in the right-hand corner and wait for it to calibrate my coordinates.

Idiot.

I shouldn't have given her my name.

Shouldn't have allowed her to poke and prod and stroke my temper to life, until I was spitting fire and harder than I've ever been and prepared to do just about anything to wipe the smirk from her face.

Facts keep me steady; data is my only book of prayer. And yet, with her finger grazing my chest and her breathing so blasted steady that she could have been touching a piece of wood, instead of a living, breathing male, I lost control.

For the first time in my life, *I lost control.*

Fucking hell.

Another sharp glance at the Tower reveals that the two guards haven't moved.

A humorless smile tilts my mouth. Seven months of house arrest may have wrought more damage on my psyche than I even know, but in this, no amount of space and time can ruin what I do best.

Spying The Cloisters on the interactive map, which sit on the backend of the Jewel Tower, I press down on the screen until a drop-down menu appears. Gunfire. Tear gas.

Grenade. It's an auditory buffet of my own design, ruthless and creative and prone to instigating all-out destruction.

Every hero has a weakness . . . even you.

"Fuck," I grunt, wishing I could eviscerate the memory of her husky voice right before I realized she was working me over like a professional.

If I'd been anyone else, I would have taken her right then and there—blind, ruined, and all—joggers tugged down and forgotten around her ankles; knickers shoved to the side with a crook of my finger; bent over, face down, my cock a hard reminder that love and hate are mirrored versions of the same indefinable emotion.

She'd love each thrust just as surely as she despised the man fucking her.

Rowena has it wrong: I'm not the hero here, and I have only one weakness that could bring me to my knees. And it's not a woman with rebellion in her eyes or a penchant for—

I select gunfire.

A second passes, and then human-made pandemonium arrives.

The air explodes with the sound of rounds unloading. Volatile. Insistent. One after another, sounding so damn realistic that if I didn't know any better—if I weren't the bastard who designed the watch—I'd be hard-pressed to believe that it isn't real.

As it is, I observe from the shadows as the two guards shove at each other. Helmets conceal their expressions, but I don't need to see their faces to know the havoc I've unleashed.

"Go!" the taller one argues, the panicked command carrying on the damp breeze.

"Me? Are you *mad*? I've been on the job for two bloody days!"

"Does it look like I care? As your superior, I'm telling you to *investigate*."

Without remorse, I tap my watch again and go for round two.

Ra-ta-ta-ta!

The guards leap in unison, helmets swiveling toward the paved path that leads to The Cloisters. They stand there, hands gripping their rifles, booted feet rooted in place.

"Bugger all," the superior finally says, "I'll go, okay? I'll go."

I wait until he's disappeared around the corner before I slide a finger under the Velcro flap of my military-grade vest and pull out a palm-sized ball. Keeping my eyes firmly locked on the remaining guard, I activate the device with a shallow push of a button and hurl it across the lawn.

It lands with a heavy *thud* in the grass.

Three.

The guard whirls around, rifle raised.

Two.

"Oi!" he calls, fear rampant in his voice. "Who's there?"

One.

A flash of blue coincides with a startling *crack!* that has the guard throwing himself to the pavement, his arms curled over his head.

I narrow my eyes. Snarl "get *up*" under my breath, as if that'll force the man to grow a pair of bollocks and do his blasted job. Jesus. Where the hell did Carrigan find these two bellends?

Finally, *finally*, he belly-crawls forward on his elbows and knees.

Not ideal, but it'll have to do.

Marking his position by the glint of his helmet under the sparse moonlight, I stalk toward him on silent feet, already reaching into my vest again.

He grunts something unintelligible.

My fingertips graze a coil of hard wire.

"What the hell—" Cutting himself off, he shifts onto his knees and taps the modified flashbang with a single finger, clearly wary of it exploding all over again.

Which it will. Fifteen seconds, if that.

Scooping the device into one palm, he turns it over in his hands. He's so focused on the weapon that he doesn't notice my approach until it's too late.

The flashbang implodes and he releases a garbled shout, and I hook the wire over his throat, each end looped around my knuckles to keep the pressure tight on his airway.

He gurgles and he thrashes, the SA80 falling from his chest to hang under his armpit while he grapples with my fists.

I drag him deeper into the shadows.

With each meter, he loses another sign of consciousness. His feet stop kicking, his legs go slack, and then, finally, his hands fall from mine to the damp grass. When his breathing slips into a shallow rhythm that barely expands his chest, I pause to stuff the wire back into its designated pocket.

Then, with my hands locked around his biceps, I pull his limp frame all the way to the Jewel Tower's arched oak door.

Quickly, I pluck the body camera off his chest and shove it into the front pocket of my trousers. Then cast my gaze to the security scanner that's bolted into the stone beside the door.

It's an unfamiliar model.

"You've been busy, Carrigan," I mutter. Not that I'm surprised.

He knew I'd come. I don't know how, and I don't know who could have warned him—especially since Rowena is currently locked away in the Palace—but it's a feeling deep in my gut that just won't quit. One look at the scanner and it's easy to deduce that he built it with me in mind: the back paneling is so deeply lodged into the ancient stone that I can't access the wiring.

I lower my chin to look at the guard.

Time for drastic measures.

Hooking my hands under his armpits, I haul him onto his feet and lean him against the Tower, careful to keep my hip against his thighs so that his unconscious body won't topple over. I rip off his glove, yank up his hand, and press the pad of his forefinger to the scanner.

It doesn't register.

Fuck.

Hastily, I pull up my coordinates again on my watch, then set off another round of gunfire within one of the enclaves of Westminster Abbey. My ears prick a second later when I hear the echoing charge of fake bullets firing, and then I'm back in the game.

I pat down the guard, searching for a badge, and come up with absolutely nothing. I shove all ten fingers on the scanner, one by one. When all that fails, I tear off his helmet, shove his face against the screen, and grunt, "Smile for the camera, mate."

My thumb lifts his thin, fragile eyelid.

The scanner awakens with a soft *beep-beep*, a half-second before the door audibly unlocks.

Without preamble, I plant the heel of my boot against heavy oak and step inside, dropping the guard's body just within the entrance and nabbing the helmet off the pavement before the arched door swings closed. I jam it on my head—it would be just like Carrigan to install cameras all over this place—and prowl up the spiral stairwell.

I haven't stepped foot in the Jewel Tower in years, but its stone interior hasn't changed. Carved into the curved ceiling are the grotesque faces of animal heads with their twisted grins, bared teeth, and taloned fingers, all of which would look more at home if they were sheathed in blood.

The helmet muffles the clip of my footsteps, but it doesn't hide the double doors that come into view when I hit the landing of the second floor. They yield without trouble, as I figured they would—because if Edward Carrigan is hiding anything here, it's in the turret room.

A room that's blockaded by an iron door.

I move swiftly, noting *1621* embossed in the iron—marking the year King James I began using the Tower—and dart a glance at the vaulted ceiling . . . and at the security camera I knew would be waiting.

Predictable.

Yanking the grenade off my vest, I pull the fuse and toss it toward the corner of the room. It activates with a soft *pop* and, almost immediately, wisps of smoke become thick and impenetrable plumes that shield me from view as I crack the lock on the iron door and step inside.

All over the room, papers are piled atop desks and tables, even on the floor. Backed into one corner is a bronze bust of King James I himself—and I laugh, low and dark and gritty, because only Edward Carrigan would convert this room to be exactly what it was under James I's reign. A place to hold secret documents. A place fit for only a king.

Turning on the overhead light, I move from desk to desk, tearing through paperwork, searching for the one thing we'll need to pin Carrigan's ass to the wall. The thought of finally catching him . . . of forcing him to suffer the way he's made *me* suffer . . .

Death shouldn't make me smile.

It shouldn't make me feel this alive.

But it does.

Fuck, it *does*, to the point that my pulse races like I've taken a hit of the most potent drug.

I was never innocent; life in Holyrood strips naivety early on, until it's forever erased, never to be resurrected from the broken fragments at your feet. But I was hopeful, once. Dedicated to the cause and the Crown and my brothers. Determined to one day find happiness outside the death and the bloodshed and the never-ending battle of keeping the royal family alive.

And then it was gone.

A rasp of movement behind me, darkness shoved down over my head.

An unfamiliar hand pressing a taser to my spine, its voltage sharp and painful. But not nearly as painful as the knife that plunged into my right shoulder a moment later—then twisted.

Fire engulfed my body. My voice gave way to a groan. And my hands, always accustomed to building and deconstructing, went limp as I hit the pavement. Carrigan's men had dragged me into the alley behind Christ Church Spitalfields. If they'd been smart, they would have stabbed me again, just to make sure that I wouldn't come back from the grave to tear them each limb from limb.

Except they'd done nothing but lean over my paralyzed body, dig the knife deeper into my flesh, and laugh.

Guy found me. Matthews saved me.

Rowena can say all she wants that her father and the king were best mates, but if that were true, John would have told Carrigan about Holyrood, about *us*. He would have stayed lenient with Parliament, allowing MPs the autonomy they've had for centuries. He wouldn't have sent me to the House of Commons at Westminster because he suspected the prime minister of foul play.

And I never would have been left for dead.

Rage blurs my periphery, and, for a moment, I allow myself to sink into its embrace.

Its claws grate down my spine and its heat wraps like a vice around my heart, and I breathe the anger in, swallowing it deep into my lungs until I'm forced to grit my teeth to smother the furious scream demanding release.

Reaching out, I snatch the next sheet of paper from the desk and press it flat before me.

Force my eyes on the words, and stop, dead-cold, at the mention of a name I recognize. A name that, as of a month ago, anyone in London would recognize from the news.

Ian Coney.

CHAPTER 12

DAMIEN

"Back so soon?" comes an accented voice.

Stopping in front of Rowena's door, I spare Hamish a sharp glance. With his mobile in one hand and a tumbler of whisky clasped in the other, the Scot peers up at me from the plush armchair he clearly commandeered from the library. "Ye can't tell me to leave, ye know. Guy assigned me."

As if I need another reminder that my brother's word is law around here. "I'm aware."

Looking contemplative, Hamish idly taps the corner of his mobile against his thigh. "I've lost count. Is this yer second visit with her? Third?"

"It's not a—" Realizing that he sounds a little too cheerful, I narrow my eyes and fight the urge to flip over the armchair, just to wipe that godawful smirk from his face. "This isn't a social visit."

"'Course it isn't."

"She's a prisoner," I edge out thinly. "I'm interrogating her." Hamish only makes a dramatic show of drinking his whisky, which has me praying for some bloody patience. "Spit it out, MacDonald."

Clearly recognizing that I'm *this* close to introducing my fist to his face, Hamish sets the tumbler down on the flat armrest. Then, like a proper wanker, he steeples his fingers and taps his knuckles against his mouth. "All I'm saying is, *fuck a woman* isn't generally something I bring up in interrogations. New tactics of yers, maybe. Keep me updated on how they work, yeah?"

"Were you *eavesdropping*?"

He doesn't even have the good grace to look sheepish. Rolling one shoulder in a lazy shrug, he props up his feet on a matching ottoman. "I've a lot of time on my hands now that Guy's promoted me to nanny duty. Can't say I miss being out in the field when the alternative is this." As if to make his point, he waves a hand at the elaborate setup—the armchair, the telly he's brought in from God-knows-where, and the magazine featuring a naked woman on the front. The latter he tosses onto the ottoman, out of my line of sight, when he catches my hard stare.

"Hamish?"

He doesn't even blink. "Yeah?"

"You have five seconds to leave or I'm going to murder you."

"So defensive," he tsks. "Keep that up and I'd almost think that ye didn't like me anymore. Which would be a bloody shame, really, because who else will watch tennis with me if not—"

"Four," I growl.

"Ye're really counting down? My heart is broken, Priest. Ye've gone and shattered it."

"*Three.*"

"I suppose this means that ye don't want to hear about Miss Carrigan's latest visitor?" When my mouth promptly snaps shut, his curves in a grin that toes the damn line at gleeful. Clearly intent on testing the threadbare limits of my patience, the bastard offers a silent toast of his whisky. "That's what I thought," he murmurs with an infuriating wink.

Jesus.

"Now, I could make ye guess *or* I could quit playing coy and just say—"

"*Get on with it.*"

Unfazed, Hamish gestures at the door with his tumbler. "He's inside."

There's no need to ask him to elaborate.

We both know there's only one *he* who would be interested in talking to Rowena—who even knows that she's here, save for me and Matthews.

I don't waste another second with the Scot.

Wrenching the door open, I step inside, my gaze moving swiftly past the floor-to-ceiling tapestries detailing William the Conqueror at the Battle of Hastings to the diamond-paned window that I cornered Rowena against yesterday morning. Her fractured breathing had fogged the ancient window while her ass ground against me in a dance that's only rhythm was blatant defiance. She'd made me hard and she'd made me crave, and even then, with her body weak and defenseless, I knew that giving in would mean letting her sink her claws into my hide.

A she-wolf out to make me her prey.

"Come for another visit, brother?" comes Guy's dark drawl.

Palm flat against the wood, I shut the door slowly and allow myself a second to breathe in the irritation, and let it run free before turning around to find my brother seated in the alcove that was used for prayer centuries ago. Intricate artwork details the plasterwork with blooming flowers and winding vines, as if to sit within means entering the Garden of Eden.

The irony. Guy Godwin doesn't do temptation.

"We were just discussing how you've acted rather . . ." Guy turns to Rowena, who sits opposite him at a table that wasn't here yesterday—another commandeered piece from the library, by the looks of it. "What's the word you used for Damien again, Miss Carrigan?"

Rowena doesn't even hesitate: "A bastard."

The wry grin he offers doesn't reach his eyes. "Ah, my mistake. Two words." With his long legs sprawled out before him and his hands clasped over his stomach, he meets my stare straight-on as though he expects me to drop to my knees and beg forgiveness. "You've been bad, brother."

My expression stays neutral. My breathing never alters.

But inside . . . my emotions are in *riot*.

The irritation flares and it devours and it fucking drowns me whole.

Bad. Such a mild word for an entire lifetime of doing very evil things to achieve extraordinary ends. I felt the prick of guilt, once—a long time ago when I returned to Paris and the cemetery where we buried Mum. It took twelve years for her body to decompose and only three hours in the dead of night to dig up her remains. Fragile bones. Dirt caked between skeletal joints. And a precious silver chain that I snatched from her neck and buried in my pocket.

You've been very, very bad, Damien.

Anger skates a ravaged finger down the length of my spine, reminding me that I'm a man with war in my blood and hate in my heart, and I never had much hope of being good. But to hear my brother repeat the same words that have haunted me for years . . . I feel the dirt from my mother's coffin like mud in my veins.

Poison.

Desperation.

Soiled, down to the roots of my battered soul.

Smothering the turmoil, before it crests the surface, I hold my brother's gaze. "Do you have a point?"

"I couldn't find you last night," he replies, his tone deceptively pleasant, "so imagine my surprise when I learned from Paul that he saw you leaving the Palace." Propping one forearm on the table, he inclines his head toward Rowena. "He isn't supposed to do that, you know."

Her violet eyes remain fixed on the wall. "You mentioned."

"So I did," Guy murmurs, never once looking away from my face. "It wasn't nice of you to leave Miss Carrigan wondering what side of the war we're on." His blue stare sparks fire, and I know, even though he won't say so out loud, that he's furious with me. Furious enough to air out all of our dirty laundry, audience be damned. "You locked her up, brother. You put her in handcuffs. And then, like that wasn't enough, you made her think that we might actually kill—"

"Get up."

At my brusque order, his brows snap together. "What did you say?"

"Don't make me repeat myself, *brother*." Prowling forward, I reach into the back pocket of my trousers for the slip of paper that I nabbed from the Jewel Tower. "Rowena and I are going to have a little talk." The smile I give him stretches unnaturally wide. Predatory. The look of a madman. "Feel free to stay. But that"—I nod toward his seat—"is about to be mine."

Then, as if he weighs nothing at all, I haul Guy off the chair and take his place. Spread my long legs wide, locking them on either side of Rowena's bare feet, and drop my elbows onto the compact table. The antique wood trembles beneath her clasped hands while dark satisfaction threads like silk through my body.

"Hello, Rowena."

A muscle works in her jaw, but to her credit, she doesn't turn and run. "Damien," she greets, her tongue rolling over the syllables of my name like she'd prefer nothing more than to see me dead and buried. "Always a pleasure."

"How much did it pain you to say that?"

"On a scale of one to ten? Only a five, maybe even a four." Had she any hair, I'm sure she'd flip the strands over her shoulder. As it is, she props her chin on an upturned palm and parts her lips in a cool, dismissive smile. "You'd actually have to mean something to me to rank any higher."

Rowena Carrigan is a liar, possibly even a fraud, but the armor she wears is weathered with dents and holes. For better or worse, I'm already in her head. Driving her mad. Pushing her closer and closer to the edge of no return. And maybe I'm as bad as all of England believes because instead of smoothing the waters, I lean forward and trace the back of her hand, directly over a delicate blue-green vein, just to shatter her ramshackle emotional shield.

A tiny gasp slips past her lips.

"Only a four?" I drawl, my gaze trained on her flushed cheeks when she tugs away, severing contact. "Rowena, I'm so far under your skin—"

"Like a nasty infection that won't go away."

"—that I can practically smell the brimstone off you."

"Figures you'd recognize the scent, since you're probably a repeat offender." Eyes narrowing in my direction, her chin angles upward. "Does Satan still bother rolling out the red carpet for you or is it just limited to special occasions nowadays?"

I bare my teeth in a merciless grin. "I've my own key

to the kingdom."

"Funny," she quips with mocking sweetness, "but I'm sensing an onslaught of predictability coming on."

"Yeah?"

"Oh, we've definitely already been here before. You're the big, bad wolf on the hunt and I'm the innocent—"

"Not that innocent," I mutter darkly, remembering her ass pressed against my cock.

"—prisoner intent on escape. Insert appropriate screaming from me and some unintelligible growling from you. And while we're at it"—she throws me an arch glance—"ditch the handcuffs this time. Turns out I'm already over your high-handed, arrogant—"

"Who's Ian Coney?"

The abruptly asked question renders her mute, just as I knew it would.

In an obvious attempt to buy herself time, she runs a finger over the back of her ear, like she didn't hear the question. "I'm sorry . . . who?"

Oh, Rowena. Who's predictable now?

Reclining backward, I angle my legs so that she's good and stuck—my little captive audience. And, because I'm willing to wait all day if it means dragging the truth out of her, I draw a small, idle circle on the stolen paper from the Jewel Tower.

She lasts all of fifteen seconds.

"I think maybe . . ." Her fingers curl into fists that she sinks beneath the table. "I've heard the name."

"I'm sure you have," I murmur silkily, my finger still circling, round and round, my gaze still fixed on her face. On that full mouth of hers that whispers untruths like my very own Apate.

A goddess of lies who sits on her throne of deception.

I'll enjoy breaking her.

Delicately, Rowena clears her throat. "Coney was a professor at Queen Mary, wasn't he? At least, that's what I saw on the news." Her spine visibly straightens. "What does any of this have to do with me?"

That's what I plan to find out.

I want to tuck my fingers into the collar of her shirt and drag her across the table, until her eyes are wide and her tongue is loose and all the truths come tumbling out into the open. But that would be . . . *high-handed* of me.

Arrogant.

Sweet, fucking temptation.

With effort, I stay sprawled on the wooden chair, my only movement the whispered staccato of my knuckles drumming against the table. *Tap. Tap. Tap.*

Rowena flinches.

And I strike: "He was strangled."

"I heard." Her black lashes sweep downward, shielding those violet eyes from view. "It seems a gruesome way to die."

"Oh, it is."

"Why are we talking about this? Whatever happened to that . . . man has nothing to do with me."

"Have you ever fired a gun, Rowena?" Behind me, I hear Guy moving, rustling around. But my eyes never leave her face. I track the furrow of her dark brows and the way her bottom lip catches behind straight, white teeth. "No handcuffs on the line here," I murmur, "just a yes or no answer."

Her plush lip whitens under the pressure of her teeth, unease scripted into every line of her body. Finally, she blows out a short breath. "I've held one."

"But did you fire it?"

A slow shake of her head brings me to my feet. Rounding the table, I skate my fingers over the chair separating mine from hers, making sure to jostle it as I pass.

The feet scrape the wood floor.

Her head jerks to the left, following the unhurried tread of my footsteps.

I stop directly behind her.

Time lulls, a moment frozen where my gaze drifts over the gentle curve of her skull to the bare skin of her nape. From this vantage point, there's no mistaking the way her inner thighs kiss, like she's prepared to bolt, and I almost tell Guy to get out.

To leave us alone.

But some secret corner of my soul, battered and bruised, screams that I can't be trusted. A good man would soothe her worries. A better man would lead her to freedom. A bad man . . . Well, I don't allow myself to think twice. Within the Garden of Eden—a place once dedicated to peace and book and prayer—I commit the biggest sin of all.

I fold my body forward, hunching my shoulders to avoid hitting the sloped wall, and slip one hand around the front of Rowena's throat.

Her shoulders heave with a sudden gasp. "*Godwin*—"

"Damien."

I feel her hard swallow against the heel of my palm. "Damien," she breathes, both hands darting north to clutch the table. "What are you . . . what are you doing?"

"Demonstrating."

Ignoring Guy's steely glare, I plant my free hand on the table next to hers, then lower my face so that we're cheek to cheek. I surround her on all sides, my chest to her back, my arms keeping her enclosed—an embrace of power, a prison of human flesh. Her shaky breath echoes in my ear, a sound that shouldn't feel like an invitation to edge closer but somehow does, and I almost circle her tighter, just to hear her make it again.

"It takes less effort to strangle someone than it does to pull the trigger on a handgun," I tell her, voice low. "Cut off the carotid artery and you have ten seconds, maybe twenty, before bliss hits and reality disappears."

My thumb grazes the length of her throat, soft flesh interrupted by fragile blisters that are an instant reminder that the woman seated before me isn't some helpless victim. She bartered with me when she was handcuffed, and she used her sexuality to prove that I'm a man like any other. A man who wants, a man who succumbs. And so, I tighten my grip, just enough to keep the upper hand, only to feel inexplicable heat flood my veins when she doesn't claw at my fingers.

No.

She fucking blooms like the flowers painted on the archway of the alcove.

Her shoulders drop and her head falls back, against my collarbone, and she releases a noise that's as tangible, as erotic, as if she wrapped her hand around my cock and squeezed. Hard. My heart hammers ruthlessly against my rib cage.

"Why are you telling me this?" she whispers.

Turning my head, I allow my lips to graze the sharp cut of her cheekbone. *Whimper for me again.* The demand dances on the tip of my tongue, ready to be unleashed—to hell with the consequences. And the consequences . . .

"There's something on the table for you."

"Is this when I'm supposed to scream?"

"If it is," I utter for her alone, "then this is when I promise to fill your mouth and shut you up."

"Predictable," she rasps. "The world would be dis-appointed to know that the Mad Priest is nothing but a B-grade villain."

"The world? Or just you?"

"I rated you a four, remember?"

My lip curls. "You gave me a five, at first."

"Clearly, a miscalculation."

"Reach forward, Rowena."

"In case you haven't noticed, your hand is at my jugular."

I tsk under my breath. "All I hear are excuses."

With an irritated growl, that feels like a purr against the clasp of my palm, she stretches out an arm.

"To the left," I instruct, whispering the command against her ear.

Her fingers dance across the wood, searching, seeking, before finally making contact with the slip of paper. Instead of picking it up, she pins it to the table with her forefinger and drags it close. I hear her teeth grinding, the uneven pitch of her breathing that she can't mask, just before she bites off, "I have no idea what I'm holding."

Your destruction.

"I'll summarize." With one hand still clasped around her throat, I fold my other around hers. Broad fingers slipping between slender. Calloused flesh meeting soft wounds. My hand spans twice the size of hers, and her pulse leaps beneath my touch. "It's a bank wire transfer to Ian Coney for fifty-thousand pounds. Dated to a month ago."

She inhales sharply.

I lift my gaze to find Guy watching us, unblinking. He mouths something that looks suspiciously like, "What the hell are you doing?" but I don't answer.

We all have a method to our madness.

Saxon with his rough brutality.

Guy with his mind games.

And me, somewhere in the middle, a seamless blend of the two that strikes at the vulnerable underbelly of my opponent and destroys any chance of escape. Humans aren't unlike the coding that I manipulate and bend to my will. We're conditioned to fear the unknown, to shirk away from danger. And when the fear does take hold, it's too late to pretend that we haven't already entered the realm of the inevitable.

I know that better than anyone.

Listening for the telltale hitch in Rowena's breath, I revel in the way her body strains closer, her cheek running against the grain of my stubble, her fingers flexing against the table. She's desperate for something she won't dare admit out loud, the dents and holes in her armor knitting closed to keep me out.

No mercy.

"Coney would have been fully aware of everything until those last few seconds," I say, drawing a tiny circle over her racing pulse. "Every kick of his feet as he tried to work himself free; every breath he took that got him nowhere. He was dying, and he knew it, and it makes me wonder . . . in those moments, just before darkness fell, what would a man like Ian Coney think of?"

I'd thought of vengeance.

As my body lay prone on that dirty street, unable to move, there'd been no thought of lost love or last regrets or hope that I might see my brothers one final time.

I'd *been* rage.

Seven months has changed nothing.

"Damien, I—"

"I'm going to ask you one more time," I tell her softly. "Who was Ian Coney to you?"

Finally, at this, she jerks wildly in my grip. "*Nothing*, okay? He was nothing to me."

Another lie.

I shouldn't be surprised. And, hell, maybe I'm even a little . . . relieved. Because if she'll lie about this, then I don't need to feel any remorse for what I do next. With one last stroke of my fingers over her quivering throat, I step away, taking the paper with me. "Your father had him killed."

"*What?*"

I stop beside Guy, making sure to look him in the eye when I mouth, "Play along." To Rowena, I pretend to clear my throat, a pitiful offer of condolences for the goddess of deceit herself. "The wire transfer," I say, noting the way she turns in her chair to follow my voice. "Fifty-thousand pounds to have Ian Coney murdered."

"But the news . . . the news said that—"

"My brother was cleared as a suspect, if that's what you mean." I pause, letting that sink in. Then, "You seem awfully worked up. I thought Ian Coney was nothing to you?"

Her lips press firmly shut.

And I smile, slowly.

Oh, Rowena. I have you.

Cornered.

Squirming.

Ruined.

Folding the slip of paper crisply in half, I hand it to Guy, who immediately takes it.

Rowena pushes to her feet, stumbling a little. "I'm tired of interrogations, Godw—*Damien*." Her naturally husky voice carries a touch of unease. "Every part of me is hurting and I'm ready to go home. Your brother said I could leave."

Still scanning Carrigan's email, Guy shifts his weight beside me. "I did promise her."

I tuck my fingers into the front pockets of my trousers. "I think interrogations are over, anyway."

Clearly unconvinced, Rowena's brows lift. "You're going to let me go . . . just like that?"

Not a chance.

But I know when I've pushed an interrogation as far as it'll go without resorting to violence. Snug in her home, with her guard down and her hackles lowered, it'll only be a matter of time before Rowena lets her secrets slip—and I'll be waiting to collect each and every one.

"I'm going to let you go," I lie smoothly, "just like that. Unless you have something else to tell us?"

"I'm pretty sure that I've said more than enough." Her violet eyes swing in my direction, stopping just short of my body. "But I want to see you."

Startled by the unexpected request, my lungs constrict. "What?"

"Before I leave," she murmurs, taking one step toward me, "I want to see you."

A deafening roar silences everything but my heartbeat. "You're blind."

"Just because I can't see doesn't mean anything. Isn't that what you told me?" She takes another step, this one a bit wobbly, and then yet another. Until she's standing an arm's length away and staring up at me with those violet eyes that can't possibly be real. Too otherworldly, too feminine for a woman more likely to shoot a man than nap in a field of heather like some fairytale princess. "Come here."

It's not a request, not quite a command.

I swing my gaze over to my brother, who stands like stone beside me. He's studying Rowena with an expression that I can't nail down, and I have this . . . Fucking hell, I don't know what it is. A want. A desire. An *urge* to step between them, so that he can't see her.

Can't see *this*, whatever the bloody hell this even is.

"You owe me, Damien," she says. "You cuffed me. You dangled me in the air. You put your *hand on my throat* like you were five seconds away from strangling me to—"

I'm not aware of my feet moving, of destroying the distance between us in two powerful strides. I look down at her shaved skull and the fresh scars gleaming an angry red under the soft, overhead lights. She tips her head back, as if assessing the size of me—how the top of her crown only comes up to my chest—and then she lifts her hand, fingers loosely curled.

The request doesn't need explanation.

This is insane.

Utter madness.

And yet I touch her wrist, gently circling the delicate bone. Place her fingers on the scruff of my jaw and suck a harsh breath deep into my lungs when the heat of her palm cups the side of my face.

Ten minutes ago, I had her at my mercy and now . . .

Her forefinger traces the shadow of my stubble, the bridge of my nose. She skims the crest of my cheekbone, pausing to discover the tiny scar that creates a shallow groove just below my left eyebrow. And then that one finger sweeps downward, taking a direct path south, until her thumb brushes my lower lip. She tugs on the flesh, gently.

My cock hardens to the point of pain.

"And?" I demand on a husky rasp. "Am I what you expected?"

"No horns," she whispers, "no elongated incisors. Turns out that you're human, after all, Damien Priest."

"Monsters hide in us all."

"That might be the only thing you've said that we can agree on."

A small smile quirks her lips, and I can almost picture

her . . . before. The sweet mouth. The flirtatious laughter. The long, flowing hair that would no doubt feel like silk wrapped around my fist. She had the face of an angel and now she's something entirely different.

Fallen.

Cast down from the heavens to unleash destruction on the rest of us mere mortals.

And none of that explains why I'm desperate to grasp her hand in mine and nip at her fingers. To draw them into my mouth, one by one, until she's whimpering again—a sound meant only for me—and I'm showing her all the ways that we monsters know how to make a woman beg.

I'd drive her to her knees. Spread her legs wide. Run my tongue over the curve of her ass and circle my fingers over her clit while her forehead kisses the floor and her hands curl into trembling fists. She'd beg for me to stop, she'd beg for me to make her come, and if she was good, maybe I'd—

The curve of her smile deepens, one corner hitching slightly higher than the other. Dropping her hand away from my face, she traces the seam of her lips with the same finger that she used on me.

It's deliberate. A challenge.

Men are easy to break—her words, not mine. Fucking hell. In this moment, with my cock throbbing in my trousers and my heart racing in my chest, I feel unmoored.

Unchained.

Forcefully, I step back and plant a hand on Guy's shoulder, so that he has no choice but to follow me.

"We'll have Hamish bring you home," I tell her, needing to . . . Jesus, I need *away*. Out of this room. Off this bloody estate. As far as I can go because I can still feel her throat under my palm and her thumb dancing across my lips and the hitched pressure seated on my chest that's yet to ease.

I want to throw her on the closest flat surface and fuck her raw.

Her, the liar.

Her, the enemy's daughter.

Her, the woman who sees nothing and too much of everything, all at once.

Before I can escape the room, though, her voice stops me in my tracks:

"What color eyes do you have?"

I glance over my shoulder, rejecting the relentless tug in my gut that urges me forward to where she waits, outlined by the alcove of the Garden of Eden.

I should lie and tell her that they're an unearthly green like Saxon's or as black as the devil's—as black as my soul, even. But the truth slips out on a rasp that I wish I could snatch back: "Blue, like the water in Cornwall." The same color that I share with Guy, and with my mum. For whatever that's worth. I fall back another step. "Goodbye, Rowena."

Her head tips to the side. Then, low and soft, she replies, "Goodbye for now, Damien."

CHAPTER 13

ROWENA

've barely closed the door to my flat when a voice from within remarks, "So you're alive."

Four nights.

It's been nearly ninety-six hours of fear and hate and heat, and I—

I slam my eyes shut, despising the way my fingers instinctively creep up to my throat. He held me, he threatened me, and I have no idea what it says about me that all I felt was *relief* in that moment. Freedom. A dark desperation that curled in my veins and tasted unmistakably like desire.

Damien Priest may very well be the devil incarnate, but with his hand locked around my neck, and his breath hot on my cheek, he felt like the savior I never knew I needed instead.

Fuck me.

Forcing my hand down by my side, I mutter, "Were you expecting to find me dead?"

"You went dark for days. Honestly, I began to think the worst."

I'm pretty sure that our versions of "the worst" exist on

two polar axes. "I was held up."

"You're never held up."

"Well, there's a first time for everything because, oh, that's right"—I snap my fingers—"Buckingham Palace caught on fire."

A tiny pause precedes a rather disgruntled, "Sarcasm doesn't become you, Rowan."

Nothing becomes me.

Biting back the hot retort, I turn around slowly. Move forward, expecting to hit a stray piece of furniture, but I've had this flat for so long that the darkness doesn't eviscerate muscle memory. *Thank God.* Four steps take me to the closest sofa, and, without any show of grace, I drop to the cushions in a heap of exhaustion.

"I told you this would happen—didn't I?"

Ignoring the snide comment, I let my head fall back. Then drag in a heavy breath that doesn't do me any bit of good in relieving the coiled tension from my body. "You failed to mention the fire."

"Well, I didn't know there *would* be a fire."

"Isn't that why I pay you?" I ask, my face still turned up to the ceiling. "To find out everything that I need to know, so—oh, I don't know—maybe I won't end up *blind*?"

A strangled noise erupts, followed by the quick pounding of a fist on a hard chest. "Sorry, I could have sworn that you said . . . Did you just say—"

"Turn the light on."

"Rowan, I think that—"

"I know that you get a kick out of waiting for me in the dark."

"It's less of a *kick*, really, and more that it's bleeding hard to catch you off guard."

"The light. Turn it on."

The sofa's springs whine with the release of weight, and then heavy feet pad across the herringbone-wood floor. Tonight will be the last time I use this flat, and I can't help but feel a tug of regret about being forced to give it up. It's not the least bit posh but it's *mine*. Mine when I fled Father's home ten years ago, and mine in all these years since—a safe haven, and then, later, a place of secrecy to gather round when we needed a change of scenery.

My heart beats in time with the antique clock on the fireplace mantle. *Ticktock. Ticktock. Ticktock.* The switch audibly clicks, signaling the arrival of light that I can't see, and then those footsteps return, momentarily pausing beside me before continuing.

The sofa creaks again.

And then I sit forward, elbows propped on my parted knees. "Take a good look," I murmur, "at what happens when you don't follow through on bloody intel."

"Good God."

I raise my brows, and promptly ignore how the skin on my forehead pulls uncomfortably tight. "Anything else you want to add?"

"You look—" A hard swallow that I couldn't miss, not even if I lived halfway across the world in the States. "Well, that's to say . . . You've . . . looked better."

A harsh laugh climbs my throat. "I liked your brother more."

The ensuring silence is punctured by the audible grinding of teeth. "I've never thought otherwise, Rowan."

I refuse to feel guilty for saying what's in my heart. For speaking up when, for years, I swallowed the truth until I choked on it. "I almost died," I growl, pointing at my face, at my ribs that are covered by the same loose swing of fabric that I've worn for three days now. "*She* almost died.

And Clarke—*fuck*."

"He's not one of us."

"Does it matter?" I pinch the bridge of my nose, then smooth my palm over my shorn hair. Gone, all of it. I won't mourn something that'll grow back in a matter of months, but still, it feels like yet another loss that's stripped something from me that I didn't willingly give. "He's dead," I say sharply. "He's dead, just like Margaret almost died, and all because you—"

"Kidnapping, Rowan. I had word that she was going to be *kidnapped*, not that the entire place was going to bloody blow up! I wouldn't have sent you in there alone if I'd known."

"Well, you did," I grit out, leashing my temper before it unravels completely, "and now the Priests have the queen. We have one job. One *job* and so far, we are spectacularly cocking it up."

"It's not . . . Bloody hell. They're impossible to kill!"

I think of rough hands on my back. A big body pushing me into a cool, glass window and stealing the very air from my lungs. Broad features and the softest pair of lips I've ever touched. It ought to be illegal for a man to have lips that soft, particularly when they belong to someone like *him*.

The villain.

The enemy.

"They're flesh and bone," I utter softly, "which means they're just as fallible as the rest of humanity."

"I don't like the look on your face, Rowan. The last time you looked like that, I ended up knee-deep in a pile of shite. Metaphorical shite, obviously. Not literal."

"Coney."

"It's goddamn eerie." I hear him shift around awkwardly. "Your stare, I mean. Are you really blind?"

"*Hugh.*"

"Sorry, sorry. I'll stop talking. Please—continue."

Goddamn, I miss Ian something fierce. Unlike his younger brother, Ian Coney was magnificent to watch in the field. A fighter. A peacemaker when he needed to quiet the always present hum of rebellion amongst our members. A friend to me as much as Margaret has always felt like a sister.

And now I've lost both Ian and Mags to the Priests.

Damien can tell me all he wants that Father had it out for Ian, but I know the truth. Jack, the arse who worked for the Priests at The Bell & Hand, watched it all unfold from the upper galleries at The Octagon. It was that woman Isla Quinn who strangled Ian, and Saxon Priest who killed my other men before sweeping her away to safety. And now Margaret . . . Margaret is in their so-called *Palace*, a place she begged me to bring her, without me realizing who they really were until Damien revealed himself.

How can she be so *naïve*?

This Holyrood . . . this vision they have of themselves is nothing but a lie.

Swallowing the lick of worry that rises swiftly, I dig my fingers into my thighs. "We took an oath, Hugh. Repeat it for me."

"*Now?*"

"Now."

"I think . . ." He clears his throat. "Well, I'll be honest, Rowan. I don't remember it."

My hands ball into fists and I grit my teeth so hard that I'm surprised my molars don't turn to ash. What I did to lose Ian and be stuck with his brother for all eternity, I don't know. Penance, maybe.

Pressing my fingers into my pounding temples, I exhale

slowly. "In the king we trust," I say slowly, *emphatically*, "for the king we obey."

"Ah, yes. I was missing the trust bit."

"Hugh?"

He hums noncommittally, a sound that sets my teeth on edge.

"If you *ever* send me into another mission without gathering all the facts, I'm going to hand you over to Gregory and wash my hands clean of you. Understood?"

The gurgling sound that comes from Hugh Coney tells me everything I need to know. "I hear you," he says. "Trust me, I hear you loud and clear."

"Brilliant. Now get the hell out of my flat."

He beats a hasty exit, only stopping long enough to ask, "Lights on or off? Does it matter one way or another if you can't see?"

I turn my head toward him, and I like to think that whatever registers in my expression, Hugh notices it immediately. He flees a second later, the door clanking shut behind him.

It's only then that I sink to the floor.

My head falls to my bent knees and a single tear slips free. It burns over my blisters, a small fire of heat that doesn't even compare to the hell that I experienced four nights ago. A kidnapping, Hugh had learned. We'd expected Margaret to be kidnapped and, yes, we'd suspected the Priests. But never could have I predicted everything that happened then, and everything that's happened since.

The sob that's been begging for release scratches at my throat once again.

Ian is dead, and his killer walks free. Margaret thinks I've betrayed her, that I'm *untrustworthy*, when it's always been the opposite.

The king chose me, and that's my curse to bear.

Kill the Priests, he said.

Protect my daughter at all cost, he told me.

In the span of four nights, I've failed them both.

And just for tonight, I crack open the dam and allow myself to feel.

Broken.

Defeated.

A shadow of misery that follows me like the worst kind of living nightmare.

CHAPTER 14

DAMIEN

The sweetened scent of cloves permeates the intel room.

Elbow on the desk, the heel of my hand supporting my forehead, I take another drag of the cigarette and let my eyes slide shut.

Jesus.

I've given up alcohol and women and every other thing that could ruin me for good, but this . . . Smoking is my last vice to purge.

Soon.

The motto of my life, that. Soon, I'll have Carrigan and Guthram begging for mercy. Soon, we'll wrangle the anti-loyalists back under control. Soon, I'll be—

"Don't go there."

My words are muffled by the cigarette. Jaw clenching, I pluck the fag from my mouth and stick it on the ashtray near my elbow, then turn my attention to the computer. Backlit against the otherwise dim room, the script on the monitor gleams with untold secrets.

Edward Carrigan's email account.

It's not the first time I've invited myself to his inbox. In the last seven months, I've made it my personal mission to comb through every email that comes or goes—but the prime minister is no fool. I've hacked his government accounts, his personal ones, too, email addresses that date back twenty years and haven't been touched in nearly as long. I'll give him that, at least. The man cleans up his messes and erases every trail before there's even a remote chance of gaining ground.

Still . . .

Pressing a hand flat on the now crinkled paper that I stole from the Jewel Tower, I skim it again:

Stay away from my daughter.
50,000 pounds or I'll

Or *what?*

Timestamped to five weeks ago, the email offers no other information. There's no reply from Coney and no follow-up on Carrigan's end to finish the threat. Hell, there's nothing to even indicate that the two men ever interacted before Carrigan hit SEND.

For the third time in as many minutes, I tab over to the Queen Mary University website and stare at the ERROR message glaring back at me. Less than a month after Isla strangled him to death, Ian Coney's administrative account is already gone. No amount of hacking can resurface what's been deleted, not after the university's tech team clearly went through the hassle of permanently erasing every trace of the professor from their databases.

It's a literal dead end.

Clasping the base of my skull with both hands, I dig into the stiff muscles there with a low curse. Four days after questioning Rowena and I'm no closer to figuring out her connection to Ian Coney.

He was her friend, maybe, or a mentor.

Or maybe they were lovers.

The unbidden thought goes down as smoothly as swallowing barbed wire.

And this time when the beast inside me rears its ugly head, I don't bind him into submission.

No, I pinch the still-lit cigarette between my fingers and bring it to my lips, because it's the only thing that settles the destructive chaos thrumming to life in my veins. I've barely managed a single pull when the door cracks open behind me and footsteps enter the room.

"I thought you were quitting."

The rampant disapproval in my brother's voice is as familiar to me as breathing, which I do now, sucking the nicotine into my system like the addict I've always sworn that I wouldn't become.

A grim smile touches my lips. "I am."

"Yeah?" Guy scoffs. "When? Before or after you—"

"I'm not in the mood for a lecture." Smoke curls in fine wisps as I exhale. Stabbing out the cherry on the ashtray, I glance over my shoulder. "Any updates from Benji?"

"No movement yet." Guy leans against the massive desk that dwarfs half the room, his arms coming up to fold over his chest. Steely blue eyes zero in on my face. "You really think she'll leave the flat when she's as roughed up as she is?"

If I've learned anything about Rowena Carrigan in the last eight days, it's that she's relentlessly stubborn—and far too cunning for her own good. "She won't let blindness keep her from making a move." No, she'll use it to her advantage. A disability that she'll play against anyone who might ever make the mistake of underestimating her.

Like you did.

The visceral memory of her tracing the lines of my face

settles like burning bricks in my gut. Oh, I'd underestimated her, all right. Had she heard the battered breath caught in my lungs? Seen, without actually seeing, the sudden craving for softness that had infiltrated my bones, down to my marrow?

The burning bricks turn to toxic lead.

Meanwhile, my brother's astute gaze flicks to the computer before returning sharply. "You're banking on her making a move, which we don't know if she will."

She will.

She was too quick to run out of here, without even a backward glance at the queen. There's no doubt in my mind that Rowena's hidden motives will reveal themselves—it's just a matter of how and when.

Lucky for me, patience is a virtue that I've been spoon-fed since birth.

I reach over the ashtray for the discarded notepad. Tossing it in my brother's direction, I point to my messy script at the top of the page. "That's what she said to me the other day. *Goodbye for now.* She was baiting me."

Guy studies my hastily written scrawl, his brows knitted. "You're overthinking things."

"We're in the business of overthinking everything," I counter sardonically. In thirty-one years, I've never had the luxury of taking a gesture of goodwill at face value. Friend or foe, greed is indiscriminating, and everyone wants something—power, love, hope . . . vengeance.

It's just a matter of knowing where to look to pull back the layers of deceit.

"Here's what we do know," I say, clicking through a series of files on the monitor. "Coney was involved in that cult with Jack." An image of the brown-haired professor loads on the screen, and then I flip to a picture of him standing, arms slung across another bloke's shoulders, with the other men whom Saxon killed at The Octagon. "They've all come to The Bell & Hand."

Dropping his hands to the desk, Guy angles his head closer to the computer. "You're sure? I don't recognize them."

"I'm sure." With three clicks of the mouse, I bring up another series of images. Unlike the first set, these are all black-and-white stills captured from the security cameras within The Bell & Hand. "I ran their names and coordinated credit card purchases to within minutes of them entering the pub. Amateur mistake on their end but a boon for us. They were coming in for months, and look"—I point to the next frame—"they always took this seat by the window. God knows how many times you and Saxon saw them there without thinking twice." A rough laugh itches to fly free. "They disguised themselves well enough, but you can clearly still see—"

"Their features," Guy murmurs, catching on without me having to elaborate. Reaching out, he taps the screen to zoom in. "They walked right in, just like Ian Coney, and we never suspected a thing." He cuts a hard look my way. "What does this have to do with Rowena Carrigan?"

Stay away from my daughter.

Those are the words of a man with something to lose.

"I couldn't find any direct ties linking any of the men with Coney. Even the two uni kids weren't actually his students at Queen Mary. Which means that however Coney handled recruitment, it wasn't through some obvious connection."

"Nothing ever is," my brother mutters, shaking his head.

"And there's nothing tying any of them to Rowena, either, but something . . ." I thread my fingers through my hair, tugging on the strands. "Carrigan wanted Coney away from her, which means one of two things: he caught wind of the operation, which she was maybe a part of, and he wanted his daughter safe, or he was—"

"Possibly running it all himself," Guy finishes, "and he wanted to make sure she was out of the picture."

I nod slowly. "It's the only logical explanation, but it still doesn't make any sense."

"Hence the fag." Guy jerks his chin toward the abandoned cigarette.

The muscles in my back coil tightly.

Averting my gaze from the disappointment lurking in his expression, I drop my hand to the desk. "Coney wanted us dead because he thought Saxon killed the king. Carrigan wanted me to *kill* the king. Their motives don't line up, but it's the only thing that might link them together with Rowe—"

An ear-splitting siren rips through the room, shattering the quiet into a thousand shards of dread.

Dread that propels me forward, fingers landing on the keyboard.

Dread that whips Guy's head toward the flashing alarm bolted to the wall, his knuckles turning white where he grips the desk.

"Damien, which place—"

"I'm looking."

The dread manifests into something far more sinister when the map of Holyrood's properties finally loads, and I see a flashing dot hovering over The Bell & Hand like a calling card for doom.

For the first time in years, I hesitate.

The siren shrieks and the door crashes open, voices corralling within the intel room, and still, I sit frozen. Because I know . . . Fucking hell, I *know*. This is no random security breach or some random break-in to raid the register at the pub.

This is personal.

This is war.

The Bell & Hand is a heartbeat unto itself, the first thing my brothers and I ever truly owned—a legacy of our own creation that bears the stamp of our sweat and hopes and whatever few dreams we've ever allowed ourselves.

"*Damien*," Guy barks over the cacophony of Hamish and Jude arguing, and the piercing alarm, and the awful *thud-thud-thud* of my pulse roaring in my ears. "Do it."

With heat barreling down my veins, I do.

One click of the mouse on the security camera positioned on Commercial Street, across from The Bell & Hand, and every monitor in the room turns on.

Hamish curses.

Matthews gasps.

Jude and Paul fall absolutely silent.

And all the while, I feel what's left of my heart snap in two at the sight of flames engulfing the pub.

Trapped behind centuries-old paned windows, the fire flickers with life, crawling through the crevices to lick at the outside world with talons painted red. An untamed mistress, it dances along the corridors of Guy's flat, visible to the naked eye, and teases the sky with outstretched arms that mask the clouds and the moon and the spire of Christ Church Spitalfields.

"*Who.*"

The single word from Guy is a battered whip that flays us all.

"*Who!*" he roars again, twisting around to shove past a startled Matthews.

He gets as far as the hallway when the siren is compounded with a sound that turns the fire in my veins to ice. Gunfire, nearby. It punctures the air in rhythmless beats, and I see the moment when my brother realizes what's happening.

His shoulders stiffen and his expression bleeds cold fury when he turns to Paul with deceptive slowness. "The drawbridge."

Pa's old second-in-command visibly pales. "It's down. I didn't . . . It didn't seem necessary—"

Guy locks a hand around the older man's throat. "You fucking *fool*."

"Priest," Paul grunts, his fingers tugging fruitlessly at my brother's wrists, "Jesus, man. We have bigger problems right now. Do you hear—"

BOOM.

The floor trembles beneath my feet. The secondary monitor drops right off the desk, crashing to the stone floor and shattering into a million little pieces. There's no point denying it: we're under siege.

Before another grenade can hit and do us all in, I turn to Hamish. "Get the queen out. *Now.*" He nods, quickly, and cuts around Paul. I look to Matthews next. Of everyone here, he and Paul have been with Holyrood the longest. This is their home, as much as it's been my prison, but there's no time to grieve. "Get what you can."

The surgeon's dark eyes burn with regret. "I won't be able to—"

"I know." Bitterness slithers into my veins, and I force myself to hold his gaze. "Whatever the queen needs, you take that with you. Do you hear me?"

Adam's apple bobbing, he steps backward. "For the Crown."

My chin jerks in a clipped nod.

For the Crown.

I watch for only a second as he tears out of the intel

room, and then I look to Guy. Though his hand is still clamped around Paul's throat, his blue eyes are zeroed in on my face. Wide. Panicked. We're locked and loaded in what's about to become a battlefield, and it's obvious that he's stuck in the past, not seeing me as I am now but as I was behind Christ Church Spitalfields.

Immobile.

On the cusp of death.

My blood coating the pavement a dark, glistening red.

I hold his stare. "Go."

His head jerks, once, in rebuttal. "Fuck protocol."

"*Go.*"

"Priest—"

At Paul's pathetic gurgling, Guy flings the older man to the side. Paul's body hits the floor with a crack of his elbow against stone, but still, my brother's attention remains pinned on me. He advances one step. "There's nothing in this room that we don't have elsewhere."

"You know we can't risk it."

"*Jesus.*" He cuts his gaze away, long enough to see Jude dragging Paul from the intel room. Shoulders hunching, Guy reaches for the pistol holstered at his waistband, only to stop halfway. His hand curls into a tight fist at his side. "Didn't you hear what I said? *Fuck protocol*, Damien. I won't let you stay."

Beyond the open door, the Palace shudders under the impact of another grenade. In the century that Holyrood has held Ightham Mote, no one has ever identified our location. We've played up the stories of being an insane asylum. We've bolstered the fears of the locals, keeping them far away from the estate with electrical fences and traps set out in the surrounding forest to discourage trespassers. The ancient walls of the medieval manor, sturdy as they are, won't withstand much more.

We have only minutes.

"Everything we have is in this room." With the stroke of a few fingers, I could rain hell down across all of England. Explosives would be the least of our countrymen's worries. That magnitude of power, especially in the wrong hands . . . "No one can get in here, brother. *No one.*"

Something desperate flares in Guy's face, and I anticipate his attempt to stronghold me into submission a second before he launches forward.

Ducking under his outstretched arm, I grab his dominant hand and fold it behind his back. My knee drives into the soft flesh of his right leg. His weight crumples and a grunt bursts from his mouth, and then he teeters forward, his lean frame grappling for control.

I don't let him gain any control.

With a hard elbow to his lower spine, I force him out in the hall. Regret burns in my lungs as I snag the doorknob at the same time that his head snaps up, those blue eyes of his making me feel as though I've peered into a mirror.

They reflect fear.

All-consuming despair.

Guy lurches to his feet, my name an anguished shout on his lips, and I give him the smallest slice of hope I can offer before I slam the door in his face: "Don't bury me before I'm gone."

CHAPTER 15

DAMIEN

The siren blares incessantly as I turn for the shadowed wall to the right of the desk.

Dark paneling stretches from floor to ceiling, wall to wall. A quick glance gives nothing away, but I know this room inside and out. It's been my haven when I had none, and my refuge when I was desperate to escape. There isn't a scratch I don't know or an uneven stone that I haven't marked a thousand times over. And so, with efficient ease, I dig the heels of my hands into the right notch and feel the wall give way under the pressure.

Dropping to my haunches, I begin piling up equipment on the threshold of the safe.

The armored vest, which I draw over my head. The myriad of weapons, which I dump into my kit, sealing off its Velcroed pockets with a practiced flex of my fingers. The small wooden box, which sits inconspicuously in the corner.

Let it go.

Except that I'm already reaching forward to knock off the flimsy lid and fist the silver chain from its bed of plush velvet. The metal glints under the overhead lighting as I thrust Mum's necklace into the front pocket of my vest.

Clamping a hand around the sniper rifle resting behind the box, I draw the weapon close to my chest.

The rules of Holyrood dictate that I stay in this room—*die* in this room—with our secrets. But, like Guy said: fuck protocol.

With one last glance at the intelligence room that I designed from the bottom up, I drift toward the opposite wall. Pressing a palm to a hand-sized scanner, the stone shifts before my eyes and cracks open to reveal a hallway known to no one but me. I step through, then shove the solid stone back into place with both hands.

Only then do I plug the code, *503,* into the dial pad positioned at waist height.

The existence of the intel room is extinguished with an almost quiet groan of despair. Material crashes against stone, the implosion destroying everything within, and dust sweeps beneath the makeshift door to settle at my feet.

There's no time to mourn.

Hugging the shadows, I follow the trajectory of the hallway as it winds toward the inner perimeter of the manor before forking off in two different directions. One leads to an underground tunnel that'll spit me out in the forest, just beyond the gardens, while the other heads for the Palace's interior courtyard.

I go left.

Gunshots echo like cracks of thunder, disturbing the peace and rattling the calm.

Picking up the pace, I sprint the remaining distance, then sling the rifle across my back as I slip through the narrow gap in the outer wall and grip the steel ladder. The cool breeze from the open courtyard kisses my face while the butt of my rifle clanks against the retainer wall.

And then I begin to climb, up and up and up, until I'm

reaching for the metal rod fitted to the Palace's steeped roof and hauling my body to a flat, horizontal position.

Sparse moonlight guides my forward momentum.

On my elbows and knees, I crawl into place and mount my rifle against one of the wooden beams that line the old roof. One glance down reveals the drawbridge extending over the moat, both exposed to slivers of night sky.

There's a harsh yell followed by a panicked tread of feet.

I wait long enough to catalog the hair and build. Recognizing that he's not one of ours, I aim, pull the trigger, and fire.

The man collapses with an audible cry.

No mercy.

When I draw forward for a better angle, the toes of my boots scrape the ceramic tiles. The sound is whisper-soft, barely audible against the backdrop of screams mingling with chirping nightingales in the surrounding forest. The grim melody strikes a shiver down my spine. A breath later my eyes narrow when I catch sight of two men emerging from the Palace onto the drawbridge. Their conversation is lost to the fray, but there's no mistaking the rhythmic way they step, haul something along, then move again.

It's a body they're dragging.

A body that's still alive, based on the way the legs kick and jerk within the shadows.

"Look at me," I growl under my breath, *"look at me, dammit!"*

As if heeding the demand, moonlight casts a warm glow over the man's face.

Matthews.

"Fuck. Fuck, fuck, *fuck.*"

The men pause. One bends down to yank Matthews' medical bag from the doctor's arms before hurling it into the moat. The other grasps the surgeon's bicep and snaps him upward. Words are exchanged but don't reach my ears.

It's a bloody impossible shot.

They grab Matthews again, towing him along like a rag doll, their voices muffled by gunfire and chirping birds and the sound of my heart rate spiking. Dark shadows splice across the drawbridge. The surgeon's battered cry cinches my lungs into a vice.

They're going to kill him.

Matthews, who's been with Holyrood for over thirty years. Matthews, who brought me back from the brink of death. Matthews, who routinely reminds me that humanity is not a given but a choice.

I line up the shot, prepared to damn the surgeon to hell, even in my attempt to save him, and—

Pain explodes in my spine.

A groan rumbles deep in my throat, and I make a desperate grab for the rifle as a booted foot skates past my periphery. The firearm clatters over the edge of the roof while unfamiliar hands grip my shins, dragging me backward. Then a voice, dark and sinister, cuts through the night:

"Looks like I found me a runaway Priest."

Instinct kicks in, and I slam a palm down to catch hold of one of the tiles, a last-ditch effort to stall my backward momentum—only, instead of gaining leverage, the tile pops loose completely.

Fucking hell.

Rolling onto my back, I allow my legs to twist in the stranger's grip. One glance upward reveals that the bastard out for my blood is huge, arms like tree trunks, thighs like bloody anchors. I'm no shrinking violet, but the man has to outweigh me by at least two stone—a rarity that sparks a thread of unease. Spotting my expression, a sinister grin splits across the bastard's face. The silver moon, now out to play, highlights crooked upper teeth.

"I's been waitin' for this day." He cranks one hand off my leg. "Waitin'," he says, his brows diving together over the sharp bridge of his nose, "and waitin'. And Rowan, she tells me, over and over, 'ave some patience, Gregory. But patience is just—" His fist collides with my chin, snapping my head back. Blood explodes in my mouth, the gunmetal taste smearing over my teeth. "That's what I 'as to say. No patience, Priest. None for me."

Rowan.

The name—*her* name—resonates through my ringing skull seconds before Gregory swings his fist again. This time, I manage to dive to the right before he can make contact. Tiles come loose under my weight, turning the dangers of a pitched roof into a twisted game of Russian Roulette where one wrong move means instant death.

I roll again, evading another kick, and pry at a tile with a prayer burning in my throat. It loosens with a shrill squeak. Fingers curled over the sharpened edge, I turn and snap it forward like a projectile.

The tile nails the bastard in the throat.

His big frame wavers, wobbling in place, and I launch to my feet.

Invisible needles prick my throbbing skull. *You're going to fall. You're going to collapse and it's going to be just like last—*

Goodbye for now, she'd said.

Rowan. *Fucking Rowena.*

Vision swimming with the memory of violet, I manage five steps toward the ladder when a burst of air suddenly rushes past my ear. With a low curse, I weave my body to avoid the punch. More tiles give way under my right foot, the broken fragments hurtling down the sloped roof to disappear over the edge.

Jesus.

I'm going to die.

I knew this would happen. With enemies like Carrigan and Guthram, I'm a man working on borrowed time. But some part of me—so deep, so buried, so easily ignored—hoped it would feel differently than that day behind Christ Church Spitalfields. I wanted a bed. I wanted my brothers close. I wanted anything but the same aggression surging in my veins, calling for me to destroy and survive and fight until the very end.

Then and now, I've been sentenced to death by the Carrigan family.

Refusing to glance down, I dart across a narrow ridge board that's barely as wide as the width of my hand.

"Coward!" the bastard growls behind me.

I hear his shoes scrape the crossbeam. *Keep moving. Don't slow down.* Lowering to my thighs, I slip down the valley rafter, only far enough so I can jump onto a perpendicular ridge, this one even narrower than the last. Oxygen drives into my lungs. My arms swing outward, level with my shoulders, as if that'll keep me airborne when the bloody roof buckles beneath me.

This goddamned house.

Seven months of house arrest and now—

Gregory's meat-sized hand pummels my right shoulder, exactly where Carrigan's men stabbed me, and then I'm falling, falling, *falling.*

Tiles slip and slide, scattering everywhere and providing no opportunity to stop my descent. Nightingales sing, and a hoarse shout climbs my throat, and in that split-second before I go over the side of the ancient roof, I spot Gregory's satisfied expression.

His smirk deepens and he yells something that I can't hear over the thunderous roar in my ears, and it wouldn't matter even if I could.

We both know I'm a dead man.

And it was Rowena Carrigan, my very own Trojan Horse, who damned me to hell.

CHAPTER 16

ROWENA

"Tight." Chin tucked down, I press my palms to the stone table for balance and hold myself still. "Wrap it tight. Please."

"Rowan . . . With your rib, you really oughtn't put any—"

"I'll be fine."

Like every other member of our motley crew, Dr. Sara Grafton does as I say with mute obedience. Tearing a new bandage from the pack on the table, she tugs on my shirt to indicate that I hold it up for her. With a hard swallow, I grasp the hem and lift, already dreading the moment when—

Her low gasp is exactly what I feared.

Another hard swallow. "Well?" I ask, feeling her cool fingers graze one of the gashes from the shattered windows at Buckingham Palace. "How bad does it look?"

"You shouldn't even be alive."

Truer words have probably never been spoken.

Then again, I've spent thirty-three years dying in a thousand little ways. And each time that I've grasped life with both hands, too blasted stubborn to let go, I find myself resurrected once again—a chameleon adopting new shades; a magician willing to put forth new tricks to entertain a perpetually restless crowd.

Here, under this roof, I'm the king's chosen one.

Never to be denied, always to be obeyed.

"Probably looks a good deal better than it did the first night. Which I guess isn't saying much." Refusing to reveal any discomfort, I force a smile over my shoulder. "Anyway, it's really not that bad"—*lies*, my soul screams, *stop lying*—"but when the cuts rub against fabric, it's just that I . . ."

I could cry.

"You need to rest," Sara mutters, proficiently tucking my shirt into the band of my sports bra. "And, before you argue with me, I already know that the likelihood of you actually following orders is nonexist—"

"They killed Ian."

"*Goddammit.*" Sara's breath comes hard and fast on my right, her elbow knocking into mine when she jerks away to tear open the bandage's plastic wrapping. "It's too soon, all right? I know what you're going to say and it's *too soon.*"

If only emotions could wait on the sidelines until we're ready to face them in all their glory—a lever we might switch on and off whenever hate swarms our hearts and defeat pools in our guts and we're nothing more than anger primed by madness. But that sort of luxury isn't meant for people like us—rebels, loyalists, spies—and the hollow smile on my face turns grim. "The Priests killed Ian, Sara, just like they killed your father."

"Rowan, stop—"

"They killed Frederick and Russ and Victor and Gregg. Nineteen. Gregg was *nineteen.* Do you know he'd never even left England? Not that he could with our borders being closed. But still. He wanted peace and he wanted hope, and he bloody well wanted to get pissed in Amsterdam, but instead he . . . instead he—"

Tears threaten and I stiffen my jaw, hoping to eradicate the sorrow before it swells and consumes me whole. What happened that day at The Octagon wasn't murder—it was slaughter. Like a pack of animals deemed utterly useless. Strangled. Shot. Diced and sliced. No matter what Damien says about Holyrood protecting the Crown, I know the truth.

Misguided monsters make the most horrific heroes.

"I'll rest when we've got the queen." And only then.

"You've a strained rib."

"Trust me," I mutter, my lips twisting, "I can tell."

Silently, Sara wraps the clean bandage around my stomach to bring it together over my spine. Huffing under her breath, she says, louder, "You're covered in blisters. Don't listen to me, if you don't want to, but at least listen to your own body."

Rest. Recuperation. Rebirth.

I'll do it all when I've fulfilled my oath to the king.

"I haven't any on my legs," I tell her, thinking of how I sat in my room four nights ago, after the Holyrood agent left me at my Hurlingham flat, and ran my hands over my body to feel the extent of the damage done by the fire. "My forearms and stomach got the worst of it from when I was caught under the beam." And my hair, and the upper half of my forehead, but there's no point in acknowledging the obvious.

After adhering the bandage to my back, Sara steps away. "They'll all leave scars—"

"And show I've lived. That I live *still*, and sometimes that's all we have going for us. We're alive, we're breathing. My heart beats. So many others can't say the same." I take an experimental step away from the table and peer out into oblivion, tugging my shirt back into place. When the material doesn't graze the cuts for the first time in twenty-four hours, since I tried to re-bandage myself, I nearly sob with relief. Smothering any trace of weakness from my voice, I say, "The lads will be back from Sevenoaks soon, and we need to be ready for the worst."

"They can handle themselves."

"We said the same thing just weeks ago and we both know how that turned out."

"Nothing can be worse than The Octagon," Sara utters quietly, and I know that she's thinking of her father. Dead from a bullet to the heart. It'd be poetic, if it weren't completely devastating.

Wishing I could burn that day from my memory, all I offer is the gritty truth: "It can definitely get worse."

With the Priests at the helm, there's no telling what other destruction might unfold.

As if the universe hopes to prove Sara right, I hear the telltale sound of car doors slamming shut, followed by a distinct release of breath from the other side of the room. Sara paces toward the corridor, her shoes clipping eagerly against the wood floor, before stopping in place. "Do you want me to wait with you?" Her voice is clear, like she's turned to look back at me. "Because I will."

"No." I shake my head. "Just send them here."

"Will do." She manages two steps before I call her name. "Did you need something else?" she asks.

I think of the man locked away in the windowless attic of the house. *Benjamin Lotts*, he'd confessed, after feeling the wrath of Gregory's hulking fist. I wonder how long it'll take the Priests to realize that we've commandeered one of their precious agents. "Take care of our own, first, but then check on our guest."

A small pause precedes her halfhearted, "And if he

spits on me again?"

A cynical grin curves my mouth. "Then spit on him back."

Sara makes a choking sound—muffled laughter to cover her surprise, I hope—and then she's heading down the hallway and leaving me to stand alone in the drawing room.

I've wandered the mansion so many times over the years that it's impossible to forget every detail. Wooden beams line the ceiling and moonlight seeps in through Gothic-styled windows. A portrait of the property's original patroness, a wealthy Victorian baroness, sits poised over the marble fireplace in a gilded frame. Bracketed on either side are ivory sconces lit with flickering gas flames. Beneath my feet, a soft Aubusson rug covers the center of the room, where an antique chaise waits, tempting me to sit and rest my aching body.

Resting seems impossible when coming face to face with the unknown.

I swallow, tightly, and reach up to slip a strand of hair behind my ear—only to remember that the nervous gesture can't be satiated anymore.

Bald. Broken. Blind.

A costume I never anticipated wearing, but the most permanent one of all.

Just because you can't see, doesn't mean you don't already know too much.

The words infiltrate my head, and *bloody hell.* I can't think of him—can't *afford* to think of him—not ever again. And especially not like this, as I stand here and wait for news that the attack on the Palace went according to plan. Because if did go well, then Damien Priest will hate me with every breath he—

"Rowan?"

At the sound of Hugh's voice, I launch forward.

"Where is she?"

Bodies gather into the drawing room—their heavy feet sounding like a herd of elephants stampeding forward—and I strain my ears, listening for any sign of Margaret amongst them. A whisper of her voice. A lighter stride. But when the blokes all settle down, as if everyone has claimed a spot before me, something that feels an awful lot like dread clogs my throat as I realize that Hugh . . .

Hugh hasn't answered.

"Coney." Another step forward. I look from left to right, seeing nothing. "Coney, where is the queen?"

Someone clears their throat.

A shoe scuffs along the floor.

And then, from the back-right corner, nearest to the windows overlooking the front drive, "We 'asn't got her, Rowan."

"You haven't . . ." I blink, just once. The dread twists and turns, surging forth like a fountain of rage that I feel all the way down to my toes. Turning from Gregory, I sweep a furious "glance" over the room. "Hugh, where the bloody hell are you?"

No one comments on the obvious.

I should be happy—*grateful*, even—that there aren't any snide remarks that I'm somehow less than who I was a week ago, when Buckingham Palace caught fire and I was caught inside its walls. But all I feel is fury that Hugh hides like a coward, knowing that I can't see him worth a damn.

Bastard.

"Three seconds." The words escape past the rage, whisper-soft and just as deadly. "You have three seconds to step forward or—"

Samuel coughs awkwardly, and then someone stumbles, their feet audibly tripping over the rug like they've been unceremoniously shoved forward.

"Rowan."

Hugh.

My chest tightens with unreleased air. "Where is she?"

"We've good news," he says, "and some bad—"

"You're going to tell me where Queen Margaret is, right now, or I'll—"

"They've got her, okay? They've still got her."

If this were the theater, it'd be an appropriate time for an actor to drop a pin, just to send the audience into a fit of hysterics. But this isn't a play, and this isn't some fairy tale with a happily-ever-after. We're at war, and if the Priests still have Margaret then . . .

Fuck me, I can't breathe.

I can't breathe.

Stumbling backward, I spin away from all the heavy stares that feel like knives jabbing into my spine. They watch, and they wait, as if expecting me to fly off the handle and lose my temper. Or, worse, cry.

But Rowan Carrigan doesn't lose her temper and she certainly doesn't cry.

Not *this* version of myself, at least, the woman who King John chose, the woman that the entire organization looks to for guidance in leading the cause. No, the woman I am today bottles up every trace of emotion until even the slightest dent in my armor reveals only another impenetrable wall. My nakedness—both the emotional and physical—is shown to no one.

Even so, my lips feel numb when I scrape together every last trace of composure and utter a single word: "How?"

"We . . . We checked every room," Hugh says, a quiver evident in his voice. "All those we could find on our own and every one that was on that blueprint you had us find. She wasn't there, Rowan, not even a trace of her."

"Like she was a ghost," Gregory adds.

Worst-case scenarios pummel me from all angles, everything from death to torture. Was that the real reason why Damien wouldn't let me see her? Because she hadn't come out of surgery at all, as Dr. Matthews claimed, but because she's *dead*?

Nausea curdles in my stomach.

My shoulders press backward, chin lifts another degree. Anything to pretend that my heart isn't racing with fear. "We'll go back," I tell them, already mentally sifting through possible plans. "We'll *have* to go back. But we'll need to be stealthy. They'll be expecting us."

"That won't be a problem."

My head jerks in Gregory's direction. "What are you saying?"

"We took care of them, didn't we, mates?"

A litany of "yeses" infuses the room, a few shouted, others more subdued.

"Gregory," I whisper, clutching the base of my throat, "what did you do?"

"I pushed 'im."

The pure, unadulterated satisfaction in that one sentence is enough to weaken my knees. "Who? Who did you push?"

"The Mad Priest."

Blood roars in my ears. "No. *No*, Gregory, I said to—"

"Bring 'im to you," comes the surly reply, "but Rowan, 'e was up on the roof and shootin' us, and I followed 'im up, yeah? And I was thinkin' of Coney—not *you*, Coney, the other one—and I couldn't just let 'im go."

"You . . . you pushed Damien Priest"—I lick my lips—"off a roof."

It's not a question, and, at this point, further confirmation is pretty much unnecessary. But Gregory seems only too pleased to add, "Right over the edge, Rowan. 'e never stood a chance."

I should be jumping for joy. Or, at the very least, pouring us all a drink to celebrate one Priest down and only two more brothers left to go. But instead . . .

Oh, God, I think I'm going to be sick.

The heel of my palm flies to my mouth, like that'll be enough to keep the vomit down. People aren't shoved off roofs, not in real life. Suspense novels, sure. Action films, absolutely. But in real life . . .

Fuck. Me.

Damien Priest—*dead.*

I'd planned to interrogate him. I'd planned to force his big body into a chair, his wrists tied behind his back, and take every one of his secrets, the way he'd done to me. I wanted him humbled, I wanted him vulnerable. Nowhere in my plans—in the assignments that I gave out before Gregory and the others left Holly Village for the Palace— was there an order to kill him.

Monsters hide in us all, Damien told me.

Right now, in this moment, I feel like the vilest monster alive.

"Rowan." At Hugh's smooth baritone, I turn toward him stiffly. "I know you wanted Priest for questioning," he goes on, unfazed, "and obviously that didn't work out like we planned—"

"'e 'ad to die," Gregory interjects, completely unrepentant.

"What I'm *trying* to say is," Hugh mutters, raising his voice to be heard over Gregory, "we brought you someone else."

Did Damien struggle the way Ian had during those last few minutes of life? Hell, did Gregory at least have the decency to kill him *before* pushing him from the roof? Or did his body hit the—

"Rowan. *Rowan*, are you listening to me?"

"You can't take credit for Benjamin Lotts." Somehow, I manage to sound completely at ease with the conversation, like we're discussing the weather or football and not the death of our enemy. *Oh, the lies we keep*. Running my tongue over the back of my teeth, I force my hand from my neck to hang listlessly at my side. "Gregory nabbed him when he was getting me out of the flat this morning."

"The Holyrood agent? No. No, I'm talking about—Samuel, be a good man and"—a heavy *thud* hits the floor—"there. See? We've brought you someone you can interrogate, if you want. Find out where the queen might be now."

Except that I see nothing, a fact that makes itself abundantly clear when Hugh mutters something under his breath, prompting a groan from the "someone" on the floor. "Give her your name," he commands tightly.

The statement is punctuated with the smack of a hand on flesh.

And then a masculine voice bites off, "Where the bloody hell am I?" and I swear to God, I whimper right then and there.

Of all the people in the world, they've brought me the one I could have gone without seeing for the rest of my life.

Alfie fucking Barker.

CHAPTER 17

ROWENA

It takes three hours to rehash every moment from arrival at the Palace to departure, including pausing everything to grieve the death of one of our own: Micah Jenkins, a thirty-two-year-old from Exeter who lost his mum to a riot two years ago.

After making my way downstairs, alone, I light a candle for Micah in the mansion's private chapel, not because he struck me as particularly religious, or because I am, but simply because it feels . . . right.

The pew is hard under my arse, the wax from the candle tacky on my fingers. Guilt pecks at my heart, like a vulture scavenging for scraps from the already ravaged, and I bend my head, elbows landing hard on my knees, and whisper, "I'm so sorry."

For dragging him into this war, when he was only ever an onlooker. For sending him to the Palace tonight, even though he eagerly volunteered. For believing—for even one, measly second—that we might come out of tonight unscathed.

I was foolish to underestimate the Priests.

And yet, in the somber silence of the chapel, I find

myself sliding off the bench and moving back toward the altar, a path I've tread hundreds of times over the years. My elbow knocks against something as I fumble for a new candle, then set about finding the matches. Fingers spread wide, my palm skids across the marble. *Stay patient. Stay calm.* Victory sings in my veins as I close my hand over the cardboard carton. The head hisses to life when I strike it against the matchbox.

Heat from the tiny flame warms my fingers.

It takes me three tries to align the lit match with the wick of the votive candle and, even though I really, really shouldn't, I find myself imagining blue eyes the color of the teal sea in Cornwall. Soft lips under my fingertips juxtaposed by the arrogance of rugged features. A voice like velvet and a touch like steel.

Had he realized that I didn't ask to see his face for anyone's benefit but my own?

He had me at his disposal for days, my hope a beating thing that he could either save or crush within his fist, my life his for the taking, if and when he wanted to take it. And all I wanted was to understand how a man can make me hate the very ground he walks on while still sparking heat between my legs. Heat that I've never felt for anyone—not a man, not a woman, not a single person, ever.

I wanted Damien Priest to break for *me*.

The hot wax drips onto my thumb, and the heat enflames, and finally I lean forward, patting around for the wrought-iron candle rack. *There you are.* Looping a finger around its heavy base, I pull it toward me and place Damien's candle next to the one that I lit for Micah. Since there aren't appropriate words for a man like Damien, I bow my head and offer a parting farewell that I know he'd appreciate:

"May the keys to Hell always be within your reach."

Then, with agonizing slowness, I make my way through the chapel toward the old servant's staircase. My palms drift over the curved stairwell, my feet climbing, one step after another, until I come to the landing. Turning right, I head down the corridor, counting the doors as I pass with a tap of my fingers, so that I won't accidentally miss my own.

One.

Two.

Three.

When I reach the fourth, I turn the knob and step inside my bedroom. It's habit that has me reaching out to flick on the light, and a desperate need to strip out of my own skin that has me peeling off my shirt and tossing it to the ground.

No guilt.

No remorse.

I said yes to this life, said yes to the king. Given the opportunity, I'd say yes all over again—which doesn't explain why I stop in front of the wardrobe, situated in the corner of the room, and stare blankly at the glass mirror. Fifteen years ago, I gave my virginity to a man twice my age. A man who posed a threat to the up-and-coming Edward Carrigan, who'd already set his cap on becoming prime minister.

Just kiss him, Father told me, his desk a massive crater that separated us on every fundamental level. *See what he might tell you.*

Alexander Harlton told me to undress.

And then he spilled his secrets into the slope of my neck while he came.

I sold a small piece of my soul that night. Sold even more of it over the next five years, whenever Father pointed his chin in the direction of his next political conquest, until I was nothing more than a mosaic of shattered fragments, held together by glue and grit and not much else.

Ten years ago, I vowed to never feel that way again.

Tonight, I do.

Self-destruction tastes bitter on my tongue, and I feel its skeletal arms wind around my waist like a long-lost lover, one I'd hoped to never see again. Only this time, I didn't sell my body to get the job done but what's left of my conscience.

Two men dead, and all because I said *yes*.

I touch the mirror and feel thick paper under my fingertips instead. A humorless smile flits across my face. "You're a right bastard, Hugh," I mutter under my breath. Because only Ian's younger brother would ever think that he's being helpful by taping a mirror into obscurity for the woman with cortical blindness.

The paper crinkles as I pull the wardrobe open. Dropping my fingers to the drawstring of my joggers, I freeze when I catch the squeak of the mattress' coil springs behind me.

Not again.

With a resigned sigh, my head falls forward. Once was funny. Twice, annoying. A year later, I'd give just about anything to nail him in the bollocks.

"Don't be such a wanker, Hugh." I snag a fresh shirt from one of the hangers, not caring which one it is, or if it even matches, and yank it down over my head. Scars or not, sports bra or not, my body is not up for public consumption. Not anymore. "For once in your life, will you just act your bloody—"

A lock turns over with an audible *snick*.

My mouth turns drier than sandpaper.

Definitely not Hugh.

Slowly, I angle my head toward the bedroom door, listening for the sinister sound of footsteps padding over the rug or the soft, raspy breath of an intruder taking cover in the shadows.

There's nothing.

No one.

I know you're there.

Lifting onto my toes, I reach into the wardrobe and skate a hand over the top shelf, patting around, searching, and—

No.

My pulse skips, ears ring. No, no, *no.*

Whipping around, I shove backward and curse when the wardrobe echoes with a hollow thud. "Who's there?" My eyes search the room fruitlessly. When the only response is more silence, I retreat again, wishing the wardrobe could swallow me whole. "Tell me who you are. Do you hear me? *Tell me who you—*"

The hammer of a pistol cocks back.

Icy terror grips my lungs.

I'm going to die by the same revolver that I keep stowed away, and if that isn't irony at its finest, I don't know what is. The gun was a gift to myself the minute I walked away from Father for good. No more men breathing down my neck. No more hands grabbing where they oughtn't be touching. I'd shoot them first.

There's no chance of shooting anyone now.

No chance of screaming for help, either. The walls are thick oak, all the bedrooms between mine and Hugh's empty. The rooms of the dead—they never made it back from The Octagon—which means that no aid is coming.

Do not beg. Do not cry.

"Who sent you?" My nails scrape the wardrobe. "Was it my father?"

My imagination paints shadows across the room, revealing a lithe form angling toward me with a predatory, unhurried stride—a man dressed in all black, his face obscured. I hear the tread of footsteps, the grate of a calloused palm skating over something equally rough. Bristles, maybe. Trousers. Something that remains entirely elusive, no matter how I narrow my eyes and wish I could peel back the layers of darkness. More irony. My world is a shroud even as the bedroom light unveils all.

I have seconds.

Long enough to envision a future I'll never live, never know. Short enough to feel a burst of regret that after thirty-three years, it's all come down to an assassin whose face I'll never see.

Anonymity has never been so overrated.

"Do it," I hear myself bite off, cool, confident—a façade I'll wear like a second skin until my very last breath. "You want me dead? Then go ahead. *Shoot me*."

Unseen hands grip my wrists and a hard thigh wedges between my legs.

I arch my back and a whimper rises in my throat and before I can even think to struggle, lips graze my cheek, warm breath heats my skin, and the voice of the devil himself husks in my ear, "No, I don't think I'll make it that easy for you."

CHAPTER 18

ROWENA

His name escapes on a ragged breath across my lips.

"Oh, Rowena," he purrs, his voice low, mocking, "don't sound so shocked." The shadow of his scruff scrapes past my cheek, but I barely have time to register the sensation before he clamps a strong hand around my wrists and boldly pins them to the wardrobe above my head. "And here I thought you'd be happy to be reunited."

Oh, God.

I've been submerged in a nightmare, the kind that clings like seaweed, dragging you down, down, down, until the pocket of sunlight kissing the water's surface turns a murky gray and disappears altogether.

This can't be happening. This can't be *real*.

"I didn't think . . ." Stretching onto my toes, I swallow a gasp when the blade of his nose nudges my jaw. "I thought you were—"

"Dead? No. Men like me never stay dead for long."

The gritty words are whispered against the shell of my ear, and this time, there's no smothering the startled whimper that begs for release. Everywhere I am, he is, too. His muscular leg thrust between mine, his calloused hand clasping my wrists against the glossy grain of wood, his soft lips drifting south to claim the hollow of my throat.

I'm surrounded, *contained.*

This is not the man who cradled my hand and let me trace the bold lines of his face.

No, this is the man who handcuffed me without remorse.

The man who caged me within his arms and danced his fingers across my throat.

This is the Mad Priest, the man who destroyed Parliament, and any chance of escaping his wrath disappeared the second Gregory took it upon himself to shove him from the Palace's roof.

He's going to kill me.

Desperation floods my veins and I squirm in his hold, hips churning futilely against the muscled plane of his thigh. "Damien, what happened tonight . . . what happened to *you,* I mean, it's not what you think."

He shifts closer, presses into me harder, chest to stomach, thigh to core. Not even a sliver of space remains between us, and air comes thin and reedy through my nose when he snarls, "You have no fucking idea what I was thinking then, what I'm thinking right this second. If you did, you'd run and you'd never look back."

"Is that a suggestion?"

"It's a promise that you could try, and I'll always find you. Catch you." A merciless chuckle reverberates deep in his chest, and I feel its twin echo in mine. A shattering bleakness howling its fury. "I'll haunt you from the bloody grave, Rowena. You'll pray for safety and only ever find me."

"The big, bad wolf."

"No one would ever mistake me for a saint."

Every pull of oxygen into my lungs carries with it the

scent of cloves from his skin. It scrambles all conscious thought, leaving me scattered and aching for something I don't dare name. Grasping the last threads of my sanity, I flex my fingers and roll my wrists within their constraints of human flesh. "Is that why you're here?" I demand. "To give me a head start before you hunt me to the ends of the Earth?"

"Oh, you won't make it that far." His lips hover over my pulse like he enjoys me trembling under his touch. A man pleased by fear. Submission. "You won't even make it out of this room."

The pit in my stomach freefalls.

His mouth curves against the slope of my neck, a smile that feels like the beginning of the end. "Poor Rowena Carrigan," he rasps, his voice seductively dark, "blind, alone. Defeated. You spun such a pretty tale—an estranged father, a heartbreaking past. And like a fool, I fell for every bloody trick in the book."

"Damien—"

"Ask me what I thought of in those last few seconds."

His thumb presses down on my inner wrist, immobilizing me against the wardrobe, his body the nails that anchor me in place. He wants to crucify me, to bring me to my knees with intimidation and power.

"No."

It takes me a second to realize that I've spoken out loud, the single word ringing with absolute authority even though it would be so much easier to submit to the fear spiraling through my veins. But I'm already one step closer to the end, and so I twist my head and hiss the rejection again, "*No.*"

He goes eerily still.

"Blind. Alone. Defeated." A harsh laugh rattles my chest. "You're the villain I don't ever want to meet on a dark, quiet street, you said, the monster in my dreams. But Damien"—my lips brush his ear—"you never stopped to realize that I'm the devil in *yours*."

His fingers go taut around my wrists.

And then the mouth of the revolver touches my temple.

Chilled.

Firm.

Deadly.

I don't allow my legs to buckle, not even to sway.

It's fight or flight, and I'll bury myself twice over before I ever break again. Not even for the man I thought was dead, whose life I willingly mourned for the span of a heartbeat. A lit candle. A hushed prayer. All in all, a serious lapse in judgment that I'll carry with me to the grave.

"It's all coming together now, isn't it?" With my shoulders squared off, I ignore the muzzle getting firmly acquainted with my forehead. *Do your worst, Damien Priest.* "A supposed insane asylum. A secret estate hidden away from the world. How was anyone to know Holyrood existed when you and your brothers clearly took such care to keep it off the grid? It must have hit you, right before Gregory threw you over, that Margaret was never my target."

"Then who."

A demand, not a question. And I'm not so disillusioned to think that he's actually clueless. No, he craves the confirmation off my lips, and hell, I want to give it to him. For Ian. For Sara's father and Frederick and Victor and Russ and Gregg. For every single person in this blasted country who's met their end at the hands of the Priests, supposed guardians of the Crown and yet deceivers to all.

"You," I whisper, angling my chin upward, wishing I could capture his gaze. "Every hour of every day, it was you."

A noise rumbles deep within his chest, but I press

onward toward the realm of no return. Reckless, in a way that I never am. Brave, the way I've only ever been in my dreams. A woman who knows her fate and reaches for it with wide, open arms.

Finally, my soul sings, *finally.*

"The irony," I say, "is that I hunted you, searched for you, and I almost walked away without ever knowing the truth. But you just couldn't resist, could you? Pride goeth before the fall. You wanted the upper hand—*no one escapes the Mad Priest*, you vowed—and then you gave yourself away, just like that."

The air thickens.

The revolver never pulls away.

I feel every breath that Damien draws into his lungs, the rhythmic expansion of his chest touching mine on each inhalation. *In, out. In, out.* If I were to ask to see his face, to read his expression with my fingers, there'd be no softness waiting for me. Not a single hint of mercy. Firm lips, furrowed brows. Harsh. Furious. I want to tear at his shirt, to fist the material and tell him to explode, to let me feel his rage and match it against my own.

But he only stands there, his arms a cage with no escape, his breath a ragged melody of death and retribution.

"Don't you have something to say?" Something dark and twisted and desperate gathers in my stomach. "You hid in here with something prove, to kill me the same way Gregory tried to kill you. And here you are doing *nothing*." When the revolver remains perfectly steady, and the seconds tick by, one after another, I let out a choked laugh. "You may be the villain, Damien Priest, but somewhere, deep down, you're just begging to be the hero."

He pulls the trigger.

I hear the lever catch with a dull *click*, feel the sob of

relief that rises like grace in my throat. *Finally, finally.* My eyes slam shut. Only—

"Boom," comes his gruff whisper.

Slowly, as if waking from a dream, muted awareness prickles over my blistered skin. Metal clatters onto the rug at our feet before skidding onto the hardwood floor. The gun, I think, being discarded like yesterday's rubbish.

Empty. The gun was *empty.*

Oh, my God.

Panic wells and I twist my body, heedless of strained ribs and jagged cuts. I need that head start. He can catch me wherever he wants, in Australia, in Egypt, for all I care, but not here, not *now.*

Except that there's no escape.

Damien towers over me, his legs pressing into mine, his free hand finding the empty spot beside my head. The wardrobe shudders, the paper Hugh taped to the mirror crinkling, as if they, too, know that the man before me is a force to be reckoned with.

Strong fingers grasp my chin, then tilt my head back.

"I'm going to say this only once," he growls, his thumb sweeping over the tiny indent beneath my lower lip, "and I want you to hear me loud and clear. Nod that you understand."

I obey, every part of my body strung tight with adrenaline.

"Good girl." He lowers his head and presses his cheek to mine. As one, we breathe. The shadow of him beside me, the blistering heat of his skin on mine—it powers through my limbs like firelight. "Own the darkness or it'll own you. Revel in it. Consume it and bend it to your will. But never, ever let it drown you."

CHAPTER 19

DAMIEN

The length of her body jerks against mine.

Not from pain—not the physical kind, at least.

"Why are you telling me this?" Her breath is hot against my ear, unsteady. "Why even bother when we're not . . ." She swallows, hard. "One of my men tried to kill you tonight and you just had your chance to even the score—why not take it?"

Because it'd be like putting a gun to my own head.

The darkness always bleeds devastation. It pollutes every thought and sabotages every moment of clarity until clawing your way out feels like an insurmountable task. Killing Rowena lost appeal the moment she egged me on, her violet eyes glittering with a desperation I've only ever seen once before. She craved the abyss, wanted the fate she saw for herself, and it's unfortunate for her that I won't ever be that man.

I couldn't kill her, *can't* kill her.

Fucking hell.

Forcing my hands off her warm skin, I turn on my heel. Prowl deeper into the room, noting the drawn curtains over the windows and the perfectly made-up sleigh bed. Beside it, on the nightstand, is a well-worn copy of *England's Grandest Homes: Architecture & Design.*

Aware that Rowena is still waiting for an answer, I tell her, "I said that I wouldn't make it easy for you."

Smart as she is, she doesn't miss a beat: "Torture is pulling the trigger when the gun isn't loaded. It's knowing that you have a piece of me that I can't ever get back."

When she inhales sharply, I cut a quick glance over my shoulder just in time to see her sink to the ground like her legs can't support her weight for another second. Exhaustion presses purple thumbprints under her eyes. "Damien, just tell me why you didn't kill me. Please."

My fingers find a dog-eared page. Cracking open the book, I glance down to see the Palace staring back at me from the depths of a black-and-white photograph. There's no sign of the drawbridge we installed a few years ago or the moat that was re-dug in the early 1930s. The next page reveals a blueprint of Ightham Mote's original foundation, back when the property was built with King Henry VIII in mind. Rowena knew where to look, knew where to find us and flush us out like bees from a hive.

I should grab the revolver and finish off what I started.

Instead I hear myself confess, "Because I've stood in your shoes too many times to count. I've worn the soles down to the threads and kept on walking."

"And does it . . ." She clears her throat. "Does the darkness ever fade?"

"No."

Her fingers dig into the outside of her bent knee. "I wish it would. I wish—"

"You harness it," I tell her, "then weaponize it until it's an asset, not a curse."

A wry smile tugs her mouth to one side, only to slip

away, like she hasn't yet mustered the strength to wrangle her emotions. "The Mad Priest at his finest. You're impossible to beat."

"But you've tried."

Her violet stare remains clear, unburdened. "More times than you'll ever know."

For a second, I can't help but wonder if Edward Carrigan had nothing to do with the attempt on my life. Had Rowena set her sights on me, even then? Trailed along after me on Fournier Street, all while making sure to hug the shadows so that I never anticipated her attack?

I study her face, looking for a sign, confirmation—and find nothing.

Whatever her sins, I don't think my almost death behind Christ Church Spitalfields is one of them. She'd boast about nearly taking me out, if that were the case. Rowena Carrigan isn't exactly shy.

"They won't let you leave Holly Village alive, you know," she says now, clearly distrustful of my prolonged silence. "If I scream—"

"I wouldn't."

"Because you're worried that they'll find you here?"

"Because I'll kill them all the second that they come through that door."

A hiss escapes past her clenched teeth. "Was that your grand plan, then? You came here to slaughter us?"

"I came here for you."

Her chin snaps back, suspicion weaving a thread through every line of her body. "You came to kill me, you mean."

Yes.

But while taking her out might satisfy the vengeful corner of my soul, it won't give me what I need most: answers. Whatever reason she and her . . . cult have for targeting Holyrood, it's either fundamentally rooted in insanity or a fragment of some warped reality that'll do us no good in leaving unmanaged. Tonight, The Bell & Hand went up in flames and the Palace met a fate not much better. At the end of the day, getting information trumps all plans I have for her father. The prime minister can wait a little while longer.

And, fact is, you can't kill her.

The bullets from her revolver sit like iron weights in the front pocket of my trousers, removed from their chambers before she ever entered the room.

"I want information," I clip out, sidestepping honesty to leave it dead and strangled behind me. I have a mission, a goal. And Rowena Carrigan is not a new addiction I can afford. Grabbing the book off the nightstand, I tuck it under my left arm. "Who do you take orders from?"

Scoffing, she lets her head fall back against the wardrobe. "You're delusional if you think you can barge in here and interrogate me in my own home."

"If handcuffs aren't involved, then it's not an interrogation."

She doesn't look amused. "I have nothing to say to you, Priest."

"Really?" Sardonically, I raise a brow. "Nothing at all?"

Her jaw tightens mutinously. "Are you wanting an apology?"

"It wouldn't be a bad start."

Just to keep her on her toes, I make a point to grab the spindle-backed chair from the desk and set it down in front of her. I sit with my long legs to the left of her outstretched one, leaving space between us because I need this conversation not to devolve into an argument, because if I touch her, hear that goddamn whimper of hers again,

I might—

Don't fucking go there, Godwin.

"I'll hand it to that big bastard of yours," I drawl, opening the book in my lap to the dog-eared page, "he tried."

"And failed."

At her grim tone, my lips twitch with morbid humor. "I caught the drawbridge's pulleys on my way down. Total stroke of luck. Couldn't recreate the moment even if I wanted."

Her eyes narrow. "You're cocky."

"Don't let that stop you—I'm waiting."

Nostrils flaring, she clutches her knee like it's either that or tackle me to the ground. I watch with silent fascination as her shoulders lift with a slow inhale. Then, in a tone carved from mock reverence, she murmurs, "Damien, I am so sorry . . ."

Satisfaction flares. "Wasn't that hard, was it?"

". . . that the pulleys got in your way."

Every comeback, every scathing retort, dies on the tip of my tongue.

And the blasted woman knows it, too.

Her full lips lift into a cunning smile that leaves me feeling strangely winded. I press a hand to my chest, fingers drifting up to clutch my right shoulder. Before I even have the chance to scrape together a mediocre response, she primly adds, "Your ego, Damien. It's seriously overinflated."

Jesus.

I open my mouth, then clamp it shut.

Rowena only taps her fingers against her kneecap. "Now that that's out of the way, should we begin with our non-interrogation?"

The she-wolf strikes again.

Torn between applauding her little performance and

dragging her over my lap, ass up, I grit my teeth. "This is the way it's going to work. You aren't going to scream and I'm not going to—"

"Threaten me?" she offers, one dark brow arched. "Intimidate me and then remind me of all the ways you can put me in a corner and make me cry?"

"Yes."

"To which part exactly?"

"All of it," I bite off. "These are peace talks. You, me, and our good mate transparency. Think you can manage that, *Rowan*?"

At my deliberate use of her nickname, Rowena leans back, head bolstered by the wardrobe behind her, one wrist propped atop her bent knee. She looks cool, poised. A queen prepared to squash a revolt with just the toe of her shoe.

"I have nothing to hide," she replies smoothly, "and now that we're both fully aware that you can't stomach the thought of actually killing me . . . Well, it looks like I have more leverage than I previously thought."

My chest tightens.

Lowering my voice, I growl, "Talk like that some more, Miss Carrigan, and I'm going to look at it as an invitation to take you down a peg or two."

Her gaze shifts, locking with mine, however incidentally, and I feel pinned in place—known without being seen, understood while having told her none of my past. Unchained for the first time in so many years that my wrists actually ache from the release of their phantom shackles.

"I didn't think a man like you would need an invitation."

"It's my only courtesy before I bring a woman down to her knees."

A wash of color darkens her cheeks. Then, with an

audible swallow, she straightens her shoulders. "I want to know how you found us. You couldn't have followed Gregory here, not without risking getting caught."

"Alfie Barker."

"*What?*"

A dark smile curves my mouth. "You didn't think we let prisoners go untapped, did you?"

Her reply is slow, measured. "What exactly do you mean by . . . *untapped?*"

"I track them."

"Hunt them, you mean."

With my feet on the rug, I drop my elbows to my knees and hang the book between my spread thighs. "Track," I repeat, firmly. "A little device I insert under the skin, not even the size of a penny."

"Where?"

"Wherever I think it won't be noticed. Barker's is just above his kidney."

I watch as her tongue darts out to slip across the seam of her lips. Then track its return, a second later, when she does it again.

A nervous tic.

Ask the question, Rowena. I know you're dying to.

Finally, she caves. "And mine?"

"What of it?"

"The tracker," she grinds out, "where is it? Above my kidney like Alfie Barker's? In my arse cheek?"

Nowhere at all.

She arrived at the Palace too wounded, and I couldn't risk her getting an infection. But clearly she thinks that I've embedded it somewhere; with agitated sweeps of her hands, she runs her palms over the length of her legs, pressing here, digging there. The devil on my shoulder quips, "Tell me who you take orders from and I'll give you a clue. Might even help you remove it before I leave."

"Sadistic bastard," she mutters, not quite under her breath.

Casually, I cross my legs at the ankles, keep my mouth shut because I know the silence will drive her mad. And it does, bringing a deeper flush of color to her cheeks just as she clamps a tight fist over her extended leg. "They take orders from me."

"Why?"

"What do you mean *why*?"

"Why," I repeat, dipping my chin, "would they listen to the prime minister's daughter? You've no military experience. No relevant history at all to prove that out of everyone in this country, you're the one to lead them."

"That's none of your business."

"And here I thought you had nothing to hide."

She shoves onto her feet with a nimbleness that I wouldn't expect from someone so injured. But move she does, stalking past me with a surprising elegance that twists me around in my seat, elbow propped on the back, so that I can follow her with my gaze.

I wait until she's halfway to the bed. Then, "I know who you are, Rowena. I don't understand the reasoning behind it, or why you've banded together the way that you have, but I know enough to put together the basics."

That stops her in her tracks.

She whirls around, her face bearing a mask of righteous fury. "You know *nothing*."

I set the book down by my feet, then stand. "Listen here—"

"No, *you* listen. You murder and you scheme, but don't think that I don't see through every one of your lies."

"When the hell have I lied to you?"

"Guardians of the Crown," she scoffs, "protectors of the queen. Isn't that a lie?" She steps in my direction, as if she's pinpointed my place within the room by only the sound of my voice. "Your own brother murdered the king. And *you* . . ."

Heart thudding, I rasp, "What, Rowena? What about me?"

"You're the reason for all of this."

I stare at her, unable to wrench my gaze away. "The reason for *what?*"

She laughs, this jagged, aching sound that buries itself inside my chest, reminding me of so very long ago when I stood under a starless sky and broke consecrated ground.

You've been very, very bad, Damien.

As if she can hear every guilty thought, Rowena approaches, one foot in front of the other, until she's a hair's breadth away. Her head tips back, the air practically buzzing with a visceral tension that tastes of hate and vengeance. And then, with little more than a finger to my chest, she cuts me at the knees: "You betrayed the king, Damien, and so he came to me."

CHAPTER 20

ROWENA

The sound of madness is deafening.

Words uttered by King John on the day that he invited me to St. James's Palace. I'd interpreted them as a warning then, a barely leashed threat that sank into my bones and rattled me to my core when I picked up the red porcelain teacup placed before me by one of the staffers.

Red carpet beneath my pumps.

Red cushioned chair under my arse.

So much red that it felt like a metaphor for the king's life displayed for all who entered his domain—the power that he wielded, the blood spilt in his name. And there, on the king's finger, a ruby glinted like the brightest star in the midnight sky.

He had the power of the whole world in his grasp while I was alone, uncertain as to why I'd been asked to come, in a room cut off from the rest of the palace. For the first time in years, I felt sweat dampen my palms. Nausea swirled, so very hot in my stomach, like the tea that I couldn't swallow down. All while the king spun a tale of a rabid anti-loyalist keen on murdering Margaret. I'd heard only my pulse.

Thud-thud. Thud-thud. Thud-thud.

Madness.

"You went to him," I hear myself say to Damien, my voice so very faint, as if I've been stuck in a barrel and put out to sea, "and you told him that Margaret would be next. You said she'd be done in just like Evangeline."

A calloused hand slips around my wrist then presses my palm flat to his chest. Tendons ripple, pectoral muscles constrict, and beneath it all, a heart hammers wildly, a frantic tattoo that feels ridiculously human for a man who regularly conducts himself like a god.

"Why you, Rowena? Why did he choose *you*?"

Isn't it obvious? "Because I'm alone. Because I've always been alone, except for Margaret, and he knew that I'd care that she was in danger."

"In danger from *me*?" Damien barks out a harsh laugh, the sound like shards of ice that pierce the skin, and I flinch. "Fucking hell. Rowena, he used you."

No.

Thud-thud. Thud-thud. Thud-thud.

I let my fingers coil in the fabric of Damien's shirt. All the better to hold myself steady as I rise onto my toes and thrust my face close to his. "You're wrong. He didn't *use* me. I was always the logical choice. No one knows Margaret the way I do. We have twenty years' worth of history, friendship. Sisterhood."

The roughened pad of Damien's thumb slips under my captive hand, burying itself in the center of my palm. "You were used."

It's all a matter of perspective, though, isn't it?

Father used me; the men of Westminster used me. I spent years avoiding anyone and everything that might do the same, wrapping myself in a cocoon of isolation so thick, so impenetrable, that I might as well have existed on my own little island for all the interaction I had with the outside world. But I'd gone willingly to King John, willingly took tea with him—and I'd said *yes*.

Yes to protecting my best friend.

Yes to hunting down the rabid anti-loyalist.

Yes to it all.

In the end, the king had no more used me than I'd used *him*.

Frustration heats my cheeks, and I fist Damien's shirt a little tighter when I spit out the words itching to scrape free: "You make me sound *naïve*."

Naïve like a young girl playing dress-up in a man's world.

A girl like I was, a million years ago, who twirled from one man's arm to the next, none of them ever suspecting that I was anything more than a beautiful face. It was never meant to be that way with King John. The decisions were mine to make. The control mine to wield, when and however I saw fit.

In this house, *I* wear the crown.

"I knew what was expected of me," I bite out, nearly giving in to the temptation to pound my fists on his chest and demand that he *see me*—how I am, how I've always been, had anyone ever cared to look deep enough. "And I knew what he wanted from me. I *knew*, Damien. You can hate me for what I've done, especially after tonight, but the fact is that the king—"

"Lied."

I suck in an angry breath. "Are you really going to pretend that you didn't go to St. James's? Or is that just another pretty lie that the king spun for me, too?"

"Oh, I went," he sneers, his breath hitting my cheekbone as he lowers his head. "I went knowing that I was only wasting my time."

"Then why even bother?"

"Because I was willing to sell my soul to the devil to get the information I needed."

"And the king was the devil, I'm guessing."

At my undisguised sarcasm, Damien scoffs under his breath. "For King and Country, right? A pledge forced on us all since John took the throne. But allegiance isn't blind, and there's always a tipping point. Tell a person to sit, and they will. Tell them to sit while balancing a book on their head, and they might get on with it just because you asked. But tell them to do all that while placing their bare feet on a bed of nails . . . Yeah, the look on your face tells me you understand. Obedience is earned, Rowena, it isn't freely given. After the Westminster Riots, I knew it was only a matter of time before someone, somewhere, remembered that Princess Evangeline's killer was never found."

That stops me cold. "You thought there'd be a copycat killer?"

"I knew there'd be one sooner or later."

"That's why you went to St. James's," I say slowly, hearing the grim edge to his tone.

I don't need to see his nod to know that he's dipped his chin in confirmation. "John wouldn't let the Met handle the princess's autopsy report. He had everything handled in-house—not even Holyrood could touch it. I was only six, then, but I grew up hearing the rumors from the older blokes. Said that the princess had been receiving secret letters leading up to the assassination. I figured that if it was true, the king would know. And if he knew, and he still had the letters, then I needed to see them. Try to piece together whatever I could so the same thing wouldn't happen to Margaret."

Or so he says.

He thinks me naïve to have trusted the king, but it'd be

exponentially more naïve of me not to question everything that falls from his lips.

"And why should I believe you?" Stubbornly, I lift my chin. "You say that a copycat killer is waiting on the horizon. You *say* that the king lied to me. Since I just spent three days undergoing your special brand of interrogation, excuse me if I don't take your word for it. In case you've forgotten—you didn't earn *my* obedience, you bloody well stripped it from me!"

"Because you'd have done it any differently?" His calloused hand reflexively tightens around mine, his voice lowering to a deadly pitch. "You may have sent your men to collect the queen tonight, but it was *me* you hunted. And had they brought me to you, I have no fucking doubt that I'd have been shoved at your feet and forced to grovel."

I hate that he's right.

Hate even more that he knows it.

"Then give me proof." I try to tug my hand away from his, but he doesn't let me go. "Give me something tangible."

His nose brushes mine and *holy hell*, he's close, so blasted close, that I feel the vibration of his every word when he growls, "I owe you *nothing*, Rowena." His breathing shifts, roughening. "The fact is, you're too scared to even consider that you've been wrong this entire time. It's always easy to hunt the monster when the monster isn't *you*."

Something splinters inside my chest—a vulnerability I thought long dead—and I slam my eyes shut out of pure habit. "Don't go there," I rasp. "Damien, *don't*—"

"Do you know, John felt the same way. One mention of Evangeline's name and you'd think I took a knife to his throat. He was scared, just like you. Only, England's king was too busy with his head up his ass, thinking about his ghost of a daughter, to acknowledge that his heir might end up the same way."

It feels like I've been put in a corner and taken to task with a ruler across my knuckles.

Worse, there's also the irrefutable fact that Margaret *has* almost met the same fate as Princess Evangeline. Only eight days ago, she crawled herself into a stairwell to die, her fingers coated red with blood, her blue eyes dead with exhaustion.

I kept her alive that night.

I did it because, whether she trusts me or not, Margaret is the only family I have. Would she truly have wanted to go to the Palace if she distrusted the Priests and Holyrood? She'd *begged* me. Begged me like her life depended on it, and I'd done it, knowing full well that I could have brought her here to Holly Village in North London instead.

My lungs expand with a heavy breath.

If I dig deep and peel back the layers of my armor, I'm terrified that I'll find the arrow that's nicked my flesh from Damien's bow. *If he's telling the truth* . . . "The king said you ran," I say, desperately. "He said that the guards couldn't catch you."

Damien snorts derisively. "I left the same way that I walked in—with a small bow to His Royal Majesty and a two-fingered salute the second that I was out of his sight. And there were no guards."

Just as there weren't any when he invited me for tea. "Did the king say anything to you before you left?" I ask.

"Only that love is, and will always be, carnage."

I grimace. "That's . . ."

"Morbid?" A low, gritty chuckle. "Call me a bastard for saying so, but the king is better off dead. His one redeeming quality was his love for his children. Anyone could see that he'd move Heaven and Earth to keep them safe. But losing Evangeline . . . Jesus, it stole something from him. His sanity, his sense of compassion. His humanity. All of it, gone. To him, I was the pest who threatened his only living daughter with the reminder of what had happened to his dead heir. And *you*, Rowena, you were . . ."

The arrow plunges deeper, spilling blood.

"What?" I whisper thickly. "I was what? Say it."

His thumb slides from the center of my palm to hook itself between my fore and middle fingers, then continues, his palm coasting along skin not damaged by the fire, until we're holding hands, mine sandwiched between his and the hard plane of his chest.

"You were alone, with just one tie to the world. And a man like John . . ." His hand squeezes mine. "He knew what would happen if you and I crossed paths. He knew what I am."

"The monster," I say, the word sounding utterly bleak now that it's on my tongue. "If we'd met any other way, you would have killed me without a second thought. That's what you're trying to say."

"The king chose you."

He says it with barely concealed pity, and I struggle to find something noteworthy to tell him when everything in my soul is screaming. "I was dispensable."

Then, gruffly, "The blind are loyal to a fault."

Not my vision.

He means blinded by my friendship with Margaret and my hope to do something good. Something, anything, to reverse the misdeeds of my past. So much so that I willingly said yes to a king who didn't care whether I lived or died, so long as I threw myself headfirst into protecting his daughter from the man who scared him with not weapons or fists but a dose of uncomfortable reality.

I'm a *fool.*

The splinter in my chest cracks wide open, a gaping, searing chasm that somehow feels more devastating than any other loss, any other sorrow.

Unable to breathe, I wrench away from Damien and catch my arms around my middle. Though not nearly as severe as a week ago, pain still erupts, and I almost laugh. Hysterically. My head thrown back, my arms spread wide. A request to be struck down that won't ever be answered because this is *me.* In reality, I only hug myself tighter, fingers digging relentlessly into my waist, absorbing all the hurt and the agony with a gasp that sticks in my throat.

"Your proof is Henry Godwin."

I slick my tongue over the dry roof of my mouth. "Another Godwin," I say, barely above a whisper. "There are so many of you."

"A Godwin with a big heart, just like yours." A single step in my direction, the clip of his shoe a now familiar approach. "He had the sort of laughter you could hear from three rooms over. He was . . . a good man. Smart. Innovative. He'd give you the shirt off his own back, if he thought it might help. At the end of the day, though, he was just another spy in a long line of Godwins in service to the Crown."

Hearing the rueful note in Damien's voice, I turn my head to the left, just enough to pretend that I can see him standing there out of the corner of my eye. His shadow, the breadth of his shoulders. Anything at all. "What happened to him?"

The laugh that greets my ears is one without mercy. "He made the unfortunate mistake of not finding Princess Evangeline's killer."

I frown. "I don't understand how that—"

"He was killed, Rowena. Henry Godwin was found

dead on Marlborough Road, right behind St. James's Palace, twenty-five years ago."

My legs grow weak beneath me. "And you think that the king had him . . . *murdered?*"

"I think we'll never understand a person's motives, no matter how well we think we know them."

"That's not an answer. Do you really think King John—"

"Perception is the only mirror we're given. The king didn't want a crack in the fortress, and my—Godwin—didn't get the job done. Do I think he killed Godwin himself? No. Do I think he had someone else do it for him? I do. But he couldn't risk all-out rebellion, couldn't risk anyone thinking that he'd had a hand in it, so he still allowed Godwin's ashes to be scattered over Holyrood Abbey, the way it's always been done. Just like he wanted you to carry out killing me. The man couldn't stand getting his hands dirty."

Bring me to Holyrood, Margaret had said at Buckingham Palace.

I thought she'd meant the old ruins in Edinburgh. Had said so out loud, even. Because it wouldn't have occurred to me, in that stairwell that was on the cusp of going up in flames, that there had been an alternative.

The king never mentioned Holyrood or the Godwins. He'd only talked of assassinations and a madman out for Margaret's head. He wove the thread of panic so tightly within me that there'd been no other option. How could I let my best friend die? How could I stand aside, in my cocoon of isolation, and let them come for her?

The Priests.

Damien.

"He said you were mad," I say, turning on my heel so I can face him directly. Because Damien deserves my transparency, my humiliation. *And my penance.* Every death—Ian's and Gregg's and Micah's—sits at my doorstep. Eight in total. A number that would have come to nine, tonight, if Gregory had succeeded. "I'd heard of you, obviously. There's not a single person in London who hasn't. Rebels. Anti-loyalists. Hell, you run a pub dedicated to—"

"It's always been a way to gather intel."

Wretched laughter bubbles to life inside my chest, and *bloody hell.* I press the heels of my hands to my throbbing temple, fingers curled into my palms. A fool. I am an absolute *fool.* "Of course, it is," I manage weakly. "Because clearly, it's not just enough that we came for Ightham Mote tonight when we've also spent *months* targeting an anti-loyalist pub that's never been anything but a cover. Oh, my God. Oh, my God, I need to—"

Retch.

Spinning on my heels, I stumble for the desk with its rubbish bin.

I barely cover half the distance when familiar hands fall on my shoulders and swing me back around. Warm breath hits my lips while calloused palms surge north to slide against the back of my neck and hold me captive.

"The fire," Damien growls fiercely. "Was it you?"

This time, I let the hysterical laugh run free. It pours out of me, low and volatile. "Do you seriously think that I would *choose* to light myself on fire?" In his arms, I'm acutely aware of the blisters peppering my skin. Skin that was, just eight days ago, completely smooth and unmarred. "I'm *broken*, Damien. Literally, figuratively. In every single way that matters. I refuse to drown in self-pity—you told me yourself that it isn't a good look—but can you honestly ask me whether I'd start a fire, only to do this to myself?"

"I'm not talking about Buckingham Palace."

"We didn't set the Palace on fire."

"The pub, Rowena," he grinds out. "I'm talking about The Bell & Hand."

The Bell & Hand caught on fire?

Shock floods my system and, not for the first time, I wish that I could see his expression. See *him*. Anything beyond registering every nuance of his voice before matching it against my limited knowledge of him.

With his hands clasping the base of my skull, as he does now, is he staring at the pinkened burns that stretch across my forehead and cheeks? Burns that, Sara informed me this morning, will turn shiny before healing further? Or does he hold my gaze, knowing that there's not a chance in hell that I can decipher the look in his blue eyes?

I don't realize that I've moved, not at first.

Not until I feel the corded muscle of his forearms when I raise my hands past them. Not until his breath catches audibly and my fingers feather over the bones of his face. The blunt-tipped fingers on my neck curl inward, biting into my flesh like he's about to embark on a battle that he'll never win.

"You're tense," I murmur, lightly tracing the throbbing muscle just below his hairline. The thick strands tease the back of my knuckles. Black, I imagine, like his brother Saxon's, who I watched more than once from a tea shop across from The Bell & Hand. I never found any photos of Damien online, though not for a lack of trying. *He's a ghost*, I always thought. My hand shifts now, wanting to discover every facet of him, and a lock of soft hair hooks over my forefinger, begging to be tugged.

Don't do it, Rowan.

Snatching my fingers away from temptation, I slip them down over the slope of his nose instead, feeling its crooked bridge and flared nostrils.

He's holding on by a thread, his emotions barely leashed.

"And angry," I add, shaking my head to dispel the fog creeping in, "so, so angry." I allow my hand to flatten over his defined jawline, feeling the bristles against my palm. "There's a lot I can own up to, Damien, believe me, but not this. Is the pub salvageable?"

"No."

"I'm sorry," I say, and mean it.

In the last year, I've spent a good number of my afternoons spying on The Bell & Hand while never stepping foot within its notorious walls. The prime minister's daughter visiting an infamous anti-loyalist pub? Not in this lifetime. But from a little bay window overlooking Commercial Street, I'd watched Ian and the rest step over its threshold, the pub's glossy black door luminous in the afternoon sunlight as it swung shut behind them. It was a hub of activity, rarely ever quiet, and—

Fire.

First Buckingham Palace, now The Bell & Hand. All in a matter of days.

Both times Damien has questioned my possible involvement, and I understand why he might think so. On the king's orders, I've pursued him and his brothers relentlessly for months. For the most part, we skated by unnoticed—hiring Jack out from under their noses, sitting at their tables and drinking their ale. If it weren't for Isla Quinn appearing at The Octagon—and Ian's reckless need to make a move, without waiting for my consent—it's possible that the Priests would still be unaware of our existence.

And we could have all been fighting this war together.

It's a bloody Shakespearean tragedy.

Which begs the question: Had the king really thought

that Damien would hurt Margaret? Or was it all a ploy to test the Priests' loyalty to the Crown? Because if it's the latter, then that means every death that's followed my afternoon at St. James's Palace has all been for nothing. And it won't be love that's carnage, as the king told Damien, but what's left of my soul.

To say nothing of the ashy remains of The Bell & Hand and Buckingham Palace. The chance of both fires being a mere coincidence . . .

A shiver chases an icy path down my spine. "You're being hunted, and not by me."

Beneath my palm, Damien's jaw goes impossibly rigid. "I know."

"No one would have expected you or your brothers to be at Buckingham Palace on the night of the fire—not unless they know who you really are." When Damien's hands fall from my neck, I fight the insane urge to snatch them back. *Focus, Rowan. Focus.* "It's possible . . . Well, I guess it's possible that the king may have recruited someone else after me, and actually filled them in on Holyrood's existence."

"Rowena."

"But even that doesn't make any sense, because if they were hired by King John, then they wouldn't chance hurting Margaret—or, obviously, *shooting* her. Which clearly is what happened. Shite. I have no idea—"

"*Rowena*," Damien grunts, "I need you to move."

My chin snaps back. "What?"

His fingers slide around my wrist, circling gently, before easing my hand away from his face. "You saw what you needed to, and now I need you to step back."

"Did I . . ." Feeling awkward, I reach up to tuck my hair behind my ear, only to remember that it's gone. My fingers graze peach fuzz instead. "Did I offend you?" When Damien curses under his breath, I hastily add, "I should have asked first. I'm not"—a self-conscious laugh scratches at my throat—"clearly, if there's an etiquette to this, I haven't discovered it yet. I'm sorry." Despising the burn of embarrassment flooding my body, I shove my hands into the front pockets of my trousers and shuffle backward. One step, two. *Please don't let me fall into the rubbish bin.* "It's an adjustment, like Dr. Matthews said, and I just wanted to understand what you were feel—"

"Don't apologize."

"I think I should. It was rude."

"Fine. Apology accepted if you let me stay."

"Stay—" Startled, my mouth drops open. "Sorry. You want to stay *here*?"

"That's what I said."

He sounds determined, and I . . . "Damien, in case—oh, I don't know—you failed to miss this small nugget of information: there are currently sixteen people downstairs who would love nothing more than to rip your spleen out from your spine. One of whom *shoved you from a bloody roof!*"

"It'll make for interesting dinner conversation."

"You're absolutely mad."

"Nothing I haven't heard before."

"They'll *kill* you."

"They won't," he replies smoothly, "because you won't let them."

"Even I have my limitations. They hate you."

"To be fair, all of England hates me."

"Damien," I try again, feeling the most ridiculous urge to grab him by the shoulders and shake some common sense into him, "logic says that leaving you in a house full of people who've spent the last month believing your family is the root of all their problems is not—and I repeat, is *not*—a brilliant idea. You leave this room and you're a dead man walking. I promise you that."

The darkness explodes with a burst of movement—footsteps approaching, closer and closer, only for them to stop just out of reach. The fine hairs on my nape stand tall. He's behind me. Biting down on my bottom lip, I touch my chin to my right shoulder and peer back. Dr. Matthews said that my vision should return—that the cortical blindness will heal on its own—but *soon* isn't fast enough when I'm already eight days in.

My bedroom is a landscape of the unknown and, in the center of it all, the man I understand least of all. A ghost, I once thought, when I searched for him all over London and came up empty-handed, time and time again. But never would the moniker have fit as well as it does now.

Like a shade come to haunt me from the Underworld, I *feel* Damien. The change in the air, rife with tension and anticipation. His gaze on the back of my shorn head, assessing and intense. The way he holds himself completely still, wholly content to see me freeze like prey caught in the gunman's scope.

And then he steps forward.

His chest to my back, his mouth at my ear: "I come as your prisoner. Cuff my wrists, if you want. Make me the villain of your nightmares. But let me stay."

My heart pounds so loud, so furiously, that I hear almost nothing beyond the roar of blood in my temples. "Why are you doing this?" I turn my head, feeling the fabric of his shirt soft against my cheek. "Why not leave while you still can?"

"Because there's only one person I can think of who might connect the fires at Buckingham Palace and The

Bell & Hand. To test my theory . . . I'll need resources that aren't my own."

What resources could I possibly have that he doesn't?

With fortitude and determination, I've pulled this ramshackle organization together on my own. Members recruited from all walks of life and wages paid from my own pocket. The king offered me nothing. Maybe he'd expected me to handle the scope of his demands all on my own. *Or maybe he expected you to fail and didn't see a point in bothering to help,* like a spoiled child lashing out with his hurt, heedless to the consequences of the whip he snapped. The thought feels like lead in my stomach, and I force it into nonexistence with a mental crush of my fist.

Regardless of what the king intended, I'm proud of what I've built—even if it is, essentially, all for nothing. But that doesn't mean we're Holyrood. To think we can provide Damien with resources that his own family can't is ridiculous.

I open my mouth, prepared to tell him just that, when he speaks.

"The king sent me to Westminster because he suspected the prime minister of foul play." His voice is painted black with unveiled secrets. Dark, enthralling. Edged with a fire that heats my skin like the flames at Buckingham Palace never could. "But when I got there, your father was already waiting for me. Told me that if I didn't want anything about that night to be revealed to the public that I'd kill the king."

"My father? You're saying that *my* father told you to assassinate King John?"

"He was there, in the middle of the night, waiting. And when I told him to sod off, he made good on his promise." Damien's fingers dig into my waist, pulling me closer. "He made me the Mad Priest. He turned me into *this,* and

I need to know if it was all a coincidence—that the last seven months are exactly what I thought they were—or if I was damned to this hell because the king set me up for a betrayal that was all in his fucking head."

"And you think that my father started the fire at the pub?" I shake my head. "If he's already backed you into a corner, why would he bother destroying The Bell & Hand on top of it?"

"I don't know but I intend to find out."

"You need me," I breathe, clarity hitting me like a sledgehammer to the chest. "You need me because you need access to my father." The man who used me for years, who turned a blind eye when I went to him, four years ago, in a frail moment of hope to salvage our fractured relationship, and who ignored me again at the Jewel Tower. The man whose actions have sent me on a path of ruination for which I've yet to recover.

Edward Carrigan, widower by choice, and father to none.

A flurry of heat warms my body.

Not lust, not desire, but anger.

Anger on behalf of the little girl who only wanted love and acceptance and found none. Anger that blossoms in my heart and fuels my soul and hastens my breathing. Finding Damien's hand on my hip, I squeeze it tightly. "Even if I let you stay, it doesn't erase the fact that it's a bad idea. What good are resources—what good am *I* to you—if you're dead?"

"You assume I can't handle myself."

"I *assume* that one against sixteen aren't great odds."

The bridge of his nose finds the back of my ear. "Are you worried about me, Miss Carrigan?"

"*No.*" The lie leaves me on a forceful exhale. "No, that's not it at all."

"Is it guilt, I wonder?" he husks, a bemused edge to his tone. "Or something else completely?"

I feel as powerless as I did when he held me in one hand and dangled me in the air. "Maybe you're delusional," I manage past a dry throat, "and maybe I don't want to handle the cleanup after they inevitably kill you."

"Oh, ye of little faith."

"Careful, your ego is showing again."

"Then agree to the terms."

I lift my head. "What could you possibly say that'll keep me from scrubbing your blood from my floors for the next week?"

The bite in my tone pulls a dark laugh from him. It twines around me like smoke, wrapping tighter, knitting closed, until I feel his hand slip out from under mine. One settles over my breastbone, like he seeks the rhythm of my heart, and the *other* . . .

The other cups my face.

A startled breath escapes me when his thumb grazes my bottom lip. "Damien . . ."

"If they hurt me, then I'll touch you, and I won't wait for an invitation."

Oh, my God.

Like a jar that's been unlatched, butterflies flutter to life in my belly. The rasp in his voice. The heat of his chest against my back. That damned thumb of his tracing back and forth, back and forth, over my mouth. The sensation is lulling. Hypnotic. He's seducing me with nothing more than a promise, terms that bear a curse, and I fear . . . I fear that he can feel me swaying now, like a moth drawn toward a flame.

Drawn to *him*, inexplicably so.

"I need you, Rowena. Say yes."

CHAPTER 21

DAMIEN

"'e's *what?*"

The big bastard from the roof, Gregory, throws me a wild-eyed look from where two other blokes restrain him behind an antique sofa—as if they'll actually be enough to keep him from hurtling the sofa and stampeding toward me. *Doubtful.* He elbows the shorter man in the gut, then growls, "Rowan, you've lost your bloody mind. 'e should be dead!"

No one in the drawing room speaks up to contradict him.

Beside me, Rowena only folds her hands primly behind her back. Like a queen confronted by rebellious peasants, she lifts her chin, visibly steels her spine, and announces, "Damien Priest is our prisoner. He stays."

Two of the men exchange perplexed glances before the redhead pulls out a chair from a dainty-as-hell table and collapses onto it. "Can you actually be classified as a prisoner if you've turned yourself in? Prisoners aren't willing. It's not the way it works." Crossing his legs at the knee, he shifts his arms across his wiry chest, a man clearly content to debate the philosophies of hostage situations all night. "Who does that? No one, that's who." He meets my gaze. "Uri said you walked through the front door like you owned the place."

Not exactly.

These men stormed the Palace tonight.

In their quest for revenge, they breached walls that have stood for centuries. Rare books were torn from the shelves in the library, for no other purpose than that they could. Vintage stemware thrown to the ground in the dining room and medicine filched from the cabinets in Matthews' operating room. I found his medical bag floating in the moat, its contents soaked. In every room, glass crunched under the soles of my heavy boots.

No corner of the Palace was left untouched.

Rowena's motley crew of misfits may take orders from her, but that doesn't lessen the deep-seated anger they clearly harbor toward me and my brothers. I don't blame them. My brothers and I have spent a decade spreading rumors about the Priests to endear us to anti-loyalists everywhere. It was a price that we willingly paid, knowing that we learned more than we ever would have otherwise. But any chance that *these* people might trust us, let alone forgive us, was obliterated the minute Isla put her hands around Ian Coney's throat and squeezed.

To them, I'm a wolf in sheep's clothing.

"Actually," I drawl, making a point to hold the redhead's stare, "I climbed the trellis."

The trellis outside Rowena's room, like I was the Romeo to her Juliet. No one saw me scaling the flimsy ladder—because for all their success at laying siege to the Palace, these people are not trained spies. Not like Holyrood.

Except, maybe, for one, and his jaw just came unhinged.

"The trellis," Gregory enunciates slowly, glancing back toward the bloke he elbowed with an air of astonishment, "'e climbed the bloody trellis *after* I killed 'im." His narrowed gaze swings back to me. "'ow many bleeding lives do you 'ave?"

A grim smile twists my lips. "Not nearly enough."

"And you won't be risking any more of them," Rowena tells Gregory pointedly. "Understood?"

"'ow can you just forget what 'e's done?"

"I forget nothing."

Though issued quietly, Rowena's voice is laced with steel. When she starts forward, I can't help but skim my gaze down the length of her spine to where her fingers are still linked together, her knuckles white with tension. I watch as she ducks a quick look over her shoulder, her sightless gaze searching for me.

Whatever his motives were in approaching her, *this* is the woman King John chose to run a counter-op against Holyrood. The she-wolf. A queen without a crown. During those tense moments in her bedroom, when she'd sought to read my emotions, I saw what I hadn't before: Rowena Carrigan may be the prime minister's daughter, but she has more integrity in her soul than anyone I've ever met.

She owned her mistakes and humbled herself before me.

Had I told her to drop to her knees, she would have—without question.

And *fuck*, I wanted to. With her hand cupping my face, and her voice hoarse with sympathy for the loss of The Bell & Hand, I'd wanted her to beg for my forgiveness, for no other reason than to see those violet eyes of hers peering up at me as she kneels at my feet.

Blind. Ruined. *Mine.*

Her chin dips in a curt nod, like she's reached some internal debate that I've not been privy to, before turning to address the room again. "I would never ask you to forget your loved ones. But Mr. Priest is one of us—he's been one of us before an *us* even existed—which means that he stays, whether you like it or not, and he does so under my watch."

"His brother murdered the king!"

At the outburst, I fix my gaze on a round-faced man seated near the curtained windows—as far away, I note, as he can get without stepping out of the room completely. When he catches me staring, color creeps up past the collar of his jumper.

"What?" he snaps, shifting his weight. "I've only said what everyone is thinking." Instead of responding, I keep silent and let him run his mouth. Which he does with obnoxious ease: "We all know what Saxon Priest did at St. Paul's. Hell, all of England knows!"

The irony being that of the three of us Godwins, Saxon has always been the least likely to betray the royal family. Until Isla, anyway, who *did* kill the king. Since I never plan to admit the truth, I only ask, "Did you ever meet John?"

A strangled noise emerges from the bloke's mouth like he's appalled at my using the king's given name. Still, he responds exactly how I expected him to—he has that sullen, *holier-than-thou* look about him—and bounces up from the chair to straighten to his full height. Which is still a head shorter than I am.

"I saw him once," he boasts, puffing out his chest, "up in Manchester."

"And did you speak to him? Say hello? Do anything besides fawn over him from two blocks over while he ignored your existence?"

"Well, no." The wanker shrinks backward. "But he's the—"

"Then don't waste your breath defending him."

There's a collective gasp from around the room, and I almost bark out a laugh. All those horrified expressions . . .

they'd know real horror if they ever learned the truth about their precious king. Murdering Pa, scarring Saxon when he'd only been a boy. At my side, my hand curls into a fist. No, a man like John doesn't deserve reverence. He doesn't even deserve the air we breathe.

If Isla hadn't done him in, someone else would have soon enough.

And it may have been you to pull the trigger.

I grit my teeth. Flick my gaze from man to man, then to the only other woman besides Rowena. "For whatever it's worth," I edge out, forcing my hand to relax before anyone misinterprets the gesture as a threat, "Saxon didn't assassinate the king. He might have thought about doing it a million times over, but it wasn't him."

"You say that like you know who did it."

I glance over at the woman. Blond-haired, blue-eyed. She sits on a bench before the grand piano, studying me like I'm the devil come out to play. "Do you?" she prods angrily. "Do you know who killed the king?"

"Does it really make a difference?"

She jerks back like I've delivered a physical blow. "*Yes*," she hisses, "of course it does."

"Then yes, we have a suspect in custody." A small pause. "And no, it isn't Saxon."

"But your brother *did* kill my father at The Octagon. I saw the pictures Jack took from the upper gallery. I know what really happened there."

Rowena's shoulders visibly stiffen. Behind her back, her linked fingers separate into individual fists like she's two seconds away from throwing hands and wrangling everyone into their separate corners.

I don't let her step forward.

Touching my fingers to her shoulder, I bypass her on

my way to the piano. "Dr. Sara Grafton, am I right?"

The woman visibly flinches. "How do you know my name?"

"Because I know every person who died that day." *Because I've spent hours trying to make a tangible connection between every person at The Octagon and Rowena and found none.* Still haven't found any. Although it's becoming increasingly obvious, just by standing in this room, that Rowena cares less about recruiting people with tactical experience and more about giving these misfits a home.

I don't allow myself the chance to look over at her.

"Because I know the first job that they ever had out of uni and their favorite takeaway. Curry, for your dad, from a place over in Mayfair. I know that you lost your mother three years ago, Dr. Grafton, and that your father was all you had left." I take another step, careful to keep my gaze trained on her face. "He was ex-military."

"Army," she says with a shaky nod that matches the way she shoves trembling fingers under her thighs, "he was in the army."

"Love is carnage," I reply, and hear Rowena's hushed intake of breath from behind me. "That's the last thing the king ever said to me. Dramatic, I thought, but it's true, isn't it?" Dropping to my haunches, just beyond Sara Grafton's reach, I prop my wrists on my bent knee. "Love is ruin—devastation wrapped in a pretty package—but what happened at The Octagon was carnage, plain and simple. My brother was saving the person that he . . . loves, and I think, if you let yourself, you can understand his motivation." When her lips press flat, I add, quietly, "You can love your father, Dr. Grafton, but you can't save the man when he's already dead."

"Trust me," she snips, her gaze hyper-focused on my

chest, "I'm well aware that he's gone."

Slowly, I extend my arm, palm to the ceiling. "Give me the knife, Doctor."

"I have no idea what you're talking about."

"The knife," I repeat, firmly, never looking away from the hand that she slipped under her leg. "I'd hate to have you bleeding all over Miss Carrigan's rug."

It's a thinly veiled threat.

The doctor swallows.

I flatten my palm, waiting.

Under the loose sleeve of her pullover, her wrist rotates like she's debating making a move. One upward glance at my face, though, steals the fury from her gaze and leaves behind only weariness. She thrusts the knife out to me without ever making eye contact.

I make a point of tucking it, flat, against my forearm while I turn back for Rowena. Standing across the room, her violet eyes are wide, frantic, the color high in her cheeks.

She couldn't hear me, I realize slowly.

And while everyone else, including Gregory, watched me take the knife from Dr. Grafton, Rowena didn't.

Correction: she *couldn't*.

Jesus.

She hasn't complained, not once. Hasn't asked anyone to make allowances for her, even though she'd absolutely be in the right to do so. I'm not sure any of my brothers-in-arms would be able to say the same if they were in her position. Hell, Jude would howl like a fucking banshee, and I'd be only too happy to knock him out and shut him up.

Fifteen pairs of eyes follow my path from the piano to Rowena's side. I lower my head. Put my mouth next to her ear, so that my words are for her alone: "Make them fall in line, or I will."

At the command, Rowena's chin jerks in my direction and her hand locks around my wrist. Her lips part on a near-silent hiss when she comes in contact with the cool metal. "Damien, are you . . . is that a *knife?*"

"Tell them."

"Tell us what, Rowan?"

I turn my head toward the new voice entering the room and recognize him instantly. Brown hair. Lanky build. The man Ian Coney stood with in the photograph that I found. With their arms slung over each other's shoulders, the similarities between them had seemed miniscule. Staring at him now, however, it's more than obvious that they're related—*were* related. Brothers.

Pulling her fingers away from my wrist, Rowena greets, "Hugh. Good of you to finally join us."

Hugh.

The same name she uttered in her bedroom before I spoke and gave myself away. How often does Hugh Coney make a habit of waiting for her, alone, that he's where her mind went first?

"I was seeing to our guests." His dark eyes slick down over Rowena's hourglass figure, deliberately pausing at her breasts and hips. Possession bleeds from his gaze before disappearing altogether when he turns on me. "So, the Mad Priest has graced us with his presence."

Jaw cinched tight, I merely stare at him.

Hugh steps farther into the room with all the flair of the Pope emerging from the Vatican. He presses a hand to Dr. Grafton's shoulder and pauses beside the redhead to exchange a quick word. Then, sweeping into the center of the drawing room, he folds his hands behind his back and smiles thinly. "Did Rowan mention that we have Alfie Barker?" he asks. "Grabbed him from the cell myself. Never met a bloke so happy to see me."

I just bet he was.

Alfie Barker would be happy to see King John's ghost if it meant being released from his cell, and he's an anti-loyalist through and through.

"You're welcome to him."

Hugh's mouth tightens at the corners. "And we have another one of yours—Benjamin Lotts. Locked him in the room with Barker just to see how that might play out."

Benji, who took great joy in beating Saxon in the woods for choosing Isla Quinn over Holyrood. If Hugh hopes to break me, then he'll have to try a little harder. There are only a few people in this world that I would sell my soul to save and Benjamin Lotts isn't one of them.

I smile, slowly. "You can have him, too."

Hugh's expression shutters like curtains that have been snapped closed. "I should put *you* in that room," he snarls.

"I'll have to pass."

"Pass? Priest, you don't have the luxury of *passing.* You're our—"

"He's not a proper prisoner," the redhead grumbles from the sofa, eyeing my unbound hands speculatively. "This doesn't follow any sort of protocol. In case anyone was wondering, of course."

"Shut *up*, Samuel," Hugh snaps before fixing me with a scowl. "Listen here, if I tell you that you need to stay with—"

"Rowena offered me the room beside hers. Can you blame her?" My smile grows wider, crueler. Vicious. "A man with a reputation like mine needs to be leashed."

"Leashed?" A crease puckers the center of Hugh's forehead seconds before the glint in his gaze turns ruthless. "You deserve to be put down! I should finish what Gregory started," he bites off, storming toward me. "Do you hear me, Priest?"

Obviously knowing when he's not wanted, Gregory says nothing.

I deliberately slip my hands into the front pockets of my trousers. Then move forward, so that I'm shoulder to shoulder with the man who clearly wants me dead. Because of what Isla did to Ian? Or because the thought of me sleeping in a room beside Rowena's is a thorn in his ass? Probably both.

"You have two choices, Hugh," I murmur, "and neither of them end with you killing me. Personally, I recommend that you simmer down."

"You don't get to waltz in here and make demands, Priest. You are *bottom* of the barrel."

When he aggressively knocks my arm with his, I make a point to roll my shoulder. "Careful, now," I utter softly, meeting his glittering stare. "I'm more than willing to leave the past behind us. You want Barker and Benji? Keep them, mate. They're yours. No one is standing in your way."

"That's not what I mean, and you know it." Turmoil is a razor-edge that hardens his features. "Your blasted brother and that bitch killed Ian, and I'll never get him—"

Hugh hasn't even finished his sentence before his fist comes flying.

Dodging the blow, I spot Gregory break his human restraints to lunge for Rowena, his big body creating a barrier around her from the altercation. She claws at his arms, demanding that he let her go, before being spun away. Someone screams—the doctor, I think—and then a chair is soaring across the drawing room. Could be aimed at Hugh. Probably at me, though.

Fuck it.

Like it's nothing but a feather caught in a cross breeze,

I snatch the chair's leg out of thin air and swing with all my might.

Crack!

The wooden back catches Hugh in the solar plexus. His features fracture, a pained grunt breaking from his mouth. Unable to stop the downward momentum, he falls on his ass with a heavy-hitting *thud*.

"*Jesus.*"

"He's a bloody madman!"

In one swift move, I palm the doctor's blade and plant a hard knee on Hugh's collarbone before he has the chance to clamber to his feet. The tip of the knife meets his quivering throat, pricking the skin. All around the room, chaos stalls in a frozen time lapse, all eyes trained on me. *The Mad Priest has arisen*, those looks scream. *We're so fucked*—the wanker by the window. I'd know that panicked expression anywhere.

Hugh's eyes are latched on me too. Wide. Petrified. He tries to swallow, his Adam's apple bobbing, before belatedly remembering that he's being held at knifepoint.

I allow my knee to sink deeper, keeping him restrained. "Are you done?"

Giving into temptation, he swallows, shakes his head quickly, then strains his chin away from the knife. It doesn't do him much good. A bead of blood pebbles beneath the sharp tip. "I think—"

"Louder, for your mates."

His gaze promises mutiny even as he gasps, "I-I'm done."

He's nowhere close, and we both know it.

I've pricked his pride, literally knocked him down to the ground in front of his comrades. Unfortunately for his wounded ego, Hugh Coney can take a number behind Carrigan and Guthram.

"Good man." Sweeping a glance over the rest of Rowena's crew of misfits, I offer them a humorless smile. "We won't be friends. Not today, not tomorrow. But I'm telling you right now, do not cross me." I look to where Gregory has Rowena bundled, his massive arms circling her like a straitjacket. "Let her go."

Lip curling, his stare shifts from me to her, then back again. "Or what?"

"Gregory," she mutters, squirming to be set free, "don't argue. Just let me—"

I throw the knife.

It sails through the air, very nearly skimming the bridge of his nose like a lover's caress, before embedding itself in the wall behind him.

His jaw drops.

A chair squeaks as if someone has literally dropped into it, like the whole night has just gone to shit.

"You had me at a disadvantage on the roof," I acknowledge, my eyes never wavering from Gregory's, "and I promise you, it was your only chance. Now let her go."

Like a mechanical toy that's been injected with new batteries, the bastard's arms spring open. Only, when Rowena steps out, Hugh tries to rise again.

My knee keeps him trapped.

"Rowena." Turning toward the sound of my voice, she takes an instinctive step in my direction. "Why don't you fill everyone in on our terms?"

Her lips part on an uneven breath, and fucking *hell*, I can already feel her now: the warmth of that ragged inhale striking my throat; her nails biting into my shoulders as she cries out my name; the shudder that'll rack her frame when I make her come on my cock, my fingers, and sweet Jesus, on my tongue, too. Until she's wrung out and limp and I roll her over, my hands pinning hers down to the mattress, and take her all over again.

I was the devil to give her an ultimatum, to bargain my safety against her own.

Because I knew what would happen the minute that she announced my presence—the unforgiving glares and the sharp verbal blows and the rash attempts to put me in my place. I predicted it all, and I anticipated every damned moment.

All so I can fuck her.

Squirming beneath me, Hugh pushes on my thigh. Exertion reddens his cheeks and contorts his features. "Rowan." He shoves again, and I move my knee to his throat. Press downward until he gasps, "*Rowan,* what terms? What the hell did you agree to?"

"Mr. Priest believes that . . ." Her throat visibly ripples with a hard swallow. "He thought that there might be some unresolved . . . feelings you all had toward him, and he . . . and he—"

"Say the words, Rowena."

Her eyes slam shut at my demand, and her arms slowly peel backward so that she can lace her fingers together again at the base of her spine. I bet she's white-knuckled, bet she's quaking in her trainers and wondering how likely I am to keep to my promise.

Oh, Rowena, I never break my word.

"Rowan?" Gregory's brows furrow. "Just tell us."

"Don't touch him."

Dr. Grafton pushes up from the piano bench. "Sorry?"

Rowena inches backward like she can sense the doctor's approach. "No one is allowed to hurt Mr. Priest. Those were our terms. Because if you . . ." Her nostrils flare. "Because if *any* of you hurt him . . . then he'll touch me."

And I won't wait for an invitation, I'd husked in her ear.

"I agreed," Rowena adds on a hoarse rasp to the deathly silent room, "two hours ago."

Before we came downstairs for my introduction.

Before Dr. Sara Grafton broke out her knife and Hugh Coney lunged for me.

"Bastard," Hugh roars now, thrashing beneath my knee, "you fucking *bastard!*"

I look to Rowena.

And regret nothing.

CHAPTER 22

ROWENA

Dropping my hands onto the desk in my bedroom, I tuck my chin to my chest and feel the healing flesh stretch across my back.

I welcome the ache.

It's a reminder, however gruesome, that agreeing to Damien's terms has no bearing on the reality of my life ten years ago. Back then, I traded pieces of my soul to the men most likely to cause problems for Father's career.

Tonight, I'll give myself to the most hated man in England.

Who also faces Edward Carrigan's wrath.

It's an ironic twist of fate, and one I want no part of—even if I do want Damien. Crave him despite the fact that I've never craved anyone. His hand on my throat, and his fingers on my hips, and his velvet baritone whispering in my ear.

I agreed to his terms because it was easier than confessing to the want, and the craving, and the dark ribbon of desire that winds itself around my chest, my heart, and squeezes the air from my lungs.

I am not Young Rowena.

Rolling my shoulders back, I push away from the desk and pass a hand over my shorn hair. The welts from the fire have made way for peach fuzz. It's a far cry from the thick hair that once swung freely down my back. Dwelling on it, though, won't miraculously lengthen the strands.

For better or worse, *this* is who I am for the foreseeable future: powerful in a way that has nothing to do with the beauty of my face and everything to do with the steel in my spine.

Broken, but never defeated.

I knot the sash of my silk robe with my head held high.

My bare feet slip over the soft rug.

The bronze doorknob is chilly against my palm.

A warm draft from the ceiling ventilator heats my shoulders when I step into the hallway and turn left, toward the floor's landing. Powerful or not, I pray that Hugh won't leave his bedroom to find me fumbling my way down the hall. Pray even harder that none of the others will decide on an impromptu visit to my room, only to find it empty.

They were all horrified by Damien's terms.

And disgusted.

It goes without saying that the Mad Priest hasn't made friends in this house.

I stop outside Damien's room and touch my fingers to the doorknob. It's warm from the overhead ventilator, or maybe it only feels that way because I'm burning up inside. Nerves gnaw at my stomach and sweat pools in my palms. I should be just as horrified, just as disgusted, as Hugh and Sara and Gregory. Hell, it wouldn't be hard to dredge up a sliver of self-loathing. Not when I've basked in it for years, smothering myself in hate and desolation and the never-ending frustration of despising what I once allowed to be done to my mind, body, and soul.

With my hand still on the doorknob, I wait for those long-ago emotions to surge again, prepared to turn my arse back around at the slightest hesitation. Only, all there is more heat, more want, more—

"The house isn't a secret, brother."

Damien.

Releasing the knob, I press my cheek to the door.

"How long have I known?" There's the squeak of coil springs like he's sat down on the bed inside his room. "It doesn't really matter, does it? I never would have said anything if not for what . . ."

A drawn-out pause has me white-knuckling the door frame.

Which brother is he talking to? And, for his sake, he better not be discussing *this* house. God only knows what might happen if Holyrood catches wind of Holly Village on the same night that we laid siege to the Palace.

Unmitigated disaster seems like a gross understatement.

"Holyrood is in your *blood*," Damien goes on, his voice slightly muffled. "It's who we are . . . Don't you think I know that? It's not like . . . Saxon, she was *shot*. I had no idea what I'd be up against coming here, so I rang Guy . . . Then say nothing. For once in your goddamn life, don't do the honorable thing . . . She'll never even know."

Who won't know *what?*

Like the cat that ate the canary, I shove my ear flat against the door.

"Paul will keep his mouth shut if he knows what's good for him. As for Hamish and Matthews, they respect you. They won't turn around and backstab . . . I know. I *know*. Jesus, I've never heard you so worked up . . . Listen, the queen can stay there and still be fucking blissful in her ignorance that Isla killed John. No one—"

The gasp slides out unbidden.

Loud enough for Damien to stop talking and the bed to creak with the release of his weight. Loud enough for me to estimate that I have only seconds before he finds me eavesdropping outside his door, and . . . oh, *fuck me.*

I run.

Without thought, without a plan.

Vertigo turns my limbs weightless, uncoordinated, and I careen into the wall with a pained grunt. *Don't stop. Don't stop!* The world around me spins and spins and spins like a swirling fog that won't dissipate. Desperate, I thrust out my arms to grope my way along the hallway.

A door cracks open.

Footsteps enter the corridor.

And then we're both running, him chasing me, as he promised he would, just hours ago, and I-I—

Isla Quinn killed the king.

The same woman who murdered Ian. The same woman who Saxon Priest loves.

We have a suspect in custody, Damien said. Not, *we've let the suspect go free.* Or *we'll make sure to never put the suspect and the queen under the same goddamned roof.* He planned to keep Isla Quinn's past a secret, to never reveal the truth of her, and the lie—

When the hell have I lied to you? he'd demanded of me.

The bloody nerve of the bastard.

The wall gives way on my left and I tumble into the abyss. The old servant's stairwell. It leads to only one place but it's too late to turn back now. With air trapped in my lungs, I take the narrow steps two at a time, tripping over my feet, cursing my lack of sight with every bump of my head on the sloped ceiling.

Damien bellows my name from the top of the stairwell.

There's no stopping now.

I run and I flounder, my shoulder bashing into the wood-paneled walls as the stairwell winds me in, winds me out, and cool stone abrades the soles of my feet when I hit firm ground. The pure silence of the undercroft reaches into my chest, and twists. There's nothing but the exacerbated sound of my breathing and the scrape of my bare feet shuffling over the floor.

Memory paints brushstrokes over where only darkness thrives: the solemn candles flickering on either side of the arched door to my left and the wooden sideboard pushed against the stone wall to my right—a sideboard weighted with framed photographs of different sizes— Mum and her parents and their parents, all standing in front of the Victorian mansion.

Mum died in the fire and I inherited Holly Village.

Blood inheritance.

With my heart lodged in my throat, I wrap a hand around the iron handle and wrench the door open to duck inside the private chapel.

The scent of melted beeswax still perfumes the air, cloying and sweet. Nothing in this room has changed in over twenty years. Stone floors contrast dark-stained pews congregated on either side of a narrow aisle. Matching wooden rafters run parallel across the ceiling, giving the impression that the room is small and suffocating. Pointed Gothic windows along the far-right wall overlook the garden. And, before me, past the six rows of pews, an altar.

I head there now.

The air crackles with tension and a draft from a cracked-open window sweeps around my ankles. Goose bumps flare. The skin on the back of my neck tingles. Hearing movement behind me, I twist around and edge backward on silent feet.

And then, so low, so gutturally visceral, his voice: "You ran."

Because you're unpredictable. Because you're harboring the woman who killed King John and see no problems with that. Because you terrify me in more ways than I could ever imagine, and this time, there'll no be resurrection when you leave me ruined.

Like he's an animal that I have no hope of outrunning, my hands come up slowly, palms out. Another step back. "I did."

"You ran," he growls thickly, "like a coward."

Instead of answering, I continue to inch backward until my arse bumps into the altar. I've hit a dead end. Nowhere to turn, nowhere to flee. It's becoming a ridiculously familiar turn of events for the two of us.

I grasp the altar with both hands. "You weren't going to tell me about Isla Quinn."

"You didn't need to know."

A startled laugh bursts from my lips. "I didn't need to know? Really, *that's* the angle you want to take with this?" That maddeningly arrogant stride storms down the aisle, shoes clipping against stone, bringing him closer and closer until the aroma of beeswax is eclipsed by the scent of *him*. Cloves. Spice. A virile masculinity that curls my fingers around the altar's edge, gripping the marble even harder as I hang on for dear life. "I had orders to kill you, your brothers. I took an oath—"

"An oath is nothing but a vow and vows are broken every day."

Disappointment hardens my jaw. "Spoken just like a man."

"Not even close."

"Then *what?*"

"He chose her."

"And that's enough?" I shake my head, bewildered. "Saxon *choosing* the woman who assassinated the king is enough for you to break your oath? Enough for you to disregard what every single Godwin before you has done to protect the Crown?"

"It's enough," Damien edges out, "for me to do what's right for my brother. Saying that Saxon was living was only a matter of technicality. He was dead—in his heart, in his goddamned soul. The king said that love is carnage, and it must be, because Isla Quinn destroyed everything that made my brother cold and she made him *human*."

He steps forward, steps into *me*, his hands locking on either side of my hips to grasp the altar. Calloused fingers slide over mine. The fog returns with swift vengeance and, once again, I'm spinning, spinning, spinning, a round top with no hope of ever falling still.

"You're a closet romantic," I mutter when his knuckles slip between my fingers, locking me in place, "the hero that you so desperately don't want to be. Don't even bother to deny it."

"Is that what you really think?"

No. Yes.

I don't even know.

I can't even remember my own name when he stands this close. His muscular legs bracket mine, and the hard edge of the altar cuts into my lower back, and my hands, now pinned beside my hips, are trapped under the delicious weight of his.

I've never been the woman who melts for a man, never been the sort of woman who falls prey to the big, bad wolf. No. I *am* the wolf. Always have been. But holy hell, here, right now, with Damien's broad frame plastered against mine, I might as well be drowning—kicking my legs, pumping my arms, anything to break to the surface when the undertow is intent on swallowing me whole.

Needing to assert myself, I squeeze his fingers between mine, all too aware of the confession burning in the pit of my stomach.

I think that I ran, knowing he would follow.

I ran, because it's the first time in my life where I haven't chased a man, a target, for anyone else's benefit but my own.

I ran, because *I wanted to be caught.*

Not by the hero, not even by the closet romantic, but by the Mad Priest, a man with heat in his veins and arrogance in his bones and a voice that leaves me shaken, shattered. Without my vision to piece together the rest—the nuanced expressions and humanizing tics—it's all I have of him. A voice that beckons me closer, a voice that drags me deeper into the shadows. A voice that thrusts every dulled, unpolished desire of mine into the light.

In Damien's arms, every broken shard of my soul feels beautiful. And I want . . . I think that I want to be *worshipped.*

Mustering the nerve, I tilt my head back. "You lied. That's what I think."

He growls deep in his throat. "How? Because I didn't tell you who really murdered the king? Or because I tricked you into a bargain that you never had a hope of winning?"

If they hurt me, then I'll touch you, and I won't wait for an invitation.

Words that caused warmth to explode in my blood. Words that I knew, deep down, would change my life forever. Damien Priest is universally despised, for reasons that aren't necessarily his doing, and it was a foregone conclusion that someone would be out for his head once introductions were made.

I knew all of that and still said *yes*.

"No," I answer honestly, straining under the prison of his fingers, seeking the irrefutable tension of him keeping me restrained, "not because of that."

"Then what?"

It's now or never.

As I suspected he would from the very second that I heard him at the Palace, Damien Priest has the ability to push me from the cliff with nothing but a crook of his finger and the purr of his voice. I leap, recklessly, and fall into the crashing waves below: "You told me that you break the weak and wreck the strong, and that I'd never hear you when you came for me—but Damien . . . that was a lie."

His breath hitches, and mine expands to fill my chest.

"Feet thundering down the stairs, the way you roared my name. You came for me, and I heard you every step of the way."

"What exactly are you trying to say?"

Gruff. Rigid. If I could tease my fingers across his face now, he would be stiff as stone. A man holding on, a god preparing to fall. "You followed me," I murmur with a softness that I know will unravel him, "and you chased me. Not for Saxon or Isla Quinn or the Crown, but for *me*. For a man not willing to be cut down at the knees, Damien, you sure are—"

A gasp flies from my mouth when he grips my waist and abruptly spins me around. Like a sacrifice, I'm flattened against the altar. Hardness digging into my pelvis, my arms flailing for purchase. I strike something solid, and iron grates against marble, a shrill shriek in the otherwise silent chapel. Damien's palm goes to the base of my spine, holding me still, and then he leans over to—

The candles.

Oh, fuck. *The candles.*

"Damien." Trapped between earthen hardness and human steel, I squirm to no avail. Desperation brings my foot down on top of his, anything to stop him from realizing that—

"The wick is still warm."

Saliva pools in my mouth. "Someone must have come down here." *I* came down here. While Damien sought out Holly Village to kill me, I sat in this chapel and lit a candle for him. Ridiculous. *Pathetic.* Feeling the hounds of hell on my heels, I blurt, "Gregory is religious."

The incriminating silence stretches on, and on, until, "Religious?" Without waiting for an answer, the firm hand at the small of my back slips under my robe and scorches my skin. "What made him come down here tonight? What prayers"—the pitch of Damien's timbre roughens—"do you think he whispered when he thought no one could hear him?"

"Forgiveness." Tasting the truth through the lens of a lie, I run my tongue over the back of my teeth. "Gregory wanted forgiveness."

A small pause. "For?"

On a rasp, I answer, "For killing you."

The iron candle rack clatters to the marble, abandoned.

The hand under my robe slips back out, taking with it my sanity, then begins its upward ascent. It skims my waist and follows every curve. It avoids each wound and cut as though the landscape of my body is one that's already been intimately learned. Except that Damien wouldn't . . . he *couldn't—*

Oh, my God.

He knows.

He knows because he's already seen me.

Naked.

Vulnerable.

At his mercy.

A sound rises in my throat, and my hands ball into fists on the marble, and then the softest pair of lips known to mankind are on my pulse, right below my jawline. Testing me, stripping away every layer of armor before I even have the chance to don another. "Don't tell me that you're nervous now," comes that silken voice, the mocking words resonating against my skin like a venerable prayer.

A throwback to that day in the cell when he found me locked away with Alfie Barker. When he cuffed my wrists and started us down a road that has no other destination but perdition. "I'm not nervous," I whisper back, succumbing to the memory, to the rapid beat of my heart pumping loud enough to wake the dead. "You don't make me nervous."

"Your pulse would argue otherwise, Miss Carrigan."

I feel him smile. Predatory, victorious. *Wicked.* And then the hand that had paused now edges north, past my shoulder, to collar the back of my neck. A whimper catches in my throat, and I strain backward with my spine arched, fingers stretching across the altar.

I breathe his name.

He drapes his chest over my back, so that I'm tucked beneath him completely, the outside world narrowed down to only this room, only this altar, only our flushed bodies. I'm bound, not by metal or pain but by brawny muscles and the scent of cloves and the knowledge that whatever comes next, I want it. Deep down, in a place known to no one but me, I *crave this.*

"Do you know what I think, Rowena?" Damien husks, his thumb caressing my throat. When I give a tiny shake of my head, a dark chuckle reverberates against my back. "I think *you* lit the candle. I bet you kneeled real pretty for me. So solemn, so very somber. Did you pray for my forgiveness?"

Fire sparks in my veins. "I wished you entry to Hell."

His hand flexes on the back of my neck like he's not sure whether to laugh at my impertinence or fold me over his lap and take a palm to my arse. Instead, he yanks all the oxygen from the room with a gravel-pitched drawl that leaves me wrecked: "No, it wouldn't be like you to want forgiveness. Not then, when you thought you were doing the right thing. Not even now."

I swallow, hard. "Damien, I—"

"You mourned for me."

CHAPTER 23

ROWENA

My chest heaves with a harsh breath. "I don't. I *didn't*. You and I, we're nothing more than—"

"You mourned," Damien growls in my ear, "for what I could never give you if I was dead. And what you wanted most is *me*." His fingers slip from my nape to gently clasp my throat. With nothing more than that tangible hold to tether us, he pulls me away from the altar. I'm encased in shadow, his hand my only anchor, until the hard planes of his chest cushion the back of my head and I'm embraced. "Am I right, Rowena? Am I what you want?"

Yes, yes, yes.

My nails bite into the forearm clamped across my breasts.

"A shared glance from across the room." Damien touches his fingers to my chin, then angles my head to the right. Warm breath mists over my lips, and a shudder of want slips down my spine as realization hits: I'm the center of his attention, the sole focus of blue eyes the color of crystal waters.

A shared glance, even if it is one-sided.

"A brush of fingers when no one is looking"—the hand

at my throat tightens imperceptibly, his thumb drawing lazy circles on my collarbone—"and a whisper in her ear when she wavers to do the right thing."

He demolishes the remaining distance between us with the slightest shift of his hips—and oh, my God. *Oh, my God*. Air drives into my lungs and my hold on his arm turns brutal, wild, when he deliberately rolls the hard ridge of his denim-sheathed cock against my back. Once, twice. It's a goddamn siege of sensuality. The pressure. The *heat of him*. A moan wrenches from my throat.

"Do you feel me?" he rasps against the shell of my ear with another roll of his hips. "Do you feel how hard I am for you?"

I give a feeble jerk of my head.

"Say the words, Rowena. Give them to me."

Fuck.

I'm swaying and swallowing fistfuls of air like that'll do me a world of good when it's so incredibly obvious that I'm two seconds from collapsing at the foot of the altar. Burning from within, I press my knees together. Flex my toes against paved stone. Claw at Damien's forearm. Only . . . I'm not clawing him at all but kneading the corded muscles like a cat preening for affection. Another second of this and my pride will be demolished beneath the sole of his heavy boot.

In the end, all I manage is a hoarse, "I'm going to die."

Damien clicks his tongue like I'm some naughty schoolgirl who's displeased him.

The fingers clasping my chin let go. A moment later they circle the nip of my waist, beneath my bent arms, to find the knotted sash of my robe. He pauses for only a moment, then tugs sharply. The bow unravels, the silk over my shoulders loosening and rippling down to expose my upper shoulders. "Give me your hands."

I swallow roughly. "You'll tie me up?"

"I chased you to the ends of the earth and you brought us here," he murmurs, already hooking the sash around one wrist while he reaches for the other. With deft movements, my hands are pressed together, the silk knotted tight. "Far be it from me that I should sin and keep you from being a proper sacrifice."

I Samuel 12:23.

Only Damien Priest.

Only *this* man would bastardize a verse from the Bible, in a chapel, while binding me like some Pagan princess. I would laugh, if it weren't for the fact that his nimble fingers are untying the knot of my pajama bottoms and destroying every last train of thought.

I glance down and see nothing.

But I imagine the dark hair dusting his forearms, his thick wrists. I imagine my tied hands pressed to the altar, where he placed them, and those strong fingers teasing my hipbone with tantalizing back-and-forth caresses.

And then I imagine nothing more because the elastic waistband is being eased down.

Down over the width of my hips, down over the curve of my arse, down far enough that I'm completely bare, save for a pair of knickers. His hands glide south and then his tall frame sinks down, too. Soft lips find my nape, then claim the spot between my shoulder blades. He lifts the back of my robe, and the shirt beneath, exposing healing skin to his perusal. And then comes another soft-as-silk brush of his lips to the devastated flesh.

"*Damien.*" Trembling, wrists kissing, I clutch the altar. "Damien, what are you—?"

"Finding the wreckage that you promised me."

"The wreckage?" I ask breathlessly.

"Do you see any angels here?" One big hand sweeps over the place where my thigh and bum meet, his fingers pressing deep into skin untouched by fire. "There are none," he answers gruffly, "just me. There's only me."

The angel dead on the floor, defeated. The devil on his shoulder.

A memory flashes—my cheek against the window, his body a shield behind me, these same words tripping off my tongue in a bold attempt to catch him off guard. He remembered everything that I whispered in the dark, and now . . . Oh, my God. *And now*—

"You have me on my knees, Rowena." I suck in my stomach when I feel his calloused palm graze the inside of my knee. "A man brought down," he adds, sliding his hand up, up, up, until it's snug between the apex of my thighs and cupping my core. "A man fully prepared to do the wrong thing and enjoy every fucking second of it."

"*Damien*—"

"Tell me what you want."

I'm crumbling, unraveling, the fragile mosaic of my reconstructed being coming apart at the seams. This is not . . . this is so much more than I could have ever thought possible. But when I try to speak, only another moan comes.

"*Beg for me.*"

At the roughened command, I tumble headfirst into the darkness. "A kiss," I utter, my voice sounding thoroughly strangled. "Please, Damien. I want . . . a kiss."

His hand turns sideways, shoving my legs apart at the same time that he tears my pajamas down to my ankles. "Where."

There's no hope in surviving this, no hope for much of anything besides praying that I'll still be left standing when he's had his fill of me. He is my ruin. My complete and utter devastation. I turn my head, just enough to pretend that I can see him there on his knees, as he promised, and give him what he's demanded of me on a breathy whimper: "My cunt."

He purrs, this guttural, masculine sound that bloody well *kills me.*

And then I'm being forced to lean over the altar, arms splayed, wrists bound like the sacrifice that he's made of me. He crooks a finger under the seam of my knickers and yanks the cotton to the side, baring me completely to his gaze. I feel the heat of him, the *warmth* of him, and then his tongue. Oh, God, his tongue.

There, at the hood my sex.

Noise shatters the room, and it's only when I claw my fingers over cool marble that it registers that the broken sobs belong to me. My head falls forward, hanging between my hunched shoulders. Fuck, *fuck.* I'm mewling, circling my hips against his face, unable to stop when the sensation of him is so completely blasphemous.

So utterly unholy.

Firmly gripping the outside of my thigh, Damien angles my hips to thrust my arse out. He nips my right cheek, his teeth offering a sharp, unexpected bite of pain against sensitive, untested flesh. Then the blade of his nose nudges my core. His tongue flicks my clit, over and over, alternating between tiny swirls that bring me up onto my toes and flat, barely-there licks that drop me back onto my heels like an addict whose only thought is *give me more.*

Uninhibited, I bend my knees and follow the retreat of his mouth.

He doesn't let me.

With an audible *crack!* Damien claps a hand down on my arse, then smooths the sting away with a circle of his palm. My knees tremble before turning weak when he gives the cheek a second smack. Heat spears my core and I let out a sharp cry.

I'm going to fall. I'm going to fall right now, and it'll all be over before—

My elbows skid across marble as he forces me back upright.

Ruthless. Merciless. A man who demands that I take it all—and submit.

Like a pagan god intent on enjoying his offering, Damien drags his knuckles over my slit. A delicious, long stroke followed by the tease of his fingertips at my entrance. Never slipping inside, only ever tracing. Back and forth, back and forth, gathering wetness that he uses to slicken my clit on every other pass.

It's deliberate, exquisite torture.

Then he sucks on my clit and the rhythmic pressure is like liquid heat in my veins.

My forehead unceremoniously hits the altar.

"I can't," I whimper, panting hard. "Damien, I've never—"

Come.

I've never come, never orgasmed. Not in all those years, so long ago, and not in all the years since. My body was a weapon used against others until it became a weapon that I no longer wanted to wield, even for myself. No touch could rid me of the grit, no embrace was hot enough to eviscerate the memory of what came before. I lived in skin that I couldn't remove, was stuck with a past that I didn't want to remember, and now . . . *and now—*

Damien releases out a throaty groan.

A furious blush crests my cheekbones.

With a dominance that leaves me aching, he snags the waistband of my knickers and pulls the material down the length of my legs to leave in a discarded pile along with my pajamas. Then both hands claim my arse and spread my cheeks wide.

I'm completely exposed.

Devoured in a way that I thought existed only in fantasies.

He licks at me with unrepentant strokes then uses his fore and middle fingers to hold my folds open. His opposite hand snakes between my spread legs, and, in a simultaneous move that shatters me completely, he circles two fingers over my clit and plunges his tongue inside my pussy.

I die.

Right then, right there.

Limbs shaking, mouth gaping.

"Damien," I cry, "oh, God, *Damien*."

He thrusts his tongue, mimicking exactly what he plans to do with his cock, and I come. For the first time in my life, I *come*. It's glorious and terrifying and beautiful. It's everything I never knew it would be and yet everything I could have ever hoped for and more. A splintering of the soul, a loss of control. It's trust placed in another's hands and also the most inherently selfish feeling that I've ever experienced, and God, I want to be tangled in its grip again.

The hands on my arse smooth upward to grip my hips, and then I hear Damien's knees pop as he rises from the floor. Still naked from the waist down, I push up from the altar so that I'm no longer resting on my elbows. Turn my head, lick my lips, and—

"When you ripped off that bandage, you asked me what I saw." Damien grasps my chin, and I smell the fragrance of sex off his fingers. Spiced. Feminine. Sweet. "Do you remember?"

I remember cool stone beneath me, much like it is now.

I remember a tremor in my limbs and a searing weight of despair carving out a place in my chest, where my heart ought to be. And I remember fire—the fire that ravaged my skin and the fire that ravaged my soul until I would have clawed my way out of that cell, had I only been able to rise to my feet.

"Yes." The word is torn from my chest. "*Yes.*"

"Ask me now what I saw when I looked at you then."

"Now?"

He ducks his head to hover his mouth over mine, not so much a kiss as it is consuming my very essence. "Now."

My throat constricts.

Turning around in his embrace, with my restrained hands lowered between us, I lean my arse against the altar for balance. Pretending that the shape of him is there, just waiting for me to blink and watch him appear before me, I drop my head back. "What did you see?"

"Me," he growls. "I looked at you and saw only *me*. Every blade of rage that scrapes at my being, every shard of hope that begs to be seen. I saw madness and I saw destruction, and I knew then that it'd be best for the both of us if I walked away for good."

It's an unexpected punch to the gut that leaves me gasping.

Raw. Vulnerable. *Humbled.*

Despite my silk restraints, I fumble for his hand. "Damien—"

"I'm not going to walk away, Rowena," he says, the devil on his tongue, "and I'm not going to do what's best for either of us. I'm going to strip you naked and fuck you so hard that you'll be old and gray and still remember that it was me who made you feel this way. And if you have a problem with that, then you better say so right now because in five seconds, it's going to be too bloody late."

If he hadn't offered a choice, I may have walked away.

But Damien Priest isn't content with dragging me into hell, kicking and screaming, with shackles locked around my wrists. No, the blasted man wants me stumbling into the devil's lair right alongside him. He wants my submission in the same breath that he wants my iron spine, and any chance of me telling him no died the second that he chased me down the halls of this mansion.

Earlier, even, when he put the revolver to my temple and refused to let me sink into the abyss. *Own the darkness or it'll own you,* he'd said. I'm not sure that he intended sex with him to be my first foray in harnessing the restlessness that bleeds beneath my skin, but fuck it, there's no time like the present.

"Five."

Without thought, I begin shrugging out of the robe.

"Four," he husks.

The silk slips to my elbows to reveal my cotton tank top. Bending my arms, I try to rip at the fabric and tear it free, but the binds around my wrists curtail all further effort. Gritting my teeth, I smother a frustrated groan.

And then I beg, just as he wanted: "Help me."

Damien doesn't need further encouragement. But any expectation of him loosening the knot goes up in flames when he plucks the thin strap of my tank top between two fingers, his knuckles grazing my skin, and *pulls.*

The fabric tears in half, down the middle, leaving me in nothing but silk and bandages.

I'm naked.

Completely and utterly naked.

My mouth goes dry. "You just . . . you just—"

"Three," comes the tick of the clock even as his hands find my hips and squeeze. And while I can't see him, I know that he's studying the pink blisters that dart across my collarbone like a constellation of devastation. Stars formed by fire rather than an accumulation of gas and dust.

Broken. Defeated. And still standing.

Always.

Lifting my gaze, wishing I could meet his, I reach out. "Two."

My fingers find the waistband of his trousers and then the metal tab. Pulse racing, I pop the button free and slide my thumb down the length of his zipper—and his cock—in a blatant tease that has him swaying closer.

I smile, slowly.

Harness the darkness.

He should have specified if we had boundaries.

With hands still bound by silk, I drop to my knees and kneel before him. My hands go to his right thigh for balance and my tongue to the tab of his trousers. Then, with my teeth biting the metal, I tug it down.

"Fuck. *Fuck*, Rowena."

Hands find the back of my head, careful of my scars, and I don't need my vision to know that I've rattled the unpredictable Mad Priest. He grunts beneath his breath and holds me to him with such possession that even if I wanted to stand up and walk away, there'd be no chance of doing so.

I glance upward. "Tell me what you want."

At his own words thrown back at him, he swallows audibly and chokes back a curse.

Swaying forward, I part the fabric of his trousers and recall the sensation of him rocking against me. I lick my lips, dragging my teeth over the fullness of my bottom one, just to make him sweat. He does, releasing a hoarse groan that sounds like music to my ears.

"Give me the words, Damien," I say on a low murmur,

my lips nearly kissing his sheathed cock, *"beg for me."*

He hisses from between gritted teeth. "You're a goddamn she-wolf."

Whatever I might have said next is lost as he clamps his hands under my armpits and hauls me from the stone floor. The silk robe flutters when he lowers me to the altar, his finger coming to my shoulder, away from my wounds, to push me down until the marble is cool against my back.

I hear denim scraping over skin and then feel his hands on my wrists.

Shock registers a moment before I ask, "You're untying me?"

"I want you free."

I bite down on my lip, hiding a smile. "And so the hero reemerges."

"No," he replies on a short, rough laugh, "no, he doesn't."

And then he loops the sash behind my neck, like he's making the beginnings of a proper tie, before fisting both ends of the silk in his hand above my head. Briefly, his knuckles graze my cheek. Then he pulls on the sash, and I rise, spine arching. He releases, and I sink to the altar.

A sacrifice.

His sacrifice.

My heart thuds against my rib cage and I strain my neck, testing the new silk restraint at my nape, and then there's nothing but him—*Damien.*

His hand on my right leg, bending it so that my foot hits the edge of the altar, his fingers dipping between my legs to sink deep into my pussy. One finger, then two. He curls his fingers, and a tremble shatters through me. Then I feel the silk go taut, lifting me upward, so that I'm forced to plant my hands down on either side of my hips.

"Last chance to run," comes his dark rasp, his fingers

leaving me empty and aching when he pulls them free.

"Even if I do, you'll chase me."

"To the ends of the Earth," he vows.

Darkness clamps down on my lungs, squeezing, and then he's there, the length of him brazen against the inside of my thigh, then at my entrance. The tension in the silk sash goes slack, until I'm hovering just above the altar, a veritable buffet for Damien's hungry gaze.

Take me, I want to tell him. *Please, please now.*

Need unfurls in my veins and I move my hands, finding the hard balls of his bare shoulders, and—

He thrusts deep, plunging in to the hilt.

I cry out his name.

"Fuck," he grunts, his hips stilling immediately. "Rowena, *fuck*, you're so tight."

He's bigger than I anticipated, and I squirm beneath him, hips churning, nails clawing down his back. The silk sash catches the weight of my head even as I arch my spine and bite back a sob.

Good God, I've been impaled.

"How long has it been?"

I grit my teeth and breathe through my nose. "Just move."

He slides out, slowly, until only the tip of his cock remains within me. "How long, Rowena?"

Squeezing my eyes shut, I twist my head to the side. "Don't ask this of me."

"*Tell me.*"

Embarrassment is a poison, and its toxin licks at the flames of my desire. There's no shame in admitting the truth: I made a decision to reclaim what I'd lost. Only, I never expected my celibacy to last as long as it did. I never expected the distrust I had for men to turn to fear, so that every graze of a masculine finger, whether sexual or not, left me chilled to the bone.

I was once the big, bad wolf. And then I became terrified of my own shadow.

Until now.

Until *him*.

"Ten years," I whisper. "It would have been four, but I couldn't . . . I couldn't go through with it."

A slow, heavy breath is expelled above me. "Do you trust me?"

The answer should be no.

I've hunted this man across London. I had orders to kill him. Just hours ago, he came to take his own revenge. We're enemies that have found each other on the same side of a war. And while the answer should be no, all I hear from my lips is "*Yes*."

"Then hold onto me, and don't let go."

He starts with tiny pulses of his hips that barely bury him inside me. But each smooth retraction of his cock steals my breath. Again, he pulses. Again, I fight for air.

The silk sash tugs upward, and I follow the silent command blindly.

Soft lips kiss my neck. He thrusts a little harder. Another kiss, this one on my jaw, followed swiftly by a second thrust that plunges deeper. It's a calculated onslaught designed to make me lose my mind, and holy hell, he's succeeding.

"Yes." Wanting leverage of my own, I plant one hand on the marble and hook my leg around his waist. "*Yes*."

Against my calf, the muscles of his arse flex with every roll of his hips. I gasp, then feel Damien's mouth brush my earlobe. He nips the sensitive flesh, tugging on my earlobe. Growls low in his throat when I squeeze around his cock and throw my head back, heedless of the silk.

It's the only invitation he needs.

He doesn't take me. No, he bloody well *devours* me.

His cock plunges deep and his free hand grips my hip, fingers biting down on the soft flesh like he relishes the feel of me. He holds me steady, refusing to let me wriggle myself away from his punishing thrusts. One deep, two shallow, two deep, three shallow, three deep, and so on, until sweat sticks to my skin and I'm begging for him all over again.

"Please. Oh, God, Damien. *Please*."

I hear the slick glide of his cock pulling out before he rocks forward, pressing deep. My toes curl, heels digging into his lower spine. I hear his satisfied purr and, like the addict that I've quickly become, I succumb to the desperate, clawing need to churn my hips and meet him thrust for thrust.

"Fuck me, Rowena," he bites off, dragging me down on top of his cock so hard that I hear him, hear *us*. "That's right. *Yes*. Use me."

The silk restraint slips free as Damien's hand takes its place. He holds me captive, drawing me closer. His forehead touches mine and the heat of his ragged breath teases my lips with every exhale. He's consuming me again, inhaling me without actually kissing, never closing that last remaining gap. Both of my legs go around his waist, and the angle—

"Like that," I whimper, clinging tight to his shoulders, "just like that. Don't stop. *Please don't stop*."

He reaches a hand between us and touches my clit— and I lose the last thread of sanity.

Sobbing, I turn my head from his and let my temple hit his shoulder. My hips move restlessly, sinking down every time that he thrusts upward. We meet as one, the slap of our skin painfully erotic in the chapel.

I'm dying.

A slow unraveling that starts with his hard cock and segues to the calloused finger that rubs over my clit in tiny, aching circles and ends with his roughened, "Come on me. Fuck, I need to feel you."

I don't want the moment to end.

I don't want to ever stop spinning.

And yet even now I feel the tightening in my core. Feel the way that I quiver with every brush of his finger on my clit—delicate, feathery caresses that make me pant and want and moan.

Damien's thrusts quicken, the carefully set pace demolishing on his next breath. He's losing control, fucking me harder, faster, and then he roars, "Now, Rowena, come *now!*" and I come with a cry that ravages my throat. With a tight, pained groan that shakes the very foundation of my being, Damien pulls out of me not even a second later. Hot jets of come hit my inner thighs, an instant reminder that we were reckless, wanton.

A lifetime of loneliness and then him, the Mad Priest.

The villain.

The enemy.

The god refusing to don the crown of the hero.

My heart hammers in my chest. I should say something. Tell him that I'm on the pill, although I'm not, or that we shouldn't do this again, although the thought of never doing so leaves me feeling strangely frantic. There are so many things that I should say to clear the air but all I manage is his name.

"What?" he rasps, his hand finding mine when I touch his face. "Tell me."

"I lied earlier."

A small, pregnant pause. Then, gruffly, "In what way?"

I offer him a tremulous smile. "I mourned for you, Damien Godwin. For a moment, when no one could see me, I mourned for you."

CHAPTER 24

DAMIEN

The living can't be mourned.

They can be forgotten or despised, and some-times, if the person in question is particularly lucky, he might even be loved—but mourning is reserved for the departed. And I'm not dead.

Which doesn't explain why Rowena's words have haunted me for hours.

She has haunted me for hours.

I chased her because there was no other choice but to catch her. Stripped her naked because I needed, for once in my goddamned life, to be flesh on flesh—no barriers held, no pretenses made. And I took her on the altar because if I was going to break a vow, then I planned to savor every bloody second of my reckoning.

Unrepentant bastard that I am, I want to take her again.

Fuck her again.

Make her come on my cock *again*.

Like a thief stealing into the dark crevices of my mind, the early morning sun creeps in between the gap in the cur-tains. Blinded, I tear my gaze away from the window to look again at the shared wall that separates me from Rowena.

Guy would tell me to keep my prick in my trousers.

Saxon, pre-Isla Quinn, would remind me not to forget about the mission.

I have no idea what Saxon post-Isla Quinn would say—probably something about chasing rainbows and choosing happiness and fuck Holyrood until our dying breath. Especially the last one, if our tense conversation last night is anything to go by.

With my wrists propped on my bent knees, and my shoulders pressed against the side of the bed, I lean my head back against the mattress and close my eyes. Familiar exhaustion lingers on the periphery, a traitorous beast prepared to sink its claws into me and claim me permanently, if I let it.

I mourned for you, Damien Godwin.

Fucking hell.

Lifting my ass off the floor, I snatch Mum's necklace from my back pocket and hold it up at eye-level. The silver links glint under the rays of sunlight. Every night, she would carefully unclasp the hook and set it on her bedside table. And she'd stare at it, this faraway look in her blue eyes that troubled me, even at six years old.

She always wound it around her fist when she struck.

Then she would sob for hours, her shoulders shaking so hard that I used to wonder if a person could die from sadness. Nowadays, I know better. Now, I know the grip misery can have on a soul, how the darkness, like I told Rowena, can own every piece of you until there's nothing left to even scrape together.

I wind the chain between my fingers, running my thumb over the links. "Why was this so—"

A scream shatters the quiet.

Feminine. Bone-chilling. *Rowena.*

Shoving the necklace back into my pocket, I snatch my blade from its ankle holster and launch to my feet. Another scream, this one sounding strangled. No, *terrified*. I'm out the door in under three seconds. A hard glance down the hall reveals Hugh Coney stepping out from his bedroom, as well.

His gaze falls to the knife.

I beat back the snarl that rises in my throat and give him my back. I shimmy the doorknob. Locked, as it should be. *Unless someone else took inspiration from me and climbed the trellis.* The thought turns my blood to ice. With all my strength, I ram my shoulder against the wood.

The door concedes with a battered whine.

When my eyes slowly adjust to the darkness within, I finally understand what it's like to mourn the living—because there, on that bed, Rowena Carrigan looks like she's in the throes of death.

The heavy comforter has been kicked to the floor and pillows hang precariously on the edge of the mattress. The sheets wrap around her knees like a noose. A whimper dredges to the surface, sounding nothing like the ones she breathed in my ear last night and every bit afraid of whatever hunts her in her dreams.

Closing the door behind me, I set the blade down on a small table and monitor the weight of my steps as I approach her. On nights that Guy stays—*stayed*—at the Palace, I could hear his screams from the other side of the medieval manor while he slept. I made the mistake of waking him only once, years ago, and found myself on my back with a knife pressed to my throat.

Keeping my voice to a low hum, I utter Rowena's name.

Her hands twitch, her chin straining upward.

Slowly, I reach for the sheets tangled around her bare

legs and loosen them with a gentle pull. I pull again, and again, steeling myself against the sound of her cries and her whimpers as I work to get her free.

"*No.*" She kicks her feet. "No, no. Help!"

She's as imprisoned in sleep as I am by life.

Broken, kindred souls.

The acknowledgment burns within me. This, I would spare her, if I could. The chains, the shackles that never slacken no matter how you try to shake them free. The fear that follows, like the reaper stalking its next victim, until you're frozen, paralyzed, and know that the end is near.

I toss the sheet to the floor.

Dropping one knee to the mattress, I reach for her clenched hand. She fights against me. "Rowena, love, you're free now." Behind trembling lids, her eyes jerk right and left. A tiny gasp inflates her chest, and, clasped within mine, her fist tightens then unfurls like she's battling a war known to no one but her. "I would chase it for you," I rasp, my gaze moving over her face. "If I could, I would chase—"

She comes awake with a sharp cry, her hand jerking free from mine as she scrabbles up the bed to press her back against the headboard. "Who's there?" Her eyes dart left then right, searching the shadows. "Please. Please, tell me *who's there?*"

Pressure caves in on my chest.

Last night, I stormed this room and kept to the darkness, never revealing myself until I could smell the fear on her. Because I wanted her scared. Because as I fell from the Palace's roof, all the anger and rage had unleashed within me, until I could have decimated all of London without a single trace of remorse.

It would be so easy to do the same now.

The Mad Priest would capitalize on the trepidation

raking her expression. But the little boy who once hid beneath a rickety kitchen table, away from his mum, can't find it in himself to bring this woman any more pain.

Even villains have their limits.

The pressure deepens, carving a space where my heart ought to be. I feel hollow, gutted. "It's me."

Me, the man you sought to kill.

Me, the man you mourned.

"It's only me," I repeat, gruffly.

Like I've flicked a switch, the tension in her shoulders deflates as she whispers my name. Bringing her knees to her chest, she wraps trembling arms around her bent legs. Against the headboard like that, she looks small and vulnerable. Too damned innocent for the life that she's lived.

"Can you ..." She rubs her lips together like her mouth is parched. "Can you please open the curtains? It's probably silly, considering everything, but I—"

"I have you, Rowena."

Pushing up from the mattress, I cross the room and sling the drapes wide. The sun scatters within, flooding the bedroom with natural light. When I turn back around, it's only to find her unmoved on the bed.

"Do you believe in karma?" she asks quietly, her fingers tightly knotted around her bent knees. "No ... no, karma isn't the right word."

I approach her on silent feet. "What's the right word, then?"

She pauses, her violet eyes downcast. "Penance. The word I'm looking for is penance."

Mum's necklace burns a hole in my pocket.

"When I was younger, I had nightmares." Blearily, she glances up when the mattress dips at her side. I keep my space, giving her a wide berth. *I'm here*, I want to tell her, and the unspoken encouragement seems to register because she gives me a shaky nod. "Darkness always lurked on the horizon. It made me fearful. And so I would run—in my sleep, I would *run*."

I feel my brows lower. "Sleepwalking, you mean?"

"All night long," she allows, her thumbs crisscrossing anxiously over each other. "Once, when I was seven or eight, I managed to get lost in Regent's Park. We lived nearby, just a block away, and I slipped out into the garden. Mum cried when the Met found me, but my father only put his hand on my arm and marched me back home without a word. After that, he . . . he had me lock my bedroom door."

A hard swallow sticks in my throat as I drop my elbows to my thighs. "You locked yourself inside."

"I was my own jailer," she answers, her naturally husky voice lowering to a pained whisper. "A few years later, stuck in that perpetual nightmare haze, I dreamt of creeping down the stairs like I did as a child. Only, I woke to find myself twisting the knob. No matter how hard I tried, the door wouldn't open."

I'm half-aware of my hands balling into tight fists on my thighs even as I latch onto her words and run them through my memory bank. "At the Palace, you told me that your door was bolted shut on the night that your house caught fire."

The right corner of Rowena's mouth turns up. Nothing in her expression exudes joy. "Before that night, the darkness always chased me in my dreams. Since then—and especially after I met with the king—I dream of only fire."

With one elbow still planted on my knee, I shove my fingers through my hair. "What kind of man leaves his wife and daughter to die while he saves himself?"

"It used to make me feel better to believe that he

planned to come back. That, when he looked up at my window, maybe he didn't actually see me standing beyond the glass."

The fucking bastard.

Although Rowena can't see me, I bow my head to hide the rage bleeding to the surface. "But he saw you," I edge out.

"Oh, he saw me. And then . . ." With a roll of one shoulder, she lifts her face up to the ceiling. "Once in a while I'd think that maybe he and Mum had a row. Maybe they argued and it was so godawful that by the time the fire started, he didn't even stop to think that I was still in the house. He needed to get out and I was just . . . forgotten."

Dispensable, she called herself yesterday.

I despise the word.

It crawls under my skin and spreads to my lungs.

You've been very, very bad, Damien.

Mum's favorite thing to tell me whenever she felt that I acted out of line. Oh, she played the victimized saint around my brothers. Always weeping, always fragile. They catered to her every whim—helping her to the loo when her legs felt weak or pouring her water when she couldn't reach the jug on the nightstand by her bed.

Then they would leave and it would be only us.

And she would show me no mercy.

"I keep wondering," Rowena says, dropping her chin to one knee, "if it's penance that's brought me here." When I start to speak, she holds up a hand. "The king tricked me. I don't want to believe it but I can read the writing on the wall. All those people downstairs . . . I took them from their lives to help with a cause that was nothing but a lie. Sara blames your brother for her father's death and Hugh thinks that Isla Quinn is the devil for killing Ian. And I won't lie to you—I thought the same."

"She did kill the king."

Rowena stares just beyond my right shoulder. "We're all running from something, though, aren't we? We run, in our dreams and in life, like that'll save us from what we've done. Isla Quinn may have killed the king, but I don't know the toll that it took on her soul. All I know is that I was blind—literally, figuratively—and it's not you or your brothers who caused my friends such hurt . . . it's *me*."

My shoulders twitch like she's struck me. "You can't shoulder all the pain in the world, Rowena. Not even if you think that you deserve it."

"I can't, no. But I want to apologize to them—your brothers, I mean—and to Holyrood as a whole."

Jesus.

Feeling unsteady, I push to my feet and stride away from the bed. I look to the wardrobe, where I held her last night, and feel ruined, down to what's left of my soul. I came to Holly Village with selfish intentions spurred by seven months of hatred for her father. Meanwhile, Rowena has the wherewithal to accept her wrongs with humility and grace. She sits there, stripped of her sight, humbled by a nightmare overheard by everyone on this floor, and *still* seeks to make amends.

I want to shake her.

I want to press her flat on that bed, spread her legs wide, and thrust inside her until she feels as shattered, as tortured, as I do.

Mistaking my silence for rejection, Rowena lets out a small, uncomfortable laugh. "Apologies are given without any expectation of their being accepted, and I don't expect forgiveness. But I'll apologize anyway because it's the right thing to do."

"We aren't innocent in this," I tell her roughly. "Don't humble yourself when we . . . when *I've* done so much worse than you could ever dream of."

"You took an oath. Whatever you did—whatever you've *done*—I'm sure it had a purpose."

Even now, I can feel the sweat in my palms from gripping the shovel as I dug and dug and dug. The dirt under my fingernails, the emptiness in my heart. Rowena would be horrified to learn the truth, and all the warmth she gave me last night would be extinguished, as easily as the flame of a candle blowing out in the wind.

Wishing I had a cigarette, I force my fingers to relax at my sides. *Breathe, Godwin. Just fucking breathe.* "And if it's only purpose was hate?" I ask, my tone hard. "If you knew it was wrong, and you reveled in it anyway?"

Her brows knit together. Slowly she extends her bare legs over the side of the bed. "I'm not one to cast stones, Damien. I *can't* be, not after everything." When she stands, it's only for me to realize that she isn't wearing any pajama bottoms at all. Only a rumpled shirt that catches in the elastic waistband of the same knickers that I stripped from her in the chapel.

My cock hardens.

Rowena Carrigan is too good for me. I'll burn her in a way that Buckingham Palace never could. Drag her so far deep into Hell that she'll feel its embers stoked over the coals of her spine until she's all but ash. And if she runs, I'll chase her—because good has never had a place in my life and my first inclination is to destroy it.

Destroy *her*.

I nearly come out of my skin when she presses a hand flat to my chest. "Do you want to tell me what happened?" Her tone is kind, empathetic. So damned *gentle*.

It snips at the already frayed thread of my control. "No."

Her throat visibly works with a swallow. "You can, if you want. Obviously, we got off on the wrong foot, but I thought, maybe—"

"*No.*" Against all better judgment, my palms find her upper arms. I sweep my thumbs over skin untouched by fire. *Forgive me.* The thought bleeds into my consciousness, just as I husk, "The only thing I want is you on your knees."

CHAPTER 25

ROWENA

I don't know when exactly I got a read on Damien, but as he orders me to my knees, I know that he's banking on me telling him to sod off.

The truth lurks in his rigid posture, like he's preparing himself for my rejection, and in his hard-edged tone that barely overshadows the raw vulnerability he's clearly trying to hide. And when he barks, "Well?" all I feel is the rapid thud of his heart fluttering beneath my palm.

I see you, Damien Godwin. For the first time, I see you.

This man has challenged me from the moment I awoke in Dr. Matthews' operating room. He's pushed at my restraints and boundaries. He's tested the limits of my temper and loyalty. To all of England, I'm the prime minister's reclusive daughter. To the people in Holly Village, I'm the one rallying the troops against the Priests. No one knows my soul. No one knows my triumphs.

Not even Margaret.

In life, I run the same way that I do in my dreams—forever reaching, forever grasping for that elusive *something* that will wipe my past clean and bring me long sought peace. Nothing has ever come closer than waking in my bed, skin teased with perspiration from a nightmare, and hearing this man call me back to the realm of the living.

Coiling my fingers in the fabric of his shirt, I tip my head back. "Confess something first."

His gravel-pitched reply is immediate: "What?"

"Would you say the same thing to any woman in my place? Would you tell her to get down on her knees and make you come?"

"*Jesus*. Rowena—"

When he cuts himself off, I steel my shoulders.

I won't wilt for him. I won't *break* for him. Regardless of whether I want to blow him or not—and, God help me, but I do—I won't bow to him or any other man. I'm a fool to want anything with Damien to mean more but I won't do it all if it'll only mean *less*.

"Well?" I demand, smothering the tremor in my voice before it can expose the soft shell of my underbelly. "Would you?"

The hands on my upper arms squeeze then draw me hard against him. My breasts flatten against his chest, and his forefinger hooks under my chin. Firm but gentle. Calloused yet unbelievably tender. His breath mists over my lips when he growls, "You want me to *confess?*"

"I do."

He hisses between clamped teeth like I've personally scorched him. "Then here's my confession: I want nothing more than to put you on that desk. I want you naked, Rowena, all but those knickers of yours. I want you flicking your thumb over your nipple while I watch, and then I want you to take your hand lower and lower, fucking still. I want you trembling, I want you panting. I want you so turned on that you'll *beg* me to touch you."

Oh, God.

"But I won't," he continues on a husky purr before I can even catch my breath. "I won't lay a single finger on you. Not then, when you're begging, and not even when your fingers dance across your thigh to cup your pussy. Because I want that, too—I want to watch you make yourself come."

My legs threaten to buckle, and Damien grips me a little tighter, his mouth finding my ear. "Does that turn you on? Does it make you wet to know that I stayed up all night thinking of this very thing?"

It makes me *whimper*.

My head lolls to the side when his lips find the hollow of my throat, the sensation so deliciously sensual that I can't stop myself from rocking against the muscular thigh he wedges between my legs.

"*Confess*, Rowena."

"Find out for yourself," I throw back at him.

He lets loose a ragged groan that rakes gooseflesh across my skin before turning me around in his arms. His hands land on my hips, pulling me back against him, and then he brings one palm to the apex of my thighs. I'm wet. Drenched. Unable to keep quiet, a keening cry escapes me as I rise onto my toes. His hold on my hip tightens and he grinds the heel of his palm against my core.

Yes, yes, yes.

The bristles of his jaw scrape my cheek as he folds his body around mine, keeping me tucked against him. And all the while he circles his palm, so slow, so arduously, that it's bloody torture. I cant my hips, seeking more friction, but he only snatches his hand away to remind me that he's the one in control and I'm left . . . bereft.

Aching.

"Please," I whisper, reaching for his wrist but finding his forearm instead, "don't stop."

Warmth from the sun dances across my bare toes. I'm burning, wanting for him, and with a dark groan, he brings his hand back between my legs like he can't last another second without touching me. "I shouldn't want you this much," he breathes. "Jesus fucking Christ, I shouldn't want you."

"Why? This—us—isn't hurting anyone."

"It's going to hurt *you*."

"Because there's someone—"

"There's no one," he grits out, "there hasn't been anyone in three years. It's how I wanted it. No distractions. No new addictions. And then you—" He slips a finger under the seam of my knickers and plunges it deep within me, wrenching a gasp from my lips. "You are the last woman I should want. You, who apologizes for your mistakes. You, who feels empathy for a man you barely know. In ruining you, I'll find salvation for myself and *goddammit*, Rowena, tell me to stop."

I don't tell him to stop.

I couldn't, even if I wanted.

Hooking my calf around the back of his leg, I grip the arm that he's locked over my lower stomach and grind myself down on his hand. He thrusts his finger, slowly, like he did with grinding his hand against my clit—and I whimper a small protest. He doesn't give me what I want. Instead, *in* and out, *in* and out, slow glide after slow, damnable glide, until my legs are a quivering mess and he's forced to hold me upright. Only then does he slide in a second finger, stretching me, while his thumb finds my clit and presses down.

I'm a woman without a single addiction—and then Damien had to show me the stars.

"I don't want to live like I'm already dying," I hear myself gasp, "so ruin me, Damien. If that's what you need, if that's what you want, then *ruin me*."

A strangled noise reverberates in his chest, and with my cheek pressed to his pectoral muscles, I feel its resonation all the way down to my toes. His lips find the crown of my head, and instead of remarking on my lack of hair or the scar that I've felt with my fingers, he husks, "You'll ruin me, too, Rowena. Fucking hell, you're going to ruin me."

I tense around him, my lips parting on a hard pant, and then he begins to drive his fingers inside me in earnest—a hard thrust followed by his thumb grazing my clit. A third finger that makes me cry out even as I circle my hips against him and seek everything that he'll give me.

And he does.

Damien kisses my throat, dragging his mouth up to my jaw. His velvet baritone is a dark, illicit melody in my ear, urging me on, telling me to let go. It's heaven and hell and the *more* that I've craved for years, and it's all that I need to come apart, legs shaking beneath me, throat quivering as I gasp for air. I'm spinning again, the way I do in my nightmares when I can't escape the flames, but now there's only this.

Only him.

Only us.

"Tell me," I say, when the stars finally dim, "tell me what you want."

His fingers grip my thigh, still wet from making me come, and I fight the blush that burns across my cheeks.

And then, quietly, "Get on your knees for me, Rowena."

There's not a single shred of doubt within me as I lower myself to the floor at his feet. I want Damien in a way that I've never wanted anything or anyone else in my life. There's freedom in submitting—when it's submission to a man who gives as much as he takes.

Only I suspect that it's not me who's being tamed here

but *him.*

My hands link around his calves and, for a moment, I merely breathe. Air seesaws inside my chest and I roll my shoulders backward. The denim is coarse beneath my palms, the man beneath nothing but hard muscle. And then I begin to move, my hands gliding up, up, up, until I have to rise to my knees so I can reach the button of his trousers.

Above me, Damien's breath audibly catches.

Enflamed by his reaction, I dance my fingers across the zipper and tease my way up to slip them beneath the hem of his shirt. The rigid abdominal muscles spasm, and I swallow a small smile.

I may be on my knees but it's not me who trembles.

Wanting to rattle him to his core, the way he's done to me, I make short work of pulling down the zipper and parting the material. A quick tug on the waistband pulls the fabric down over his arse then farther to his thighs. He stands perfectly still, like he's half-terrified that I might leave him with his trousers down, and then he comes to life when I press a palm to the heavy erection straining past his pants.

We both groan, his pitched erotically low, and his big hands close over the back of my head. It's a line drawn in the sand, a battle for who's really in control—and I stake my claim by rubbing my thumb over the velvet-soft head of his cock. "Does this turn you on?" I breathe, victory singing in my veins at the chance to toss his own words back in his face. "Because I think it does. You're leaking, Damien."

His cock twitches against my hand.

"Jesus," he grunts, "you should see yourself."

"Paint me a picture."

"I'm no artist." His hips push forward when I roll his pants down his thighs and his cock springs free. "I orchestrate death—it's all I've ever done and all I'll ever do—but with you . . . fuck, grip me harder . . . harder, *yes*," he hisses, thrusting against my palm, "like that. Just like that." The hands on the back of my head flex. "I wish I knew beauty. I wish I could paint it for you because you, Rowena . . . you're a dream I don't ever want to wake from."

Beauty is a man as roughened as he is—the villain, the monster—who breaks for only one woman.

Circling the root of his cock, I grip him hard, the way he likes it, and then . . . And then, with a surge of vulnerability quaking in my limbs, I lean forward on my knees and touch my tongue to the crown.

"*Fuck.*" At the guttural curse, I lick away the bead of moisture and drag the flat of my tongue down over the hard length of him. His fingers press into my skull, the internal war within him breeching the surface as he pulls me closer. "Open your eyes," he orders.

I hadn't even realized that I closed them.

As I lift my gaze, I take him into my mouth and swallow him as deep as I can. A throaty groan escapes him, and I feel my heart lurch. He's enjoying the hell out of this and I . . . Oh, God, I love it. With him, for him, I *love* it.

It's sensual, painfully erotic.

His hips rock gently against my mouth and the noises he makes sound wrenched from his soul. I'm warm from the sun and burning from him, and I can't stop myself from following the descent of my hand as it sinks to the root. I pepper open-mouthed kisses over his cock and moan when he gruffly utters my name. My palm skims north, feeling a ridged vein that I stop to lap with attention before twisting my hand around the crown.

And then I do it all over again, bringing him deeper into my mouth, nearly preening when his hands begin to tremble. He smooths a palm over my head, breathing, "Oh, fucking hell, Rowena, it feels so good."

I've never . . . Oh, God, I never thought it could be like this.

It's need and want that has me clutching his arse, my fingers digging into the muscle. It's a desire to make it last that has me monitoring the pace of his thrusts, so that I pull back when he tries to wrest away control, only to swirl my tongue over the head of his cock when he finally relents and cedes power back to me.

Whatever line we've drawn is now blurred by the tread of our feet running in the sand.

He curses my name, and my knees press together in response. *I'm going to come.* If I don't finish him off quick, I'm going to come before I've even let him orgasm once. I pull back long enough to whisper, "Take what you want."

He doesn't need to be told twice.

With one hand cradling the back of my skull, Damien feeds his cock back into my mouth and begins to pump. He slowly retracts, rubbing the damp crown over my lips, once, twice, before plunging deep. My eyes water and my throat knits closed, and then I hear him growl, "Wrap your hand around me."

The tips of my fingers touch as I grip his base, and the calloused hand on my neck retreats again to my head. I'm ashamed of how wantonly I whimper with every thrust that he gives me, but not ashamed enough to stop myself from slipping my free hand between my thighs to satisfy the growing ache.

"Yes," he growls, "fuck *yes*."

I know he sees that I'm touching myself, my finger wet, my clit even wetter. And I paint a portrait of him in return: his dark head thrown back, the veins in his neck throbbing to match the way his corded forearms flex to hold me still as he fucks my mouth.

It's messy.

It's beautiful.

It's a slow ruination of us both and I don't regret a thing.

When I come with a cry, I choke on his length, and he releases the deepest, most delicious moan I've ever heard. "I'm going to come," he warns, his voice guttural. "You've got to pull back, Rowena . . . Jesus, *pull back*."

I don't.

Damien orgasms with a roar, and, for the first time in my life, I give all of myself to a man. I suck him down, and lap him up, and when his legs give out and he pulls me over his prone frame on the rug, I allow my limbs to tangle with his.

If this is ruin, then I'll gladly die happy.

CHAPTER 26

DAMIEN

Thin pink scars stretch across Rowena's bare back. They expand and contract with her every breath, and no matter how she tries to angle her arms to reapply a fresh bandage, she can't finish the job.

And I can't tear my gaze away.

Those wounds were red and bleeding when I pulled her from the moat. Even hours later, when I extracted the glass myself, there was no telling how Rowena managed to escape Buckingham Palace with her life. She should have died right alongside the queen.

"Let me," I husk.

She freezes with her arms clamped awkwardly behind her, then peers over her shoulder at me. "You weren't so kind the last time around."

"Should I apologize?"

Her mouth pulls to one side. "I don't know, Damien. Do you feel bad?"

No.

Yes.

Skimming a hand down the back of my neck, I rest my palm over my nape and squeeze tight. Do I *feel* bad? After a lifetime in Holyrood, my relationship with pain is . . . complicated. I expect it because I've been the one to suffer a hundred times over. The same goes for every Holyrood agent. We've all been hurt. But none of us can claim innocence—we're thieves in the night, snatching anti-loyalist lives with just another mental tally on the chalkboard.

Pain has its place in the world, its purpose, and I . . .

"Apologizing for something I believed in seems insincere."

Dark brows furrow over the bridge of her nose. "And you feel differently now?"

"I feel . . ." At the expectant expression on her face, my hand drops to my side. Heat scalds my cheeks, and I lower my gaze to the bandage she's holding, where her thumb worries the latex edge. A quick glance at the tight set of her shoulders tells me she's actually holding her breath, waiting for my answer.

Her uncertainty in me is a punch to the gut.

When did I become the man who trades only in the currency of violence? When did I *become* the Mad Priest, when the moniker alone makes my skin fucking crawl?

Deep down, I can pinpoint the exact day, hour, minute—and I despise myself for it.

Carrigan's men stabbed me and along with my blood, spilled out my conscience. It ran in rivulets over the pavement. Morals, gone. Ethics, destroyed. I started the day as one man and ended it as another. And the half-dead man who left the alley behind Christ Church Spitalfields didn't care, one way or another, who he hurt in his quest for vengeance.

Rowena included.

Something that feels like embarrassment propels me forward. I duck my head, cutting eye contact that's already severely one-sided. Nine days ago, I stood over the exam table and ran my gaze over her blistered body, and I felt . . . nothing. Nothing but rage. Nothing but vindication that she practically landed on my doorstep to do with as I wished.

Blind. Ruined. *Mine.*

The heat on my face spreads south to squeeze the air from my lungs. I've been no better to her than Mum was to me—the only difference being that whereas I once hid to make myself invisible, Rowena Carrigan has claws that draw blood the moment she's threatened. A she-wolf who will bend to no one, even when she's backed into a corner and left to fight for her life.

Swallowing tightly, I touch my fingers to the bandage, to take it from her, but she yanks it out of reach. "Do you *feel* bad?"

"Ashamed," I admit, my voice hoarse. "I feel ashamed."

When her violet eyes lower, black lashes casting twin shadows over her cheeks, I feel downright condemned. "*Rowena,*" I start, only to clamp my mouth shut when she turns around and presents me with the slope of her naked back.

Salvation.

I taste it on my tongue, foreign and holy.

Bowing her head, Rowena thrusts the bandage over one shoulder. "Apology accepted," she says, "because I have no doubt that if our roles were reversed, I probably would have castrated you first and asked questions later."

I give a short bark of laughter. "Would you have at least taken pity and sterilized the knife first?"

"Oh, I don't know, Mr. Godwin. Someone once told me that self-pity isn't a good look."

Jesus, this woman.

Plucking the bandage from her fingers, I shake my head with the ghost of a grin on my lips. "Anyone ever tell you that you have a twisted sense of humor?"

"Generally speaking," she drawls, "people tend to find out when it's already too late."

I want to taste that sharp mouth of hers.

A new addiction to devour. A new flavor to learn. The thought of crushing Rowena to me and lowering my mouth to hers feels as dangerous, as forbidden as the cigarettes I continue to smoke, knowing all the while that I'm damning myself with every inhale.

My fingers curl around the bandage, the latex edges crinkling.

Don't do it, Godwin.

Sweet, fucking temptation.

When she hums my name, I force myself to look away from her profile to the expanse of her back. Up close, with sunlight streaming in from the window, the gravity of the scarring is undeniable. The affected skin is textured, raised. With every intake of breath, they ripple like water tucked away behind a shard of glass.

"You lived," I say, carefully fitting the fresh bandage over her back, "when so many others didn't. How?"

She doesn't ask me to elaborate.

With her head still bent, she waits until I've finished and then reaches for a new shirt from one of the wardrobe's many hangers. "I ran."

I feel one side of my mouth curl. "A habit of yours."

"It comes in handy. Sometimes handsome men even catch me." Snapping up a pair of denim trousers from where she slung them over the wooden door, she adds, quietly, "It was my nightmare come to life. Windows were shattering and the smoke was so thick that I could have choked on it. But I didn't hear a single scream. It felt like . . . I had this sixth sense that, for the first time in my life, I was running in the wrong direction."

"You didn't think to leave Margaret behind and save yourself?"

She tugs her trousers up the curve of her thighs, all while vehemently shaking her head. "I'm loyal to a fault." She gives a low laugh. "*Foolishly* loyal, even. It's what I thought as I was running toward Margaret's apartments. But I couldn't not save her. I keep such a small group of friends—just Mags and . . . and well, there was Ian."

Ian, who tried to strangle Isla, only to end up strangled and dead in return.

Lifting a hand, I scrub my palm over my jaw. "You have the people in this house, don't you? The doctor? Gregory?" My molars grind together as I bite off, "And Hugh."

Buttoning her trousers, Rowena leans back against the closed door of the wardrobe. Her violet gaze is unerringly astute. "I pay their wages, Damien. I appreciate them all, and I treat them like family, but we aren't friends."

I narrow my eyes. "*You* pay their wages."

On a slow nod, she replies, "I do, yes."

"How?"

"The usual way, I guess." The blasé shrug she gives me reeks of unspoken secrets. "I have their IBAN numbers and I deposit money into their accounts like the rest of the—"

"*How*, Rowena?" Despite the fact that she can't see me, I gesture toward the bedroom. "How do you afford this house and their wages and—*Jesus.*" I rake my fingers through my hair. Only last night, they stormed the Palace. The drawbridge being down worked in their favor, but even if that hadn't been the case . . . "And the weapons," I growl. "The lot of them had *grenades*, which don't come cheap."

Her jaw works side to side as she drums her fingers against the wardrobe. "I don't feel comfortable saying so."

"You don't feel comfortable? Rowena, you just had your mouth on my—"

"Don't you dare say it."

"—cock," I finish, gritting out the word. "I think we've reached the point where being comfortable is second only to our good-mate transparency."

She presses a hand to her ear then hastily nods her head like she's heard something. "Oh," she murmurs sweetly, "that was our good-mate transparency ringing to say that you're a bloody *hypocrite*, Damien Godwin." Her arms fold over her breasts. Clearly worked up, she jabs a finger in my direction a second later. "Confess, you said, so I did. But now you're wanting more of my secrets while revealing none of your own."

I don't deny it.

Can't deny it when I'm standing less than an arm's width away with my mother's necklace buried in my back pocket—a necklace that I ripped from her dead body.

"Then ask me something," I tell Rowena. "I'll answer, and then you tell me how it is that you afford everything."

"I've half a mind to make you pinky promise."

Laughter climbs my throat when I notice that she's grinning. "Only you, Rowena Carrigan, would think that a pinky promise with me would mean a damned thing."

"Are you saying that I can't trust your word?"

"I'm saying that you should know better."

"If you're trying to convince me to keep my silence, you're doing a bang-up job of it."

"Then let me shut up before you change your mind completely."

With a nod to allow that the battle lines have been drawn, she closes the wardrobe behind her and carefully picks her way through the room until she's perched against her desk, her legs crossed at the ankles. "You have an accent."

My brows lift in surprise. "I don't."

"You do," she retorts swiftly with a tilt of her head. "I noticed it the first time that you spoke in Dr. Matthews' OR. It's so soft, honestly, almost undetectable, but I once spent an insane amount of time schmoozing with politicians from all over the world—I can recognize an accent when I hear one."

"And Guy? Did you hear one from him?"

"A little but his is even fainter than yours."

She watches, and she listens.

Didn't she tell me that only days ago? At the time, it seemed particularly dramatic—only now, I have a gut feeling that she wasn't exaggerating at all. Fucking hell. It's unnerving to be confronted with someone who's so eerily like myself. If I were to wave right now, I half expect her hand to come up instinctively and wave on back.

"I lived . . . *we* lived in Paris."

A frown tugs at her mouth. "Holyrood allowed you to leave?"

"In theory, no."

"Which means what exactly?"

"It means that we were exiled."

I utter the words matter-of-factly, but still, they send her jaw flapping open. "Exiled," she repeats on a hushed murmur, "the lot of you were *exiled*? Is that a thing that still happens nowadays? One minute everything's going brilliantly and then *surprise!*" Her hands clap together. "You're banished, just like that?"

Not *just like that.*

I don't remember every detail in the days leading up to when we were sent to France. But I do remember Mum crying hysterically and Guy, at only twelve, trying his best to calm her down. I remember Jayme Paul standing in the middle of our cramped Whitechapel flat with his cap clutched in one hand and the other rooted firmly on Saxon's shoulder while he informed us that, for our *safety*, it was best if we left England until Holyrood could make sure that whoever attacked Pa wouldn't come for us next.

Pain and fear followed us across the Channel.

The City of Love broke me irreversibly. Saxon, too, after the butcher cut his mouth and left him forever scarred. If Guy suffered during those five years, more so than the rest of us, at any rate, he's never said a word. Then again, his midnight screams lead me to believe that he probably did.

Aware that Rowena is still waiting for an answer, I give her the unvarnished truth: "Henry Godwin was my father."

Her expression instantly falls. "Oh, Damien."

It's all she says, but really, is there anything else that *needs* to be said? We were sent to Paris because Paul wanted us Godwins away from the Crown while he assumed Pa's place in Holyrood. Four generations of Godwins in power and then Paul saw an opportunity and he snatched it with both hands.

I can't say that I wouldn't have done the same.

"No one's ever mentioned me having an accent," I go on, as smooth as I can, "but if you hear anything at all, it must be what little I've kept of Paris." Even though I'd give just about anything to have retained nothing of that city at all. "It's your turn, Rowena."

Her sightless gaze slips down to the thick rug. "I told you that I can't cast stones—I meant it, Damien. I really meant it."

Voice low, I murmur, "Tell me."

Her fingers tighten around her upper arms. "After I stopped . . . working for my father, I found myself at a crossroads. I was only twenty-three but I felt ancient here"—she briefly presses a hand to her chest—"and, more than anything, I was a realist. Dreams were for good people, *honest* people. And I was, admittedly, quite adept at doing nothing but spreading my legs."

Those words, *her* words, are ones I'd uttered in her ear while pressing her up against a glass window at the Palace. Arrogant. Patronizing. Crude. Any lingering trace of salvation dissolves on my tongue. "Rowena, I was an ass. I shouldn't have—"

"*No*," she interjects firmly, shaking her head, "no, you were right. And I recognized it even then. England . . . the whole country was already taking a turn for the worse and I had nothing but this house. I inherited it when Mum died and I could have sold it. Sometimes I wonder if I *should* have sold it, but the satisfaction I felt knowing that Father couldn't take it away from me . . . it was worth every bit of hardship."

Bloodthirsty thing.

I want to kiss her even more for it.

"Did you live here?" I ask.

She laughs. "No, I leased the flat that your man Hamish brought me to the other day, the one in Hurlingham. Realist. Pragmatist. It's all the same, isn't it? I couldn't bear to part with Holly Village but leasing it would at least keep me afloat."

One glance around the elegant room around us is confirmation that, at some point, Rowena managed to do a whole lot more than just keep herself afloat. The sleigh bed alone must have cost a fortune. Bringing my gaze back to Rowena, I watch as she lifts a hand to her head, only to hover her palm above her skull.

A nervous tic that she tries to cover up by tugging on

one ear.

"You did something else," I say, eyeing that hand on its trajectory back down to her side. "You might as well just spit it out."

Her shoulders square off. "I had information."

The implication of that one statement is enough to rock me back on my heels. "Jesus, Rowena," I breathe. "Tell me you didn't."

"I set up a private forum under an anonymous name." Her chin hikes up, as if daring me to find fault with a decision she made ten years ago. "It turns out that that the old adage is true: it's better to smile at your enemies than it is to frown at your friends."

"No one says that," I edge out.

"Matshona Dhliwayo did."

Oh, bloody fucking hell. "Rowena, it doesn't matter *who* said it. The fact is, you turned a profit on selling intel from MPs. You could have been caught."

"Instead I grossed nearly a million pounds in the first year alone and I re-invested all of it."

Torn between the ridiculous urge to applaud her ingenuity while also calling her damned sanity into question, I run my hands over my face. It doesn't matter that it's been years, my mind paints an image of her behind bars or, worse, dead—and it sets my blood on fire.

I demolish the space between us in three strides, and, before I even realize it, my hands are on her elbows and my face is in hers and I'm locked back in the darkness that I once told her to harness before it consumed her.

Right now, envisioning her limp and broken, I am *consumed.*

"Do you know how bloody easy it is to hack a website?" I growl, shaking her. "I can do it in my fucking *sleep,*

Rowena. I can do it with my hands tied behind my back, or blindfolded, and I'm telling you right now, the fact that you're standing here is proof that either all politicians are idiots or that you are the luckiest woman—"

"I hired someone in the field."

My lids fall closed and I pray for control. "You hired someone," I manage on a tight whisper, "to create a forum where you *sold private information?*"

"I'm not—" She struggles in my arms and plants a firm hand on my chest. "I'm not naïve."

"In this," I clip out, "you are."

She pushes against me. "After some major digging around that lasted months, mind you, I found someone who'd done some work for MI5. He must have thought me ridiculous." A wry grin deepens the curve of her bottom lip. "But I'm nothing if not savvy. I used a fake name and an account that I opened just for this venture. And I knew, Damien—I *knew* that I could never let any of it get back to me or my head would be on a pike. All I needed was the skeleton of the site, anyway, and I could manage the rest. So, I had him build me a website that catered to selling second-hand clothing worn by England's rich and famous because—"

All I hear is the roar in my ears.

Beyond it, there's the sound of her voice.

Beneath it, the quickening of my pulse.

I step back, then step back again. Twist around at the waist and find myself leaning against the window, staring blindly at the garden that overlooks Swain's Lane beyond a brick outer wall.

My hands furl into fists at my sides, which I plant heavily on the window frame. "The name," I utter, my gaze trained on the sycamore trees bracketing the street. "What was the name of the clothing site?"

"I . . ." She clears her throat, and I hear her feet pad in my direction. "I actually never took the time to make one up. In the email I sent, I said just to leave that part blank."

Jesus Christ, I think I'm going to be sick.

"Damien?" comes her soft voice, just behind my right shoulder. "Are you okay?"

No.

No, I don't think I am.

"It was me," I rasp, looking back at her. "You hired *me*, Rowena."

Her porcelain skin pales to a ghostly white. "I didn't. There's no way. I hired—"

"You paid me twenty-thousand pounds." Turning around, I face her directly. Openly. "And you spent five paragraphs rattling on about how you wanted everything to be top-notch and anonymous, so that celebrities wouldn't feel embarrassed that they were forced to sell the clothes straight off their backs to make ends meet."

"But you . . . but, Damien, you—"

"I took it on as a whim." Because *M.* had sounded desperate in her emails. Plus, turning down a twenty-K gig, when the job itself only would take a matter of two or three hours, was the very definition of madness. "And I said yes."

"You work for Holyrood!" Her eyes are wide, the color in her cheeks swiftly returning to bloom a furious red. "You *worked* for Holyrood. Why in the world would you take on anything else?"

Boredom, mostly.

But also because, back then, it had amused me to peel back the clandestine world of MI5 and steal their secrets for Holyrood.

"Thanks to me, you managed to—what did you say?—

make almost a million pounds in a year."

Before she can respond, my mobile goes off and I reach it for in my pocket. One glance at the screen and the pit in my stomach grows. "I have to take this," I mutter, flicking my gaze back to Rowena. Something compels me to add, "It's Matthews."

"Is it about Margaret?" she asks, worry creeping into her voice. "Is she all right?"

"I'll let you know." The mobile continues to vibrate in my hand, and I hover there, wishing that I could ignore Holyrood's surgeon. But he wouldn't be calling unless he had news, and I'm not ready to face the consequences of avoiding the outside world to stay in this bubble with Rowena. "I may have to step out this afternoon," I tell her.

Her lips press together in a straight line. "Is that a smart idea when there's a bounty on your head?"

Because the Mad Priest is wanted. Fortunately for all of England, they only have to wait a little while longer to get what they so desperately crave. Unfortunately for me, with Carrigan and Guthram on the hunt, I already have one foot in the grave.

CHAPTER 27

DAMIEN

The Bell & Hand is a husk of ash and rubble.

The windows are gone, the outer walls nothing but mangled, half-melted steel piers that reveal Christ Church Spitalfields across Fournier Street. The stairwell leading up to Guy's flat stretches north toward an open night sky, and Saxon's bar—once a hub of activity—sits like a soot-covered cavern near the back of the pub.

It's a fucking disaster.

Hunching my shoulders against an icy breeze, I light a cigarette and bring it to my lips. Inhale slowly, drawing the nicotine into my system, before exhaling on a soft breath. I shove the Zippo into the pocket of my armored vest. "I know you're there."

Debris crunches under near-silent feet. "You're playing a dangerous game, brother."

"Not dangerous enough, apparently, because you still came to meet me in the middle of the night." I glance over my shoulder at the darkened frame picking its way through the rubble, and feel a twist of relief to see him after all these weeks. "Where's your other half?"

Moonlight splices across Saxon's harsh face, revealing

the snarled upper lip and those eerie green eyes that he inherited from Pa. Dressed in his customary black-on-black, he carries a duffel bag in one hand, which he tosses at my feet when he steps in close.

He jerks his chin toward the fag. "Put it out."

Fighting the urge to take another drag, just to mess with him, I drop it to the ground and stub out the cherry with my boot. "Happy—"

The rest of my sentence is bludgeoned to death by my older brother's massive arms coming around me.

A hug.

He's *hugging* me.

My hands stay suspended mid-air. "What"—I clear my throat, frantically searching the pub beyond his right ear—"are you doing? Has Isla addled your brain? Swapped you out for a different model or—"

One of those big fists leaves my back to grab a handful of my vest and—*crack!* Teeth rattling, my chin snaps to the left.

Jesus fucking Christ.

Staggering backward, I flex my lower jaw. Press two fingers to the sore flesh and come away wincing. "What the hell is *wrong* with you?"

Saxon only stands there, the lower half of his face concealed in shadow. "The hug is because Matthews told me how you almost died up on the roof. You were reckless, Damien. Absolutely goddamn reckless."

"And the punch?"

"That's for sending me the queen. And Guy. And *Paul,* you sadistic bastard."

"At least you don't have Benji," I mutter, letting my hand drop after prodding my aching jaw one last time. "He's currently locked away with Alfie Barker in Holly Village's loft. I hear they're mates but couldn't tell you if it's true."

"You haven't gotten him out yet?"

"Benji? No. I figure he can do with a bit of penance after attacking you in the woods. Justice by Damien Priest—he should be glad that I didn't have any of my toys." Angling my chin toward the duffel, I say, "I'm assuming you brought everything I asked for?"

"You're lucky I had most of it on hand."

Luck has nothing to do with it. When I rang Saxon this afternoon, after meeting with Matthews, I figured he'd have everything that I needed and more. A man doesn't leave Holyrood without being prepared for the moment when Holyrood decides to bring you back. There's only ever been one agent to retire: Robert Guthram, who once stood side by side with Pa. But the old man has been shut away in an asylum for the last ten years, and I doubt he's enjoying his days post-Holyrood.

Especially not with a son like Marcus Guthram.

Shoving a hand into my kit for the cigarette pack, I fish another fag free from the carton. "Have Isla and the queen . . ."

"Interacted?" Saxon gives a rough chuckle that carries on the breeze. "Currently, the queen thinks Isla is the sweetest woman she's ever met. They've had tea."

Fucking hell.

After lighting the cherry, I take a slow drag. Then swing my gaze over to Saxon's inscrutable face. Spontaneous hugs aside, my older brother has always been the one person who I've never been able to read. He plays his emotions close to his vest—whatever he has of them, at any rate—and rarely reveals anything. Still. The thought of the king killer sitting down for tea with the queen of England, of all people, sounds so far-fetched I'm almost positive that he's taking the piss.

"And what does Isla think of her . . . newfound friendship?"

"She finds it problematic that the queen isn't half bad, especially since Margaret spends most of her time sniping at Guy. They share a common enemy."

Laughter kicks free from my chest. "If we've nothing else going for us, at least we don't have to worry about the king killer making her debut as the queen killer—doesn't really have the same ring."

Saxon's mouth barely tips up in a smile. On him, though, it's as close to a full-blown smirk as I've ever seen.

Turning his gaze from mine, he sweeps a hard glance over the ruined pub. "You really think Carrigan did this?" he asks. "There's nothing for him to gain by torching the place."

The confession burns within me, as does Guy's warning that I can't hide from Saxon forever. I never intended to keep Carrigan's appearance at Westminster a secret. He posed a logistical problem that none of us could have ever predicted. Hell, until the king told me his suspicions, there was no reason to suspect the prime minister of any foul play. Carrigan fulfilled what few responsibilities he had as PM and he did it all with little fanfare. That he wanted me to kill the king was a major red flag that I never saw coming.

Just as I never anticipated the attack.

If Guy has always taken on the disciplinary role of father figure, then Saxon has always sought to be my fiercest protector. It's only thanks to a riot in Leeds that he was away from the Palace when Guy brought me to Matthews. There's no doubt in my mind—one word about my brush with death would have had Saxon nailing Carrigan's ass to the wall before ripping the bastard's entrails from his body.

Then and now, vengeance belongs to me.

And while Saxon deserves to know the truth, I can't bring myself to reveal anything that might ruin the measure of peace he's finally found with Isla Quinn.

Grimacing, I take one last pull of the cig before stamping it out on the ground. "Carrigan wanted the king dead."

Saxon's head snaps in my direction. "What?"

"Dead," I mutter, staring at the dimly lit entrance of Christ Church Spitalfields, a view we'll never enjoy again unless we go through the hassle of rebuilding the pub. "When I showed up at Westminster that night, Carrigan was already there and waiting to propose a bargain: kill John or he'd make my life a living hell."

My brother curses under his breath. "That's an ultimatum not a bargain."

"Generally, my favorite kind," I drawl. "Unless, of course, it's being used against me."

Ignoring the sarcastic quip, Saxon's eyes narrow on me. "You told him no."

"I told him no," I confirm. *And I've paid the price for my loyalty every day since.* A loyalty that was all for naught because the king hired Rowena to kill us anyway. Mouth flat, I tear my gaze away from the church. "Imagine what people would think if they learned the prime minister had hoped to take out the king."

"At least half the country would cheer him on."

"And the other half would revolt—it'd be the Westminster Riots all over again but so much worse. Anarchy. Bloodshed. And Carrigan would go from being the country's last hope for democracy to the fanatical Grim Reaper." *Spit out the words. Just fucking say them.* "I know too much," I say quietly. "I hold his entire life in the palm of my hand and can snap his neck anytime I choose."

"Is there a chance that his daughter—"

"*No.*" The word leaves me on a battered snarl. "No, Rowena hates Carrigan." He's the monster in her life, just as Mum was always the monster in mine. Broken, kindred souls, the two of us. Raking my fingers through my hair, I drop my chin. "She and I have had our differences but she wouldn't lie to me about this."

"The queen seems to think that Rowena had a hand in the fire at Buckingham Palace."

I shake my head. "The group that Rowena's pulled together . . . there's no chance in hell they could have coordinated an attack of that caliber. It's just not possible."

"And yet, they still found us in Sevenoaks. Guy said that she's blind."

Scrubbing a hand over my jaw, I say, "She has a book about English architecture dog-eared to an entry on Ightham Mote. I'm guessing that someone—Hamish or Matthews, probably—let the name drop and thought nothing of it." But she remembered because Rowena Carrigan is cunning in a way that no one ever suspects of her.

Particularly when it comes to selling the country's deepest, darkest political secrets to the highest bidder.

Saxon stares at me for a beat too long, and I steel my spine to keep from averting my gaze. If I know a person's move before they ever think to make it, then my brother has the uncomfortable ability to look someone in the eye and steal every one of their thoughts. It's uncanny, bloody unnerving. When he finally looks away, my shoulders fall with relief.

"I told Isla that I was done with Holyrood," he says, dropping to his haunches to pick up a charred picture frame off the floor. Turning it over, he stares down at the image that's completely blackened from the fire. "And even when I left Oxford tonight, I looked her in the eye and said, *I choose you.*"

"Saxon, I know."

"I don't think you do, brother." He lets the frame go,

and it splinters completely when it hits a pile of equally charred wood. "Isla is my fire, my fucking soul mate, and life without her is no life at all. But you . . ." With both wrists leveled on his bent knee, he twists at the waist to stare up at me. "You're running from something. The rage, the panic when you think no one is watching—I've seen it for months now."

My throat constricts. "You're overthinking shit."

Those cold, green eyes don't even blink. "You've lost at least a stone."

"House arrest tends to dampen one's hunger."

"Don't fuck with me, Damien." He pushes to his full height, which is still a few centimeters shorter than me. Thrusting his face close to mine, he shoves a hand against my shoulder but we're evenly matched, when he's not catching me by surprise, that is, and I don't budge. "Tell me what it is," he growls, "tell me what you need because, Christ, I know the look in your eye. I've seen it before— that soul-wrenching bleakness—and I'm willing . . . Bloody fucking hell, I'm willing to step back into this life for you."

He's already been roped back in.

I told Guy about Saxon's safehouse in Oxford because desperate times called for desperate measures. But in every other way, Saxon has walked free. He rang when Buckingham Palace went up in flames but didn't return to the fight. He must have heard the alert when The Bell & Hand caught fire but didn't make a move. He chose Isla Quinn over Holyrood and his brothers-in-arms, and I . . .

I don't fault him for it.

"You deserve better, brother." Clapping a hand on his wrist, I pull him away from my shoulder. "You deserve *happiness.* And we both know that Holyrood is the tidal wave that'll drown you."

The severe lines of his face go taut. "Damien, just—"

My gaze snags on something moving along Fournier. A shoulder turning. A body bending down. And then, far off to the right, the unmistakable shape of a long barrel that turns my blood to ice.

Saxon lets loose a grunt as I tackle him to the soot-covered floor.

I don't move fast enough—fire sears my right bicep and red swims on my periphery, and *fucking hell*. Hissing through clenched teeth, I deaden my weight so that Saxon can't push me off. "Stop," I snarl. "Jesus, *stop moving*."

"You're not a goddamn shield. Get up."

Gunfire erupts above us, and I flatten my body over my brother's, prepared to take every hit that comes our way. He has Isla. For the first time, he has a future worth living at his fingertips, and I have—

Bullets ping off the only remaining interior wall.

Moonlight shimmers over the rubble, bathing what's left of The Bell & Hand in a pearlescent glow. Without the pub's roof for cover, we're ripe for the picking.

Dropping my head to Saxon's ear, I demand, "How many do you see?"

I feel him angle his head. "Six. No, seven."

We're either dead men walking, or dead men buried, and since I have no plans to see my brother dressed in his funeral best anytime soon, it's going to have to be neither of the above. With small, incremental adjustments, I move off him.

"*Damien*," he hisses.

Debris coats my fingers, and the taste of ash sits on my tongue. Planting one bent elbow in front of the other, I use my forearms and the toes of my boots to propel me over broken slats of wood. Rewind the clock nine days, before Buckingham Palace went up in flames, and Commercial Street would have been heavy with pedestrian traffic, even past midnight. But beyond the discharge of gunfire, there's only stillness. It's only us, only *them*, while the rest of Whitechapel locks their doors and prays for daybreak.

Bang!

I jerk my head up to see Saxon on his back, a pistol clamped between his hands. He fires from the darkness, the devil cloaked in shadow.

I don't wait to see if his aim is true.

Belly-crawling the remaining distance, I tear open the duffel Saxon brought me. With my head lowered, I shove a hand inside and rummage around, pushing aside fresh clothes to find—

"Reunited at last," I mutter, grasping the rifle and hoisting the stock against my chest as I roll swiftly onto my back. My fingers move fluidly over the weapon that I designed a few years back. Lifting it, I stare down the scope, find my mark, and—*crack!*

The man goes down.

Sweat beads on my temple, a sweep of red encroaching on my central vision. Not again. *Not again.* Familiar panic claws at my chest and I breathe hard through my nose. Ash rises from the destruction. It hangs like death in the air, drying my throat and stinging my eyes.

Relying on muscle memory, I aim, fire.

Another falls.

Under the cacophony, I hear someone yell "throw it!" and my gaze flickers over the shadows, trying to locate the source.

Something hard lands on my right, less than an arm's length away.

I twist my head, the rifle still cradled to my chest, and

spot the tear gas grenade, its safety pin already removed.

Fucking hell.

"Out!" I bark at Saxon. "Move, move, move."

Grabbing the duffel bag, I hook the strap over my shoulder and launch to my feet. I run, bent at the waist, to keep low and to the shadows, then grasp Saxon by the arm and pull him along behind me. We zigzag through the ruins of The Bell & Hand and slip out into the night through one of the bare window frames.

In unison, we turn left down Fournier where Christ Church Spitalfields stands sentry to the chaos.

A round sings past my left ear, and I bite back a curse. "Take Wilkes," I tell Saxon. "I'll head for Brick."

"Sod off," comes his grunt, a second before he shoves me down Wilkes Street. The moonlit sky reveals crooked pavement and boarded-up windows. Without exchanging a word, we make the first left, ducking into a narrow alley lined with cobblestones and cast-iron streetlamps.

It's as good a place as any.

The duffel bag squishes behind me as I press my back against the brick.

"I should punch you all over again," Saxon growls, settling in beside me. With his shoulders leveraged against the building, he swaps out the magazine clip of his pistol with perfunctory proficiency. "You knew you were being tailed."

"I suspected it," I mutter, fixing my gaze on the corner of Wilkes and Puma Court, "and now I know for sure. Thanks for the gear, by the way."

"I'm going to *kill* you."

"Does this mean that hug time is over?"

The barrel of a SA80 edges past the corner wall, and I lift my rifle and aim. A scream rips through the air, followed by another threat from Saxon: "There won't be enough of you left to even show the queen when I'm done." He pauses, then grits, "Christ, you're bleeding."

"It grazed me."

"No, you're *bleeding*."

I twist my wrist so I can peer down at the back of my right arm. Sure enough, the sleeve of my jumper is hanging from my elbow to swing in the breeze. The skin is torn, too. There's nothing but blood oozing from the wound, smeared across my elbow, nothing but the reoccurring nightmare of a very different day when I was immobile on the pavement, unable to scream, unable to shake myself free.

Paralyzed. Frozen.

A man who deserved better than to die with a sack pulled over his head, just a stone's throw away from where his brother waited for him.

I hear the duffel bag hit the cobblestones as it slides from my wounded arm.

Hear Saxon shout my name, ordering me back to his side.

And then I hear nothing at all as I turn the corner onto Wilkes and walk straight into the line of fire.

No mercy.

Not today, not tomorrow.

Not until the day I die.

CHAPTER 28

ROWENA

One staggering step takes me away from the loo, and then yet another and another, until I'm running clear across my bedroom. My feet are bare, my naked flesh damp from a late night shower. It doesn't stop me from throwing open the heavy drapes, heedless to wandering eyes down in the garden, and shoving my nose against the chilled glass.

Light cuts through the darkness—a car winding through the dense sycamore trees that bracket Swain's Lane.

I follow the glowing head lamps without blinking, terrified that if I do, it'll prove to be only a mirage, a bout of wishful thinking after days of quashing every seed of hope within me. The car disappears a moment later, around the bend toward Highgate Cemetery, but it's enough.

Enough for me to face the cavern-like darkness of my bedroom and make a break for it.

I dive for the desk and put greedy fingers to the lamp string. One tug and warm, yellow light splices across the wood. I stare at the varying shades of oak, my heart racing fast, fast, faster, before I'm rushing to each nightstand, and the switch by the door, and, finally, to the loo, where it all started with a feather-like shadow darting across my vision when I reached for the bath towel.

A *shadow* when I was already encased in total darkness.

I want to laugh.

Instead, with my arms locked across my middle, and water droplets dripping from my body to the rug, I slowly turn around. *Please, please, please be real.* My shoulders curl inward and a sob aches to burst free and this time, I don't do a single thing to stem the tears that burn the backs of my eyes.

Light pervades the room, revealing everything I've seen for years but never thought to see again. The rocking chair in the far-left corner, where my grandmother used to hold me as a child. Behind the sleigh bed, a mural of Ben Bhraggie overlooking the tiny coastal town of Golspie, its blue-oiled bluffs sharp and distinct against a cloudy afternoon sky. The yellow-striped blanket that rests over the footboard, its hand-stitched threads looking worn with age and love.

A birthday gift from Mum the year before she died.

Choking back a sob, I reach for something solid to support my unsteady frame—and graze wood.

The wardrobe.

I step toward it, toward the mirror that Hugh covered, only to slam to a halt when an unexpected shadow flies from my periphery to the center of my vision. It hovers there, a black mark layered over the wardrobe's filigreed wood.

No.

No, no, no!

Shoving down panic, I close my eyes gingerly. *Don't you dare think the worst.* Dr. Matthews said that the woman . . . the woman who fell—hadn't she seen dark streaks when her eyesight returned? Floaters, Matthews called them. An improvement, some might say, over seeing nothing at all.

A floater, if that's what this is, will not be the end of me.

"Broken, but never defeated," I whisper to the empty room.

Damien told me to harness the darkness, to own it with all my heart, and I do that now. My eyes remain closed as I trace the hills and valleys of the ornate wood before coming to the thick sheet of paper which covers the mirror.

I tear it free.

Opening my eyes, I first spy my feet. The black mark now rests atop the big toe of my right foot. Another joins it as a slightly oblong shape that remains on my right peripheral, followed swiftly by a third that dances across the rug as I bring my gaze upward.

Disappointment is the thief of joy, and I smother it into nonexistence.

I step close to the mirror.

Brace my hands on the glass.

And *see*.

The slope of my calves, which are leanly muscled from hours spent walking Highgate Cemetery. The unmarred flesh of my inner thighs and the width of my hips, both soft and curved. *And here we are, the beginning of the end.* Pulse quickening, I look to my belly and stifle a small gasp. The skin there is textured from the fire, the blisters having formed thin layers of pink that crisscross atop one another. Not daring to tread any closer, I touch a finger to my waist.

My vision shimmers.

I don't allow myself the luxury of turning away.

Instead, I absorb the yellow bruising over my sternum, from the fallen beam, as well as the constellation of nearly translucent burns that burst across my collarbone. With a deep breath that barely expands my chest, I look up, up, up, and feel my heart rate spike.

The woman staring back is not me.

And yet, somehow, she is more *me* than I've ever been.

The armor of black hair is gone, leaving behind a face that's both foreign and familiar. Shiny blisters kiss my forehead and the right side of my jaw, turning my porcelain skin a muted peach, as if the fire from Buckingham Palace still burns furiously beneath my flesh. Exhaustion is a curse that's turned me gaunt, pressing fine lines to either side of my mouth. And my eyes, a deep, effervescent blue that Mum always called violet, give entry to my soul—there, I see the most foreign feature of all: unmasked hope.

A woman brimming with *life*.

A tear escapes, and as I watch it descend in the mirror, I feel its charted course over my cheek. The floaters follow, clinging to my vision, a reminder that the darkness has been my closest friend for years, and that it'll swallow me whole if I slow down long enough for it to catch me.

The sound of a car door closing snaps my attention to the window.

Damien.

His name is a rhythmless beat inside my veins as I throw open the wardrobe and grab clothes off the hangers—a black shirt that I draw down over my head, a pair of joggers that I tie off at the waist with a lopsided bow. Trainers forgotten, socks dismissed, I hurry into the empty corridor. My heart pounds with a burst of awareness—*I can see, I can see*—and then I'm tearing down the hall and flying down the stairs that I've taken a thousand times over the years.

But with every blink, floaters scatter across my vision like billiard balls springing toward waiting pockets. Nausea weakens my legs. An aching throb pulses to life in my temple. Slowing down, I press a hand to the wall outside of the drawing room and slam my eyes shut.

It's not weakness.

It's not even pain.

It's complete and utter disorientation.

Another adjustment to make, that's all. Just another step toward recovery.

I need to find Damien.

I need to *see* him.

Masculine voices lead me to the entrance hall where a blockade of shoulders cuts off all access points. Beyond them, I hear Hugh arguing and Gregory making one of his unintentional sly jokes and then: "I'm not here for *you.*"

My left elbow lands in Samuel's gut and my right nudges Uri aside. Both men stare down at me with wide-eyed expressions but I shove my way through the horde of bodies without ever stopping.

"You have some real nerve showing up here," Hugh snaps. "Not even your brother is—*ow!* Bloody hell, Rowan, that hurt."

I intended it to.

Another step, then a semi-circle spin that angles me in front of Gregory, and there, standing in front of me is—

"Miss Carrigan," greets Saxon Priest, "tell your guard dog to stand down or he's about to find himself without fingers."

Not Damien.

A quick glance over the entrance hall reveals that he isn't here at all.

As if the blisters on my skin have turned to sieves, the giddy anticipation that carried me down two flights of stairs seeps away. I feel my shoulders fall and my pulse slow to a crawl, and it's a miracle that I manage, "Welcome to my home, Mr. Priest." I pause, running my eyes over the discoloration on his jumper—and do my best to ignore the trio of dark floaters that tag along for the ride. "From the ash on your shirt, I'm going to guess this isn't a social call."

His gaze—a strange, brilliant green—narrows. A rare display of surprise, I think. Did he really expect me to throw him out onto his arse? If he's found us here, that means Damien showed him the way or at least pointed him in the right direction.

Saxon Priest is not my enemy.

"You're not blind," he says, the words coming low and curious.

I raise a brow. "And you're more observant than I ever gave you credit for."

His mouth twitches from a straight line into something that barely qualifies for a smile. Then, with a hard glance at the men behind me, he confirms, "I'm here for Benji Lotts."

"But not Alfie Barker?"

"He's the trade-off. We'll get Benji but you'll keep Barker."

Hugh shoves himself forward, nearly knocking Samuel out of the way. "You can't just *take* either one of them," he growls. With his shoulders pressed back, he jams a finger into Saxon's chest. "We stole them from you—the both of them. And if you aren't careful, Priest, you're about to find yourself locked away, too."

I fully expect Saxon—the man who murdered so many of us without remorse—to break Hugh's fingers, as promised. But he only stands there, like a brick wall that breathes, and lowers his inscrutable green eyes to Coney's face. A beat passes. Hugh balls his hands into fists at his side.

Saxon simply sidesteps him, as easily as he would to a toddler having a tantrum. "Show me the way, would you,

Miss Carrigan?"

A hysterical laugh bubbles to life inside my chest, and it's all I can do to tell Hugh to back off as I brush past him and lead Saxon Priest toward the main flight of stairs.

Will there ever be a day when Damien and his brothers *don't* catch me off guard? Guy let me go free from the Palace when he absolutely shouldn't have. Saxon didn't break Hugh's fingers just now when he deserved it. And Damien . . .

"Is your brother all right?"

The question escapes before I can snatch it back, and Saxon's dark head jerks in my direction. Layered over his right eye is a floater, and I give a subtle shake of my head, hoping to send it scattering. When the mark barely moves, I beat back a sigh and grasp gratitude with both hands.

I'm alive. I'm breathing. *I can see.*

If Saxon Priest thinks anything of the random tic, he doesn't say so. Instead, he merely lifts his gaze to the stairwell and takes the steps two at a time. "Would you care if I said he's not?"

Yes.

God help me, but I do.

"He said that he had things to take care of," I murmur, after nearly missing the next rung when a shadow streaks past my vision, "and I'm going to guess, based on the ash on your shirt, that one of those errands had him meeting you at The Bell & Hand. He sent you to grab Lotts, didn't he?"

"You're perceptive."

"I try to read between the lines and it helps when the lines are visible."

Coming to the loft's landing, I motion for Saxon to step behind me, so that I can access the locked door. As a child, my grandmother kept this space as a play area for me, the same as she'd had it for Mum. I'm not sure she would approve of its use today. Two men shut away, one of whom who tried to kill the queen. Meanwhile, the man whose girlfriend—wife? I'm not even sure—*did* kill the king stands at my back.

No, I don't think my grandmother would approve at all.

When I reach out to input the security code, something compels me to look back at Damien's older brother. His eyes are hard like emeralds and the scar in his upper lip lends him a perpetual snarl that should have me recoiling. But I've never been one to cower from trouble, and I'm pretty sure that I can give Saxon Priest a run for his money on the scarred front.

Society dictates beauty, but what society never acknowledges is that the most beautiful amongst us are often the ugliest within.

He was dead, Damien told me, *in his heart, in his goddamned soul.*

Staring at Saxon now, I can see how that might have been true. And probably still *is* true, in many ways. *Here goes nothing.* Lifting my chin, I make a point to hold his gaze. "I'm aware that you didn't kill the king."

A muscle in his jaw flickers.

"And," I continue, picking my words carefully, "I'm aware that Isla Quinn is the one who actually pulled the trig—"

My back hits the wall with jarring force.

"You won't get within a fucking *mile* of her, do you hear me?" Saxon thrusts his face close to mine, his forearm locking across my breastbone. "I'll rip your heart out first."

Thud-thud. Thud-thud. Thud-thud.

Madness.

Damien was wrong.

Isla Quinn may have made this man whole, but she

hasn't made him human. Not completely. And I'm glad for it. Because Saxon Priest is still the man who slaughtered my people at The Octagon, and I'm still the woman who led an attack on the Palace, all with the intention of ending the Priest brothers for good. The day we become friends will probably be the day the world ends.

"I want to apologize," I tell him, my arms hanging loosely at my sides, "for what I've done."

His feral expression shutters.

Having second thoughts about snapping my neck?

Biting back the caustic remark, I push onward. "Your brother said that it's insincere to apologize for something you once believed in. I agree with the logic, with *him*, but I'm going to apologize anyway—for any fear you faced, for the hurt I caused. But, mostly, I'm sorry that it's because of me that you were forced to choose between Isla and your brothers."

Stilted silence envelops the landing, and I'm distinctively aware that though I hear air rushing past my lips, Saxon appears unmoved. His breathing, his coloring, are as if we've been discussing nothing more controversial than the weather. The man has all the emotional dexterity of an iceberg.

After searching my gaze, he pulls back. "I didn't."

My head snaps up. "Sorry?"

"Have you ever been loved, Miss Carrigan?"

The unexpected question rocks me back on my heels.

Have I ever been loved?

I'd like to think that Margaret loves me, and that Ian did, too, in his own way, but something tells me that's not what Saxon means at all. He's talking about the sort of love that's reserved for a partner, a soul mate, the person who will move Heaven and Earth to keep you safe, and it guts me that if he has to ask, then the answer must be painstakingly obvious.

"No." The forced smile on my face wilts then disappears altogether. "No, I've never been so lucky."

The hardness in his eyes softens. "It wasn't a choice between them or her," he rumbles, putting his hands on his hips, "it was a choice between Holyrood or the woman who loves me—and that wasn't a choice at all."

"But you're here, aren't you?" I gesture toward the door. "You're here while Isla isn't, so have you really chosen at all?"

"Damien asked me. And I couldn't tell him—"

A heavy *thud* hitting the floor to my left has me twisting at the waist, and when I see the . . . the *body* there, I wish that I hadn't looked at all.

Mangled.

Bloodied.

Ruined.

The unfamiliar man remains curled in a ball where he fell, his dark hair matted to his dirt-streaked forehead. His clothes are disheveled, his bruised wrists shackled. And his fingernails . . . all but two have been ripped clean from their beds. I don't know why that, more than anything else, disturbs me most. Feeling weak in the knees, I press the back of my hand to my mouth to keep the bile down.

"Christ," whispers Saxon.

And then I hear footsteps coming up the stairs. Heavy, commanding. Deadly. A tread I recognize almost as well as my own. It's not how I envisioned this moment unfolding. Not with his brother standing an arm's width away or with the battered figure of a stranger, half-alive, in the fetal position at my feet.

There's no chance to run.

The toe of a dirtied black boot appears first.

It pauses on the landing, the sole pressing flat against

the rung, as if its owner recognizes the scent of fear—
unease—that's rife in the air, and then the boot flattens.
Pushes forward, carrying with it the man himself.

I don't allow myself to raise my gaze and no one says
a word.

He stops before me, and the distinction between my
bare feet and those boots is staggering. One freshly showered, the other caked with dried blood. I kneeled before
them just this morning. Was *bound* before them just last
night. Dark denim trousers pull my eyes up past long legs
and rock-hard thighs. At his sides, his calloused hands flex
and unfurl.

There's no hiding the blood.

No pretending that he wasn't the cause of the stranger's suffering.

And so I continue my upward trajectory, hearing my
heart in my ears, feeling the sweat in my palms.

I take in the black, armored vest that clings to an impossibly broad chest and the wide shoulders that look as if
they've been carved from the Highland's most formidable
crags. The right sleeve of his pullover is missing, exposing a
thickly muscled arm and a deep gash that spills blood over
a canvas of inked skin.

A shattered breath spills over my lips.

More tattoos peek out past his tattered collar, leading
up to a tan throat and a hard jawline dusted with dark
stubble—a jaw that I've touched, cupped, and which is now
dirtied with blood. His or the stranger's? I don't dare ask.
Not yet. Not until I'm done. Those impossibly soft lips are
firm, pressed flat under my slow, thorough perusal. Flared
nostrils, a crooked, once-broken nose. High cheekbones
that ought to belong to a model on a catwalk, somewhere
else in the world, but not here, not on this man who's been

kissed by Death.

And then I arrive at my final destination.

The windows to the soul.

Eyes that are nothing like the teal waters of Cornwall but belong to the deepest, hottest blue of a flickering flame. I feel their warmth, even now. The rage that burns beneath his tattooed skin, the darkness that clings to him as it always has to me. Every chaotic, merciless desire lives in that distinct shade, forever tumultuous, forever vengeful, and I feel their narrowing like he's physically traced a finger down the length of my spine.

My chest expands with a sharp breath. A beat later, his inflates just the same.

We're tethered, bound.

For better or worse.

"You see me," he rasps.

His face is smeared with blood, his body tense like he's prepared to chase me should I run, but I never avert my gaze from his. The blue enflames me, the chaos there consumes me, and I only whisper one thing: "I see you, Damien. I see all of you."

CHAPTER 29

DAMIEN

Violet eyes stalk my every move.

She watches as I haul a furious Benji out of Holly Village's makeshift prison.

She watches as I replace him with the sole survivor from tonight's attack on The Bell & Hand, never missing a beat when I make a point to re-shackle the man's wrists at his spine, so that he has no choice but to sit uncomfortably until I return.

And she watches while I stand on the front drive to see Saxon off, the curtain in her bedroom window casting her in shadow—but I know she's there, waiting.

Her watchful gaze is a blessing just as much as it's a curse.

Because now she sees you for who you really are.

The monster.

The villain.

The man with war in his blood and hate in his heart.

I don't know when Rowena became my judge, jury, and executioner, or when our roles became reversed, but each dried speck of blood on my skin feels like a strike against me—a reason, as if I haven't already given her plenty, to keep her distance. To keep her warmth.

Discreetly, I scrape my palms over my trousers for the fourth time since feeling her gaze on the back of my head.

It does me no good.

I'm still stained, still tainted.

"You're a bastard," Benji throws at me, over his shoulder, as he jerks open the back door of Saxon's car. Twisting around, he juts his chin forward. "You left me in there with fucking Alfie Barker!"

"Did you get anything useful out of him?"

The dangerous flicker in the man's gaze dims. "Tell me you're taking the piss. Tell me, Priest, that you didn't leave me *locked in that room* all so I could spend a little one-on-one time with Barker."

Two birds, one stone.

In Holyrood, it's explicitly forbidden to go after another agent. Locking Benji in that room was the only penance I could dole out after what he did to Saxon. But I'll be lying if I say that his taking advantage of the situation didn't also cross my mind. If he's half the spy that he thinks he is, he'll have jumped on the opportunity.

"Well," I say, "did you?"

With a heavy sigh, Benji shoves his fingers through his hair. "Just more of the same shite. According to him, it's a whole network that he was involved with and he was just the grunt taking orders from the top."

"Except we know it was just one person," Saxon cuts in. It's the first time he's spoken since he saw me in the loft, and I recognize the glimmer in his gaze. My always silent brother has something he wants to say, and I'm not surprised that he's waited until we're out of earshot from everyone in Holly Village. "Isla said something to me on the night that Buckingham Palace caught fire," he goes on stiffly, "said that a man like Barker has something to lose and we should cut a deal with him. Use him instead of punishing him."

Benji's mouth drops open. "He wanted to kill the queen! We can't just . . . do you *hear* yourself, man? Treason is a crime."

"He's just one man."

Both men turn to look at me, Benji's expression revolted and my brother's contemplative. "Right now, he's nothing but collateral damage," I add, meeting Saxon's gaze with a brief nod, "when we could be putting him to work. He does what we want, and we give him back to his daughters. It's a win-win."

"It's illegal."

I look at Benji. "Illegal according to who? No one oversees us."

"Your brother, for one."

"Guy wants answers. I don't think he cares how he gets them."

Benji's gaze shifts from me to Saxon and back again. "I want it known that I think it's a bad idea." And with that, he climbs into the backseat, sprawls out on the bench, and throws an arm over his face like he can block out the sight of us. I shove the door closed behind him.

Fucking prick.

Instead of following Benji's lead, Saxon visibly wavers.

Eyeing the muscle ticking in his jaw, I say, "Get it off your chest."

Under the moonlight, Saxon's gaze slips past me, up to the window with its parted curtains, and I know that he's spotted Rowena when his shoulders stiffen. "You said that you'd be right behind me after you took care of the dead, and then you showed up looking like . . ." Lowering his stare to the pavement, he scrubs a palm over his mouth. "*Christ,*

Damien. I don't even know who you are right now."

The blood itches my skin.

"It's nothing that we haven't done before." The words leave me calm, easy. My brother might be a mind reader but even he can't see that I'm close to the edge of no return, that my veins are black with sludge and sin and secrets. We've done worse for Holyrood, for the Crown, but never for our own personal gain. Tonight was about vengeance. Tonight was contained rage finally spilling free and an irrational need to make someone else suffer as I have. It was spotting an opportunity and taking it, to hell with the consequences.

And the consequences were dire: I've never felt hollower than I did climbing the steps to Holly Village's loft only to find Saxon and Rowena already there. Her expression . . . the *revulsion* that I first spied—

I slip shaky fingers into my trouser pockets, though it's too late to hide what I've done. The Mad Priest took action, and all bore witness to his misdeeds. *My* misdeeds. "I needed to know who was tailing me. Whether it was Carrigan or—"

"It could be anyone and you—" He goes to grab me by the kit but yanks back at the last second after another glance at Rowena's window. Breathing heavily, he drops his hand onto the car's bonnet. "You are not the man who bloodies someone for the hell of it. You are not the man who loses his temper. You're *good*, better than me, better than Guy. Boy genius with a heart of gold, remember?"

The old nickname feels like an actual knife to the heart.

While growing up, my brothers kept me swaddled in a protective bubble that they never dared to pop. When Guy finally put me to work, he kept me cloistered away from danger, up on the rooftops where I scouted anti-loyalists or sandwiched between Robert Guthram and Jayme Paul for safekeeping.

But what Guy and Saxon never realized was that the bubble existed only to them.

Boy genius I may have been but I've never had a heart of gold. More times than not, I never had a heart at all.

"You have the wrong man, brother," I utter softly, "because I'm not him."

"I don't," is Saxon's gruff response, "and you are. There are things in this world I won't claim to understand but *you*—bloody fucking hell, you aren't one of them. You base every decision on reason and you don't act on emotion. You're stability, the only person in Holyrood without a goddamn screw loose. *That's* who you are."

It's possibly the most Saxon has said to me in years.

It's also nothing but his perception.

Reason keeps me grounded when I'm wound so tight that it's only a matter of time before I implode and take out everything around me in the aftermath. It wasn't until Guy sat me down before a computer that I tasted tranquility. The numbers provided intrigue, the coding provided structure—the combination of both was a balm to the chaos, a glimpse of bliss like I'd never known. I took to it the only way a lad bent on saving himself can. Obsessively. My very first addiction.

Sometimes I wonder if Guy wasn't saving us all by locking me inside the Palace.

"Damien," Saxon growls, "are you listening to me? I said that . . ."

His raspy voice fades to a hum as my bloodied fingers grasp Mum's necklace from my bloodied vest. I pull it free, the silver links clinking together when I hold it tight. Silently, I reach for Saxon's hand. There's no turning back from this confession, and some long-buried part of my soul screams to stop, that it's not too late to end this here and now.

This is not how you want him to remember you.

No.

But, fucking hell, it'll feel good to be seen.

I see you, Damien. I see all of you.

Rowena saw me all right.

Never mind that it was because of her that I put down my wire coil when the man begged me to spare his life. Shame had invaded me then. She would know, wouldn't she? She'd recognize the pungent, unmistakable scent of blood on my skin. And I'd feared her disappointment. Dreaded the heat in her touch disappearing when I reached for her next. It wasn't a risk that I was willing to take, I decided.

I found mercy too late.

Because when her violet eyes finally held mine, she saw every part of me.

Bloodied. Depraved. Shattered.

Ignoring the inexplicable heaviness in my chest, I apply pressure to the inside of Saxon's wrist. His hand flexes open, and I drop the chain into his waiting palm.

"The clasp," I tell him, voice low.

Saxon's fingers work over the necklace in the dim moonlight, his body angling toward the headlamps so he can get a good look at the inscription. Benji sits up in the backseat to bang a fist on the window. I shift in front of him so that he can't see my brother.

This is for no one but Saxon.

Slowly, my brother's head comes up. His face is drawn, his stare shuttered. Then his Adam's apple bobs down the length of his throat, and it's all the confirmation I need.

He might not want to believe it, but he knows.

The chain loops over his forefinger as he straightens. "We buried this with her."

I nod. "We did."

"No." When he shakes his fist, the necklace jerks like the legs of the hanged. "We buried this with her, Damien. Twenty-four years ago, we *buried this with her*."

Feeling strangely unburdened, I hold his stare. "She hasn't had it for twelve."

My teeth rattle as I'm shoved against the car.

Saxon grips my vest in both fists. "*Why?*" His green eyes are wild, troubled. "Why the hell would you . . . Christ, I can't even say it. *I can't even say it*."

"No mercy, brother."

"No mercy? She was our *mother*."

"Not to me," I husk, "never to me."

His hands loosen their grip on me but don't pull away. "There was something wrong with her. Guy knew it, I knew it. Pa probably knew it, too, before he died. But she never . . . Bloody fucking hell, she didn't deserve to be—"

"Unburied," I finish, because if he can't bring himself to say it then I will. "And I felt nothing—no remorse, no grief. *That's* the man I am, Saxon, the man I've always been." Nodding my chin toward the car, I mutter, "You made a choice, Holyrood or Isla, and you chose happiness."

"Damien—"

"You *deserve* that," I growl, giving him a push. "What happened tonight is for me to handle, not you. Go back to Oxford and stay there."

"Ask me for help. Fucking *ask* me—"

Quietly, I utter the words that I know will break him: "You aren't Holyrood. Not anymore."

His chin snaps back like I've plowed a fist into his face.

"I'm your brother."

Always.

But I won't have Saxon trading his life for mine. He walked away. He chose love. I want that for him. Fucking hell, I want that for him so bad that it feels like I'm being torn in two. I should never have sent Guy and the queen to him after the attack on the Palace. I should never have had him meet me at The Bell & Hand. *Selfish.* So goddamned selfish when he finally has a reason to put down the gun and live for a future that doesn't carry with it the scent of death and misery.

I've spent a lifetime on a solitary track—it's no different now.

"Keep the necklace," I tell him, angling my shoulder past him so that he has no choice but to let me walk free. "No doubt she's been turning over in her grave ever since I took it."

CHAPTER 30

DAMIEN

My heart thunders in my chest as I stand before Rowena's door with my fist raised to knock.

I ought to fill her in on what happened tonight. Explain about the men who followed me all afternoon and the fight at The Bell & Hand. At least she can take small comfort in knowing that her father wasn't behind today's clusterfuck.

No, according to the confession that I wrought from my little interrogation, that particular honor belongs to the Met's police commissioner. Not that I'm surprised. Courtesy of Marcus Guthram and The Metropolitan Police, I'm the UK's number one fugitive. And, thanks to Guthram, Saxon was recently put behind bars for a murder that he didn't commit.

You'll thank me for this, brother.

Maybe not today or tomorrow, but one day he'll look back at this moment and he'll be grateful. Because there's only one way to make a dog like Guthram heel, and it's to put him down.

More death.

More needless bloodshed.

Don't do it, Godwin. Don't go to her like this.

Bloodied. Depraved. Shattered.

The veins in my forearm pop as I clench my fist, tight, and wrench away from Rowena's door. Spinning on my heel, I force distance between us when every chord within me is singing only one note: *I need you, I need you, I need you.*

Her warmth.

Her iron spine.

That cunning smile of hers that makes my bones fucking ache.

I slam my door shut with the heel of my boot, then cut across the bedroom in five long strides. My palm hits the switch for the loo, flooding the room with light. Avoiding the mirror, I lean into the shower, past the curtain, and turn the water to piping hot.

And then I begin to strip.

Bloodied clothes hit the tiled floor. Pain pulses in my right arm from the round that grazed me. Need and want war within my soul, a tumultuous battle that has no victor because Rowena deserves more than I can give her. She rose from the ashes of Buckingham Palace, burned and blind, and she's fought for life every step of the way. She's a phoenix rising and I'm a man wreathed in violence.

I won't have her see me like this again.

The first hit of water is like stepping past the gates of Hell. Hot, scalding, and still not enough to eviscerate the memory of Rowena's horrified gaze when she finally laid eyes on me. Blood and shame run in rivulets down my legs. They stain the marble red. Circle the drain but don't go down as the old pipes back up and water rises at my feet.

Caustic laughter scratches at my throat.

If only purging my sins was as easy as washing the grime from my flesh.

But I try.

Fucking hell, I *try*.

With soap and water, I scrub until my skin is raw and the water is ice. Pa warned me of this. The only time I can remember him sitting down with me, away from Mum's always-narrowed eyes and my brothers' antics, he put me on his lap and said, "There's no hope for a man who falls to madness."

He'd meant the king.

The words have always resonated with me. There's no hope. No possibility of salvation. And I'm tired, so fucking *tired*, of the rage and the fear and the goddamn need to keep fighting when I've already fallen. I feel the fatigue in my marrow. Feel the exhaustion that sits heavy on my chest because I'm terrified to sleep for even a second. The same terror shadows me even now as water slips past my lowered head to my spine.

With my forearm planted against the marble wall, I feel it wash over my left shoulder blade and sense nothing on the right.

Dead, nerveless skin.

"Damien."

Peeling my eyes open, I meet violet through a cascade of water.

I need you.

Had she heard my unspoken plea while I stood outside her door? Had she sensed the raw desperation within me that demanded that she let me inside her room, inside her bed, inside her sweet cunt? Or had she known, from the very second that Saxon's car peeled off and I turned to look up at her window, that I'm a man walking a path straight to purgatory and I don't trust myself not to take her down with me?

I'm doused in a sheet of ice and feel only the grips of fire, and my fingers dig into the soaked tile to keep from reaching for her.

As if she's heard my thoughts, Rowena sucks her bottom lip behind her upper teeth. Her fingers grip the curtain under her chin, the material bunching between her knuckles like she's aching to touch me, too. But she doesn't give in to temptation and she doesn't pull the curtain back for a better look.

She lets me keep my privacy.

She lets me have the moment to myself, should I want it.

Such a subtle show of respect when anyone else would have stopped to stare at my cock. But Rowena's body was once her father's greatest political asset, and I'm not surprised that she doesn't feel comfortable forcing others to reveal what they haven't personally chosen to share. Because while she's felt all of me twice now—her hands greedily conquering every piece of me—that was before her sight returned.

Now she sees all of me, and I feel wrecked.

Tortured.

"I didn't . . ." My throat burns, tongue scrapes against the dry roof of my mouth. The cold water continues to drench my skin. "I wanted to be clean." *For you.* "I wanted to be . . . better."

Her throat works with a convulsive swallow, and the smile she gives me . . . Jesus. It's not cunning, not even remotely lethal. No. It's soft and gentle and *sweet.* My heart kicks against my rib cage and I'm half-aware of pressing my palm flat to the tiled wall as I turn myself toward her. I drift closer. Lower my head and breathe her in, absorbing the sweetness of that smile and the soft, beckoning look in her gaze.

Would she let me kiss her?

A shudder rolls down my spine, and I briefly close my

eyes against the intensity of the want.

I need you.

"Rowena—" I start at the same time that she blurts, "Do you trust me?"

"What?"

She pushes the curtain down, just enough so that I can see her from the neck up. Steam has plastered her cotton shirt to her skin and turned her cheeks a rosy pink. Violet eyes blink up at me, then narrow slightly like she's gathering her nerve. "I want to know if you trust me."

A little over twenty-four hours ago, I fell from a roof thanks to her men. Twenty hours ago, I buried myself inside her with no other motive than the purely selfish—I wanted to make her come just as much as I wanted to feel alive. Rowena Carrigan is an addiction that I never could have foreseen. I wanted her even when I hated her, and I chased her even when I should have kept my distance.

I should still keep my distance.

In the end, though, my need for her is merciless. And I want . . . for just a little while longer, I want to own all that softness.

"Answer me one thing."

Her brows lift in question. "Another confession?"

"Yes." Turning off the shower, I let the water drain at my feet. The blood is gone but not the shame. The latter slips over me like a second skin, cinching tight around my throat, my heart. "Do you fear me, Rowena?" I ask softly.

Violet eyes meet mine, steady, intensely focused.

The phantom shackles around my wrists tremble, desperate to unlock. And then they clatter to the tile at my feet when her reply comes barely above a whisper: "You make me feel too much, Damien. You make me feel like I'm dancing with madness. So, yes, I fear you—I fear you like I've never feared anything else in my life. But if you're asking if you *frighten* me, then my answer is no. I'm not sure you could, honestly, even if you tried."

A breath that I didn't realize I was holding floods my lungs. I gasp it in, and then give in to temptation to touch a finger to her chin. God, she's beautiful. "My answer is yes—I trust you."

She clasps a hand over my wrist. "Then meet me in my room in ten minutes. And don't be late."

CHAPTER 31

ROWENA

Damien enters my bedroom on silent feet.

Even with my back to the door and the rush of water hitting the porcelain tub to muffle the sound of his footsteps, I know it's him. The air changes with his presence. It thickens and electrifies, and any hope I had of faking casual indifference after my *not*-so-indifferent confession goes out the window when his velvet voice rasps my name.

Moving my hand on the standing tub, to better balance my weight on the stool, I turn and watch him approach.

He's beautiful.

Brawny frame. Thick, corded muscles. Each step he takes is a lesson in sensuality. Lithe, powerful. He advances toward me like a predator, and I have the distinct impression that he's chasing me all over again even though I'm stationary. His blue eyes home in on my face, never wavering. He offers no smile, no pleasantries. It's him and me, and the escalating tension between us, and the carnal look on his face that reads, *You'll break for me, and enjoy every second of the wreckage.*

Feeling off-kilter, I slide a trembling hand between my clamped knees and tilt my chin toward the tub. "You mentioned that you wanted to feel better, and I thought, maybe, I could—"

"When did your vision come back?"

As if to mock me, the floaters in my right eye land on his gorgeous face. I smother a howl of frustration. "Earlier, when I was reaching for a towel after my shower. I didn't bother with turning on the lights but still saw a shadow out of the corner of my eye. It was just like what Dr. Matthews said—one moment I saw nothing and then I did."

"And you see . . . everything?"

"Everything that matters," I tell him softly.

Blue eyes fall to the tub that's steaming with hot water, and a muscle leaps in his jaw.

A seed of awkwardness blooms in my stomach.

In the span of nine days, I've been with this man in every way that matters—angry, naked, vulnerable—and I think . . . I think that if I'm being truly honest with myself, there's been a sense of relief in not being able to physically see him. Oh, I heard the different nuances in his tone and I read his mood in a heartbeat whenever he brushed his hands over my body. But when he fell to silence, or when his expression contorted with anger or lust, I saw none of it.

I existed in a vacuum that was, in many ways, a shelter from the storm.

There's no hiding now.

Instead, I feel unsteady, like he's set me down in a tiny boat and pushed me out to sea without a single oar to carry me back to shore. I feel every wave that crests the hull and every sharp gust of wind that sets me farther off course.

My grip on the tub tightens. "When I first looked at you—when I *saw* you—you were lost to the darkness."

Those blue eyes of his flicker to my face, startled, and I almost say, *I understand.* Because, God help us both, but

I do. He looks haunted, and hunted, and if I thought he'd accept it, I'd leap to my feet and take the five steps separating us to wrap him in a hug. Uncertainty, however, keeps my arse planted on the stool after I shut off the water tap.

"You let it win tonight, didn't you?"

"I drowned, Rowena. It didn't just win, I . . . *Jesus*." His Adam's apple bobs with a hard swallow, and he presses his shoulder against the wall closest to him. His entire body sags into the support while his big hands slip into the front pockets of his trousers. Deep down, I can't help but wonder if he's ever allowed himself to appear so vulnerable. After a moment, he admits, "I let myself drown in a way that I haven't in years."

"Why?"

His dark brows furrow. "What do you mean why?"

"What happened tonight that made you lose self-control?"

That unsmiling mouth quirks at the corners, and my heart flutters hopelessly. "Self-control is a figment of our imagination. It's the rules of society telling us that we need to keep silent when we want to scream or that we ought to walk when all we want to do is run."

"You're saying it's a social construct?"

"I'm saying that I can act as well as the best of them, but I'm the man screaming when no one is listening and I'm running when the rest of the world is down on their hands and knees."

"And tonight?" I prod gently. "What happened tonight?"

The muscle in his jaw jumps again, and then he confesses, "I let the world hear me scream."

Oh, Damien.

As if my hand belongs to someone else, I watch myself reach for him. Palm up. Fingers loosely curled. Not so unlike how I found Clarke at Buckingham Palace. My heart constricts with the thought. Had he reached for Margaret when he fell? Did she take his hand, just once more, before making her escape? And if she didn't . . . how had he born it?

Because I don't think I'll survive if Damien turns away from me now.

I stare at my fingers, silently begging them to drop before the humiliation of rejection really kicks in. But here I am, still reaching, still hoping, when slowly I lift my gaze—and am ensnared by the hottest, most visceral shade of blue that I've ever seen.

Take my hand.

Please *take my hand.*

"I thought of you," comes his deep baritone, his cheeks flushed with color.

Instinctively my fingers curl against my palm like his voice is a tangible caress that I feel down the pearls of my spine. "Tonight, you mean?"

"Every moment since we've met, Rowena." He gives a low laugh, then combs his fingers through his still-wet hair. "Even when I wanted you dead, I thought of you. I was *dying* and, fucking still, my mind went to you. Always to you."

"What happened at the Palace, up on the roof, I never meant for you to be—"

"You were the angel." When my brows shoot up in surprise, he ducks his chin like he's uncomfortable with the admission. "The devil on his shoulder," he adds stiffly, "and the angel dead on the floor, defeated. Except that you're not dead"—vivid blue eyes swiftly meet mine—"and I was fully prepared to add another death to my tally tonight." Lips pressing flat, he brings a hand to his hard jaw. "Only, I couldn't do it. After a lifetime of doing what has to be done, no matter the cost, I *couldn't do it.*"

The god who dons the crown of the hero . . . Somehow, I knew it would always come to this with him. Damien Godwin is only the villain in his own nightmare.

"Why?" I ask.

"I worried you'd smell blood on me. Be horrified by me. And I wanted . . ."

My heart beats fast in my throat. "You wanted what?"

His gaze falls to my outstretched palm. Hunger glimmers in the blue, a flickering flame that burns so hot that I feel scorched. "I learned at a very young age that death waits for no one. Instead it waits in the wings to steal you away, always in the moment when you least expect it. Meanwhile every wish you had, every hope you ever clung to, is gone. You're lucky if you bothered to live but damned if you spent an entire lifetime waiting to die."

Shadows dance along my right peripheral.

Or maybe it's just the tears threatening to spill free.

I've amassed a fortune over the years and reclaimed ownership of my body. I've said yes to a king and saved a queen. And I don't think I realized, until this very moment, anyway, how very little room I've given myself to hope or dream. I live because I draw air into my lungs and put food in my belly, and I live because it's expected that I'll continue putting one foot in front of the other, day after day. But I haven't *wished* on anything in so long that I'm not even sure it's a skill that I still possess.

Have you ever been loved, Miss Carrigan?

Sweat dampens my palms.

That would be my one wish—to love and be loved.

To feel its heat in my veins and its courage in my bones. To know that when I wake each morning, it's to a face that I dream of when I sleep. I want laughter and the adventure that comes with tackling life beside your soul mate. I want the fierceness of safety while facing the risk of falling ever deeper. And if I let myself hope, if I really let myself dream, I wish that this man would chase me to the ends of the Earth, just so he could catch me in the end.

"Is that what you wanted?" I ask, my voice hoarse with unshed tears. "To make a wish?"

Damien pushes away from the wall.

His long legs demolish the space between us until he's right there in front of me. Tall as he is, his eyes are level with mine when he drops to his haunches and clasps my outstretched hand. Calloused against soft, big against small. He traces my lifelines with his forefinger before gently bringing my hand to his mouth.

He kisses the center of my palm with his eyes closed.

"I want to live," he says on a rough breath, "I want to live long enough to know happiness. I want to feel it, Rowena, here"—he presses my hand to his heart, which beats solidly inside his chest—"and I want to be the man who loves first and loves hardest. That's what I want, but what I *wish* . . ." Steadily, he meets my gaze. "I wish that I could kiss you, just once. I wish that—"

I crush my mouth to his.

A harsh sound rises in his throat and then his hands clasp the back of my head and he's dragging me close, close, close until my arse is nearly off the stool and it's only the strength of his body that keeps me from falling to the floor.

His kiss isn't patient or gentlemanly because Damien Godwin is no Prince Charming here to whisk me away on his white steed, and I'm a woman who will always save herself.

No.

Our kiss is a brutal clash of lips, a spiral of desperation when the world around us is crumbling at our feet. Our kiss is heat and burning fire when my heart has been frozen and neglected for years. Our kiss is *us*, a perpetual battle of the wills that has me sinking my fingers into his hair and tugging on the strands, hard, because I want to hear him *groan*.

Like melody in my ears, he feeds it to me guttural and low against my lips.

His fingers flex over my shorn head, and he seeks retribution with a nip of his teeth. *God, yes.* I pull away to seek out his chin, the underside of his jaw. My nails rake through his thick hair, over the slope of his nape, and then my lips find the hollow of his throat. I press an open-mouthed kiss to his racing pulse, and then another, because I live for the way he curses beneath his breath.

Then he tugs me back up for more.

Against my mouth, he growls, "Open for me, Rowena."

I can't find the strength to tell him no.

My lips fall open and his tongue swoops in, and he consumes me like I'm the oxygen he needs to see another sunrise. My head falls back into the cradle of his hands and he angles our mouths at a slant, pressing deeper, invading me completely.

I'll die if he stops.

So when he lifts me in his arms and carries me into the bedroom, I cling to his shoulders. And when he lowers me to the bed, I all but whimper as he separates us to pull his shirt over his head. It lands on the floor with a whisper.

"Touch me," he husks, bringing my right hand to his chest, "please touch me."

Dark scrolls of ink bleed across his sculpted upper body.

There's little rhyme or reason to the abstract tattoos on his biceps; they're as tangible as wisps of smoke slipping through my fingers. But my pulse quickens when I spy the figure inked over his hard chest: a raven in profile, the lower half of its body morphing into a skull with wings of burnished red. My gaze catches on the inscription below, and I drag my fingers over the words written in Old Norse. "What does it mean?"

He catches my wrist. Flattens my palm over the ink like he hopes that I'll feel the words in my soul just as he feels them in his. "'Two ravens flew from Odin's shoulders,'" he says, "'Huginn to the hanged and Muninn to the slain.'"

"You see yourself as the dispatcher of death? Like the ravens Odin sent to the corpses?"

Damien's blue eyes are fathomless, ancient. Haunted. "No, love, I *am* Death."

And then, before I even have the chance to digest the implication of that statement *or* the endearment that tripped off his tongue, he brings his mouth back to mine in a kiss that leaves me breathless and squirming on the bed.

He pins my wrists above my head and lowers himself into the cradle of my hips. I arch my spine, an invitation for him to bring me closer, if he wants, and he takes the offering with a throaty groan. One palm slips beneath me, to the small of my back, before sweeping around my waist to press flush against my stomach. Careful to avoid my sensitive skin, he fists the fabric of my shirt and bares my breasts to his hungry gaze.

"Jesus, you're beautiful to me." Blue eyes hooded, those soft lips of his swollen. He meets my stare, studying me with that quiet, intense way of his, and then he drops his head and slicks his tongue over my nipple.

The first touch is heaven, the second downright electric.

By the time he's alternating between swirling his tongue and flicking at the hardened bud, I'm coming off the bed with desperate moans that he quiets with a hand over my mouth and a wicked glint in his eye.

Yes. Yes.

His other palm finds my hip, his fingers gripping me tight. And then he tilts his hips against mine in a slow, sensual grind that leaves me shattered and panting. My joggers are thin, his denim trousers practically plastered to his erection, and the *friction*—

I cry out against the prison of his hand.

Then, framing his face, I drag him back up so that I can feast on his mouth. I bite his bottom lip and sweep my tongue over the flesh to ease the sting. I beg for entry with a whimper and he parts his lips on command, letting me steal my way inside. The scruff on his jaw abrades my skin but I can't find it in myself to back away. And all the while, he nudges my right leg from his waist and plants it flat on the mattress, at a ninety-degree angle, so that when I pull back for air and glance down, there's no missing the way he rocks against my core with every pump of his hips. Muscles straining, ink rippling.

He's driving me to the brink of insanity, and I feel *worshipped.*

"Make me yours," I pant against his mouth.

His breath catches, his hips ceasing all movement. Slowly, he eases his forehead against mine. "A dangerous wish."

"I'm choosing to live." Leaning up on one elbow, I tug on his earlobe with my teeth. "Escape into the sunshine with me, Damien. Just for a little bit."

His only answer is to crash his mouth down over mine.

He swallows my cry of surprise and he soothes my restless whimpers with delicious strokes of his tongue. Then, with his hands gripping my upper arms, he tugs me with him when he sits up. He feeds me a frantic kiss before stripping off his trousers and then gives me another that's no less all-consuming after he pulls my joggers and knickers down the length of my legs.

Naked, he sits on the edge of the bed with his feet planted on the floor. Lets his knees fall open like he's leaving space for me to crawl between them. Voice low, he orders, "Straddle me."

Not yet.

This bubble we've created around ourselves will pop soon. Someone is hunting Margaret and someone else is still stalking Damien and his brothers, and once this moment ends, I fear we'll be forced right back into the harsh-limned light of reality. I'm not ready to return to a Britain on the brink of war; I'm not ready to let go of this small corner of the world where wishes come true and we feed the beast of hope instead of slaughtering it for putting us at risk.

Needing to make these seconds last the length of forever, I dip my chin. "Let me look at you first. Let me *see* you."

It's more than I thought to have after days where darkness swallowed me whole.

Crawling off the bed, I back up and take him in. The hair-dusted calves and the thick, muscular thighs. The heavy cock that bobs against his ripped stomach and the ink scrawled in Old Norse, and I must be overtly ogling him because Damien grips the base of his hard-on with a low groan.

"Go ahead," I murmur, my mouth dry.

"Jesus, Rowena."

I shake my head, sending floaters scattering.

And I watch, unable to look away, as he skims his big hand up the length of his cock. The vein in his throat visibly throbs, the color in his cheeks turning a muted pink that has nothing to do with hesitation and everything to do with lust, with *want*. He teases me with a short pump at the crown. Drags his palm over the head before moving down to circle the root.

I touch my tongue to my bottom lip.

A beat later, his knuckles whiten with tension when he plants his free hand down on the mattress.

Muscles ripple under his inked skin as he physically sinks into his grip, his thighs spreading wider, his shoulders appearing that much broader when he eases into his tight fist, over and over again. His flame-blue eyes are fixed on my face. I sense his anticipation of what's to come, feel his urgency for me in every thrust that he gives himself. He's a vision. Delicious. Wicked. Dark hair falls over his forehead and his lids lower to half-mast. Then his head tips back, his throat working with a deep groan, and the hand on his cock squeezes the crown and sinks back down a little rougher with every pass.

My mouth waters.

Heart races.

"I need you," he rasps, fisting the sheets in one hand as his hips begin to pump hard and fast into his hand. "Rowena, *I need you.*"

I don't make him wait.

He grasps my hips the second that I'm within reach and he brings me in, so that the mattress dips with the pressure of my knees on either side of his hips. Down past the raven and skull, his abdominal muscles clench with restraint as he palms my spread thighs. Bruised hands against unmarred legs. Supple flesh that pinkens when he grips me hard and begs for my mouth.

I say yes with my lips.

Say yes with my body, too, as I reach down to position his cock against my entrance. We're doing it again—the reckless, wanton thing—but neither of us says no as I lower myself down on top of him, fast and hard until his palms go to my arse and he stills all downward movement.

My eyes fly to his. "I thought—"

"Let me bring you to the sun." His lips curl to one side, as if he enjoys the thought of me bathing in warm sunlight. "A wish for a wish, Rowena. You gave me mine and I'll be damned if I don't give you yours."

I kiss him again, open-mouthed and raw, and my core muscles clench when I feel him lift me until only the crown of his cock remains inside. He thrusts upward, lifting his hips, then brings me down a little more.

Oh, my God.

I try to squirm, to grind my hips down, but he doesn't let me take control.

Pulling back with a gasp, I meet his gaze, only to find blue already waiting for me. His teeth sink into his bottom lip, the pink flesh turning white under the pressure. One glance down reveals the strain in his arm muscles, the control he's exerting to set the slow, anguished pace, to make it last and make it good. He lowers me again, and I clutch his shoulders at the overwhelming sensation of him stretching me.

"My left," he grits out, "mark me on my left."

There's something he's not telling me, something that briefly tugs his gaze away from mine as he utters the request, but I give it to him anyway. I press my hand flat on his right pectoral muscle while raking my nails down his left shoulder. He groans, low and throaty, and kicks his chin back as he drives his cock deep inside me in a single thrust.

A cry rips from my lips.

My head falls back on my shoulders.

Leaning forward, he brushes his mouth over my throat before dropping his head to tease my nipple with his teeth. Gooseflesh erupts over my skin. The rhythmic tug of his mouth, the relentless thrusts of his cock, the hot skin beneath my hands that trembles like he's desperate to hold on . . . I'm coming apart at the seams and there'll be nothing to stitch back together when he's through with me.

"Damien," I whisper raggedly, "this is . . . this is—"

His blue eyes lift to mine. "It's living," he growls, "and happiness, and fucking hell, Rowena, I don't care if it's madness, too. I want it and I want you, and God help us both, but I'm going to have you no matter what."

Tears sting my eyes, blurring his face. Shadows dance in the periphery, a silent reminder that danger always lurks around the corner, just waiting to strike in a moment of vulnerability. And then I give all of myself over to the moment.

To *him*.

I take each hard thrust as if it's my due; I fight his hold on my hips with tiny circles that make him breathe hard through his nose; and I drag my mouth over his, swallowing those pants of his to claim them as my own. He moves inside me, fucking me hard, without mercy, and I feel myself tighten around him.

My fingers dig into his left shoulder. "I'm going to come. Damien, oh, *God*."

His mouth finds mine while he brings one hand between us to rub my clit. "Let go," he rasps, "let go and I'll catch you."

I don't have the chance to return the sentiment because he angles his hips just right and I splinter above him. My legs tremble in his grip, my heart teeters in my chest. It's too soon. It's too soon to care to beg for more, but we're bound in a way that bears no reason or understanding. He drags me down on top of his cock, his eyes squeezing shut and his jaw clenching tight. He's lost to the moment, to the sensation of living, and when he comes, he yanks himself free of me and spills onto my thigh at the very last second.

His shoulders heave with hard breaths.

His fingers knead my thighs.

And then, so quietly that I nearly miss the words: "I would chase you to the ends of the Earth, Rowena. I would chase you forever if I could."

CHAPTER 32

DAMIEN

"Where do you think you're going, Priest?"

Déjà vu.

They're the same words I've heard a thousand times over in the last seven months but they come from an entirely different person.

Slowing my stride, I glance back over my shoulder to find Hugh Coney watching me from Holly Village's main staircase. He sits on the third lowest rung, his wrists propped on his bent knees. "Did you hear me?" he demands. "I asked you where you're going."

He and Jude are two peas in a pod, proper bosom buddies.

Hooking my thumb under the duffel bag's strap, I turn around. "Found your bollocks already, Coney?" I offer a slow, lethal smile that would send a smarter man running. "Because I distinctly remember you almost pissing yourself the other night."

Since Hugh doesn't have a lick of sense, he responds exactly as I knew he would: by launching to his feet and brandishing a knife like he's some swashbuckler out of a pirate film. Amused, I lower my gaze to the blade he's jabbing in my direction. It's a test of self-restraint that I don't do us both a favor by breaking his wrist and letting the knife clatter to the floor. Instead I raise my brows and deadpan, "Didn't your mum ever teach you not to play with pointy objects as a lad?"

Hugh's nostrils flare. "You're our prisoner, Priest. You don't get to just"—he slashes the knife in a wide arc—"leave whenever you want to. It's not how this works."

No, Hugh. It's not how this works at all.

Moving swiftly, my right hand bumps the base of his wrist and he instinctively releases the knife. I catch the base as it sails upward into the air, then sidestep his swinging fist by locking my forearm over his throat. I press my cheek to his, so that he's forced to watch sunlight glint off the blade as I twirl it in front of his face. "Hugh," I hum, my voice dark in his ear, "we've been here before, haven't we, mate?"

He struggles in my arms. Brings his foot down on my mine.

The bastard never learns.

Thrusting my leg between his, I hook my left calf around his shin and send his body sprawling forward. So close to the blade, so close to being rendered permanently mute. Lucky for him, it's my first day at turning over a new leaf. Not the villain, not the hero either. Just . . . Damien Godwin, for better or worse.

With my track record, I'm banking on the latter.

A memory of vivid violet warms my chest when I drawl, "See, Coney. I have a list of shit to get done today and getting rid of your dead body isn't one of them. In other words, you're wasting my time."

His shoes squeal against the wood when he tries to claw out of my chokehold. "It's *wrong*," he snarls. "You coming here, thinking that you can do as you want. Rowan can say whatever she wants but the rest of us know better.

We aren't the ones fucking you all over this bloody house!"

The familiar bite of anger nips at my heels.

Find mercy, Godwin. Be merciful.

"Do you know what your problem is?" Even mercy has its limits, and I allow the knife to touch his throat in warning. "You've never had to live in a world that wants you dead. If you did then you'd understand that adjustment is how you survive."

Tucking the blade against my forearm, I grab a fistful of his jumper and shove him away.

He stumbles forward, barely catching himself before going knees-down to the ground. When he turns on me, fury glitters in his dark eyes. "I've survived," he snaps, jerking on his shirt. "I've *adjusted*."

"Then don't bite the hand that feeds you or you'll be out on your ass." Spinning the base of the knife on my finger, I let a wreath of sunlight dance over the tip. "Stay out of my way, Coney, and I'll gladly stay out of yours."

I'm almost to freedom when he shouts, "Don't you think I know about the bounty on your head? I could ring it in, Priest. One conversation with the Met and you'd be behind bars within an *hour*. How smug do you think you'll be when your knob isn't being used for the next thirty years?"

The problem with people like Hugh Coney is that they push, and they push, and they *push*. And then, when they're dangling in the air with their feet kicking helplessly, they wonder how in the world fate could be so cruel.

Tipping my head back, I close my eyes.

Let the duffel drop from my shoulder to the floor.

For worse it is then.

Hugh's gaze is panicked when he's shoved clear against the wall, my hand fisting the front of his jumper to hold him off the floor. His legs squirm and his arms push, and

I thrust my face close to his when I growl, "Adjust or die. That's your last warning." Then I drill the knife into the wall a centimeter away from his right ear. Its steel base audibly vibrates upon impact.

Without waiting for a response, I turn on my heel and stride across the entrance hall, grabbing the duffel off the floor as I pass it. The fact that Coney was waiting for me is a problem for later today when I'm not short on time.

Only, when I step out into the sunshine and spot the woman leaning against the passenger-side door of my car, I find myself faltering for an entirely different reason.

I slept beside a woman for the first time in my life last night.

My arm tucked around her waist, her back nestled against my bare chest, our legs intertwined. And while I didn't allow sleep to claim me, breathing in Rowena's scent throughout the night was the closest I've come to experiencing soul-deep peace. Even now, I'm drawn to her.

At my side, my fingers curl into a tight fist of restraint.

Better that than storming across the drive and slamming my mouth down on hers, mercy be damned.

"Going somewhere?" she calls, lifting a hand to shield her eyes from the early morning sun. "Or is it that you've had enough of me already?"

The tone of her voice, that cunning smile . . . The she-wolf has come out to play.

When I reach her side, I drop my duffel to the pavement and bring my arms down on either side of her, parking my hands on the car. "Have you a confession to make?" I lower my face to hers, noting that she's done something to conceal the healing skin on her temple and jaw. And her lips . . . *Jesus*, she's painted them red. "Or is there a reason you've ditched the joggers I tore off you an hour ago for a skirt?"

Violet eyes sear mine just before she catches my mouth

with her own. Then, against my lips, she murmurs, "You aren't the only one with secrets, Godwin." From her cleavage, she produces a tiny, handheld camera. "You made the mistake of thinking that we don't watch our prisoners very, very closely here at Holly Village."

I eye the camera with disdain. "Is this payback for the tracker?"

"It's my way of ensuring that I'm not shoved aside in helping Margaret stay alive." Reaching for my hand, she closes my fingers over the palm-sized device. "So, why are we heading to Broadmoor Hospital this morning?"

Fucking hell.

"*We*," I grunt, "are not going anywhere."

When I step to the right, she follows swiftly and plants herself directly in front of me. Her gaze is sharp, her red mouth still curled in that smile that makes me want to strip her naked and fuck her ten ways from Sunday. "Don't worry, Damien, I'm willing to overlook your mistake in thinking that I'll somehow hold you back from whatever asinine plan had you bent over your laptop at the crack of dawn."

Asinine plan?

Brows lowering, I scowl at her. "I'm making a mistake, am I?"

"Men have a habit of complicating matters," she says, nodding toward the camera as if to prove her point. "Based on what I read over your shoulder this morning, you're timing your arrival at Broadmoor with its daily security check at ten-sharp. I'm going to guess, although I could be wrong, of course, that you're hoping to cut the alarm without anyone realizing that you've snuck yourself in. But are you taking documents? Seeing a patient? So many choices. Anyway, how did I do? On the nose?"

Rowena Carrigan will be the death of me.

And, if I didn't know any better, I'd swear that she's enjoying the hell out of this.

Just to rattle that smug smile of hers, I hook a finger over the collar of her shirt and slip the camera back into place between her tits. Then I grin at her, dark and ruthless. "It's called staging a kidnapping, love."

She surprises me, not by reeling back in shock, but by actually leaning forward to pat my chest like I'm a treasure that needs safeguarding.

Or, in other words, a complete idiot.

"And *that*," she chirps, "is why men complicate everything. Women—me, in particular—always know a person who knows a person. Lucky for you, I once spent a ridiculous number of hours at a charity dinner sitting next to the hospital's director. She's lovely, by the way."

It takes superhuman effort not to let my jaw fall open. "What?"

Though Rowena blinks up at me, there's a hawkish awareness in her gaze that tells me she's already strategizing her next five steps. "I'll ring her when we get there and walk right in the front door while I do it." With a sway of her hips, she bumps me out of the way and motions for me to unlock the door. "If you would, please."

"Rowena, I'm not sure if you heard me but this is a kid—"

"The door, Damien." She smiles, wide. "Don't you trust me?"

When she looks at me like that, like she can see right into my battered soul, I'd be a fucking fool to say no. Bringing Rowena to Broadmoor Hospital, however, *is* asinine. I don't doubt her ability to handle herself—but embroiling her in this mission won't just be putting a target on my back, it'll land one on hers, too. Kidnapping a former Holyrood agent for political leverage goes against every rule in the bloody handbook.

And I'm going straight to Hell.

With my jaw clenched, I plant a hand over Rowena's, where she has it ready to open the car door. "What I'm doing at Broadmoor isn't for Holyrood," I mutter, careful to keep my voice low, "and it isn't for the queen."

Her head tips back. "Then who is it for?"

I want to lie.

And yet, as I hold her gaze, I feel her silently daring me to confess the truth. To trust her with something that has nothing to do with the queen or the future of England and everything to do with *me.*

"Get in the car."

As if sensing that I want privacy for this conversation, Rowena slips into the passenger seat without protest. I close the door behind her, then grab the duffel bag. With one last glance up at Holly Village, I feel the hair on the back of my arms stand tall.

I know you're there, you bastard.

Scouring the vacant windows, I find him on the second floor where Alfie Barker and Guthram's man, Kendrick, are locked away in the loft.

Pushing the curtain wide, Hugh Coney presses both hands to the glass.

Mercy or not, if he turns me into Guthram before I'm good and ready, I'll string him up by the bollocks and let the vultures feast on his entrails.

Turning my back on him, I cut around the bonnet and climb into the driver's seat. The duffel goes in the backseat and the key into the ignition. With my hand on the gearstick, we peel out of the drive and onto Swain's Lane. The sycamore-laned street winds us down toward North Road, and I'm surprised that Rowena waits until I've merged onto the motorway, to reiterate, firmly, "Who is this for?"

"Me, Rowena." With the quiet admission, I tighten my grip on the steering wheel. "It's for Saxon, too, but mostly it's for me."

I feel her gaze linger on me before shifting back to stare out the windscreen. "Does this have anything to do with that bloke you brought back last night?"

Brought back implies that I had plans to invite him to the pub for a pint. Instead, I put him in the backseat of this car. Dead men can't talk, and those who keep their tongues and their lives . . . Well, I can't risk him running back to Marcus Guthram.

Briefly lifting my hand from the wheel, I scrub my palm over my unshaven jaw. "It has to do with that night at Westminster, when your father found me. Turns out that telling him to fuck off carries a life sentence. He's the one who had the Met's police commissioner put the bounty on my head." When I hear Rowena's small intake of breath, I cast a sharp glance her way before admitting, "My family goes back years with the Guthrams. Marcus's father, Robert, was best mates with Pa. They served in Holyrood together."

In my periphery, I see her frown. "Are there rules about who becomes involved with Holyrood? If Robert Guthram took the oath to the Crown, wouldn't that mean his son would serve, too?"

"No. Marcus shouldn't even know that Holyrood exists."

She taps her fingers on her thighs. "Wouldn't the same be said for you and your brothers, then?"

"The Godwins have served the Crown since 1899. We *are* Holyrood." Flicking on the indicator, I ease into the middle lane to cut around a lorry. "Generation to generation, we all join. It's in our blood."

"Like a title," she says slowly. "Some people inherit

dukedoms and others, like you, inherit—"

"Spy rings." I give a low laugh. "I'm not sure which one of us has it better, but it's the same concept—the eldest takes control. For us, it's Guy. Pa was an only child." Over the years, Saxon has mentioned time and again that Henry Godwin wasn't the right man for the position. I've always taken his word for it—my memories of our father are few and far between. "Outside of the Godwins, it's like any other post. Only, if you're hired, you agree to never say a word. So, no, Guthram should have never told Marcus about Holyrood."

"Then why would he?"

Because a man with a big heart couldn't find it in himself to punish his best mate for breaking the rules. Not that we'll ever know if that was really the case. When Pa was alive, we were too young to know any better. Now that we're older, Robert Guthram's health has long past deteriorated. The fault lies with all of them and we're stuck with the consequences: a bounty on my head and my brother briefly held behind bars for a murder that he didn't commit.

Saxon may be out but I'm still being hunted. If I can use Robert Guthram to corral Marcus into letting me go free, without resorting to just killing the commissioner—which was my original plan—then I'll take it.

Mercy isn't without its benefits. It just requires more devious scheming.

To Rowena, I say, "Guy will tell you that he thinks Guthram pushed his case to Pa. Probably even pointed out that the three of us—me, Guy, and Saxon—were growing up in the same world as our father and he only wanted the same for his own son."

She rests her elbow along the window, gently knocking her knuckles against the glass. "But you don't think that, do you?"

I shouldn't even be surprised that she's read me so well. "No," I answer, reflexively squeezing the steering wheel, "I don't." Switching gears, I push the car a little harder. "I look for signs, patterns in behavior. Whenever Marcus comes for us, it's not motivated by envy."

"Power?"

My stomach tightens with the memory of seeing my name appear on the UK's Most Wanted list. For seven months and counting, I've remained the number-one fugitive. Without a picture of me, Marcus Guthram was forced to stick with Damien Priest's fake profile. A lifetime of serving this country, and the Crown, only to end up with *Domestic Terrorist* captioned beneath my name.

I grit my teeth.

It was a power move on Guthram's part, all right. It was him staking claim over a city that he views as his, done as rashly as whipping out his prick and pissing all over the streets of London. But no matter how hard he tries, the Met's commissioner will never stretch his fingers as far or as wide as we do—my brothers and I rule from the turquoise seas of Cornwall to the dark, turbulent waters of the Shetland Islands.

We may not wear the crown but all of Britain is our throne.

"For whatever reason, he likes the idea of us down on our knees. Guy terrifies him, but Saxon and me, he seems to think that he can pick us off one by one. Yesterday he had me followed."

Her voice kicks up a notch when she demands, "From Holly Village? You were followed from my *home*?"

"No, after I met Matthews by St. Paul's."

"So the man that you . . ." Clearing her throat, she taps her knuckles against the window again, a restless tempo that picks up speed when she says, "He was one of Guthram's?"

"*Is* one of Guthram's," I correct, darting a quick look at her. "I didn't kill him, though God fucking knows I'll probably regret that soon enough." Easing the car into the left lane, I merge onto M3, heading for Southampton. *Almost there.* "Today isn't for Holyrood or the queen, Rowena. It's for me and it's for Saxon, whom Guthram put in prison for murder. Even though it wasn't him who did it but Jack."

Rowena's hand falls away from the window. "Who did Jack kill?"

"The priest from Christ Church Spitalfields."

She clutches her stomach. "I had no idea. That's not . . . I hope you know that in no way did I tell Jack to kill—"

"I know," I cut in, wanting to ease the stricken look on her face. "Guy had Saxon released. And we . . . Guy and me, I mean, we may have taken things too far." Thinking of the way I severed Jack's head and left it for Guthram to find in his bed chills my blood to ice.

Madness.

Life is a series of cause and effect, and while I may not have started the war with Robert Guthram's son, I plan on being the one to end it.

"For putting the bounty on my head, I always planned to kill him," I tell her on a rough exhale. "The only way to make a cycle stop is to end it in the most permanent way possible."

Hiking her leg up under her skirt, she turns to face me in her seat. "Are we finding ourselves an accomplice at Broadmoor?"

"No," I mutter, grimly, "we're kidnapping Robert Guthram as leverage over Marcus, and if that still doesn't work, *then* I'll kill him."

CHAPTER 33

ROWENA

Broadmoor Hospital is a Victorian behemoth. Chimney pots dot the roofline, stretching north toward a cloudless sky. Rows of double-arched windows parade across all three stories of the red-brick structure—there's no mistaking the bars laid across each set. The grounds before the hospital offer a sparse but well-maintained lawn, and surrounding the entire facility is a tall fence, no doubt the electrical variety guaranteed to temper a flood of escape attempts.

All may enter and none shall leave.

I swallow, roughly, and dig my fingers into my thighs. Cast a quick glance to my right, where Damien has his laptop balanced against the steering wheel. Dark, messy hair falls over his forehead, and I stifle the urge to reach across the gearshift and rake those strands back from his handsome face.

"Do you know his diagnosis?" When blue eyes lift from the screen to collide with mine, I clarify, "Robert Guthram's, I mean."

"No."

Fuck me.

Returning my attention to the hospital, my antsy fingers tap out a rhythmless beat. The good news: I've never met a man that I haven't managed to charm, even with my teeth bared and my claws ready to draw blood. The bad news: I generally don't remove them from psychiatric hospitals better known for housing the country's most infamous serial killers.

Already dreading the answer, I ask, "When did you see him last?"

Damien leans over his laptop, his fingers scraping across the keyboard so fast, so efficiently, that it's like watching a magician at work. "A decade," he mutters around the pen clamped between his teeth, "give or take."

"And he's been here for all those years?"

Those nimble fingers lift from the keyboard as he looks my way. "You don't have to do this."

I don't *have* to do much of anything, but still, the idea of Damien being caught by the hospital's security team leaves me feeling strangely frantic. Whether he wants to admit it or not, the bounty Guthram placed on his head is a real threat. One wrong move, and he'll find himself behind bars for the rest of his life.

"Your plan is reckless."

"For anyone else, maybe," he allows, giving the computer screen a sideways glance, as if whatever he's doing there carries a time constraint, "but not for me."

"Your ego, Damien."

"Love, if you're concerned about the size of my ego in a time like this, then we need to work on your priorities." Plucking the pen from his mouth, he taps the end against the laptop. "In exactly thirty minutes, Broadmoor is going to sound like a bomb site during World War II. Every morning like clockwork. Which means that I either have twenty minutes to deactivate that alarm, leaving the security team in scrambles while I sneak in, *or* I'll be taking the next ten minutes to rewrite Guthram's file so you can get him out of there without a problem. I can't do both."

I raise my brows. "You can do all that from your laptop?"

"There's really not much I can't do." He says it with such ease, such unlabored arrogance, that a spark of laughter burns in my chest. Brows knitting with consternation, he passes a hand over my shorn hair before cupping my face. "I won't burden you with this," he utters, his voice dark, hypnotic, "and I won't sway you either way. But you have five minutes to decide before I'll need to—"

"You can't be seen."

Those blue eyes, always so hot and fierce, turn glacial. "Don't do this for me."

I clasp my fingers over his wrist, holding tight. "If it weren't for you, then I wouldn't do this at all."

"Rowena—"

"The way I look at it, there's really no better way to feel alive than with a hastily planned kidnapping." I feel tethered to this man, bound to him. I didn't lie when I said that, with pulling the trigger to a gun that wasn't loaded, he took something from me—and I don't think that I'll ever get it back. Squeezing his hand, I let him go. "One kidnapping it is, courtesy of yours truly. Also, I'll need your mobile to make the call to Kathryn. Mine went up in flames." I tilt my chin toward the computer. "Will you be able to find her number on there?"

"*Look at me.*"

The command is an assault on my senses—deep and velvet and laced with undisguised need. When I turn my attention on Damien, it's to find him with one hand planted against the steering wheel while the other hooks around the back of my headrest. His computer sits at a crooked angle on his lap. Under the weight of his heavy gaze, I feel slain, stripped down to my soul.

A sharp breath cuts past my lips.

"I live this life because it's all I've ever known," he expels roughly, "and I do it to perfection because that means survival. But *you*, Rowena"—he shakes his head, those dark strands slipping over his temple—"you found the strength to walk away. I won't be the one to drag you back, do you understand me? I won't be the one to use you, just to save my own fucking skin."

Thud-thud. Thud-thud. Thud-thud.

Madness.

"We leave right now," he adds, already closing his laptop, "and no one will ever know that we were here."

I stop him with a finger to his wrist.

"I could have stayed in that stairwell," I confess on a shaky murmur, "and no one would ever know that I had the chance to save a queen and chose instead to take her with me to the grave." His blue eyes burn bright, and his throat works with a visible swallow. I force the difficult words from my throat: "I could have left the Palace and fled London, and you never would have known who I am. And I could sit here now, aware that the noose is closing around your neck, and be content with the fact that at least I'm alive. Beauty is fear, Damien. It's feeling the chill all the way down to your bones and pressing onward anyway. I'm stronger than you know, stronger than anyone ever realizes. Stronger, even, than *I* realize."

His palms clasp the back of my head, startling me to my core with his ferocity, and then he drags me over the gearstick and captures my mouth with his. I taste cloves, feel heavy muscles rippling under taut skin, and hear the moan that rises in my throat like a benediction. The kiss is over before it's even begun when he pulls back to growl, "Beauty is *you*, Rowena."

Beauty of character.

Beauty of soul.

For better or worse, Damien Godwin has already ruined me.

From our vantage point, Broadmoor Hospital appears before me like Mt. Everest, a mountain to scale and defeat, come hell or high water. Its double doors beckon me closer even as its barred windows mock me for daring to enter.

"Don't let security take your jumper, do you understand?"

Ignoring the trio of floaters that have become my personal little stalkers, I glance down at Damien's fingers pinning a red poppy to my left breast pocket. The metal brooch winks under the sunlight. If he hadn't told me, I'd never know that it's been outfitted with a camera and audio. Like Odin himself, who sacrificed an eye to see all things, Damien allows nothing to fall to chance.

"Understood," I tell him.

"Good girl." Turning his left wrist over, he unfastens a black watch and motions for my hand. "This," he tells me, looping the supple leather straps around my wrist, "is if you need me. Tap this button here"—the screen shimmers to life, glowing red around the edges—"and I'll find you."

"Damien, I don't think—"

"Wherever you are," he reiterates, "*I will find you.*"

Sweat coalesces on my spine. The heat from the sun overhead, maybe, or the gritty determination in his voice. Either way, I give him a firm nod that I pray translates to

Don't worry, I have this. When I stepped into Buckingham Palace ten days ago, this is not where I imagined I'd be this morning—kidnapping a former spy when all I'd hoped was to stop my best friend from being kidnapped herself. But I've not stopped running yet, always reaching, always grasping, and I look down at the watch as if it has the power to save us all.

"The mobile," I say.

He drops the burner phone into my waiting hand. "I've already inputted the director for you."

Self-doubt is a sword cutting me at my knees. "And if she doesn't recognize who's ringing her?"

"The call's programmed to come from your number."

Nodding, I skim my palms down over the fabric of my skirt. It doesn't ease the throbbing in my temples or the ridiculous pounding of my heart. I force myself to step back, to step toward the winding front drive of Broadmoor when all I want is to crawl back into the passenger seat of Damien's car and bury my head between my knees.

Broken, but never defeated.

"Rowena."

I glance back over my shoulder at the solitary figure standing beside the car. His legs are long, his arms thickly muscled, but his eyes . . . They hunt me, even now. Chase me, as if I'll disappear at any moment and it's his very last chance to keep me with him.

"Have no mercy."

The words drive a shiver down my spine.

With a small dip of my chin, I turn for Broadmoor Hospital and shove my shoulders back. *Young Rowena, how we meet again.* My lips curve with a smile that's only skin-deep. Though I'm not nearly the vision that I was before the fire, I saunter toward those double doors like my life depends on it.

No, not your life—Damien's.

Just inside the front doors, a guard rests on a plastic chair, his legs sprawled, his head tipped back with a heavy snore that echoes in the hall. I tap his booted foot with my pump, then make sure to keep my distance when he scrambles awake.

Muttering under his breath, he shoves himself to his feet. "Visiting hours aren't until half past," he grunts. Sleepy brown eyes peer down at me through a tangle of blond hair. "You'll have to wait."

"That's not possible." I smile, wide, the smile of a woman who flits from man to man, feckless and naïve. "You see, I'm here to collect someone for my father and, oh, he'll be *so* furious with me if I don't pull through." I lean forward to whisper, "We aren't on the best of terms."

Like a dog being led to table scraps, his gaze drops to my breasts and stays there. "I don't think"—he visibly swallows—"or rather, we really aren't meant to allow anyone inside right now. There are checks we do. Daily checks. In"—he makes an exaggerated show of checking his wristwatch—"seven minutes."

My eyes go big, apologetic. "And here I am just taking up your time when you've so much to do." I cast a glance down the empty corridor. "Is there a front-desk monitor? You could just point me in the right direction . . ."

He wavers, literally.

Reed-thin body swaying left, toward the hall, while his hands shove deep into his trouser pockets. Skating a drive-by peek at my chest, he looks to the double doors, clearly deliberating, before motioning for me to pass him by with a quiet puff of air filling his cheeks.

Victory.

"Mary won't like this, you know." When those brown eyes swing my way again, he doesn't even pretend that he's not blatantly staring at my cleavage. "She's particular about the rules around here. And an angry Mary means hell for the rest of us."

"Are you saying that you can't handle a woman who knows her own mind?"

"I'm not sure I've ever met a woman who has one."

Keep smiling, Rowan. Do not *skewer him.*

Easier said than done when he cuts around the next corner, waves a dismissive arm toward me, and introduces me as, "Mary, this one here says she's on an errand for her old man. Wouldn't shut up about it, and I knew you'd be just the one to put her in her place." Dark brown eyes peel away from the infamous Mary to focus on me. "Who's your father anyway?"

Through gritted teeth, I manage, "The prime minister."

Color spears his cheeks. "Right-o, then." And with that, he spins away and scurries back down the hall like the vermin he is.

Refusing to appear rattled—or annoyed—I plaster a pretty smile on my lips.

I've played this game a thousand times over in the past: well-timed fawning, the always necessary simpering that manages to degrade my own achievements while stroking my opponent's ego. It's a role that I slip into all too easily as I turn to find Mary sitting like a queen behind her desk.

Slick-backed hair, tidy outfit, prim glasses that sit on the bridge of a perfect nose. Clasping her fingers together, Mary presses her wrists to the empty space beside her computer keyboard while bringing her pointed gaze down on me like the sharpened blade of a guillotine lowering to sever its next victim. "What's the prime minister's daughter doing in Broadmoor Hospital?"

The fact that she recognizes me isn't the least bit surprising. Once upon a time, my face was plastered on every magazine cover along with Father's. And Mary doesn't look like the sort of person who ever forgets a face, never mind the fact that she's surrounded by hundreds of them daily.

Without waiting for an invitation, I take the vacant chair opposite her.

Mirroring her pose, I cross one leg over the other and turn myself at an angle to lean my wrists on the desk. "Truthfully," I murmur with sunshine cheerfulness, "I couldn't tell you the specifics—my father rarely tells me his secrets. But when he barks out an order, I always hop to obey." I sweep a pointed glance over the cramped office behind her. "Isn't that the way of things, though?"

Her narrowed gaze doesn't falter. "I'm not sure what you mean, Miss Carrigan."

My smile says *of course you do*. My next statement, however, is carefully bland: "A woman like you maintaining order in a place like this?" I lift my shoulder in a delicate shrug. "You're so lucky to have someone like Kathryn as Broadmoor's director. I'm sure she appreciates everything you do." *More so than my father does for me* goes unspoken.

It's enough gentle praise that Mary perks up in her seat. "She does. Mrs. Levell does, I mean. Do you know her well?"

Not anymore.

I left this world behind without a single regret. Grasped the tattered shell of my life and rose to stand on my own, breaking and molding my spine until the woman who peered back at me in the mirror recognized only one strength: complete and utter independence.

Smoothing a palm over the desk, I deliberately keep my tone blasé when I murmur, "We've crossed paths over the years." A small pause, and then, "I hope you can understand that I'm working with a time-sensitive matter. My father"—I tip my wrist over in a motion that's synonymous with *what can you do?*—"is adamant that I bring him Robert Guthram."

Mary's chin jerks back. "*Guthram*? But the man . . . the man's been here for nearly ten years!"

"Your guess is as good as mine." I lift both hands, palms to the ceiling. Helpless. Ignorant. *Break for me, Mary.* "Honestly, sending *me* of all people screams desperation—I mean, the man could be downright mad. I've only my driver out front to make sure that I get back to London in one piece."

"He's not . . . that is to say, Mr. Guthram is a special case."

Bloody hell. *Special* how?

"And it doesn't matter, anyway," Mary continues, "because you aren't authorized to take him from Broadmoor."

Sending up a little prayer of hope, I sink one hand into my handbag and grab the burner phone. Place it flat on the desk like a bomb ready to explode. "I'll ring Kathryn if you need the reassurance."

"Well, I don't think that's—"

"But I can promise you that the prime minister is *very* thorough. He wouldn't send me here only to have me return empty-handed."

Her gaze swings from my face to the computer. "His son is his legal executor. Marcus Guthram is the commissioner for the Metropolitan Police, you know." When I only smile at her, patient to the bone, she worries the keyboard's wire. "Let me just . . ."

Unease swims in my gut.

Forcing my shoulders to remain loose is a burden all on its own, and I fight the urge to peer down at the poppy pinned to my jumper. Is Damien watching us now? Listening? *Do not look, Rowan. Do not give yourself away.* I'm so close. Mary holds the proverbial keys and—

Sirens the likes of which I've never heard erupt over the loudspeakers.

They wail like the banshees of Hell, so loud, so piercing, that bile rises in my throat and my palms turn damp with perspiration. Behind me, armed guards take to the hall, marching two in a row. I see their bodies form a line through the blue-tinted lens of Mary's glasses.

When I sink down into my seat, she sends a disapproving glance my way. "As the prime minister's daughter, Miss Carrigan, I'm sure you can appreciate our need for caution. It's routine procedure. No need to look so repulsed."

It's not repulsion—it's bloody fear.

If Broadmoor's patients require *armored guards* to watch their every move, I'm terrified to think of what will become of me when I plant myself in the path of Robert Guthram.

"You're doing a wonderful job here," is the only reply I can summon when my ears are ringing from the unrelenting sirens. Good God, I'm two seconds away from vomiting all over Mary's pristine desk. "It's just . . . *inspiring* to see such unity nowadays."

Her stiff nod barely indicates approval.

She taps away, unperturbed by the scene before her, and then her expression twists. Leaning forward with one elbow on the desk, she double-clicks the mouse. "I don't . . ." Removing her glasses, she uses her shirt to clean the lenses before slipping them back onto her face. Whatever she sees on the screen doesn't change. A moment later, she shifts her surprised stare to me. "You've been made Mr. Guthram's legal executor."

Oh, Damien, I could kiss you.

"My father, Mary—there's a reason why he's been

elected PM two terms in a row now. Not a single detail is ever overlooked."

Begrudgingly, she admits, "Usually there's a step-by-step patient release process. But"—her jaw clenches—"for the *prime minister*, I'm sure we can bypass with precautions just this once."

"You're an absolute gem."

Without making further eye contact, she ushers me into a waiting room and lets me know that Robert Guthram will be down shortly. The heavy door slams shut behind her the second that she releases the knob to step back into the hallway.

I don't allow myself the chance to sink into one of the plush sofas.

Don't allow myself the luxury of checking Damien's watch.

My gut tells me that she's left me in a room decked out with security cameras, and I'd be a fool to give myself away now.

Stay sharp. Stay focused.

Clamping my trembling hands together at the base of my spine, I make a point to pause before each of the paintings that decorate the otherwise blank walls. Five in total. All picturesque landscapes of Berkshire and the towns surrounding Crowthorne and Broadmoor Hospital.

My heart threatens to burst from my chest.

I squeeze my right hand over my left and turn my back toward the closest wall to hide my display of nerves.

Have no mercy.

Damien's words stay front and center when the door clicks open and swings wide.

And they remain front and center as a tall, middle-aged man steps into the room with his uncuffed hands linked in front of his stomach, as though he's been instructed to keep them visible. A guard follows directly behind him, looking nearly diminutive behind the lumbering Holyrood agent.

My gaze shifts to a face that may have been classified as handsome before ten years in a psychiatric hospital had its way with him. Impassive dark eyes. Brown hair liberally salted with strands of white that match the growth of his neatly trimmed beard. A flat nose and thin lips, and a scar . . .

It threads through his right eyebrow, splitting the hairs and stretching toward his hairline. I *know* that scar but from where? Grasping at the slip of a memory, I try flicking through a mental rolodex of the hundreds of people that I've met whilst at Father's side. But this . . . *this* doesn't feel like that. The tug at my consciousness feels ancient, like a dream swept under the rug, to be forgotten and dismissed in the light of day.

Then Robert Guthram smiles, and, in my veins, I feel only ice.

He steps forward.

I step back and collide with the wall.

"Miss Carrigan," the guard starts awkwardly, "this is—"

"Oh, she knows me," Guthram drawls. "We go back *years*, don't we?" His voice rings with mocking chastisement. "How you've finally grown up, Little Rowan. Your mum would be so proud."

Oh, God.

No.

Guthram shrugs off the guard.

Another step deeper into the room.

Then he bends at the waist, a glint of hell flickering in his dark eyes, and for my ears alone, he murmurs, "And here I'd lost hope of your father ever keeping his word. Freedom, at last."

CHAPTER 34

ROWENA

Terror grips my lungs.

That face lurking in the shadows.

That scar, blood-stained and stark, against pale skin.

That name . . . *his* name—

A lie. A sham. A complete and utter fabrication.

A cruel sneer lurks at the corner of Silas Hanover's mouth. "Nine years and counting," he hisses, low, "and your old man couldn't even be bothered to show up after all I did for him. The bloody *bastard*." Straightening from his exaggerated bow, he shoves his unshackled hands in front of him again, as though the rules of Broadmoor Hospital have been ingrained in his every movement. Mary said that Robert Guthram was a "special case," and now I know why: he's spent ten years in a psychiatric ward when clearly it wasn't for a diagnosable reason.

The sound of madness is deafening, and Silas Hanover is seething with brittle venom.

"And *you* . . ." His gaze carves a hardened path from my head down to my pumps. "Still a quiet mouse, are you, Little Rowan? Just like your mum. Except, of course, at the end." Unflinching, he meets my stare. "Such a shame that she didn't make it."

Wrathful words dance across my tongue but none emerge.

This can't be real.

Silas Hanover cannot *be* Robert Guthram. A spy for the Crown. Defender of the king. The man who was once best mates with Henry Godwin and a member of Holyrood. The one hope Damien has in making the Met's police commissioner fall in line.

Hanover's lips twist to the side and his nostrils flare like he's inhaled something foul. Leaning forward, he touches a finger to the red poppy brooch pinned to my cardigan. "Love for your king," he remarks sardonically, "the *irony* coming from your family. This is too much arse-kissing, even for me."

And then he rips the brooch free.

Tossing the delicate device up into the air, he catches it in one palm and turns on his heel. Stops only long enough to thrust the brooch at the guard before stepping into the corridor without another backward glance.

He knows I'll follow him.

I'm frozen against the wall, my heart threatening to clamber from my chest, and he *knows I'll follow him.*

Because I'm Rowena Carrigan, the prime minister's daughter, and Silas Hanover was once a man whose scarred face I saw near nightly as a child. My feet padding down carpeted steps and masculine voices drifting from Father's study, and always a glimpse between the crack in the open door before Father emerged to march me back up to my bedroom. Another nightmare, another night of the darkness stalking me. And a face that I haven't seen in twenty years, since the night of the fire that turned my life upside down.

"Miss Carrigan?" The guard tilts his head toward the door. "I'm required to escort you both to the front."

Run.

Run now.

Except that even if I do, there's no rewinding the clock. Mary spoke with me; records were altered. And the alleged Robert Guthram was discharged, for better or worse. I sway in place. *Fuck me.* One word from Hanover or any of the staffers to my father about what I've done, and I'll be dangling in the breeze before the end of the week.

Or sooner.

Moving past the guard, I glance at the red-poppy brooch clasped in his hand. Hazel eyes peer down at me, and I know—before he even shifts a muscle—that I'm staring at an anti-loyalist. His gaze burns with disgust for my show of silent respect for the fallen king. A muscle tightens in his jaw as he directs his stare to the red poppy.

"Sir, can I have—"

"We don't wear the likes of this around here," he mutters, dropping the brooch to the ground. He crushes it with his heavy boot, the silver audibly squealing against the concrete flooring. "Do we, Guthram?"

Whistling, Silas Hanover doesn't even turn around. "Not a one of us."

The guard puts a hand on my shoulder to march me down the hall. "Don't suspect that your father'd much like you wearing a red poppy, anyway, Miss Carrigan. Not after all that business with the Mad Priest and Westminster."

It takes everything in me not to slam to a stop.

Why would he mention . . . ?

Jerking my head up, I demand, "What does a red poppy have to do with the Mad Priest? The man's an anti-loyalist, same as you." I pointedly drop my gaze to my torn jumper. "Or have I read the situation wrong?"

"It's not the same." The hand on my shoulder tenses. "I can promise you that."

"Priest is against the royal family, isn't he?"

"He's an *anarchist*," the guard grunts, "and that's even worse than those damn royal arse-kissers. It means that he's unpredictable." His eyes follow Hanover, who's taken to peering through the oval-shaped window of every door that he passes. "Is it true what everyone's saying?"

"I have no idea what you're talking about." Needing space, I give my arm a sharp pull. "Now let me go or I'll—"

"The PM, Miss Carrigan. I'm talking about your blasted father. Is it true about his plans for Parliament?"

Instead of answering, I spin, fast, and let my jumper tear from my shoulders. It shreds at the sleeve, leaving the guard to stand there with a fistful of sunshine yellow fabric. Cool air hits my left arm, a dash of ice against the fury gathering in my gut.

"Do *not* touch me again," I grit, nails biting into my palms. "And if you think for even one second that I won't go to Kathryn Levell about this, then you're downright delus—"

"Guthram."

Silas Hanover wheels back around. "What?"

A single finger jabs in my direction. "Burns," he says, letting the ripped sleeve fall to the floor. He lowers his gaze to my scarred arm. "Fresh, too. Not even a few weeks old."

My gaze flies from one man to the other.

There's a familiarity between them that I don't understand. A . . . a sort of *kinship* that makes itself all the more apparent when I grip my handbag, tight, and power down the hall, my pumps clipping ominously against concrete—only to be cut short by Hanover.

He grabs my wrist, turning my arm over.

Unease sweeps over me, and I yank, hard. "Take your hands off me."

"A red poppy," Hanover murmurs, as if tasting the word on his tongue and finding it offensive, "and these scars . . ." Tracing a finger over the blisters, he gives a low, skin-crawling laugh. Pensive dark eyes flick to mine. "Connelly, bring me that brooch, would you?"

No.

Oh, fuck, *no.*

Desperation floods my veins and I dart right, ducking under Hanover's arm. But I get no farther than three steps when a forearm clamps down over my head and cinches tight across my throat. A startled cry bursts from my lips, and then Hanover drags me backward.

Feet flailing. Nails scratching.

"*Let me go!*"

Shadows dance in my peripheral as I'm shoved hard against a door. The metallic tang of blood bursts on my tongue. Turning my head, I angle my chin upward to draw air into my lungs, but the movement inadvertently gives Hanover better access to what he so desperately wants. And he takes it, the bastard. He squeezes my throat until I'm scratching at the door and struggling to hold onto the fragile threads of life.

"*Why—*" Vision swimming, I claw at his arm fruitlessly. "Why . . . are you doing this?"

"Nothing happens in London without me knowing it, Little Rowan. I have ears everywhere, friends in all places. And *you*"—that dark, caustic laugh comes again, this time directly in my ear—"everyone knows that there's no love lost between you and your old man. Just like we both know that he didn't send you here. So, the question is . . . who did? Was it the queen?"

"Maybe it was me," I choke out, refusing to give him Damien's name. "Did you ever think of that? Maybe you owe your freedom to *me*. And here you are, trying to kill me for—"

His arm flexes and the air slips away, a ghost that never was.

Firm fingers grasp my chin and force my head down, just as the mangled brooch is shoved centimeters away from my face. The guard, Connelly, growls, "Mary should've looked before she let this one through. It's a camera."

"Check the back."

The silver piece is turned over and held toward the light. "Marked with the number *503*."

"Of course it is. Fucking Holyrood."

I'm wrenched away from the door, Hanover's hand fisting the back of my shirt as he hauls me down the corridor. I trip over my pumps, one of them clattering to the floor and disappearing behind me. I want to scream. I want to cry for help. But all I manage is: "I'll kill you. Do you hear me, Hanover? *I'll kill you.*"

"You won't be the first to try."

"Which room should we put her?" Connelly asks. "With the others?"

"No," Hanover says.

"*Really.*" The guard whistles. "Solitary, then?"

"No," I breathe, throwing all my weight in the opposite direction to slow our pace. But Hanover treats me like I'm nothing more than a disobedient dog. He uses my shirt like a lead, bunching the material at my throat, and forcibly drags me behind him. "You can't do this." Desperation turns me wild, frantic. "Do you hear me, Hanover? *You can't do this.* My father—"

"Has wanted you dead for years." When my head snaps up, Hanover spares me a cruel grin over his shoulder. "Oh, don't look so shocked. Deep down, you've always known it was true."

"You're lying." The collar of my shirt nips tighter, and I pull on the material desperately. Fading consciousness blurs the world gray at the edges. Pushing feebly at Hanover's wrists, I hiss, "He had nothing to gain with me dying in the fire."

"Only a million pounds."

"At *thirteen*? I didn't even have five quid to my name!"

"Inheritance is a tricky thing, though, isn't it? Particularly when it belongs to a wife and her children." That cruel face barely flinches when he adds, "You didn't go down nearly as easily as she did."

Mum screaming.

A bedroom door bolted shut.

And my father, down in the garden beside Silas Hanover, peering up at my window while I begged him to save me.

"He'll thank me, honestly," Hanover continues, "for doing what he couldn't. Never did have the stomach for violence when he always had ample greed." He grips my shirt tighter, snapping me forward until I'm at his feet. "But unlike your father, I always give credit where it's due. So, thank you, Little Rowan, for setting me free after all these years. I'm sure your father intended to leave me to die, same as he did to you."

Pain radiates from my core.

The shadows creep forward and the darkness swoops in, and I let the world hear me scream.

Have no mercy.

And God help us all because I have none.

I swing my right leg forward and snatch the pump off my foot. Turning into Hanover's grip, I twist my body and surge upward—and plunge the stiletto heel in his gut. It sinks past fabric, sinks deep into skin. Clasping his stomach, he staggers backward from the blow.

I run.

I run to the grim melody of Silas Hanover screaming and Connelly barking orders, and I'm halfway down the hall when the sirens begin anew. The shrill of banshees. The wail of hell. Lights dim overhead, casting a red tint over everything in sight. Gruff voices enter the corridor behind me and all I need is one look over my shoulder to know that I'm fucked.

The guards have entered the fray.

"Oh, hell."

Skidding sideways, I change directions and duck down the next corridor—only to stumble to a stop when a paired column of guards comes into view. Glossy black helmets conceal their faces and terrifying guns are held diagonally across their chests. The second that they latch eyes on my paralyzed frame, they assume position. The first two rows lower to their knees, the second and third fanning out to create a blockade that I'll cross only in my dreams.

Ice dances down my spine.

Fear creeps into my heart.

On bare feet, I inch backward. Only, the guards don't follow because they don't need to—one panicked glance down the bordering hallway reveals that I've already been effectively cornered.

There's no way to freedom, no way to escape whatever comes next.

I'm going to die.

Damien demanded to know what Ian had thought of before Isla Quinn killed him in The Octagon. Friend or not, I'll never know Ian Coney's heart or soul—but I know my own. As I inhale my last breaths of life, I grasp onto the only memory of warmth that I can recall—blue eyes fixed on my face and calloused hands pressing my palm to a pair of soft lips, and a wish . . . a wish that I desperately hope will come true.

"May you find happiness," I breathe, feeling my eyes burn with tears, "and live for us both."

Slowly, my hands come up.

And then my knees sink to the floor.

CHAPTER 35

DAMIEN

If there's a Hell on Earth, Broadmoor Hospital has become its epicenter and I its devil.

One by one they all fall down.

Necks snapping, rounds flying; I grab the guard to my right and slam the stock of my rifle into his face. Blood spurts from his nose. His hands come up to shove me off but I'm already swinging his body to the left just as another comes barreling toward me. The guard in my grasp catches the spray of bullets. Dropping him to the floor, I swiftly angle my gun and fire.

Another falls.

I don't wait long enough to see him hit the ground.

Weapon clutched to my shoulder, I take the next corner and flick my gaze down the length of the empty hallway. Panic is a seed inside my gut, unfurling and growing until its tremor is a vibration that's embedded in my bones, a living, breathing thing that screams, *Where are you?*

I shouldn't have sent her in here.

Shouldn't have assumed that Robert Guthram would be the same man from my childhood who always stood up for right versus wrong and never let Jayme Paul or the older blokes mess with me or my brothers. And I—

A guard cuts down the hallway, followed swiftly by another six or seven.

Broadmoor Hospital is a house of horrors, and, on silent feet, I descend farther into the madness. With my back to the wall, I shadow the group jogging down the hall. They never once glance back.

And I fight every instinct that demands that I kill them all here and now.

They wind their way through the maze of the psychiatric ward, never stopping to look in the windows as they pass, as if the sight before them is one they've examined a thousand times over. Unable to stop myself, I allow my gaze to wander from one to the next.

One person in the first room, three huddled in the second.

I recognize the face in the third.

Run to her. Chase her.

But my heart is lodged in my throat and I can't turn away from the window, can't turn away from Caren Fitz, a famed London hotelier, who went missing three years ago. Until his disappearance, he'd been a frequent visitor to The Bell & Hand. Slowly, as if aware that he's being watched, his head lifts from where he's seated at a desk. His gaze collides with mine.

It takes him only two seconds to recognize me.

Face paling, he rushes to the oval window and pounds his fists on the door. "Priest," he shouts, his voice muffled, "get me out! Help!"

Sirens begin to blare, shrieking their ferocity, and I send a dark look down the hall. The guards have already turned the corner and *fucking hell*. Rowena. I need to find Rowena.

I watch Fitz's expression crumple as I move away, see it shatter completely when I turn.

With each step that I take after the guards, I force myself to stare into the passing rooms. Some I don't recognize but others, like Caren Fitz, are people who've come time and time again to The Bell & Hand. All known anti-loyalists in relatively affluent posts in society. Men and women both who have gone missing over the last few years, their faces plastered across all of Britain to see on the telly, in the newspapers.

Only, they aren't missing at all.

My grip on my rifle turns tight at the thought of Rowena being shoved into one of those holding rooms. I felt her terror when Guthram plucked the red poppy brooch from her jumper, saw the fear reflected in her violet eyes just before everything went upside down when the guard crushed the camera beneath his shoe. Instinct propelled me from the car before my next breath, heedless to the fact that I'm the country's most wanted fugitive. I thought of her, nothing and no one but her.

Wherever you are, I will find you.

A promise. A vow that I'll never break.

When I turn a sharp corner and see the shoulders of the guards standing uniformly in a row, rifles raised, adrenaline pumps through my veins, only to be replaced by fear the likes of which I've never known.

Beyond those black helmets, a pair of slim arms reach toward the ceiling in surrender.

Scarred skin. Yellow fabric.

No. Jesus Christ, *no.*

Her name leaves me on a violent roar.

As one, the guards whip around. Any scrap of hope I had of doing the right thing, the *good* thing, disappears instantly. I tear through them all, one after another. Beyond the cry of the siren, bones shatter and limbs sever. I duck beneath outstretched arms and slide my knife from its holster to jab between first and second ribs, there and gone again before they even realize that they've been struck. I use bodies as shields, letting the dead fend off attempts from the still-living until there is no one left standing but me.

And her.

Huddled in the corner of the hallway, with her bare arms raised over her head to shield herself from the spray of gunfire, Rowena Carrigan lives.

I stagger toward her.

Breathe her name on a hoarse whisper.

Her shorn head lifts, those violet eyes of hers red-rimmed as she chokes back a sob. Before I can cross over to her, she launches to her feet and hurls herself at me. Lingering fear guides my bloodied hands to the back of her head as I step into her space, my right palm smoothing down to between her shoulder blades, my left still cradling her skull.

"I was dead," she whispers raggedly into my chest, "I was seconds away from dying and you—"

"I'll chase you, Rowena. Wherever you are, however you got there, I will *find you.*" Against my sternum, her heart thrums an incessant beat that matches the pace of mine. Over the crown of her head, I scan the empty halls. Carnage is a disease, and within these walls, I've opened festering wounds. "We have to go before more come. Can you run?"

"We can't get out. There's no way—"

"Do you trust me?"

She pulls away from my chest to nod. "With my life."

"Then follow me."

I manage two steps before she tugs on my arm. When I glance back, she shifts her gaze to the bare corridor. "Silas

. . ." She touches her tongue to her bottom lip. "Robert Guthram—he might still be there."

My eyes narrow. "He might?"

"I stabbed him."

"You don't have a knife—"

"It's probably best not to ask questions right now, since we're short on time and all. But, Damien, we need him."

The edge in her voice tells me that whatever Guthram has done, it probably relates to the anti-loyalists locked away within Broadmoor Hospital. I think of Caren Fitz. His wife, his children . . . I attended the man's bloody funeral all while he was alive and stuck in a psych ward in Crowthorne. We can't save them all today—not with just Rowena and me—but if we have Guthram, if we have *information . . .*

"Tell me where he is."

"I'll take you to him."

"Rowena—"

But she's already jogging down the hall, her skirt riding up her knees. With a curse, I follow quickly. Her feet are bare, her jumper torn, the flesh around her throat pinkened with the shape of a handprint.

A gust of rage sweeps beneath my skin.

The red haze of the emergency lights cast shadows over the walls, tunneling the corridor so that it appears narrow and twisted. Rowena guides me with only her hand. Down one hallway and then to the next. She tracks the blood staining the concrete, as if knowing that at the end we'll find Guthram.

And we do.

He's shoved himself against a wall, his legs bent to the side. In the ten years since I've seen him, he's aged a century. Fine lines feather across his forehead and white hair tangles in with the brown. His lids flutter as I sink down in front of him, then open completely when he feels my hand fist his shirt to tow him off the floor.

"I knew it was you," he grunts, batting at my hands. "I fucking *knew* it was you."

I don't respond.

Instead, I slip one arm under his waist and brace myself as I lift him clear over my shoulder. Exhaustion threatens to send me sprawling to the floor. But I grit my teeth and readjust my grip on the bastard and, after a shaky first step, I begin to move at a quick clip.

"The watch," I mutter to Rowena. "Go to the home screen for me." With a worried glance in my direction, she does as I say. "Tap the right-hand corner like I showed you. Good . . . good, now see the coordinates? Pull them up and choose anywhere behind the hospital. Press down . . . select grenade."

A second later, mingled in with the pulsing siren, comes the heavy *boom!* of an explosion.

Rowena's lips part. "Damien—"

"It's an illusion." I shuffle her down another hall after glancing ahead. "It channels the closest WiFi connection, manipulating nearby technology to produce sound. They won't know that, though, and it'll give us a few minutes."

Slowly, as if she's half-terrified by the watch's power, she holds up her wrist. "You created this?"

"Yes."

"And the brooch? You did that, too?"

I nod.

"You really can do everything, can't you?"

We're surrounded by death, layered by grim misery, and my chest fucking swells at the awe in her husky voice. Over my shoulder, Guthram releases a pitiful groan. Ignoring him, I lead Rowena through the final maze of corridors before gesturing toward the door that I left cracked open with a rock. We push our way in, and relief nearly takes me down when I see that the room is still empty.

Beside me, Rowena stares at the bare bones window . . . and the bars that have been left mangled on the floor. "Do I want to know?" she asks mildly.

Probably not.

"Go first. You'll need to help me shove him out."

Rowena clambers through and, together, we maneuver Guthram. By the time I'm pushing my way out into the crisp sunshine, there's no mistaking the sound of a helicopter circling above Broadmoor.

Fuck.

Bending at the knees, I hike Guthram's bulky weight back over my shoulder. Grit my teeth and let my gaze follow the narrow trail to where I parked the car. We stay and we die or we move and we die. If my brothers were here, they'd tell me it's suicide. Glancing up at the sky, I note the angle of the helicopter's rotation.

"We run."

"Damien, we won't even make it past—"

"We run—*now!*"

The helicopter swoops inward, leaning in toward Broadmoor's roofline, and, briefly, allowing the trees to obscure us from view. Rowena's bare feet kick up dirt and I stay on top of her as best as I can with Guthram bouncing over my right shoulder. For once, the dead, nerveless flesh is a blessing; I feel nothing as we zigzag through the brush and follow the shelter of the trees.

Rowena's breath comes hard and choppy, her hand returning again and again to her strained rib.

"You're strong."

Violet eyes swing back to me, her dark brows furrowed from pain, and I hold her gaze for as long as I can before dipping them back to the uneven trail. "You're stronger than you know," I growl, "stronger than anyone ever realizes. Keep going, love. Just a little more for me. Just a little—"

The helicopter's path cuts directly above us, swallowing my words and sending leaves scattering from the branches. The downcast of wind plasters my hair to my forehead, and it carries enough force that I stumble under Guthram's weight.

Soft hands catch me, tangling with my fingers.

"Don't you dare give up," Rowena utters fiercely, her gaze snapping up to the tree line. "Run with me, Damien. Goddammit, *run.*"

Air pumps into my lungs as I lurch to the right and re-position Guthram's weight. The whirring of the chopper's wings pulses overhead, and I don't need to look up to know that the pilot has spotted us. It hovers in place, tracking our every movement. I look to Rowena and the sight of that handprint on her throat throws me into renewed motion.

I feel heat.

I feel rage.

I feel terror, down in my marrow, for what'll happen if they catch the prime minister's daughter in the company of the likes of me. The Mad Priest. The country's most wanted fugitive. Broadmoor Hospital will be a bloody joyride compared to what they'll put her through, and I force myself to pick up the pace, despite the fact that my muscles are now cramping, stalling, begging for relief.

"The watch," I bark, "the second button down on the menu. Unlock the car."

Ten seconds later, it comes into view, nestled within the woods just off Broadmoor's property. Rowena darts forward. The boot unlatches and I feel the most ridiculous urge to kiss her for reading my mind. Sweat beads on her temple as she holds it open and I thrust Guthram in, feeling not a single trace of regret when he grasps at my arms and begs me not to lock him inside.

Mercy isn't for traitors.

Nor is loyalty.

I meet Rowena's gaze as she slams the boot down on the former Holyrood spy. The trees shimmer with the onslaught of human-generated wind, and the blood from my hands stains her forehead and cheeks. A woman with war in her blood and courage in her heart.

I've never seen anyone more beautiful.

CHAPTER 36

DAMIEN

"**I**s he dead?"

I shift my weight, letting Rowena get a better view of Robert Guthram. His legs are twisted at an awkward angle and, after the hour-long drive back to Holly Village, the blood from his wound has completely discolored his shirt. Fortunately for us, the bastard is still breathing. Grasping fistfuls of his shirt, I haul him out of the car. "He's alive," I grunt, wrapping an arm around his middle, "and we need Grafton to keep him that way."

With her fingers gently clasping the boot, Rowena swings a nervous glance over her shoulder at Swain's Lane. "You don't think that they—"

"Look at me." Her hold on the car turns white-knuckled as she obeys, her gaze climbing my chest, then my throat, before arriving at my face. Tension lines her full mouth. "We lost them by Bagshot, remember? I made sure to stay off the motorway once we did."

"It's no secret that I own Holly Village." A visible shudder racks her shoulders, and it takes every scrap of self-restraint not to drop Guthram to the pavement and pull her into my arms. "They'd already be here by now, wouldn't they, if they were planning to follow?"

"Wherever they are, it's not here." My voice is low, husky. *Believe in me, Rowena.* "And I promise that if anyone pulls up this drive, I'll take care of them myself."

My brothers and I have spent ten years straddling England's barbed-wire political fence. We're despised in the same breath that we're adored, and I've long since forgotten the worry that comes with stepping into new enemy territory.

The same can't be said for Rowena.

Her shoulders curl forward, and I catch her darting looks back at Swain's Lane twice more before we make our way into Holly Village. Inside the mansion, Guthram's shoes drag noisily over the glossy wood floor. And, for the first time since I found him in the hallway at Broadmoor, I allow myself the chance to really look at the man who once stood side by side with Pa. His dark eyes are half-shut, all signs of consciousness out the door; dried blood paints his palms and forearms, from where he clearly tried to staunch the flow after Rowena stabbed him. Remove the impact of age and stress, though, and it's the same face that I remember from childhood.

Another mirrored perception.

The Robert Guthram I knew never would have done what this man did to Rowena today. Unlike his son, Robert lived by a strict code of moral conduct—women and children were always off-limits, no matter who they were. Ten years at Broadmoor clearly changed that, changed *him*—just as the nervous twitch to Rowena's shoulders tells me that she won't soon be forgetting the taste of death.

Kill him.

My molars grind and I rip my stare away from his face before I give in to temptation.

"Where's Grafton's exam room?" I ask Rowena.

She tilts her chin down the hallway. "Two doors past the drawing room, on the left. I'll grab her for us—I doubt she's in there."

"Rowena, I—" When she blinks up at me, I fall irrefutably silent. Words of apology beat to life inside my chest, all demanding exit though none of them take flight. *Forgive me, please.* For dragging her into this mess and putting her in danger. I stand there, holding up the man who tried to kill her and all I know is that if she demanded that I end Guthram, I would.

Her stare lowers then flickers to where Guthram is hauled up against my side. With narrowed eyes, she studies him like she would a cockroach that ended up on her plate. Distaste flattens her lips before she steps back and folds her hands at the base of her spine. "I'll get Sara."

Fuck.

Just before she disappears around the corner, I catch a glimpse of her linked fingers and it takes all the concentrated effort in the world not to chase after her. *Do what has to be done, Godwin.* It's for the sake of the mission that I drag Guthram's limp body down the hallway. Voices echo from the drawing room—Gregory and Samuel, I think—and with the toe of my boot, I shove open Grafton's door. Hit the light switch with my elbow before shouldering my way inside.

One glance reveals that that the room is nowhere close to the state-of-the-art OR that Matthews worked out of at the Palace, but beggars can't be choosers. The Palace is gone, at least for now, and I doubt Saxon's place in Oxford is outfitted with the medical supplies we need to keep Guthram alive.

Fighting the urge to drop him, I set him down carefully on the exam table and arrange his body so that he's fit for a coffin—legs straight, arms by his sides. Only the shallow rhythm of his chest proves that he's still among the living.

I hear Dr. Sara Grafton's voice in the hall before I see her: "I won't do it, Rowan. There's nothing you can do or say that'll convince me"—the door flings open and Grafton stumbles in with Rowena at her back—"otherwise."

Rowena keeps her hand on the doctor's shoulder as she lets the door close behind her. "Sara," she says, her tone sharp, "I pay you to administer to the wounded, don't I?"

Blue eyes slide toward Guthram on the exam table. "You don't pay me enough to care for anti-loyalists. And, from what you said, this one tried to kill you." She whirls around to face Rowena. "Why in the world would I keep him alive? Answer me that."

"Because if you don't there's nothing that'll stop me from ending you next."

Slowly, Dr. Sara Grafton peers over her shoulder and coolly meets my gaze. "Congratulations, Priest, you've just signed his death warrant."

When she makes an attempt to leave, Rowena is already there to head her off. She's still in that torn jumper from Broadmoor. Blood and dirt cake the fabric, her feet and face, too, but it doesn't stop her from extending an arm to block passage to the door. "You'll keep him breathing," she utters quietly, firmly, "and you'll do it because there are lives at stake."

"Whose?" Grafton demands.

"Damien's, for one, but also—"

"Seven-hundred-and-ninety-three souls."

Both women turn to stare at me, and I plant one hand on the doctor's desk to steady my frame against the memory of Caren Fitz begging me to set him free. "That's the number of anti-loyalists who have gone missing since the Westminster Riots."

"Should I care?" Grafton looks from me to Rowena. Stiffly, her arms clamp down across her chest. "I'm not the one who—"

"Would you care if they appeared at your old hospital?" I ask, watching her closely. "If they were injured and on the verge of death, would you send them away, Dr. Grafton, just because they aren't loyal to your queen?"

The arms across her chest squeeze tight and she falls back a step like I've struck her. "Why do you care?" she hisses. "You're *Holyrood*, aren't you? You've taken an oath to the Crown. If people go missing—anti-loyalists, at that—what does it matter to you?"

"Humanity is a choice." Digging my fingers into the desk, I feel my jaw clench when I grit, "I've spent ten years playing both sides and you know what I've learned? People are *people*, Doctor. They hurt, they bleed, they laugh, they love, and at the end of the day, they pray that when they wake, the goddamn destruction will end. Loyalist, anti-loyalist—you want to know if it matters to me? Then *yes*. When innocent people die, it all fucking matters."

As if her legs have gone weak, Rowena's back hits the door with a quiet *thud*. Her gaze never wavers from my face. Visceral. Poignant. She stands clear across the room but she might as well have put her hand on my heart. I feel myself grip the desk so hard that its sharp corner pricks the calloused skin of my palm.

"We need him alive," I say gruffly, tipping my head toward where Guthram lies, "because we need information. When I was . . ." Swallowing tightly, I force the words out past a dry throat: "From the moment I stepped inside Broadmoor Hospital, I knew something was wrong. It wasn't just that it's a psych ward. There are others like it across the country but *this* one—"

"I felt it, too," Rowena says. "And I knew it the minute the guard talked to . . . to Guthram like they were friends. They spoke to each other in a way that a guard and patient rarely do."

Grafton opens her mouth to speak, but I cut her off: "They're holding anti-loyalists in those rooms."

"You . . ." Rowena's hand finds the doorknob like she needs the support. "You *recognized* them?"

"Some," I admit, "not all."

"How do you know it was them?" Grafton asks. "It could have been anyone."

"They came to The Bell & Hand." *I've attended their funerals*, I almost add. They have spouses, siblings, children, who all believe them dead. If I thought . . . Jesus, if Saxon or Guy disappeared without a trace, I'd destroy the world to find them again. "We need to know how they ended up at Broadmoor, and, to do that, I need that man alive. So, you're going to keep him breathing, Grafton, even if you have to do it with my gun to your head."

Rowena reaches out and, with a single flip of the latch, she locks the door. "Save him, Sara."

"It's not much of a choice," Grafton mutters, eyeing the lock.

"It's an ultimatum," murmurs Rowena, "you're all out of choices."

Words that I told her when she was blind and shackled, and I don't know whether to throw my head back and laugh or pull her close and crush my mouth down over hers. In the end, I don't get the chance to do either because my mobile vibrates in my pocket. I answer without looking, and the familiar voice of my oldest brother greets me with seething fury:

"What the fucking hell have you *done?*"

CHAPTER 37

ROWENA

Holyrood has descended on Holly Village.

Three hours after Guy rang Damien, they trail in one after another with Guy Priest at the helm. No signs of Margaret or Saxon. Instead, all are veritable strangers to me, except for Benjamin Lotts and Dr. Matthews, who pauses awkwardly beside me to say, "I hear your vision returned."

I recognize him from the sound of his voice—genteel and smooth around the vowels. His hair is stark white, his skin brown. Eyes as black as coal peer down at me, and while they aren't warm, exactly, I think it's safe to say that Dr. Nathaniel Matthews is more than the coldhearted bastard who threw me in a cell with Alfie Barker.

Ignoring the obvious answer to the doctor's question, I clasp my hands behind my back. Angle my frame slightly toward him to keep the floaters on the wall and off his face. "Did they bring you along in case chaos erupted?"

He matches my pose, then leans one shoulder against the wall beside him. His gaze sweeps over the mismatched group of people in my drawing room. All stand in separate corners, as if the battle is only just about to begin. "I don't have high hopes," he admits.

"Does anyone?" I mutter.

It's going to be a proper blood bath.

There was no telling Guy otherwise, though, after con-firmation of Robert Guthram being taken from Broad-moor landed on every media outlet in the country. And it was a done deal as soon as Damien told Guy that he'd spotted anti-loyalists within Broadmoor. For better or worse, two enemies are converging today. Though Guy made it clear, right before he hung up, that if anyone so much as pulled out a weapon, he'd shoot us all.

From my corner of the room, I watch Damien's oldest brother as he grips Gregory's hand and introduces himself.

Guy Priest is nothing like Damien.

Both men have hair the shade of midnight, and their hips, shoulders, and chins line up, as if the universe decid-ed to draw the two brothers on a grid to get them even with each other. They easily stand taller than everyone else in the room. But the similarities end there. Where Damien is brawny, his muscles thickly defined beneath the fabric of his clothes, the eldest Priest is lean, nearly hawkish, with features just as intensely angular. And where Damien's blue eyes flicker with barely repressed heat, his brother's gaze remains calculating, cold. It softens only when he turns to Damien, and I don't miss the way he shuffles his body in front of his youngest brother with every new introduction.

"How far we've fallen," gripes a voice to my left, and I don't need to look to know that it's Hugh. "First the Mad Priest and now the rest of them. I wonder, do your terms apply to *all* the Priest brothers or just—"

My heel sinks into his foot.

"Jesus *fuck*, Rowan!"

A few of the Holyrood blokes turn in our direction and I smile and wave like I'm the bloody queen of England instead of her best mate. Hyper-aware of the fact that Dr. Matthews is doing a shoddy job of pretending *not* to listen, I turn my head toward Hugh. "Speak like that to me again, and you won't enjoy what I do next."

He shifts his weight onto his opposite foot. "Ian is probably rolling over in his grave right now."

The devil in me replies, "A tough feat considering that you had him cremated."

Letting out a dark growl, Hugh gestures to the room. "You've let his killers into our lives, Rowan." He doesn't bother to modulate his voice, not even with Dr. Matthews eavesdropping from my right-hand side. "And I can't be the only one who thinks it's wrong. The king recruited us—"

"The king recruited *me*." At the base of my spine, my fingers interlace tightly. "And then I recruited you and Ian. I don't fault you for feeling the way you do, Hugh—no one would, not even the Priests. But this is . . ." I bring my gaze to his face. "Can't you see that this is bigger than all of us?"

His stiff jaw suggests that he can't.

Frustration eats at me and I clamp my mouth shut before I say something that I'm sure to regret later. I won't pretend that losing Ian as a friend somehow equates to the loss of him as a brother, but Hugh is dangerously close to finding himself out on his arse. Aside from that first night, everyone else has managed to dance politely around Damien. Everyone, that is, but Hugh.

He's a loose cannon when we're already on the eve of war.

Either his rashness will see him dead or it'll take down someone else in his stead, and I can't . . . I *can't* allow that sort of devastation to happen. As much as I want to walk in Hugh's shoes with him, this is one trek that he'll have to make alone.

"Take the night off." Easing one hand away from the

other, I place it on his arm. "Put down the hate and rest your heart, Hugh. Please."

"I don't need—"

"It's an order," I tell him gently, raising my chin, "not a suggestion."

His dark eyes squeeze shut, and then he's spinning away without another word. Only once he's gone do I release the pent-up breath in my lungs. Falling back against the wall, I allow my hands to sink down to my sides.

"You handled that well."

I cut a wry glance toward Dr. Matthews. "You really have no shame."

"Would you believe it if I said that I was hard of hearing?"

"If you were, then you wouldn't have thrown me into a cell just to get rid of me."

The corner of his mouth quirks up. "Touché, Miss Carrigan." Bringing his gaze to the room again, he stews on his silence for all of three seconds. "Loss is a funny thing, isn't it?" He asks it in such a way that I know it's a rhetorical question. "We treat our grief like it's a curse."

"I don't understand."

"We obsess over it," he says with a roll of the shoulder that isn't pressed against the wall, "to the point that it consumes us. Where death is permanent, grief is a constant renewal of life that thrives on our pain."

My heart thuds against my rib cage. "That's . . ."

"Reality." Another small shrug. "He'll come around, Miss Carrigan. Just give him time."

But time is something we desperately don't have, especially when Damien and Guy break away from the fold and head my way not even five minutes later. From the matching grim expressions on their faces, I know that they're ready.

If death is permanent and grief is life, then betrayal is misery—and Silas Hanover may be wishing he already took his last breath by the time the Priests are through with him.

♛

"So," the eldest Priest brother drawls, "we finally meet again."

Opposite Guy, Silas Hanover is strapped to a chair in the undercroft. With his back to the stone wall, he sits with his nails biting into the armrests and his knees turned inward. Flickering gas lamps cast shadows across his face. And for every breath I take, his angry, dark eyes find their way back to me again.

It might, however, have something to do with the framed picture of Mum that I angle toward him on the sideboard, so that he has no choice but to acknowledge what he's done.

You didn't go down as easily as she did.

Fury clamps my fingers into tight fists that I shove behind my back. The Priests are leading the brigade on this interrogation, but I can't stifle the threat that crawls up my throat. "Did you know," I murmur, "that this is the only place in Holly Village where the walls are so thick that no sound escapes?" With his gaze centered on me, I push away from the sideboard. "You scream, and no one will hear you. You beg for mercy"—I drop my hands atop his on the armrests—"and no one will see your tears. You are alone, Silas, just as she was. And if it were up to me, you'd die alone, too."

His mouth tugs up on one side and, with his eyes narrowed, he spits on me.

Bastard.

Damien releases a feral growl but I stop his approach with a raised hand. Then, with the back of the same wrist,

I wipe away the spittle from my cheek. All-out defiance radiates from Hanover. No show of remorse. Not a single display of regret. Father always did choose his associates well, and Silas Hanover is no different. He's coldhearted, a murderer, and—

"She was innocent," I hiss, feeling the wrath of Hell propel my hand forward to clutch his neck, as he did to me at Broadmoor. "She was innocent in all of this and you . . . you helped him kill her, and for what? A *house*?" Against his throat, my hand visibly trembles. I'm aware of Damien and Guy staring but I can't—oh, God, I can't suppress the anger, can't pretend that it doesn't overrule every sense of reason when, deep down, I want this man to die a thousand little deaths as I have. "Whatever my father promised you, he *lied*. My only inheritance was this property, and if you think"—I draw a heavy breath—"if you think, for even one second, that I won't enjoy seeing you suffer here, then you're wrong. Justice is dying in the same house that you killed her for. You deserve no better."

My shoulders heave and the undercroft remains ominously silent, and then Hanover dips his chin, thrusts his neck farther into my grip, and drawls, "Are you done?"

All the rage, all the hate, knocks loose from my bones. I'm weightless, gasping for air and finding none.

"*Rowena*."

I turn slightly, my hand still locked around Hanover's throat, and find Damien.

How—how can a man commit such evil and feel nothing? How can he betray those he loves—Henry Godwin and Holyrood and King John—and abandon them in favor of the unthinkable? A broken oath. A discarded family-in-arms. A death that left my world in ruins. A death, if he's to be believed, that was sanctioned by my own father.

My lips part on all the words that won't come, and I seek Damien's gaze almost desperately. *Help me*, I beg him silently. *Help me understand.*

Because I understand none of this.

"Give me your hand," he rasps.

Blankly, I look down at my right arm, which hangs limply at my side. It feels weighted by stone boulders as I force it up and up and up. But when my palm is level with my waist, Damien jerks his chin toward my left, which has yet to leave Hanover.

"Let go"—Damien's velvet baritone slices through the thick, impenetrable fog to reach me, confused and irreparably wounded—"and give me your hand."

Let go of the pain. Let go of the hurt.

Dr. Matthews was right: grief is an endless cycle of life that I breathe into even now, twenty years after I heard Mum's final scream.

As if my fingers belong to someone else, I watch them slowly peel away, one by one, from Hanover's throat. My palm stings with the searing heat of mourning as I stagger backward. A retreat that lasts less than a heartbeat because Damien is already there, his arm slipping around my waist to catch my weight against his solid chest. His calloused palm skims my forearm, careful of my scarring, to tangle my fingers with his own.

He squeezes once.

I slam my eyes shut.

Focus on the mission, Rowan. Focus on what matters.

"His name is Silas Hanover," I whisper past a dry throat, "and a lifetime ago, I heard him nightly down in my father's study. He was also there on the night that Mum died."

"Is that true?" Guy demands, the staccato of his steps near-silent on the stone. "Were you working with Carrigan?"

I open my eyes just in time to see Hanover tip his head back. His posture stays loose and untroubled when he murmurs, "I have no idea what she's talking about."

Damien stiffens behind me. "Denial isn't the game you want to play with us. It won't end well."

"Because of how you've grown?" Hanover's grin is barely more than a leer. "Oh, if only Henry could see the two of you now. Though . . ." With mock concern, he cranes his head to eye the door leading to the servant's staircase. "Now that I think about it, where's Saxon? Don't tell me that you've sacked him."

My fingers are squeezed again, but this time, the gesture isn't offered in comfort. Tension ripples through Damien's frame. Against my back, I feel his chest shudder with a labored breath. "Mention his name again," he warns, "and you won't speak for the rest of your miserable life."

Before Hanover can reply, Guy drops to his haunches in front of the former spy. His wrists are tied to the armrests and his ankles secured to the chair's wooden legs, but none of that stops Guy from pushing Hanover's right trouser leg up to his knee. His hands are steady as he pulls a blade from the holster at his waist and sets it down next to his boot. Dropping one elbow to his thigh, Guy cocks his head. "We aren't the lads you remember . . . but I remember much about you, Robert."

Dark eyes land on the blade.

"The first time I ever saw blood spill was by your hand, and do you know what I remember?" The unhurried smile that touches Guy's lips sends a shiver skating down my spine. "I remember how you circled the man. He was bound, just like you, *stubborn*, just like you. And then you dropped to your heels, just as I have, and you turned to me and said, *He'll last longer this way.*" Guy traces a finger over

Hanover's exposed calf muscle. "You wanted answers and answers you would get. Tell me, how many cuts did you make before he died?"

Hanover's throat visibly bobs but he doesn't utter a word.

"That was your first test, Robert, and unfortunately . . . you've failed." With calculated precision, Guy reaches for the knife while never looking away from Hanover's paling face. "The answer," he goes on, dragging the tip of the blade across Hanover's quivering flesh in one unwavering stroke, "is seventy-one." The tip of the knife drips red when Guy pulls back. "Should we do a comparison and see where you fall?"

He poses the question so casually, so ambivalently, that my stomach freefalls as nausea catches me in its debilitating grip.

The first time that we met, at the Palace, I sensed a barely restrained energy about Damien's oldest brother that chilled me to the bone. Guy Priest is the hunter who finds his prey without ever lifting his gaze from the first print in the snow. And while I want Hanover to suffer, I still can't shake the inexplicable need to *run*.

The fact that Damien barely reacts tells me that Guy's interrogation tactics are common enough in Holyrood. After a quick squeeze of my hip, Damien even moves to his brother's side. "We'll keep it easy for you to start," he says to Hanover while pressing one hand to the stone wall and angling his body to present me with his back. "Robert Guthram is on your birth certificate, so why the fake name?"

It's only after Hanover's maintained his silence, and I hear his low hiss as the blade meets skin for a second time, that it hits me what Damien's done: with his body as a shield, he's blocked Guy completely from view so that I'm not forced to witness the violence firsthand.

I inhale sharply.

Damien's shoulders immediately contract and a moment later he catches my eye over his shoulder. Shadows tease across the hollows of his throat while the gas lamps bathe his handsome face in swaths of golden warmth. The villain and the hero forever tangled in a man who bleeds both death and salvation.

He doesn't tell me to go, doesn't demand that I stay.

The choice sits in the palm of my hand, mine to do with as I wish.

With my heart in my throat, I give him a small dip of my chin. He mirrors it, wordlessly, then returns to Hanover. "You told Rowena that you've been waiting ten years for Carrigan to get you out—what deal did you make with him?"

Hanover's gritty chuckle greets my ears. "I have no idea what you're talking about."

His new M.O., apparently.

He walked the halls of Broadmoor Hospital like he owned the place. He threatened to throw me into solitary confinement for no other reason than that I wore a red poppy and showed support for King John. And he knew— even as he planned to walk free from it all—that there are people locked away within Broadmoor whose sole crime was to stand opposite the king. Every single move he makes is a lesson in contradiction.

"Was it you?" I demand, folding my arms across my chest to contain the fury demanding release. "You have friends all across London, you said. Somehow those anti-loyalists went missing and *somehow*, they all found their way to Broadmoor. Was it your doing? My father's? The *king's*?"

"I have no idea what you're talking about."

Against the stone, Damien's hand balls into a fist. "You apparently know a whole lot of nothing, Guthram." Before Guy can move, Damien stays him with a hand to his shoulder. Then the hand that's leveraged against the wall drops to the back of Hanover's chair.

"The problem is," Damien utters, his voice pitched low, "I already know where Carrigan stands with the Crown and it's not with Holyrood. Which means that you've either been playing both sides for decades or, sometime in the last ten, you abandoned everything you knew, everything you ever believed in, to stand side by side with Edward Carrigan. Which is it?"

Predictably, no answer comes.

Among the floaters dotting my peripheral, I spy Hanover's feet jerk against the floor as Guy makes his next cut.

Escalating frustration throws me before the man who helped kill my mother. "I asked you this at Broadmoor and I'll ask you again—why do any of this?" I slash an arm at Guy, who still kneels on the ground, his fingers coated red with blood. "You know how far they'll take this, and you still won't cooperate." When he remains stubbornly mute, I growl, "Is it money that you want? Because I'll pay you, Hanover. Name your price and I'll pay you, so long as you give us answers."

Those dark eyes promise retribution as he rubs his lips together, flexes his fingers against the armrests, and grinds out, "I have no idea what you're talking about, Little Rowan."

I should have allowed Sara to let him die.

"I think you know everything and more," the eldest Priest murmurs. "So, I'm going to ask you just one more time—*what* was the deal you struck with Carrigan?"

Only, Hanover confesses nothing.

He confesses nothing as his blood hits the stone, and he confesses nothing when his cries fill the undercroft, and he continues to confess nothing until thirty-two strokes of the knife leave him unconscious and slumped over in the chair.

CHAPTER 38

DAMIEN

"We kill him."

Sparing my brother a dark look, I close the bedroom door behind me. "We aren't going to kill the man who'll get us what we want."

"And what the hell do we want, Damien?" Guy's hard stare tracks me inside the room as he uses the hem of his shirt to wipe Guthram's blood from the back of his hands. "Do we want our entire lives to end up on the telly? Is *that* what you want? Because after the stunt you and Rowena pulled today, we're one step closer to making that happen."

I grit my teeth. "Clearly, it didn't go as planned."

Agitation chases swiftly across his features and he opens his mouth like he wants to lay into me. At the last second, he turns on his heel and prowls deeper into the room instead. "Whatever's happening at Broadmoor, we handle it on our own. One call to the lads in Southampton and it'll be over within hours. Those people . . . they'll go home to their families."

"And us?"

He pauses at the window, shoving aside the curtains to peer down onto Swain's Lane. "What about us?"

"More will go in," I say, "and soon enough, we'll be heading back for another rescue mission. Is that how you want this to play out?"

"We don't know that'll happen."

"No, we don't, because Guthram won't bloody talk!" Rage crawls beneath my skin and, in a moment of weakness, I twist at the waist and slam my hand against the door. The wood rattles under my palm as my shoulders drive north to my ears. "He sat there," I bite out, "like we were nothing to him. He *sat* there like Holyrood didn't exist to him. And what he did to Rowena—" Cutting myself off with a harsh curse, I drop my gaze to the carpet before I reveal too much.

Like a snake choking the life from its victim, silence invades the room. It pulses and it thickens, until, finally, my brother breaks it with an in-drawn breath that audibly rattles his chest. "Why did you go to Broadmoor? The truth."

I slam my eyes shut. "Guy . . . don't."

"You may want to save those people—I don't doubt that—but it's not why you went."

With my temple against the door, I pinch the bridge of my nose and try to tame my racing pulse. "It doesn't really matter now, does it?"

"*Tell me, dammit.*"

"I want to be free!" The confession explodes from my soul, shattering the silence and splintering my brother's thin veneer of control when I turn on him. He physically steps back, his ass hitting the window, but still I let the words bleed out: "I want to walk down the street without having to look over my bloody shoulder every two seconds. I want to know that if someone is seen with me"—if *Rowena* is seen with me—"it's not a death sentence." Heat powers through my limbs, tightly wound and exponentially fragile. "I'm tired. I'm so *tired*, don't you fucking see it?"

Guy's gaze shutters.

His hand finds the windowsill.

And then, quietly, he destroys me: "You won't ever be free, brother."

I hear the words, see his familiar face, but he may as well have taken that knife of his to my own legs. They weaken beneath me and I throw out a hand to catch my balance.

I don't make it.

The room spins as my spine collides with the door and I sink down to the floor. I inhale only darkness and exhale only light, and no matter how I try to snatch it back—to fill my chest and collect every rare memory of stepping into the warmth of sunshine—it disappears as if it never was.

"This life . . . *your* life . . ." Breathing hard, Guy slams his fist down on the sill. "Fuck, Damien. You *won't* be free—don't you understand that? I'm trying . . . Jesus, I'm trying to keep you alive!"

Chained.

Collared.

I feel the noose tightening now, cutting off my air supply, until my only options are to accept defeat or unleash destruction.

My fingers dig painfully into my thighs. "I can't do this."

"*Damien*—"

"Did you see her?"

Guy's stare sharpens. "See who?"

"Rowena. Did you see her, really see her?"

Clearly trying to buy himself time before answering, he passes a hand over his mouth. "What does she have to do with any of this?" he finally demands. "Besides the obvious, which is that her father wants you *dead*."

You make me feel like I'm dancing with madness.

Words that heated me in a way that nothing else ever has—not rage, not vengeance, not the ever-present hum of *no mercy* that begs me to relent and succumb to sweet, fucking temptation. Rowena Carrigan isn't meant for me but damned if I won't hold onto her for as long as I can anyway.

"She breathes," I tell him roughly, "even when the world tries to destroy her—even when *I* tried to destroy her. She went into Broadmoor Hospital for me, brother. She risked death for *me*. And even just now, when I'm sure she wanted her own vengeance for what Guthram did to her mum, she passed the torch because I need the bounty off my head. The strength she has . . ." Slowly, I shake my head, even as my fingers bite into the stiff muscles beneath my trousers. "I need the chance to live and I won't let you take that away from me."

He doesn't meet my gaze when he returns to scraping the back of his bloodied hand with his shirt. "Do you love her?"

Air pumps hard and fast into my lungs.

War and hate are what I've always known. I'm the man who unburied his mother, the man who felt no remorse in bringing a wounded woman pain. Never in my life has there been a moment of kindness, softness, until Rowena stripped off that bandage and brought her violet eyes to mine. And I want to keep it—God, I want to bend that softness to my will and submerge myself in it, in *her*, until happiness is as familiar to me as breathing.

"I don't . . ." Clearing my throat, I smooth the heel of my palm over my right shoulder, squeezing the nerveless flesh. "I don't know how to love but if I could . . . I would give it to her," I husk, "I would give her all of me, if I could."

Guy's nod is barely detectable.

Without speaking, he makes a start for the door but remembers too late that I'm still propped up against it. He stops abruptly, just out of reach.

I lift my chin, the back of my head glancing off the wood, and bring my gaze to his. "I'll leave the missing anti-loyalists to you," I tell him, knowing that he won't have it any other way, "but Guthram is mine, brother. Don't touch him."

"Whatever you're planning," he replies, his voice dark, "it's suicide. You know that, don't you?"

"I would rather die trying to live than die knowing that I never tried at all."

CHAPTER 39

ROWENA

"Blackmail," Gregory deadpans with his right fist balanced on his knee, "you're telling me that you want to *blackmail* the police commissioner—and you want *me* to join *you*?"

With his arms linked over his chest, Damien crosses his long legs at the ankles. Behind him, Holly Village's patroness judges us all from her portrait above the marble fireplace mantle. "Sounds about right."

Gregory swings his wide-eyed gaze to me before turning back to Damien. "Why the 'ell not? Never did like the wanker." Slapping his thigh, he releases a maniacal chuckle that makes me squeeze my palms together in my lap. "Sign me up, Priest. I'm yours."

The corner of Damien's mouth hitches as he shifts his attention to the redhead seated next to Gregory. "Once upon a time," Samuel drawls, threading his fingers together between his spread legs, "there was a man who actively tried to avoid all confrontation. That man, in case it's not obvious, is me."

Damien arches a brow. "Is that your way of telling me to piss off?"

"It's my way of acknowledging how far I've fallen that

I didn't even bat an eye when you mentioned blackmail."

"So, you're in?"

"Damn me to hell and back, but yes." Samuel hooks a finger over the collar of his shirt, pulling on the fabric as if the conversation alone has him feeling anxious. "We aren't about to hug now, are we? Because if I'm being honest—"

With a bark of surprise, Samuel goes flying when Gregory's gigantic fist makes contact with his bicep. "Try to 'ug me and I'll 'ave more of where that came from."

Awkward laughter climbs my throat, and I can't help but tap Damien's foot with my own. "Is that about how it went when he pushed you from the roof?"

"Too bloody soon," Damien rumbles but his blue eyes glitter with suppressed humor. He waits until Samuel's clambered off the floor before leaning forward to prop his elbows on his thighs. "I can almost guarantee that the only reason the hospital hasn't released Rowena's name is because they don't want the PM breathing down their necks. But they will, soon. We need to strike first, while we still can, and I can't use Holyrood. If the commissioner spots any of us, it'll be over before it's even begun."

I cut a sharp glance in his direction. "And you honestly think that he'll believe that one of them"—I tip my chin toward Gregory and Samuel—"kidnapped his father from Broadmoor?"

"No."

I blink. "Then why—"

"Because I've already laid the groundwork." Reaching into his pocket, Damien fishes out his mobile and tosses it to me. "First photo," he says.

With no passcode to plug into the burner, I find the gallery easily and feel my heart rate spike when the photo loads. "You've . . ." Unable to finish the thought, I stare at the grainy picture of Silas Hanover down in the undercroft. Damien's cropped the image so that there are no identifiable features that might lead Marcus Guthram back to Holly Village, but there's no mistaking the fact that the former Holyrood spy has been captured. He's bloodied, handcuffed, and eerily still. "You mean to make him think that we've killed his father?"

"I mean to make him think that Alfie Barker has *almost* killed his father and if he wants to see the old man live, he'll show up when and where I tell him."

Startled, my gaze jerks up to his. "You're bringing *Alfie Barker* into this?"

"He wants freedom," Damien returns, plucking the mobile from my grasp, "and if he succeeds, then freedom he'll have."

"And if he dies?"

Blue eyes shift toward the sofa opposite ours. "If Gregory and Samuel do their job, Barker won't have to worry about that."

"Another prisoner on the loose," Samuel says with a dramatic sigh. "Soon we'll be down to none."

A dark chuckle escapes Damien as he pockets the mobile. "A dead Robert Guthram means no Holyrood pension for Marcus when he's been silently collecting it for years." He catches my eye. "I've already set the bait. Trust me, he'll show."

"And *you?*" Gregory demands. "We do all the 'ard work and you just—"

"We need Marcus feeling like he can appear alone, and Barker wouldn't even make a toddler nervous." Damien plants a down-turned fist on his thigh, leaning his weight into it. "I'll play catch and release at Tower Bridge. You lure the commissioner to me, and I'll handle the rest."

Samuel leans back to rest his arm across the back of the sofa. "When? Today?"

"Two nights from now."

Unable to contain my nerves, I tap a restless beat on my thigh. "You're planning this for the same time that Guy will be at Broadmoor?"

Damien gives me a slow nod. "We need the hospital staffers distracted if Marcus rings them. We take away his options and leave him squirming—it's the only way." Despite our audience, he lowers his head to put his eyes level with mine. "It'll work, Rowena. Believe in me."

Fear chases me up the stairs an hour later.

I follow Damien down the hall, tracing my trembling fingers over the wallpaper, and still I can't shake the disquieting feeling that this plan—*his* plan—is filled with holes that we haven't had the chance to uncover. Once we do, it'll be too damned late to crawl ourselves free.

The bedroom door hasn't even closed before I blurt, "This isn't a good idea."

Striding toward his duffel bag, Damien fists the back of his shirt without a word. His abdominal muscles ripple as he bares the script of Odin's ravens, Huginn and Muninn, and the hollow of his sternum expands as he reveals the skull and raven inked across his chest. Only once he's clutching the fabric in one hand does he lower his chin and speak. "You have to trust me."

My response is immediate: "It has nothing to do with trust."

"Then tell me what the problem is."

"Every unknown!" His blue eyes widen at my outburst but I'm already on the move, pacing the length of my room because I can't . . . I can't stand still when everything around me is spinning. "Damien, you're operating on one unknown after another. *If* the commissioner takes the bait. *If* he's foolish enough to follow a man that he doesn't know down to the Bascule Chambers beneath Tower Bridge. *If* Gregory and Samuel are able to keep out of sight long enough to see it all through. It's one risk after another and—"

"You don't think I know that?" He drops his shirt onto the duffel a second before he turns for me, *comes* for me, and prowls across the room. "Don't you think I know that one wrong move and it'll all come crashing down?"

Unwilling to concede defeat, I stand my ground. "You know all that and yet you're still willing to place your life into the hands of men who don't care if you die."

His nostrils flare. "Gregory and Samuel are your men."

"They're men that I *pay!*" Surging forward, I meet him halfway with a jab of my finger against his chest, directly in the eye of the raven. "I want to believe that their loyalty runs deeper than the money I've deposited in their accounts, but this is . . . Damien, this is—"

"This is what, Rowena?" When I don't answer right away, he catches my finger and presses my hand flush against his naked skin so that I have no choice but to feel the rapid beat of his heart beneath my palm. "This. Is. *What?*"

Each syllable that falls from his lips is like a round from a rifle, deadly and accurately aimed. I feel lightheaded, exposed. "It's insanity," I breathe, lifting my gaze to his, "to think that if it comes down to a matter of who lives or who dies, they'll choose to save you."

As if the words have struck him, Damien's hand inadvertently flinches around mine. Against my palm, the raven breathes, hard and fast, with every sharp inhalation that Damien draws into his lungs. When he finally speaks, his velvet timbre is mockingly cruel. "You seem to have the answer for everything, love. So, you tell me . . . I'm a wanted man without options—what do I do?"

Say it, Rowan. Just say it.

White noise floods my ears, drowning out the sound of my heart thudding frantically in my chest. "Choose me."

The flame in his blue eyes burns with unholy fire. "No."

His powerful frame spins away before I can press my case, and my words hit the rugged expanse of his back: "Whether you like it or not, Guthram is going to see my name on the register at Broadmoor. Today, tomorrow, the next day, it's a matter of when not if. At least this way, we do it on our own terms." When he says nothing, I fight the urge to grind my teeth. "Damien, I'm the logical—"

"I almost lost you!" he roars, wheeling back around to face me, inked shoulders heaving. His hands are clenched at his sides, those muscular, denim-clad legs spread and prepared for battle.

Thud-thud. Thud-thud. Thud-thud.

Madness.

My feet stay rooted to the rug but my body sways like a delicate flower caught in a tempest. I fight for air and feel my hand press heavy against my heart. It beats wildly. It beats with ferocious need. It beats to the rhythm of this man who has stormed his way into my life and unleashed chaos on every broken fragment of my soul until I'm nothing but a mosaic of want, need, hope.

The hope propels me forward now, one foot in front of the other. "You weren't supposed to care."

"But I do. Fucking hell, Rowena, *I do*." Those calloused hands descend upon my shoulders, intending to pull me close, but I duck under his arms to the melody of a harsh breath slipping past his lips. His blue eyes track me, stalk me, a god unwilling to let his sacrifice slip from sight. "I've only known the fear that I felt today once before," he expels roughly, that hand at his side flexing like he recalls the moment even now, "and to know that I sent you in there—that I believed, for even a second, that Robert's health had nosedived like Marcus said it had, and that we had a solid chance . . ." He gives a vicious shake of his head that sends his dark hair falling over his forehead. "It doesn't really matter what I thought, does it? Because you're not going to Tower Bridge."

He twists away.

I bend at the knees, blinking away the dark streak that chases across my right peripheral, and swipe the knife poking out from his duffel bag. Five swift steps return me to his unsuspecting back, one deep inhale carries my arm up high, and then I touch the tip of the blade to the ragged scar that stretches across his right shoulder blade.

He doesn't even flinch.

Testing him, I graze the fingers of my left hand gently over his muscled oblique. His shoulders instantly shudder, and his dark head falls back as he lays a hand over mine, gripping me tight . . . And all while I keep the knife pressed against that scar.

The seconds tick by.

One.

Two.

Three.

It's not until he turns that he spots the glint of steel. When he does, his entire body goes rigid. "What are you doing?"

"Proving a point."

"And your point is what? That you plan to stab me?"

"No," I whisper, careful not to prick his scarred flesh, "it's that I'm standing here on the side that I know you can't feel. It's you having to trust me that I won't stab you in the back—that I won't let you down when you need me most—even when your guard is still stacked like a fortress. It's me begging you to take a chance."

A vulnerable shiver visibly chases down his ridged spine. Then, gruffly, "What do you want?"

The hope unfurls, twining between my legs, looping around my waist, until I cave to its demands and give him the truth: "I want you to *see* me."

One moment I'm in control and in the next, the knife has clattered to the rug and my back is against the wardrobe and Damien's naked chest is flush with mine. He presses one hand to the wood beside my head in a move that's eerily reminiscent of the night that he came to take his revenge.

The similarities begin and end there.

"Don't you think that I see you?" he growls, his lips coasting over mine as he frames my face and forces me to meet his glittering gaze. "Rowena, I can't *un*see you. I see you on your knees, ready to die. I hear you in my fucking head, the panicked gasp that left you when Guthram ripped off the brooch. I *saw* you. Terrified and pressed up against that wall, and I knew"—his fingers scrape the wardrobe as a ragged breath fills his lungs—"Jesus, I knew then that I would stop at nothing to find you."

Tears sting the backs of my eyes. "Damien—"

"I don't know how to . . ." With a tight swallow, he smooths his thumb over my bottom lip and dips his head to taste me. The kiss is brief, the kiss is sweet, the kiss is soul-shattering in its complete and utter simplicity because Damien presses his forehead to mine and breathes,

"There's no point to being free if there's no sunshine waiting for me on the other side."

My hands tremble as a dangerous wish thrums to life within my heart.

To love and be loved.

To feel its heat in my veins and its courage in my bones.

Rising on my toes, I clasp my hands on either side of Damien's hips and brush my mouth over his. And then I pull back to let him see all of me, as no one has before: "I am not the damsel in distress, and I'm not some princess waiting for her prince." When he parts his lips to interject, I cut him off with a hard, silencing kiss. "I'll walk through darkness with you and I'll dance in the pits of hell at your side, but I will never be the woman who stands back and waits to be saved. You take me as I am, Damien, or you have none of me at all."

Anticipation teases up my spine. Gooseflesh kisses my skin. Strong fingers grasp my chin, angling my head so that all I see is him—the strong jaw and the soft lips and those blue eyes that gleam with want and need and hope.

"An ultimatum, Miss Carrigan," he purrs, his breath hot on my lips. "Am I all out of choices?"

"Unfortunately," I whisper, breathless, "you are."

A dark, wicked smile curves his mouth, and then he lowers his head and presses that wicked smile to my ear, and he vows, "Then I'll take you, Rowena. I'll take you as you are and I'll take you until you have nothing left to give, and then I'll do it again for as long as you'll have me."

CHAPTER 40

DAMIEN

War arrives under the cover of darkness.

"You bloody bastard," Robert Guthram snarls, thrashing in my grip as I push him down the shadowed stairwell, "You'll pay for this. Do you hear me? *I'll make you—*"

One sweep of my foot against his and he trips, his shackled wrists unable to break his fall. He lands face-first on the concrete steps with an audible crunch of snapping cartilage. Feeling Rowena's gaze on my back, I drop to my haunches and eye his crumpled frame with contempt. "You were saying?"

The metal handcuffs clank noisily as he tries to crawl away.

Predictable.

"You had your chance to speak and you chose silence." I close my fingers over the back of his shirt, fisting the material to put an end to his labored fumbling. "You killed an innocent woman for personal gain. You aligned yourself with a traitor. And, as if all that isn't enough, you turned your back on Holyrood." My knee lands on the center of his spine and I lower my head close to his. "You've been at Broadmoor for ten years, Guthram, but I'm sure you remember what happens to those who betray our oath."

With a grunt, he twists his head toward me and bares his teeth. "*Piss off.*"

"Actually, the correct answer is death. Turns out my ancestors weren't so keen on second chances." Beneath my weight, he squirms for freedom but I don't let him have even a scrap of hope. "You live because I let you. You *breathe* because I have use for you. Do you understand me?"

"What I understand is that you're a damned fool—"

His bloodied nostrils flare angrily as I fit a length of rope in his mouth. Aside from the muted drip of water hitting the steel accumulator tower to our left, the darkened stairwell falls quiet. With a quick jerk of the cord, I tie the rope at the back of Guthram's skull then close a hand around his arm to haul him to his feet.

"Move," I growl.

The damp air grows more oppressive the farther we descend below Tower Bridge and the River Thames. Wide concrete steps become narrow metal rungs that audibly vibrate under the rubber soles of my boots. Pearls of moisture cling to pipes fitted against curving brick walls. A glance past the metal balustrade reveals only the pitch-black cavern of our destination.

Rowena's voice breaks the stillness: "Barker has him."

Inaudible words strike the rope as Guthram wrenches his body to the left. Gritting my teeth, I shove him back into line. "What's their ETA?"

"Samuel says twenty minutes."

On a quick look back, I see Rowena shove the mobile into her joggers while her gaze rakes over the subterranean space like she's never encountered anything like it— and I doubt she has. Before the Westminster Riots, the Bascule Chambers regularly welcomed tourists wanting a glimpse of the massive Victorian counterweights which lift the Tower's suspension bridge and allow ships passage down the Thames. Nowadays, the chambers are home only to the run-off soul looking to escape London's streets.

And us.

"Let him know that we'll be ready and waiting," I tell her, fighting the flare of anticipation that sends my pulse into a quick clip. "We're almost there."

Soon.

Freedom. Happiness. Sunshine.

Fucking hell, I can almost taste it now.

But when we pass through the arched tunnel and finally enter the dimly lit, cavernous space, it's only to find a familiar figure sitting on the theater-style brick steps that dominate half of the chamber.

With deliberate ease, Guy unfurls his body from the steps and rises to his feet.

The sight of him sends Guthram lurching forward with a muffled snarl and I snatch the back of his shirt to lock him in place—but my narrowed stare never veers away from my brother. "You're supposed to be in Crowthorne right now."

"I sent Hamish." The clip of his boots echoes hollowly within the chamber, growing more distinct the closer he comes. "He'll meet the Southampton team, as planned. The anti-loyalists will go home to their families, as planned. Nothing changes from me not being there."

Maybe not but it still doesn't change one crucial fact: "You called this is a suicide mission."

His stride visibly falters.

Shadows chase across his chin, his throat, but a splice of light from the emergency lamps reveals those shrewd blue eyes scanning the exposed bascules in the brick-lined ceiling. Then, "When you go to battle, brother, you don't do it alone."

"You should have stayed with—"

"He's not alone."

My chin jerks to the right, where Rowena has stepped in beside me. She rolls her shoulders back, holds her head up high like the queen she is at heart, and throws me a fierce look. An involuntary intake of breath expands my chest, and *Jesus*. We're standing in a room submerged beneath a city, hidden away from all of London, and I swear that I can feel the warmth of the sun on my skin. Holyrood is my family, Guy is my blood, but Rowena has somehow become the hope that beats mercilessly inside my veins.

The she-wolf. The phoenix rising.

A vision of life when I've always been a man consumed by death.

"He's not alone," she repeats firmly, dragging her gaze away from me to address my brother, "but I'm sure we can use all the help we can get. They should be here in"—she pulls out the mobile, its screen glowing bright—"eight minutes."

"Or less," I mutter, checking my watch, "if Barker starts running."

Guy's palm flattens over his holstered pistol. "Why the hell would he be running?"

Before I can answer, Guthram throws his weight against my hand—I don't bother playing nice this time. Spinning his flailing frame under my arm, I shove him back, back, back until his heels hit the brick steps and he collapses onto his ass. Pulling the wire coil from my kit, I sink down to one knee and begin looping it, tight, around his ankles. Over his guttural shouting, I say, "Because I may have implied that Robert, here, will lose a limb for every minute that Marcus runs late."

"You're mad," Guy says.

"Devious," I grunt under my breath, "I prefer devious."

Reaching into my armored vest again, I pull out a wool sack that's eerily similar to the one Carrigan's men used on me. One look at it and Guthram immediately tries to scramble backward but all he manages to do is send his restrained body teetering onto his side.

"This isn't . . ." Struggling for the words, I stare down at the sack hanging harmlessly from my palm. A month ago—hell, even a fortnight ago—I would have taken great pleasure in killing Robert Guthram. It would be a lie to pretend that I don't feel that way now, too. "Pa would be disappointed in you. Everything you've become, everything you stand for"—I squeeze the wool tight in my fist, then meet a pair of dark, furious eyes—"you've become the man you once slaughtered without a second thought."

The rope scrapes the inner corners of his mouth when he clenches his jaw, looking like he'd spit on me—like he spat on Rowena—if he could somehow manage it.

"I should kill you, Guthram, but it turns out that I want my freedom more than I want your life." Lowering one knee to the brick, I angle him upright and then slide the sack down over the top of his head. Once a legendary Holyrood agent, he's been reduced to *this*: bound feet slamming against the ground and shackled body twisting wildly as he fights for escape. It's too little too late. "Do as I told you and you'll live. Whatever your son does with you after that isn't my problem."

And then I turn away from the man who once sheltered me from danger after our return from Paris. I feel the pinch of guilt in my chest. I taste the sour note of bitter regret on my tongue. None of it, however, is enough to deter me from the end game.

Freedom. Happiness. Sunshine.

Soon. Now. Fucking *finally*.

Hiking up the back of my shirt, I grasp the revolver that I took from Rowena's wardrobe and approach her. She's dressed in all black, from the jumper that covers her scarred forearms to the trainers that barely emit a sound on the brick as she meets me halfway. Her head immediately tips back, lips parting to speak, but I cut her off.

"If something happens, you shoot," I say, my voice low, reaching for her hand, "and you won't think twice about the consequences—do you hear me?"

Her surprised stare flickers up to my face. "I told you that I've never fired a gun."

"And I believed you until I found this hidden in your room." Nestling the grip in her palm, I close her slender fingers over the engraved metal. Then I meet her gaze. "You do everything with grit, with purpose. You'd never carry a firearm unless you made sure that you knew how to use it."

"Damien, I—"

"Here we go, brother," Guy mutters from behind me, "I can hear them in the tunnel. Get against the wall before the commissioner sees us."

I tug Rowena behind me, drawing her into the shelter of shadow, but it's the gut-wrenching memory of her arms slipping into the air at Broadmoor that has me growling, "Promise me that you'll shoot. *Promise me.*"

"I promise, but—"

There are no but's.

There are no if's.

In this world, there are only *when*'s, and so I slam my mouth down on hers to swallow the undercurrent of fear marking her husky voice—the same fear that marks my soul. I devour her, forcing her lips open with a thrust of my tongue. She tastes like dreams. She tastes like *life*. My body aches to curl around her, to pull her flush against me until I can feel her heartbeat flutter against my chest. Freedom. Happiness. Sunshine. *Almost there, almost there.* With a clenched jaw, I tear away before I lose myself completely.

Those violet eyes lift to my face on a shattered breath.

Her fingers curl into her palm, shoulders rising and falling with emotion, and then she presses two fingers to her lips like she can hold onto the taste of me forever. No cunning smiles to issue a challenge this time. No lethal grins to make me feel duped. Instead, Rowena slides the revolver into the waistband of her joggers, as if it's a move that she's done a thousand times over, and then she shifts onto her toes and presses those same two fingers to my own lips.

Her touch is a vow.

A vow that she'll walk with me in the darkness, that she'll dance in the pits of hell at my side. A vow that she is here, beside me, and I'm not alone.

Her whispered words hit me at the same time that I hear commotion entering the chamber: "Have no mercy."

CHAPTER 41

DAMIEN

The Met's police commissioner enters the Bascule Chambers exactly as I figured he would—with a sobbing Alfie Barker held at gunpoint.

I touch Rowena's wrist to make sure she doesn't make a sound.

We can't reveal ourselves until the right moment or this will all come crashing down on our heads. Barker knows the plan; Samuel and Gregory—who should be trailing behind at a safe distance to avoid being seen—know the plan. And while Guy doesn't know much of anything, he hasn't failed a mission in the twenty years since we've returned from Paris. He'll catch on, quick.

Stumbling forward from the brightly lit tunnel into the darkened chamber, Barker lifts his arms in surrender. Tears streak down his cheeks. Blood beads on his temple. He begins to beg, shamelessly, the second that the pistol jams, hard, into the back of his skull: "I have children. *Daughters*. Don't . . . Oh, God, please don't do this. *Please*."

Marcus Guthram's expression remains rigidly impassive. "You should have thought of that before you kidnapped him." He shoves Barker deeper into the chamber.

"Where is he?"

"I-I don't know."

"You don't know?" The impassivity contorts, revealing a fury that flares his nostrils. Like father, like son. "You sent me pictures of him nearly dead, you spineless twat! And now you want to tell me that you don't *know*?"

A tendril of light reveals Barker's trembling fingers. "He's here, I promise. He's—"

"Alive," I finish for him, stepping out from the darkness. "Although for how long remains completely up to you, Commissioner."

At the sound of my voice, Marcus's head snaps in my direction.

The gun aimed at Barker now swings to me, and he snarls, "I should have known you were behind this."

"And yet you came anyway." I hold my hands up high to show that I'm not carrying. Not that he expects me to be empty-handed—and he'd be right. I've three knives tucked away, and two handguns holstered, one at my waist and the other at my ankle. I prepared for nothing less than war. "Some might even say you came hoping that I'd be the one waiting for you."

"This piece of—" Lip curling, he slashes his arm and nails Barker in the back of the skull with the gun. The *thud* resonates through the chamber and Barker crumples instantly, his legs ceding defeat beneath him. Over the sound of his limp body hitting brick, Marcus taunts, "Having others do your dirty work now, Priest? Or were you too scared to meet me on your own?"

"You'd know all about that, wouldn't you?"

"I have no idea what you're talking about."

At the now-familiar words, I nearly bark out a laugh. "And here I thought you never missed a thing, but maybe . . ."

Rolling one shoulder, I keep my hands lifted by my ears. "Maybe you're just too busy to notice when six of your men don't return from a mission. Not great leadership on your part, I'll say that, but no one's ever accused you of knowing what the fuck you're doing."

The line of his arm barely dips. "Where are they? Priest, you better tell me—"

"Casualties of my own survival, unfortunately."

"You bastard!"

A cruel smile touches my lips. "Don't worry, they called me much, much worse."

Though the pistol trembles in his grip, his dark eyes narrow to slits of rage. "I'm going to ask you this only once—where are the bodies?"

Stopping beside Barker, I touch my boot to his shoulder and roll him onto his back. His lids are closed, all the color gone from his face—but he breathes. I feel the rise and fall of his chest under my sole. He'll wake with a hell of a concussion but still have his life. And he'll go back to those two girls of his, his debt to Holyrood paid off in full.

"Did you hear me, Priest?" Marcus barks. "*Where are the bodies?*"

Without ever turning away from him, I step backward. "Already buried."

"Where? Where did you—"

"All except for one, that is." Another backward step.

His mouth falls open and I hear only his harsh rush of breath when he slides his forefinger over the trigger. "*Who?* You tell me which one of my men you have or I'll rip your blasted heart out. Do you hear me?" He follows me as he speaks, storming across the chambers to keep the distance between us tightly knit—and I let him.

Closer, Marcus.

I retreat.

Come closer.

He advances.

On my periphery, I spot my brother on the move and purposely scuff the soles of my boots against the brick to muffle the sound of his stride. Back I go, back I move, and all the while, Marcus never removes his finger from the trigger.

A little more.

Just a little . . .

"You coward! You brought me here to the fucking *underworld* of London and now you run when—"

The words turn strangled when he spies Guthram's bound feet.

Disbelief chases rage across his ashen features. The pistol follows me south as I drop to my heels and put a hand on Robert Guthram's shoulder.

"You may recognize my guest," I murmur, kicking up my chin so that Marcus stays in my line of sight. "Since he is, obviously, the reason that you're here in the first place."

"You—you—"

"You're in a bit of a conundrum, aren't you, Commissioner?" I smile, slowly, and reach for the sack covering Guthram's head. Pulling it free, bit by bit, I reveal the rope still tied over his mouth and his bloodied nose. At the sight of his son, Guthram's struggle begins again. I return my gaze to Marcus. "You could kill me, if you wanted."

The gun inches closer.

"The *problem* with killing me," I continue, flattening my hand on Guthram's chest to keep him still, "is that you'll never know where poor Kendrick is. That's his name, right? He had a devil of a time saying much of anything after I was through with him."

The commissioner's roar hits the back of his clenched

teeth.

"Tough choice, isn't it?" Raising my brows, I lean over Guthram to make sure the rope is snug between his lips. "You kill me for your old man here or you find out where Kendrick is being held. You can't have both."

"*Why?*"

Steadily, I meet his stare. "You know why, Marcus."

His lips peel back angrily and the gun collides with my browbone. "I know what you can do, you bastard. Anytime in the last seven months you could have taken the damned bounty off your own head."

Oh, I'd thought about it.

Every fucking night, every bloody day—but it wouldn't have mattered in the end. Because while I can hack my way in, I can't convince the people of Britain that I'm not worth the thousands of pounds that the Met's commissioner put on my head. In a time where people are struggling to carry on, the green that comes with turning me in is a first-class ticket to a better life.

"It has to come from you," I edge out, despising the fact that I'm forced to grovel, "or it'll mean nothing at all."

The pistol digs in, canting my head at a sharp angle that makes me see red. "So, what you're telling me is that your life is in my hands."

I grit my teeth. "Kill me and you'll only kill yourself, Marcus."

"Take the rope off him."

My stare catches on Guy, who's moved stealthily to a few paces behind the commissioner. *Don't shoot*, I want to shout. Jesus Christ, don't shoot. Until Marcus rings in to remove the bounty, he stays alive or this—every risk we've taken—will all be for nothing. Rowena nearly died to see me go free and I can't . . . *fuck.*

"Take. Off. The. Rope."

Each syllable is punctured with the pistol shoving my head farther back. Fury swirls in my gut. Desperation claws at my lungs. If I remove the rope, Guthram will give away that we aren't alone, but if I don't . . .

There's a good chance that Marcus will decide that he doesn't give a damn about saving Kendrick. He'll shoot me, then. Paint the bricks red with my brains. And Rowena will see it all unfold. A lifetime of nightmares where she's surrounded by flames and then, in a heartbeat, she'll remember me dead in this chamber forever after.

"Ease back," I grunt, "and I'll do it."

The gun barely shifts.

Unable to turn my head, I trace the length of the rope from the back of Guthram's skull. He twists his body and thrusts his chin away. It gives me pause, for less than a second, that he's actively trying to pull back. I don't let him. Sinking my fingers beneath the rough threads of the rope, I yank him into place.

The rope tears free and the commissioner turns away to face his father and, in that split-second moment where time slows and hell rises to destroy us all, I watch my brother pull the trigger.

A shout lodges in my throat.

Robert Guthram's body spasms from the force of the blow.

And then Guy shoots again.

The commissioner's anguished cry reverberates throughout the chamber. His right leg twists inward, his weight collapsing hard and fast. He lands on the ground, less than an arm's length away from a dead Robert Guthram, but still has the wherewithal to lunge for the gun he dropped.

I launch for it at the same time.

He curses in my ear when I swipe it away and push up to my feet. Whirling on my brother, I hiss, "What the *fuck* are you doing?"

"Hurrying shit along."

His blue eyes don't bother to meet mine as he holsters his firearm. Without another word, he crosses over to the commissioner and grabs him by the arms to prop him on the brick steps beside Guthram.

Fucking hell.

Oh, *bloody fucking hell.*

"Broadmoor is looking for him." Wide-eyed, I look from one Guthram to the other. Father and son, both white-haired, both bleeding. "Jesus fucking Christ, the hospital has people looking for him and you *killed him.*"

"The commissioner will live," he mutters, "and he'll be sure to call back the hounds for us. If there's still a Broadmoor left standing at all after tonight." With his mouth set in a grim line, Guy pats down Marcus and pulls out a mobile from the commissioner's trousers. Shoving it at me, he keeps his attention firmly rooted on Marcus. "You're going to ring the Met, and you're going to have them remove the bounty."

Marcus's stare never leaves his father. Chin wobbling, he breathes, "You've killed him."

"And you've been collecting his pension for ten years now, so let's not sit here and pretend that you suddenly give a damn. We both know that you don't."

"*Piss off.*"

Grabbing the commissioner by the collar, my brother jerks him close, hissing, "The difference between us, Marcus, is that I understand loyalty. I understand *family.* So unless you want to end up like your old man, you're going to take this"—he plucks the mobile from my grasp and shoves it against the commissioner's chest—"and take him off the fugitive list."

Marcus's fingers tremble as he angles the phone toward his face.

Guy growls, low, "Where I can fucking see you."

The commissioner lowers his hands to do as he's told—but the cut of light from the screen reveals Rowena coming to stand beside me. His mouth twists with disgust. "If your father could see you here—"

"My father had my mum murdered and had *your* father make it happen. Edward Carrigan doesn't have a leg to stand on." Deliberately, Rowena lets her gaze drift to Marcus' bloodied thigh. "Justice always has a way of being served, don't you think?"

He lurches toward her with a roar.

"Trust me," I grind out, clamping a hand around his arm, "you don't want to do that."

His furious gaze flickers to me. "And you have no bloody idea what you're doing here. You'll regret this, Priest. One day, you're going to realize that you've—" A scream rips from his throat as Guy grinds the heel of his palm against the commissioner's wounded thigh.

"The bounty, Marcus," my brother says.

On a sharp glance toward his father, jagged breaths cut past Marcus's lips. His pallor turns ghostly under the sparse light. The hand clutching the mobile visibly shakes. And all the while my brother maintains his weight on the commissioner's thigh, where the round went clean through.

Had Robert Guthram not betrayed us, he'd be alive right now.

Had Pa not allowed his best mate to disregard Holyrood's rules all those years ago, Marcus Guthram wouldn't even know we exist, and he wouldn't be bleeding all over my brother's palm.

One could argue that bad things happen when rules aren't followed.

And *I* could argue that humanity, at its very core, rejects anything that limits our individual ambitions. We know greed and we know power and we know, more than anything else, that we will always put our own wants and needs first.

Mum told me that I would be shown no mercy.

But as I watch Marcus fumble with the mobile, his face contorting with pain the harder my brother pushes down on his wound, I realize that we're meant to show mercy more than we should ever expect to receive it.

"Let him go."

At my roughly uttered command, Guy's head jerks toward me. "What?"

I swallow, hard.

Say the words, Godwin.

Mouth dry, I tip my chin toward his bloody hand. "Let him go, brother."

"Damien," he growls, "you've lost your goddamned mind."

No, for the first time in my life, I know exactly what needs to be done.

I turn my gaze on Marcus Guthram, the commissioner of the Metropolitan Police, to find him already watching me. Suspicion crawls across his expression. "I went to the House of Commons that night on the king's orders," I confess, never allowing my stare to leave his, "because he suspected that Carrigan wanted him off the throne."

"Why are you telling me this?"

"Because we've existed in the same world for decades," I allow, feeling a hand settle on my shoulder in silent support. *Rowena.* Needing the connection, I slide my palm over hers and lace our fingers together. "Because I've been loyal to the

Crown from the day I was born. I'm not"—the despised word sticks in my throat—"some terrorist, and I'm not mad like the prime minister wants all of the world to believe. I'm a spy for the royal family, Marcus. I am *Holyrood.*"

"And you think that's enough?" The commissioner yanks his leg away from my brother with a stifled hiss. "Did you ever stop to think that I put the bounty on your head because it's what *I* wanted? What I still fucking want?"

"Jesus." I plow my fingers through my hair. "Until tonight, I've done nothing to—"

Rowena's hold on my shoulder tightens a second before her choked "*No!*" hits my ears.

By the time it registers that she's not talking about the commissioner, it's already too late.

The staccato of gunfire reverberates in the chamber, and I twist around before my next breath even exits my lungs. Circling Rowena's waist, I haul her off the floor as she screams over my shoulder, "Hugh, *no!*"

Cradling her in my arms, I turn my back on the tunnel. Flick my gaze over the shadowed chamber while my gut sinks like an anvil in the sea. No exit points. No way out and only one way in. I picked the Bascule Chambers because I wanted Samuel and Gregory following Barker at separate intervals to ensure Marcus came alone. Only, I didn't anticipate danger coming from within the fold.

I hear a gruff shout—and recognize it as belonging to the commissioner.

I hear a harsh curse followed by the immediate discharge of fire—and know that Guy is giving hell.

When you go to battle, brother, you don't do it alone.

I may not be alone but now I've taken them all down with me.

With my chin pressed against Rowena's temple, and

my arms caging her to my chest, I sprint toward the shadows without ever looking back at the chaos. Rowena Carrigan is a woman capable of saving herself, but I can't lose her ... *Won't* lose her. Her breathing is ragged in my ear, her voice strained as she continues to beg for Hugh to stop.

There's no end to the bloodshed.

No end to the war.

Isla killed Ian Coney and now Hugh plans to kill us. Two Priests for the price of one.

More gunfire explodes, its release utterly deafening, and pain rips through my left shoulder. I twist at the waist involuntarily, staggering sideways from the force of the round drilling past the shell of my vest.

"Put me down," Rowena begs, her fingers clawing at my shirt where I've been hit. "Oh, God, Damien, put me—Hugh, *no!*"

My left leg buckles.

The heat. The *fire*.

A hoarse groan dances across my tongue as I struggle to stay on my feet. Despair propels me forward, my arms cinching tight around Rowena. *So close.* So close to those shadows and to that safety, however temporary they each might be. Except that the fire is already spreading—climbing up my thigh, crawling down my spine. A sensation that I've never been able to erase from memory.

My body may be a shield, but like all armor, I'm not infallible.

Agony punches through my right calf and, this time, there's no stopping the fall.

I release my arms from around Rowena at the very last second, hoping to set her free before I crush her under my weight. Coarse brick tears through my trousers when my right knee hits the ground. The collision rattles my jaw, bursts a blood vessel on my tongue.

Rowena's fingers grasp mine and she pulls with all her might. "Damien, run with me."

My lips part to speak but no sound emerges.

I'm voiceless, again.

Dying, again.

"Damien, get up. *Get up!*"

She yanks on my hand and I see her—oh, fuck, I see her hands on mine, but the fire is flooding my veins and my chest is caving in with panicked breaths and *I can't feel her.* Fear jerks my gaze to hers and I try to force the words past my tongue:

Run.

I need you.

I'm not ready. Rowena, I'm not ready!

None make it past my dry throat.

Greed for life has me clenching my core to stay upright on my knees, to be strong and pretend that I haven't already traversed this path and know exactly where I'm heading—but my muscles are completely unresponsive. Dark brick comes up on me, hard and fast, when I crash facedown.

Paralyzed. Frozen.

The same as I was outside Christ Church Spitalfields.

The brick disappears from sight as I'm shoved onto my back and Rowena's beautiful face appears above me. I feel nothing but terror as she beats on my chest with her fists, feel nothing but heartache when tears coat her dark lashes. "Damien, you can't leave me. *Please.*"

A battered breath rattles my lungs when she buries her face against my chest, which burns with the heat of a thousand suns. The beginning of the end. In the alley, I had only minutes before everything faded, and I need to see her. God, I need to see her just one more time.

I try to move my fingers.

Look at me.

Her shoulders shake with heart-wrenching sobs that gut me.

Please, love, just let me see you.

"You promised to chase me." Her hands grasp the front of my kit, her throat working hard, and then she's scrambling onto her knees as if she plans to drag me from this pit of hell all on her own. "You promised to chase me to the ends of the Earth, Damien Godwin, and I won't let you die on me. Do you hear me? You are not dying on me!"

I've never been a man who cries.

Never been the man who sheds the rage to reveal the softness beneath.

But as Rowena struggles to push my unresponsive body, and fails, I finally learn what it means to break.

Silent sobs crack my chest wide open and I strain my paralyzed limbs to reach for her, to crush her to me and press my mouth to hers. I wanted freedom and I wanted sunshine, and while my body may leave this chamber to experience both, my soul never will.

I'm as chained and collared as I've always have been.

Only, Rowena keeps her vow.

As the last threads of consciousness slip away, she walks through the darkness with me, her tear-stained voice a guide that I cling to desperately, her touch a balm that soothes the panic of stepping into the abyss—even though I feel her not at all.

I'm not alone.

And, with her alone, I know love.

CHAPTER 42

ROWENA

Damien won't move.

His chest rises and falls under my palms.

His flame-blue eyes flicker with an agony that destroys me.

But his limbs remain heavy as stone no matter how hard I push. And I *push*. As Guy takes down Hugh, I shove Damien's body with all my strength. My trainers skid against brick and my heart weeps for what I refuse to believe might possibly be true—and I get him absolutely nowhere.

Looping my fingers around the straps of his armored vest, I pull and pull and pull.

He doesn't budge.

Another sob claws its way out and I taste the ear-shattering scream threatening to follow in its footsteps. Bleakness ransacks my soul, killing every seed of hope within me until I'm on my knees before him. "Don't give up. Please, Damien. *Please*." Head lowering, my throat knits closed. I've spent years shoving back tears, all traces of emotion, but I can't manage stoicism now—Oh, God, I *can't*. Heat spears my face and dampness gathers on my cheeks, and I fold my body over Damien's to interlock my hands over his chest. "Wake up for me," I beg, "please wake up for me."

Own the darkness or it'll own you, he said.

Harness it until it's an asset and not a curse, he told me.

His breath slips over his lips. Shallow. Barely a rasp. If I look at him now, there'll be nothing left of me to scrape together. Tears blur my vision as I grip his vest and bend my knees to leverage my weight against his. "You are *mine*, Damien," I grit, digging in my heels, "do you hear me? You are mine and you *are not dying*."

"Rowena, stop."

When I don't answer the gravel-pitched command, Guy's lean frame drops into view. Blood paints his profile red. Resting on the balls of his feet, his hands visibly shake as he pushes mine out of the way to grab hold of his brother.

"He won't move."

His eyes slam shut at my plaintive whisper, but his fingers never loosen their grip on Damien's shoulder. "Help me," he breathes, turning his head to meet my gaze. "I need you to help me, Rowena. I can't carry him alone."

"He's not dead. Don't you understand? *He's not dead!*"

Terror cuts me to the quick as I fumble for Damien's hand. His pulse. I need to check his . . . *Nothing*. Oh, God. Oh, God, *no*. Desperation brings my fingers to his armored vest. I tear at it wildly, pulling at straps, unzipping the metal tab, until the only thing separating me from his skin is the soft fabric of his shirt. I rip at that, too. Only, there's too much blood. It coats the raven, stains the skull. Choking back a ragged cry, I shove my ear against his heart with a prayer burning on my lips.

Breathe for me, Damien. Live *for me*.

His chest barely lifts.

I want to howl my misery and scream my despair.

Broken, but never defeated.

As if I've been thrust into a fog, I'm aware of wordlessly threading an arm under Damien's neck to cradle his head. Soft, black strands caress the scarred flesh of my forearm. The blisters. The blindness. Fire consumed me and, against all odds, I lived—I live, *still*—and Damien will survive, too.

"We'll bring him to Sara and Dr. Matthews."

"Rowena, you don't under—"

"He. Will. *Live*." With courage seated deep in my bones, I stare Guy down as though he isn't Damien's brother but rather the Grim Reaper come to collect the dead. "I won't let you write him off," I growl, curling my hand protectively over Damien's chest, where his heart still thuds softly against my palm. "Just *believe* in him."

Those blue eyes—so calculating, so cold—could melt glass as he steps over his brother's sprawled legs. He says nothing but I don't need pretty speeches. Together, we haul Damien's brawny frame off the ground. His dark head falls forward. His arm slips from my shoulder. All it takes is one intake of breath for my rib to scream bloody murder under the strain of carrying his bulky weight.

I put one foot in front of the other.

And I do not stop.

Like we've found ourselves submerged in the Underworld itself, we carry Damien past the dead. Silas Hanover and the Met's commissioner. Alfie Barker, who must have roused with the commotion, only to be laid to rest in a bloodied grave beside Marcus Guthram. And then Hugh Coney.

The devil.

The wolf in sheep's clothing.

He followed us with only destruction in his heart, and I hate him for taking what didn't belong to him. Alfie Barker's life was not his to take, Damien's life not his to steal. Barker had his daughters and Damien had . . . he has *me*. Fresh tears well and I let them fall. Then I tangle my fingers with Damien's, which hang limply over my left shoulder, and bring them to my lips.

Stay with me.

Please stay with me.

"All this bloodshed," I hear myself whisper, "only to end up dead in the end."

Over Damien's head, Guy only clenches his jaw.

In silence, we trudge through the white-painted tunnel. The bright lights contrast and reveal the acute shape of my floaters. Blood stains the concrete beneath our feet, growing into larger pools the farther along we go, until finally Guy mutters, "He was already wounded before he got to us."

Around the bend, up near the metal stairwell, we learn how.

Much like Clarke at Buckingham Palace, Samuel sits with his back shoved against the brick wall. Head slumped forward, hands clasping his bloodied abdomen. Angled awkwardly against his outstretched legs is his firearm.

Dead.

Shame crawls into my marrow to mingle with grief.

As Damien carried me in his arms, hellbent on protecting me, I'd expected to see Samuel and Gregory turn the corner into the chamber. I expected them both to align with *Hugh*. And even when they didn't appear, it never occurred to me that Samuel and Gregory might not have shown up to help because Hugh had already done them in.

The shame burrows deeper, and I feel sick with it.

Twisting my head, I seek out cold, blue eyes. "He doesn't deserve to be left here."

"We have no other choice."

"There's always a choice."

"The choice is Damien or Samuel, just as it was Alfie

Barker or Damien." A rough breath leaves Guy as he lowers his arm to gather more of his brother's weight. "We bring Damien to Holly Village. Then ... then I'll see what I can do."

Swallowing past the surging remorse, I nod stiffly.

With Damien caged between us, ascending the narrow stairwell proves near-on impossible. Our shoes clang against the metal rungs. We turn Damien sideways, shuffling him up, step by step, while never uttering a word about how much more we've left to climb. Or how, with each minute that we spend beneath Tower Bridge, Damien's chances of survival worsen.

Needing to focus on the task at hand, I steel my heart against the hurt, the agony of loss.

I am a *liar*.

Though my feet may move in the right direction, I'm all too aware of Damien's skin growing colder against my shoulders and the color fading from his handsome face. As if gravity has won, his lids fall shut—not that I'll ever forget the haunting misery that glimmered in the blue when I tried to tug him back onto his feet. And so, I press his palm to my collarbone, as if the heat that I feel within my soul will somehow escape past the constellation of blisters to keep him alive.

We find Gregory, knocked out and unconscious, near the accumulator tower.

Without needing me to voice my request, Guy silently grasps Damien around the waist while I move to Gregory.

I drop to my knees.

Reach out to clasp his hand in mine.

"Come on," I beg, "come on, you big bastard, wake up for me."

Calloused fingers jolt against mine, and I throw my arms around Gregory with a relieved cry. His hand collides with my back, the gesture surprisingly gentle for a man so brutish, and he rubs in a small circle, as though I'm the one passed out in a dank, underground prison.

"Is 'e dead?"

Damien.

"No." Feeling my lungs squeeze tight, I pull back onto my heels. "No, he's not."

"I'll carry 'im with Priest, Rowan."

It's all he says before I'm forced to stand aside while they carry Damien to freedom. His booted feet trail behind him, the laces undone. His armored vest hangs open and loose at his sides. Every few minutes, Guy pauses to check his brother's pulse.

He breathes.

He lives.

Just.

When I finally crawl into the backseat of Guy's car, not fifteen minutes later, Gregory carefully shuffles Damien in beside me, too. His legs are bent against the door, the size of him too large to be stuffed back here with me.

He doesn't utter a sound.

Gently cradling his head in my lap, I run my fingers through his hair. My lips are pressed to Damien's forehead when Guy rings Saxon, and my hand flat against his tattoo of Odin's raven when Guy phones Dr. Matthews next.

I anticipate every inhale Damien gives me, like it's my own form of communion, and dread every exhale that threatens to take him away from me forever. And I barter—with a god that I've never believed in and with myself, too, for the lengths that I'll willingly go to keep Damien alive.

Anything, my soul screams, *I'll do anything.*

It's a vow I will not break.

An oath I take for him and him alone.

CHAPTER 43

ROWENA

We reach Holly Village at daybreak.

Gregory carries Damien past the front door and immediately cuts left down the corridor toward Sara's exam room. Familiar faces peer back at me—those of my own men and others from Holyrood, whose jaws go slack at the sight of Damien—and I let their questions hit my back unanswered.

We stop for no one.

A chair props Sara's door open and Gregory slips inside first, lowering Damien to the exam table with startling care before stepping back out to give the doctors room. Both Sara and Dr. Matthews are dressed in scrubs and I taste only panic when I think of the grime down in the Bascule Chambers—the same grime that dirtied my hands as I tore at Damien's shirt to hear his heartbeat and the same grime that's buried beneath my fingernails even now.

Fuck me.

On a burst of movement, I dart past Guy for the sink, where I shove my hands under the faucet.

"Three gunshot wounds," Sara mutters to Dr. Matthews over the sound of running water. "We'll need to get him scrubbed up and ready for surgery."

My hands are still sopping wet when I twist back around. "You'll save him."

She throws me a sympathetic look. "He's lost a lot of blood but I promise that I'll do my best."

"No." I snatch paper towels from the rack and dry off my fingers. "No, Sara, you will *save* him. I don't care what you have to do but he will—"

"She can't."

Dr. Matthews utters the remark so softly, with such *resolution*, that I'm entirely taken aback. The sole of my right trainer squeaks against the tiled floor as I turn to find him standing with his head bent over Damien's prone body. Gingerly, Dr. Matthews' gloved fingers peel back Damien's shirt.

"He's alive, Doctor"—the paper towels crumple in my fist—"which means he can be saved."

For a moment, he doesn't respond. He plucks at the bloodied shirt, prods at the wound on Damien's chest, and then his somber, dark eyes meet mine. "He can't, Miss Carrigan."

"I don't . . ."

I don't understand.

The air squeezes from my lungs when I bring my attention to Guy. His dark head is bowed, his bloodied hands clamped into fists as his sides. His shirt is torn, his trousers ripped at the left shin. This man just helped me carry his brother up from the depths of Hell, and while we have no connection beyond that, I swallow, hard, and say his name. The single syllable trips off my tongue as a question.

Blue eyes lift to collide with mine and, in them, I see only the shadows of ravaged misery.

"Don't give up on him, remember?" I choke out. "Guy, he's still *breathing*."

His wide shoulders flinch. "He's dying."

"*Of course he is!*" The words explode from my core, and Sara's feet physically come off the floor as she reels backward in surprise. "We're standing around him like he's not bleeding out. Meanwhile, his damned doctor won't even try to—"

"Rowena," Guy grits, "he's *been* dying."

"No." The ground splits open wide beneath me and my entire world teeters on its axis. "No, he's not. There's nothing—"

"You hunted him, didn't you? For *months*, you fucking hunted him."

The vehemence in his voice sends me stumbling backward. "I don't—"

"And didn't you ever think it strange," he continues harshly, "that you and your little mates always saw Saxon and me at the pub while never once coming across Damien anywhere in London?"

"The bounty—"

"This has nothing to do with the bounty!" he roars. "This has to do with your fucking *father* sending men to take Damien out because he wouldn't kill the king. This has to do with Damien stabbed and poisoned just steps away from The Bell & Hand. I found him unable to move, Rowena"—the visceral pain glittering in his blue eyes nearly brings me to my knees—"and I clung to him then just as you did down in those chambers."

I can't speak, can't breathe.

Damien's shoulder, the scar that I pressed a knife to while I begged him to trust me. He hadn't felt the tip of the blade, had admitted as much when he begged me to mark his left side instead of his right when we had sex.

Paralyzed.

His body heavy like stone.

My periphery distorts with tears as I collapse against the counter. He had to have known. If he's been through this before—whatever *this* is—then he knew, down in the Bascule Chambers, and still he carried me in his arms until he could no longer stay on his feet.

Just like he could have left me to die at Broadmoor Hospital but came for me instead.

Wherever you are, I will find you.

Mistaking my silence for doubt, Guy growls, "Do you think I forced him into the Palace for all these months because I *felt like it?* Do you think I enjoyed watching my brother lose pieces of himself every bloody day? It was a choice I made to keep him alive because I couldn't—" Cutting off with a low curse, his throat bobs with a convulsive swallow. "I would rather him hate me for all eternity, for chaining him to a prison, than lose him for good. He was safe. At the Palace, away from Carrigan and the rest of the world, he was *safe*, and then you—"

"Destroyed it," I manage on a shuttered exhale. "I destroyed *him*."

In following the king's orders, I may not have harmed Damien, but I damned him all the same—but only after he was already sentenced to death by my father.

I'm sorry.

Oh, God, I'm so sorry.

I clamp my hand over my mouth but the world still hears my scream.

Dr. Matthews averts his gaze and Sara presses her lips together, like she wants to offer comfort but is terrified to step too close when I'm liable to explode. The mask Guy wears like a second skin is gone, torn away like a tattered page from a book, and all that's left is exhaustion and grief. His back collides with the closest wall and he slips down until his arse is on the ground and his hands cling to his bent knees.

"I'll admit that this isn't my field of expertise," Sara starts awkwardly, "but assuming that he's been on medication all this time then maybe we can—"

"I've had him on daily doses of Atropine," Dr. Matthews interjects. "It's not . . . The short of it is, it's not at all what he needs but it's the best I could manage given the circumstances. When he was stabbed behind Christ Church Spitalfields, the tip of the blade drove halfway through the dermis layer of skin. The poison immediately affected the surrounding tissue—nerve-endings shot, the muscles irreparably damaged. We . . ." He throws a brief, miserable glance toward Damien. "We tried everything but nothing I did could flush the poison entirely from his system."

"Another doctor could have—"

"How?" demands Guy, his head tipping back against the wall. "When all of Britain wants his head on a stake, how exactly were we going to bring him anywhere for a second opinion? On any given day, Holyrood is a logistical nightmare but when you're the most wanted man in England, it's—"

"A cage," I finish hoarsely.

Damien wanted his freedom, and I'd thought . . . God, I thought it had to do with the bounty. But that was only the first act in his plan to step into the sunshine—he wanted to live like only a dying man can.

He understood the darkness because he'd spent his days lost to it.

He refused to kill me because he'd already tasted the promise of death.

And he inked his skin with Odin's ravens, Huginn and Muninn, who attended to the hanged and the slain, because he saw himself in the abyss with no chance of crawling his way back to the realm of the living.

Sara peels back Damien's shirt. "His veins are black."

"The first time, the Atropine helped to stop the poison from spreading past here." With his mouth pressed flat, Matthews gently taps Damien's right shoulder. "It wasn't a permanent solution, by any means, and it was only a matter of time before it stopped working entirely. But this . . ." He shakes his head, his gaze downcast. "If his veins are black, then the poison is already in his bloodstream, and I still can't tell you what the toxin is. I thought botulinum, maybe, but the symptoms . . . they don't align."

"Tetradotoxin, do you think?" asks Sara, her brows furrowing.

Matthews lifts his head. "Whatever it is, I've never seen anything like it. The Atropine won't save him from this—it was barely managing when we only had to worry about muscular atrophy in his shoulder."

"Then how—"

"Medically induce him."

Three pairs of eyes swing in my direction.

On weak legs, I move toward Damien on the exam table. Curling my fingers around his, I suck in a harsh breath when I feel how stiff the digits are against my own. Within the shadowed cavern of the Bascule Chambers, it was difficult to spot the small details but now I see the black, spider-like veins that crawl from the exit wound in his upper left clavicle to spread across his chest. If I were to cut away his trouser legs, I'm sure that I would find similar markings around his thigh and calf. And while he might not be able to sense me here beside him, I touch two fingers to his lips anyway. I made a vow, a promise.

What would I do to save Damien?

Anything. Everything.

I would destroy the world ten times over just to feel his arms around me again.

"Miss Carrigan," Dr. Matthews says, "I hope you understand that while I can respect your . . . feelings for Damien, I can't—under good conscience—agree to—"

Silence grips his tongue when I cut a hard look his way. "You'll induce him."

Sara steps forward. "Rowan, you can't just—"

"And you'll remove the bullets from his flesh, so there's no chance of infection."

"His heart won't—"

"Make it?" Steadily, I meet Dr. Matthews' stare. "If you remember, you said that I wasn't supposed to make it either."

"Well, yes. But—"

"I've almost lost my life to fire twice now, Doctor, and I never should have made it free from Broadmoor Hospital. I should be dead, and we all know it, but here I stand before you." Squeezing Damien's hand, I skim my thumb over his cold knuckles. "How long did you think he'd live after my father's men attacked him?"

Almost guiltily, he turns his back on Guy. "A fortnight, maybe."

"And that was when?"

"Nearly eight months ago."

"Eight months of life," I utter, my voice laced with steel, "from a man who is too stubborn to die from a poison that should have killed him in under two weeks." My fingers trail down to search for Damien's pulse at his wrist. Though thready it still flutters with life. Without releasing him, I notch my chin. "Listen to me carefully because I'm going to say this only once: you will keep him breathing even when you're convinced that he's on the verge of no return, and you'll keep him breathing even when you believe that all hope is lost."

Commotion in the corridor comes in the form of the door slamming open and Saxon Priest storming inside. His green eyes are turbulent when they spot Damien on the exam table, and they turn downright wild when Dr. Matthews argues, "He's dying, Miss Carrigan. Do you understand what I'm saying? He's *dying!*"

I do not bend.

I do not break.

"He won't die," I return, shortly, "because I won't let him."

CHAPTER 44

ROWENA

'm slipping a knife into my ankle holster when a knock comes on my bedroom door.

With a downward tug of the hem on my trousers, I pop back up and throw open my wardrobe. "Come in!"

Behind me, the door hinges audibly whine.

Then, "I come bearing peace offerings."

My fingers still over a wool jumper, and one glance at the figure hovering in the doorway tempts me to take the knife and send it flying.

Strawberry-blond hair. A stubborn chin. Blue eyes that study me with silent reproach even as she stands there with a wine bottle clasped in one hand and two glasses hanging by their stems from the other.

The woman Saxon chose over Holyrood.

The woman that he loves.

Isla Quinn.

As much as I'd love to put my knife to use, killing her would hurt Saxon, which, in turn, would upset Damien and bloody fucking *hell*. The plastic hanger rebounds roughly as I yank the wool jumper free. Only, by the time my head pops through the collar, Isla has already invited herself in and is setting the glasses down on my desk.

"It should be noted," she says, carefully angling her body toward me, "that the wine is yours, as are the glasses."

I narrow my eyes. "Brilliant. I do love being gifted my own alcohol."

Undaunted by my sarcasm, she fills up one glass with chardonnay and then turns to the other. "I would have taken the time to buy you something, but it turns out that I've been too busy hanging out with the queen."

As if I need another reminder of the chaos that my attack on the Palace has unleashed.

Ignoring the shadowed streak that cuts across my vision, I slam the wardrobe shut. "Thank you for the wine," I mutter, my tone glacial, "but I think we're done—"

"I killed Ian Coney."

Dragging my attention away from the abandoned wineglasses, it's only to find Isla watching me again, her expression strangely inscrutable considering everything that I know about her speaks to a recklessly impulsive spirit. Stiffly, I manage, "I'm aware."

"And I killed the king."

My molars grind together. "I know."

"Because he told you." Tilting her head, her blue eyes remain steady on my face. "Damien did, I mean."

I don't have time for this.

Ignoring the offer of my own wine, I tug the wool down to hide my blistered forearms while sidestepping Ian's killer. Frustration, however, slows my hasty escape. No, not frustration. Reluctant understanding. Didn't I speak about this exact thing with Damien when I asked to apologize to Holyrood for all that I've done? Apologies are given without any expectation of acceptance, and I'll be a right hypocrite if I don't give Isla the chance to get it over and done with.

With a low growl, I force my feet to turn back around.

She stands exactly where I left her, looking complete-ly unruffled by the fact that I can't be bothered to make pleasantries.

Play nice, Rowan, and get on with it.

A pained smile stretches unnaturally across my face. "If you've come up here to ask for forgiveness, then you have it. I forgive you, Isla. Now let's just call this quits before—"

"I'll help you."

"I have no idea what you're talking about."

It's the same reply that Silas Hanover gave us down in the undercroft, over and over again, even when we knew he lied through his teeth. The same lies that he took with him to the grave, just hours ago, at Guy's hand.

Isla must recognize my unease well enough because she retorts, "Yes, you do."

Feeling the knife at my ankle and the revolver tucked into the waistband of my trousers like time-ticking explosives, I breathe, "You don't know anything about me."

The smile that she gives me isn't sweet or kind. It's the look of a warrior before she steps into battle. Fierce. Determined. If I had any doubt about her before, it's long gone now. *This* is the woman who killed King John, who murdered Ian. "I know that I would kill anyone who hurt Saxon," she says, "and I would do it without thought be-cause I love him."

My skin prickles with heat that has nothing to do with the wool jumper I'm wearing and everything to do with the growing ache in my chest. No matter what I do, I can't unsee Damien down in the Bascule Chambers.

I see him on his knees, his calloused hands clasped in mine.

I see the panic in his gaze just before he crashed down on the dirty brick.

Had he felt my hands on his body? Had he heard the terror in my voice when I begged him to live? The idea that he might not have, that his last few moments were filled with only condemning silence, makes my heart palpitate.

"I left my brother and sister in Oxford," Isla says, approaching me slowly, "because when I saw Saxon's face after Guy rang him about Damien, there was no other choice. He needed me and I ran, Rowena. But I'm standing here now—with wine that I stole from your kitchen as a shite excuse to stop in—because I overheard what you said to Matthews."

There's no stemming the tears that bleed to the surface, not when Isla stops in front of me, less than an arm's length away, and murmurs, "You'll fight for him."

I don't need to ask who she means.

Always, always Damien.

Monster.

Villain.

The man who is more a hero than anyone I've ever met.

"Yes," I whisper.

"Would you die for him?"

I'm no longer the girl who once went wherever her father pointed, not even the spy who spent a night at Buckingham Palace in the hopes of saving a queen. In her place is a woman who has been to hell and back, whose beauty is scarred by fire but driven forward by courage.

Slowly, I allow my gaze to meet Isla's. "My heart died the second that he fell, and I don't think it will beat again until he stands at my side."

She cocks her head. "You love him."

Throat as dry as sandpaper, my hands tremble as I press them to my stomach.

Love, the king told Damien, is carnage. It must be true. I descended the metal steps to the Bascule Chambers with hope brimming in my heart and an unfamiliar lightness in my soul, only to emerge from the wreckage shattered and bruised.

Each minute that Damien succumbs to the inevitable threatens the very fiber of my being. Each moment where I don't hear his silken voice promises to leave me permanently gutted. I ache in a way that I never have and burn so hot that not even the flames of a fire could compare.

He breathes and I mourn for him.

He *lives* and I don't know whether to grieve or go full steam ahead, my heart raw and my soul screaming, to save him from the abyss.

We are tethered, Damien and I, bound, for better or worse.

And if I don't . . . if I *can't* pull this off . . .

"I love him too much," I tell Isla on a broken whisper.

"That's really not possible."

"It is," I allow, "if I can't save him."

Isla's gaze falls to my trouser leg, as if she knows exactly what I've slipped under the hem. "You have a plan, don't you?"

A risky one.

The sort of high-risk move that I haven't indulged in for years, ever since I—unbeknownst to me—hired Damien to build me a forum to sell the secrets of England's politicians to anyone with the steepest bank account. And there's only one man I can think of who would possibly know the manufacturer of the poison that Hugh used on Damien tonight.

Or *be* the manufacturer, at any rate.

"There's someone . . ." Pressing my lips together, I battle

with how much to reveal. Isla and I may have found common ground with our connection to the Priest brothers, but we aren't exactly friends. In the end, I admit, painfully, "There was an MP, many years ago, that my father sought to woo to his corner. I was the . . . wooer."

Isla's brows lower. "And he dabbles in poisons?"

"He inherited the largest pharmaceutical company in all of England when his father died. On the side, he often . . . dabbled." More like he had a bizarre fascination with toxic animals from all around the world. An entire wing of his London mansion was once dedicated to storing everything from frogs to snakes. "He may know of the antidote."

"Or have one."

I nod.

Isla folds her arms over his chest. "I'll go with you."

"Not necessary."

"It is, and I will."

"Why?" I demand. "You owe me nothing and I don't—"

"It's honestly easier to accept that this is happening than to fight me on it. Don't worry, I'm particularly handy when it comes to combat, and, lucky for you, I have only one stipulation."

Warily, I ask, "Which is?"

"Saxon comes with us."

CHAPTER 45

ROWENA

Saxon Priest is a grenade without a safety pin.

As he throws his car into park on King Street, I keep my mouth shut lest he actually explode. His movements are rigid, his raspy voice tapped with a rage that would sound more at home coming from Damien. If it weren't for Isla sitting in the passenger seat, there's a pretty good chance that he would have whipped the car right back around to murder his older brother.

Nearly eight months since Father had Damien poisoned, and Saxon was never told.

Afternoon sun slants through the windscreen, highlighting the furious lines of his scarred profile. With one hand on the steering wheel and the other nestled firmly over Isla's thigh, I watch as he draws a deep breath into his lungs. On the exhale, he asks me, "Do you have enough?"

The heavy backpack in my lap could knock out an unsuspecting soul. "If he won't hand over the antidote for one-hundred-K, then we go for Plan B."

"Which is?"

"Revealing to the public what Mr. Keely docs in his spare time. I'm sure his constituents would be only too happy to learn about their elected MP's extracurricular activities."

"Diabolical," Isla murmurs, her blue eyes shifting to meet mine in the mirror, "I like it."

"Somehow," I mutter, "that doesn't surprise me."

With the backpack cradled to my chest, I push open the car door and step out into the heart of St. James's. Before the Westminster Riots, this neighborhood would have been jam-packed with visitors peering into all the posh art galleries. Today, it's empty. Bay windows are boarded up and the doors latched shut. The once pristine pavement is now home to abandoned rubbish that I kick to the side.

While I feel for the shops, which have long since closed, a twisted, vengeful corner of my soul takes solace in the fact that Quentin Keely can no longer lord it over everyone he meets that his corner of London remains un-touched by civil unrest.

It's been twelve years since I saw him last—since I found myself in his brick mansion on Ryder Street—but my feet carry me there as if it's been only days.

You are not that girl anymore, Rowan.

Although Saxon doesn't ask me how I've come to know about Keely's hobbies, the concerned glance he sends me tells me that Isla filled him in. Her shoulder brushes mine now as though she senses the wild tangle of emotion be-neath my skin. Under her breath, she says, "Just say the word and we'll take it from here."

"You won't even get inside."

Her lips tug upward. "You don't know me very well, but I have a feeling that you will."

And, with that, she pulls back to walk beside Saxon.

Clutching the backpack tight, I slow before the bold red door of 3 Ryder Street. Quentin Keely's two-story mansion is by far the most elaborate on the block. Arched windows sit against a backdrop of stately brick. One upward glance reveals a stone balcony that spans the width of the first floor while the second boasts a series of matching Juliet-style balconies. The property screams wealth and prestige. For me, it's a step in the past toward a never-forgotten feeling of self-loathing that's haunted me for years.

For Damien, I rap the iron knocker.

For Damien, I slip a smile onto my face and wait for Keely's butler to answer.

Sure enough, when the red door swings open thirty seconds later, the face peering back at me is one that I distantly recognize. The butler's rheumy, blue eyes shift from me to Isla and Saxon. "I believe you have the wrong address," he huffs, already retreating to shut the door.

I slam a palm against the red-painted wood. "I wouldn't do that."

Unease skitters across his weathered features. "If you persist in loitering on the doorstep, I'll be ringing the police, and I'll warn you that Mr. Keely is a personal friend of the commissioner."

The man now dead and buried beneath Tower Bridge.

Lovely.

Splaying my fingers wide against the wood, I tilt my head back and meet those watery, blue eyes. "Mr. Keely wouldn't appreciate you turning away a client."

"Mr. Keely is *not* home."

Just as the door comes swinging closed for a second time, I blurt, "The yellow daffodils are a nice touch," and it stalls, just like my heart.

The butler's balding head finds the narrow gap between the door and its frame. "What did you say?"

My strained rib sings as I point to the matching window boxes on the ground level. Both hold only yellow daffodils—a sign, to those who know what to look for, that Quentin Kelly is open for business. Some things never change.

Pressing my shoulder to the door, I angle my body so that there's no chance of being shut out. "I can only imagine what Mr. Keely will think when he learns you've taken a good deal of green out of his pocket."

The butler lets his narrowed gaze drift to Saxon and Isla again. "What did you say your name was?"

"I didn't give one, but I think Mr. Keely would call me an old . . . friend."

His gnarled fingers tighten on the door, as if he's internally debating the repercussions of letting us inside, and then he steps back.

The entry hall hasn't changed in twelve years.

Busts of Zeus and Hera face each other from opposite sides of the room. Plum-colored wallpaper spans from floor to ceiling. Beneath our feet, the glossy marble floor features a circular mosaic with Helios riding his chariot through a wash of turquoise skies—a priceless antique from Greece that Keely once bragged about commandeering from a museum that had gone bankrupt years ago. The MP has a habit of taking what doesn't belong to him. Women, included.

I step over the Greek god.

As the butler leads us deeper into the Victorian mansion, I'm careful to keep my attention trained forward and not on Saxon or Isla behind me. We pass the wide entry to a parlor with mint-green walls and a WC that reeks of perfumed soap, only to be deposited in a sitting room with glossy, dark furniture and three sash windows along the far wall that allow for an abundance of light.

The butler remains by the door, one hand perched on the knob. "Mr. Keely will be down momentarily."

As soon as he's out of sight, Saxon cuts over to me. His green eyes scan the room while his head lowers to mine. "Let him come in with an offer or he'll drive up the price just to push you."

I set the backpack down beside an armchair. "Since I didn't come alone, it'll go high no matter what. He won't like it that I've brought the two of you."

"Then we take it as it comes. Damien would never—" Fisting the back of the chair, Saxon ducks his head and growls, "He *won't* forgive me if I let something happen to you."

Heart lurching, my eyes snap up to meet unearthly green. "Saxon, we have to—"

"Miss Carrigan and . . . company—to what do I owe the pleasure?"

All it takes is the sound of Keely's voice to hurl me back to my early twenties.

Rough, sweaty hands. Fragile skin pinched between greedy fingers. Bruised thighs. Numb, so damned numb— mind, body, and soul—that even now, all these years later, perspiration dampens my palms at the sickening memory.

I've stood in this house before, been ruined here before, and all I want to do is *run*.

It's for Damien that I sidestep Saxon's large frame to catch my first glimpse of Quentin Keely in over a decade. He looks the same, albeit older. Heavier. Wrinkles crease his forehead and jowls soften a once hard jawline. A lifetime of dipping his fingers into his own medicinal buffet has chipped away at smooth skin to reveal pink, splotchy patches. Unsurprisingly, he has the gall to give me a thorough onceover with a condescending lift of his brows. "You've gone for a new . . . look."

I smile, thinly. "And you haven't changed a bit."

He's still the same greasy bastard that I once scrubbed

from my skin, and he preens now like I've given him high praise.

Then his gaze skates right past me and Saxon to land on Isla.

Like the yellow daffodils planted in his window boxes, it seems not much else has changed. Quentin Keely lives in a bubble that no one has ever dared to pop, completely ignoring the infamous anti-loyalist standing in his home in favor of checking out a pretty woman. His lips turn up at the corners, revealing teeth stained from countless cigars, and he pushes his hips forward to saunter toward her—only to be cut off by a quick-moving Saxon, who angles his big body neatly in front of Isla's. His expression promises murder and, sensing immediate danger, Keely snaps back around like a naughty dog caught pissing on a rug.

Without invitation, I sit in the armchair and cross my right leg over my left. "It's been a long time, hasn't it?"

"We missed you . . ." His hands land on the back of the closest chair. "For a little while, at least."

The implication is clear: he and his mates enjoyed the use of my body before moving on to newer, fresher meat.

Bile rises swiftly in my throat and I struggle to battle it down, to smash it to smithereens and hold my head up high.

I am not Young Rowena.

And even if I was—even if I *am*—I'm not at fault for the misdeeds of men. They dehumanized me, stripped me of my womanhood until I wanted only to crawl out of my skin—but they do not own me. They don't even own a *piece* of me. Keely's power comes only from what I allow him to take, and the days of breaking off fragments of my soul at Father's demand are long over.

You are strong.

Clinging to the memory of Damien's velvet baritone, my

nails bite into the armrests. "It occurred to me," I murmur, keeping my voice deliberately light, "that when I last visited, I noticed the most fascinating collection of yours."

Predictably, Keely puffs his chest out.

Just as predictably, he darts another glance toward Isla. "I do own the largest assortment of Hellenic-era busts—outside of the British Museum, naturally."

I sink back into the armchair. "Naturally."

"Did you come here for a little look-see?" Face reddening, he sinks one finger into the starched collar of his shirt. "It's not up for public viewing but for a *friend* I might consider—"

"I think we both know that I'm not talking about some Greek bust."

"And I'm not sure that I know what you're talking about."

"Don't you?" Carefully, I hook my foot around the backpack to drag it before me like bait. "Because I remember stumbling from your room, a long time ago, and when I couldn't find my way back, I *distinctly* recall discovering an entire wing dedicated to . . . toxins."

"Miss Carrigan—"

"Back around the time you weren't missing me, I couldn't stop thinking about *you*." My lips curve in a smile that tastes of gritty satisfaction. "Only, it wasn't your prick I was missing, Mr. Keely. Instead, I spent a ridiculous amount of time wondering if the authorities knew about your collection. Considering the padlock on the door, I'm guessing your pets have always been a dirty, little secret."

His shoulders heave with a sharp inhalation. "Are you . . . are you *blackmailing* me?"

"Not at all."

"Then what—"

"You have something that I want."

"I'll repeat this again for you," he clips out, "in case you didn't hear me the first time around: are you black-mailing—"

"Rowena, *move!*"

There's no time to obey Saxon's order.

No time to duck or weave out of the way when the cold muzzle of a pistol is already pressed to the back of my head. Like prey found lurking in the woods, a jolt of awareness ripples down my spine.

Slowly, I lift my gaze to Saxon.

His handgun is raised, his expression set like stone. A façade that reveals absolutely nothing, not recognition, not even the smallest dose of fear. Meanwhile dread is a poison that crawls through my veins, swift and debilitating. A hard breath escapes me as I make brief eye contact with Isla.

This cannot be the end.

The heels of my palms grind against the armrests as I bow my head. "It's a wonder you have any repeat customers," I say to Keely, gritting my teeth against a surge of hate, "when you threaten them with death at every corner."

Only, it's not the MP who answers.

The pistol's muzzle follows me forward, the air fairly crackling with tension, and then a figure drops down on my right side. I feel warmth on my neck, and inhale the scent of sandalwood and evergreen, but see nothing aside from the dark streaks of shadow that hug my peripheral.

"Tell them, Keely."

Dark. Sinister. The voice of the devil himself.

The gravel-pitched baritone punches through the brightly lit room like a death knell, and I snap my gaze to Quentin. "Tell us *what?*"

Keely's finger returns to his collar to pull the fabric away from his neck. "Don't shoot."

Except that the shakily issued command isn't directed at the man behind me but to Saxon, who growls, "Give me one good reason why I shouldn't blow his fucking brains out."

"Because—"

"Louder, Keely."

"*Because*," the MP hastily repeats, raising his voice to acquiesce the order, "I don't . . . I don't—" His eyes squeeze shut, and he creeps backward, hands leaving the chair to pass over his thinning hair. "*Fuck.*"

The pistol moves.

Its muzzle rounds my skull and skims the shell of my ear; it teases my cheekbone and dances south to find the line of my jaw. Then it cuts under to the hollowed notch beneath my chin, and terror becomes a sparked flint within my soul as the hand gripping the gun forces me to turn my head.

Sooty lashes frame eyes so black, so bottomless, that there's no telling where the pupil ends and the iris begins. I feel a chill like I've stepped into the North Sea in the coldest grips of winter, but his gaze is no match for the timbre of his voice, which rakes ice-taloned claws down the length of my spine:

"Everything that he is, everything that he's ever been, belongs to me, Miss Carrigan—and if you're not careful, so will you."

CHAPTER 46

"We're not here to cause trouble."

Those dark eyes never leave my face. "Then tell your lapdog to put down the gun."

Almost simultaneously, the pistol edges upward to put my head at an awkward angle. With his left arm looped around my body, I'm surrounded on all sides—a position not so unlike the one Damien took with me when he demonstrated how Ian died. But where I felt heat before, I taste only keen desperation now.

Every second that we waste is another where Damien might never wake up.

"Put it down."

"Rowena—"

"Put it down," I bark, the shape of the muzzle following my involuntary swallow. "Saxon, just . . . put it down."

"And your mate," adds the devil, his lips flat and humorless, "tell her to get rid of the blade."

Isla.

Hysterical laughter itches to leap free because she . . . Bloody hell, Isla killed the king and she killed Ian, and here she is still, prepared to kill this man to protect me—her enemy, the woman who stands opposite her in all things but in our love for two very different brothers.

Throat dry, I manage, "Don't—"

"Don't *what*?" The now-warm muzzle notches upward, putting my eyes level with his. Cold. Detached. The gaze of a man who has hunted his way to the top, a trail of dead bodies left in his wake, and isn't opposed to adding another to the already astronomical tally. "Speak clearly, Miss Carrigan, so we all can hear you."

No.

I am not Young Rowena.

I am not the woman who will ever roll over and accept defeat.

It's fury that has me gripping his thick wrist, my fingers finding his tucked away on the trigger. Baring my teeth, I hiss, "Keely may have served you his bollocks on a platter but I've none to give. I'm here for one thing only and I'll gladly tear this house apart until I find it—do you understand?"

"You seem so sure that you know what you'll find within these walls."

"And you're testing my patience," I bite off, thrusting my chin forward so that he has no choice but to jerk back to avoid a collision. "I might not know how Keely found himself indebted to you—whoever the hell you even are— but those flowers out front tell me that you've at least kept some of his ways alive and well. So, either shoot me and be done with it or let's move to the part where I tell you what I need and you hand it over."

The gun shoves upward. "You push a hard bargain, Miss Carrigan."

"I don't put up with fools."

"And Keely is—"

"The biggest fool of them all," I say, not bothering to temper my voice, "but something tells me you already knew that."

Digging my nails into the back of his hand, I sweep my gaze over the devil's face. Tiny scars scatter across the slope of his forehead and one cheekbone. The bridge of his nose hooks gently to the left as if it's felt the brush of knuckles more than once in the past. A square jawline melts into a clefted chin while dark bristles lend a certain sullenness to the curve of his mouth.

He's not classically attractive.

Not in a way that's elegant or posh or welcome in Quentin Keely's world, who's always made it a point to surround himself with pretty, exclusive things. Whatever stronghold this man has over the MP, he clearly earned his power with brute force and cunning savagery. And he keeps his foot on Keely's throat in much the same way that he holds me at gunpoint now—without remorse, without emotion, without anything but razor-sharp ambition.

"I need an antidote for a poison that I'm sure is one of Keely's and—"

"How *dare* you accuse me of—"

The devil cuts a hard glare toward Quentin, and any further protest from the MP descends immediately into silence. Then those inscrutable dark eyes return to me. "Go on."

I angle my head in a wordless demand that he release me.

He doesn't let me go.

My nostrils flare. "We both know Keely's side hustle has nothing to do with his pharmaceutical company. If anyone is going to have an antidote, it'll be here, somewhere in this house."

"Symptoms?"

It takes every bit of wherewithal not to remember

Damien down in the Bascule Chambers. *Focus, Rowan. Focus on the here and now.* "Immobility," I force out, struggling to subdue my quickening pulse. "Within seconds, he . . . the *victim* was paralyzed. Consciousness lasted no more than a handful of minutes. The veins are completely black surrounding the gunshot wounds."

"If they are, then it's in his bloodstream."

"Don't you think I already know that?"

Not even a glimmer of pity in his expression. "You're better off letting him die."

Behind him, Saxon releases a guttural growl and I feel his pain like a slash of Isla's knife against my own skin. The shadows creep inward, casting a dreary haze over my vision until I'm fighting for air and ripping my hand away from the gun to grip the armrest with all that I am. My arse is firmly planted in this seat but I might as well be swaying in the breeze when I breathe, "He deserves to live."

"I didn't say anything about deserving."

"Then I don't understand."

"CL-152 treats the body like a honeycomb—every muscle, every tendon, all disintegrate to make way for the flood of toxin. Recovery isn't guaranteed. You wake him up and he'll be wishing that he were dead."

The clip of Isla's stride is nearly muffled by the rug but her voice rings loud and true: "And you *sell* this?"

"For a price, I'll sell anything."

Saxon enters my line of sight as he positions himself to my left. "Who the hell are you selling this to?"

"To anyone with a pulse, Priest." The man's mouth doesn't even twitch. "I'm not in the habit of playing favorites."

Saxon's green eyes narrow. "You know who I am."

"Unlike the fool over there," he rumbles, returning the muzzle to the back of my skull as he straightens to his full height, "I recognize all of you. Saxon Priest, the man who killed the king. Isla Quinn, the woman who murdered a priest. Aren't you lucky that I don't give a fuck about politics?"

"You have us at a disadvantage," Saxon bites off, "because we don't know *you*."

It doesn't matter.

Bloody fucking hell, it doesn't *matter* who he is when Damien is suffering. How long will he last before the poison—this so-called CL-152—claims him entirely? How long will it be before nothing we do wakes him?

Panic slams my heart against my rib cage. "Name your price for the antidote."

"You assume we have one."

"No one is insane enough to create something so destructive without a way to reverse the damage—not even Keely. So, let me ask you again: how *much*?"

The backpack at my feet tips over when he gives it a soft kick, as if he's testing its contents. "How much do you think his life is worth when he's bound to wake up, realize that his body no longer does what it once could, and despises you forever?"

Damien wanted to live, to know happiness, and I . . . There's no other way. Dr. Matthews has kept Damien living by a thread for all these months and that was when the poison was somewhat contained. Now, it's devoured his body, possibly even his mind. There's no chance of searching for an alternative when the clock is ticking down and time is not on our side.

I'll bear his hate, if I must.

I'll carry the weight of it for the rest of my life, knowing that I did everything that I could to let him feel the sun—even if it means that, in the end, the two of us together will only ever be a memory.

Trapping my bottom lip beneath my teeth, I nod my chin toward my knees. "There's a hundred-K in the bag."

"You're having me stick my nose in where it doesn't belong, Miss Carrigan." That sinister voice lowers and lowers some more, drawing closer as he bends to snatch the backpack from the floor. "We all pay a price. The question is—what's yours?"

Tension steels my muscles. "How much more do you want? Twenty thousand? Fifty?"

"No."

"Then—"

"The hundred will do," he replies smoothly, "as well as a favor for a life spared."

A *favor*.

My gut twists with unease, and I fight the overwhelming urge to seek out Keely, who's gone completely mute. He's a man buried in my past, a face that I hoped to never see again. A reminder, however much I loathe it, that once upon a time, I spent my days giving out bits and pieces of myself in order to earn my father favors from various members of Parliament.

I walked away from that life.

Yet here I am, ten years later, on the precipice of re-opening the door to keep the man I love alive.

The courage in my bones threatens to wilt while tears threaten to bloom. "You're the devil," I breathe, choking on the words.

"And you're desperate. Meanwhile, every second that you sit here, he dies a little more. Fate's a fickle bitch, isn't she?"

"Rowena, there are other ways. You don't have to—"

I cut off Isla with a raised hand.

Turning my head, heedless of the pistol that follows, I stare up at the man with the heartless gaze. "You won't ever have my body," I utter, my throat tight, "but you'll have any other favor asked."

"Then it looks like you'll have your antidote after all."

I wait until he's stepped away, his broad shoulders cutting around Saxon's tall frame, before demanding, "Who did I sell my soul to?"

The devil pauses, revealing only his profile when he peers back. His dark eyes are narrowed, his sullen mouth flat and untroubled by the chaos he's unleashed. Then he smiles, just the smallest hitch of his lips, and I feel like I've been doused in ice.

"Baron Hastings. But you, Miss Carrigan . . . you can call me the Reaper."

CHAPTER 47

The antidote is little more than a nondescript blue liquid, but I carry its clear, plastic bottle to Holly Village like it has the ability to cure the world.

"We'll need Matthews to keep Damien sedated," says Saxon from my left, his hand already stretching out past my shoulder to shove the front door open for me and Isla. "If what Hastings said is true, we can't risk him waking up before we've assessed every—"

"Where the fuck have you been?"

Guy.

He stands in the entry hall with his legs spread and arms crossed, frustration chasing a ravaged path across his hawkish features. With only his body, he blocks all access to the corridor leading to Sara's medical room.

"Move."

At my roughly uttered command, his blue eyes fix pointedly on me. "Wrong answer. The lot of you disappeared hours ago, so let me ask again—*where have you been?*"

"Doing what needs to be done to keep Damien alive." Clamping my fingers tight around the plastic bottle, I press the antidote to my chest. Beneath my knuckles, my heart hammers a quick tattoo as I shift to the right. "Now, get out of my way or—"

Lean fingers wrap around my bicep, stalling my flight.

Guy jerks me close, his voice low and rough when he husks, "You heard what Matthews told us."

I tip my head back, meeting his stare. "I did."

"Jesus, Rowena—you're setting yourself up for bloody heartbreak." Jaw clenching tight, he shakes his head. "You have to let him go. *We* have to let him—"

"Back up, brother."

Brows furrowing, Guy's head swings toward Saxon. The tension in Guy's jaw prompts a visible tic of muscle, and I swear that I can hear his molars grinding to ash. "You went with her," he edges out, releasing me to face his brother, "and for *what*? To spite me?"

Saxon brushes past me, so that the breadth of his shoulders becomes a fortress between me and the eldest Priest. "I went with her," he growls, "because I have god-damn faith."

"You have no idea—"

"No, I don't, because you didn't bother to tell me that my own brother has had one foot buried in the grave for *months!*"

It's the first time that I've heard Saxon's voice rise above cool, calm, and collected. Even when he threatened me away from Isla, his eyes had burned with a fury that never crossed his lips. All that leashed aggression seems ripe to finally explode.

I step back, colliding with Isla, who tilts her chin toward the hallway. "Go find Matthews. I'll hold down the fort."

She doesn't need to tell me twice.

With a quick nod of thanks, I sidestep the brothers and escape down the corridor. The antique door to the drawing room is thrown open but the gathering space is

ominously empty. Somber silence permeates the house—
no heavy feet padding on the first floor or rambunctious
voices filtering through the walls. We lost Samuel last
night and, regardless of the destruction that he wrought,
we lost Hugh, too.

Two men who were very much key figures in our organization—both gone forever.

Swallowing past the lump in my throat, I push Sara's
door open and come to a dead stop when I spot a familiar
blonde seated beside Damien's hospital bed.

The queen.

My best friend.

The woman who turned her back on me at the Palace,
as though I haven't proved my loyalty to her time and time
again over the last twenty years. I nearly died for her, I
burned for her, in the most literal sense of the word, and
she left me to fucking rot.

Slowly, as though realizing that she's no longer alone,
Margaret twists at the waist to look back at me. Before she
even has the chance to speak, harsh words are already tripping off my tongue: "It figures that you'd invite yourself
where you aren't wanted."

Her shoulders snap back with queenly conviction. "I've
never needed an invitation."

"That was before you let me sit in a *cell* like a goddamned criminal."

"Rowan—"

"You shouldn't be in here." Not with Damien, who's
been hunted because he refused to kill the king, and not with
me, after she willingly believed the worst, even after everything that we've been through together. Slipping the antidote into my pocket, I clamp my fingers over the door and
hold it open in a wordless gesture for her to see herself out.

Though her blue eyes drift to the empty hallway, her arse never leaves the stool. Then, softly, she utters, "Cowards hide in the dark."

My mouth falls open.

"You did not just call me a-a—" Any chance of uttering the word *coward* disappears as indignation grips my lungs in a vice. Twenty years of having her back when King John sought to hide her away from the world, of sisterhood when life took a massive shite on us both and hope ceded way for grim acceptance. That she could . . . that she thinks that I'm some—

I slam the door shut.

Roughly fisting the collar of my jumper, I tug the wool down to expose my blistered collarbone. *Look at me*, I want to scream. *Look at what my loyalty to you has done to me!*

Instead, a caustic laugh escapes me as I cross the room. "You think that I'm a traitor?" I demand. "A *coward?* I was ready to die in that bloody stairwell, Mags. Do you know how easy it would have been to bring you down with me? But I didn't—I couldn't let you die—and do you even know why?" Breathing hard, I put a hand on her shoulder and roll her stool away from Damien, my broken body acting as a barrier between my oldest friend and the man who's stolen my heart. "Because you're my best—"

"*I'm* the coward!"

"I—" Surprise snaps my chin back. "What?"

As if the weight of the world sits heavy on her shoulders, she rises to her feet with a push of her palms against her thighs. Briefly, her fingers graze her abdomen, and I don't miss the grimace that flickers across her face. Then she dips those same fingers into the front pocket of her jumper to pull out a chain, the silver metal glinting under the florescent lighting a second before she clamps the necklace in a tight fist.

"I learned a very long time ago," she tells me softly, "that while half of Britain would see me swaddled in bubble wrap, the other wants me dead for no other reason than that I come from a family born to take the throne." Still clutching the necklace, her gaze skips past me to Damien. "The Godwins are the worst of them all. They'd isolate me forever, if they could. They'd rip me from society and burrow me back in the Highlands if they thought doing so would keep me alive."

"They took an oath."

"Rowan, I forgot that they're *human*."

As if she's socked me right in the gut, my palm goes to my stomach. The muscles clench beneath my touch but I feel nothing of the pain that I did on the night of the fire. Now, there's only a pervading sense of awareness that I'm looking at a woman whom I thought I knew after years of standing by her side . . . only to realize that I may not know her at all.

"All my life," she goes on, moving to the foot of the bed, "it was made very clear that Holyrood would forever bend the knee. They obey, they submit. And, somehow over the years, they became faceless subjects whose only duty is to follow our every rule." Blue eyes flick toward me, and in them, I see only strands of guilt. No, not guilt, but something intrinsically more damaging. It's *shame*, I realize with a jolt, as she curls her shoulders forward and returns her attention to Damien. "They've died in my father's name, in mine. Clarke, he—"

Hoarsely, I interject, "He was doing his job."

"He had a family. They *all* have families. And yet, because of a fluke in genetics and parentage, my life somehow means more than theirs."

"You're the queen."

"And when the monarchy comes crumbling down?" she asks, her tone hardening. "Who am I then?"

"It's not going to—"

"Tell me why he's like this."

Damien.

Her stare never leaves his ashen face, not even to take note of the myriad IVs connecting his body to the equipment lined up along the far side of the bed. The monitor beeps behind me and, unable to wait any longer, I lean over to press the button to the right of his head, to alert Sara that we've returned. It glows momentarily before fading again to a dull forest green.

Needing to occupy my hands, I straighten the thin sheet that's been pulled up to his waist. "He needed the bounty off his head. It went . . ." Stiffening my jaw against emotion, I expel the awful truth: "We had a solid plan, and it went wrong, so horribly fucking *wrong*."

"You care about him."

There's no judgment in her voice, nor even the slightest hint of disdain, just a naked curiosity that speaks volumes—not that I can blame her. After a lifetime of watching me avoid the opposite sex at all costs, her curiosity is well warranted.

Falling in love with the most hated man in England was never the plan.

"I'd chase him to the ends of the Earth," I admit, finally raising my gaze to meet hers. *See me*, I ache to whisper, *see* him. "He's human, Mags. He's good and honest, like you. He's dangerous and complex, like me. He's flesh and blood—a man, not a god—and this bounty—"

"He's dying."

Plucking the antidote from my pocket to set it down

on Sara's desk, I growl, "He's alive."

"I mean that he's dying because of *me*."

When I only stare at her, she roughly pushes her hair back behind one ear. "A coward accepts fidelity from all and offers none in return. A *coward*," she grits out, "allows her allies to fall, one by one, while she retreats to watch it all unravel at her feet. I am a queen, Rowan, and my word is law, but Damien and his brothers knew better than to come to me, or their king, to ask that we pardon him."

"What are you—"

"I would have said no." Holding my gaze, she repeats the words that snatch all the oxygen from the room: "I would have said no because, until a month ago, the Priests were faceless people whose lives catered to ensuring that mine continued. All these months and they said nothing about Damien. This morning, I found out about the imprisoned anti-loyalists from Hamish, after they'd already been returned to their families. I'm the *queen*, and it'll be over my dead body before I let Holyrood shoulder all the responsibility when I could make a difference with a snap of my fingers."

It's a pretty speech, but it doesn't change one, single fact: "You were wrong to assume that I would ever side with my father over you, that I would toss aside our friendship for a man who *brutalized* me."

She fists the metal bed railing, as if needing the support to remain standing. "Sorry isn't enough," she breathes, visibly swallowing. "It's not enough to atone for how I didn't confide in you about Holyrood and it's definitely not enough for the way that I didn't trust you when I absolutely should have. And that . . . those decisions will *haunt* me, Rowan, and I've no right to ask for your forgiveness."

Before I can respond, the door swings open in a rush,

nearly bouncing off the wall as Sara and Dr. Matthews rush inside. Almost in unison, they send a startled glance to Margaret before charging forward like stampeding bulls to shoulder me out of the way.

Picking up the bottle that Hastings sold to me, Dr. Matthews holds it against the light. "Is this it? Saxon said that—"

"There's enough for two doses," I cut in, "in case one isn't enough. The man that I . . . He said that when Damien wakes, he might—" *Despise me.* Unable to form the words out loud, without taking a dagger to my own heart, I manage a weak smile. "You'll need to monitor him. The side-effects of the antidote might prove worse than the poison itself."

"I've known him since birth, Miss Carrigan—there's nothing I wouldn't do for him."

"Is this yours?"

Turning at the sound of Sara's voice, I see her holding up the silver chain that Margaret brought with her. "No," I say with a shake of my head, "it's—"

"I overheard Saxon mention that it's Damien's," Mags tells me, backing up to the door. "He left it in Oxford, and I thought . . . Well, I thought, maybe, it might be a good luck charm." She tilts her chin toward the bed, indicating that she means Damien. "Something familiar to have nearby."

"Margaret—"

"I hope you'll have the chance to chase him to the ends of the earth, Rowan," she tells me, her blue eyes bright with grief, "today, tomorrow, forevermore. You deserve nothing less than a man who would sacrifice all of himself so that you can keep all of you."

CHAPTER 48

DAMIEN

Pain stalks me through the darkness.

Muscles spasming, I dig in my heels as my back bows upward—but there's no relief, no escape, and the nightmare continues on.

I run, and I'm caught.

I hide, and I'm found.

I pray for peace and stumble into only more agony.

Pressure clamps a vice-like grip around my throat. The weight of it, the fucking heat of it. I'm dead. No, I'm *dying*. Desperate, I seek freedom, hands grasping, body jackknifing. I scrape at flesh, at the unrelenting pressure suffocating me, and feel only more pain when the metallic scent of blood permeates the air, rife under my nose.

"Grafton, help me out over here."

Fire scorches my veins, and I twist and twist and twist, digging trembling fingers into the ground to avoid being swallowed by the abyss—but the earth beneath me is quicksand. I'm sinking, drifting.

Gone.

Gone.

Gone.

"Fuck! His heart rate is spiking."

Agony drags me down. Exhaustion slows my pulse to a crawl.

The nightmare traps me, drowns me, owning every piece of my soul until I'm gasping for air and clawing frantically at the heaviness leveraged against my throat. Then softness grazes my skin, and I cling to it with all that I am.

"I'm here and you are not alone."

That voice.

That strength.

I reach for her, stretching my arms through the oppressive darkness to find her. *Rowena! Rowena, love, stay with me.* Only, the quicksand gives way and then I'm gone again—the pain, the fire, the hope, all of it.

Gone.

Gone.

Gone.

CHAPTER 49

DAMIEN

A monitor beeps somewhere to my left and IV tubes cross neatly over my body—and I feel it all, the cool plastic against my forearms and the distinct pressure of a nasal cannula. Greedily, I lift my head to scan the length of my body that's been tucked beneath a thin, white sheet.

I wriggle my toes.

And the sheet moves.

I press my fingers flat.

And the soft pad beneath me depresses.

Hysterical laughter scrapes my raw throat as I clench and unfurl my stiff fingers, a rhythmic gesture that drags my knuckles against the textured sheet that's warm from my skin. Warm, as if I'm not . . . as if I wasn't—

Shot.

Paralyzed.

Dead.

With a surge of panic, I throw off the sheet to fumble with the hospital gown, yanking at the fabric to see if the poison—

The door slams open and then an all-too-familiar voice barks, "Don't you bloody move, Godwin."

With my body laid out flat, and facing a blank wall, there's no opportunity to turn around and watch Matthews approach. But I hear his even footsteps against the tile floor, followed swiftly by two other sets, the first tread heavier, the second almost deathly silent.

Guy and Saxon.

They're here, in this room.

This is not a dream.

Behind my rib cage, my heartbeat is a heavy drum that echoes wildly in my ears. I remember nothing after the Bascule Chambers. Only that I fell, and Rowena tried to pull me to safety. My last memory is clamoring for the sound of her voice while everything around me faded to a cold, damning emptiness.

I'm here and you are not alone.

She gave me those words, she kept her promise, and now—

"We've been through this before, haven't we, lad?"

My gaze snaps away from the ceiling to Matthews' face. He looks the same as he always has—white hair cropped short; forehead creased as he stares down at me with clinical appraisal like I'm some medical experiment gone wrong—but it's the stark relief in his dark eyes that breaks my composure.

I'm not dead.

Fucking hell, *I'm not dead.*

Emotion floods my veins and a tortured sound rises in my throat. This is a second chance. No, a goddamned *third.* Every day I feared would be my last. Every night, when all of Holyrood slept, I stalked the halls of the Palace, too terrified to close my eyes and accept defeat.

What if I never woke?

What if I died without ever having lived?

And now *this*.

I'm breathing when I should already be buried.

I'm staring at a man whose face I've always known, and it's not pity staring back at me but an unholy sense of triumph that curls his mouth. *Victory.* When Guy and Saxon settle on my left, both leaning their respective weights on the bed, I meet their gazes, first green then blue, and choke back a hoarse noise.

Not a dream but *reality*.

I'm alive.

Scraping my tongue along the roof of my mouth, I ask, "How?"

Only, the word starts and stalls on my tongue.

"What's wrong with him?" Saxon growls, turning his hard gaze on Matthews. "You gave him the antidote. Two bloody doses, at that. He should be—"

"Like I said, we've been through this before"—solemn, dark eyes remain fixed on my face—"haven't we, lad?"

Oh, I've been here before.

Voiceless. Powerless. Weak.

My body a traitor that obeyed me not at all, no matter how hard I tried to bend it to my will. Last time, it took nearly five days for mobility to return and a week for my vocal cords to produce any sound at all. My limbs are responsive this time, at least, but I'll be lucky if I—

Antidote.

He said *antidote*.

With no care for the IVs still attached to the back of my hand, I lock my fingers tight around Saxon's forearm and wait only long enough for his gaze to return to me. *Antidote?* I demand soundlessly.

His dark brows knit together. "We should probably hold off on all that until Matthews can clear you for—"

"She wouldn't let you die."

Dragging in a sharp breath, I look to my oldest brother.

His fists move from the bed to the metal railing, which he grips so hard that veins visibly throb in his forearms. Shoulders rounded, mouth flat, he meets my stare. "I saw what you did in the Bascule Chambers. You were reckless going after her," he utters, his voice low, "and you had to know that you were damned from the start."

No, I've been damned since birth.

Chained.

Collared.

Saxon once told me that if I had to ask why he gave up everything for Isla Quinn then I wouldn't understand. She made him human, he'd said. She made him *want*. And he was right—I hadn't understood how he could allow anyone to come between him and Holyrood.

I understand now.

I would stand between her and the world, my body a shield wielded for her alone, because Rowena Carrigan is the only woman who's ever brought me to my knees. I look at her and see traces of my soul. I look at her and see *hope*. Her courage is the fuel in my blood, her strength the steel in my bones. I came to Holly Village to kill her and lie here now as a man broken and shattered—but, in the end, a better man.

In her arms, I finally found mercy.

Guy is wrong. Saving Rowena—the phoenix who rose from the ashes, the she-wolf who sits on a throne all of her own, the woman who begged me to live—wasn't reckless.

It was instinct forged by fire and a sacrifice born from love.

I would do it again, brother, I mouth, shaping the words carefully with a closed fist thumping twice against my heart. *For her, I would do it all again.*

Though his nostrils flare, he doesn't have the chance to say anything else because Matthews flings back the thin sheet with a gruff, "To answer your question, Godwin, it was your Miss Carrigan who found the antidote." He slips one hand under my right calf, where I was shot, and I fight back a hiss as he angles my leg upward to bend the knee. "I'll admit to having my doubts but she's cunning, that one. Resourceful. You could do much worse."

Coming from Dr. Nathaniel Matthews, that's high praise.

"You'll live, thanks to her," he goes on, poking and prodding at me like I'm a slab of salted meat being prepped for a meal. "It did take four days for the CL-152 to dilute completely from your system but she did it, Godwin. Bloody hell, she fucking did it. Even called me out for losing faith in you. Rightly so, I'd say. And from what I understand, she gave—"

"*Don't,*" Saxon hisses.

Startled by my brother's vehemence, I look from him to Matthews to Guy, then back again. Don't *what?*

"He'll find out," grunts the doctor, barely lifting his eyes from his task. "You don't think one of the blokes in this house won't tell him eventually? Even the queen—"

Broken or not, I tear the nasal cannula free, ignoring the pinch of discomfort, and leverage myself up on the hospital bed. Matthews orders me to lie back down but I'm already gripping Saxon by the shirt.

His green eyes flare.

Four days has stripped almost all the pain from my body, and I'm sure a healthy dose of morphine has ensured that I'll feel absolutely nothing for a few hours yet. But Matthews was right—I've been through this before. I've died and survived, came crashing down to hit rock bottom and crawled my way through each and every muddied trench, prepared to fight until the end.

My last breath has come and gone, a horrible twist of fate for all that would see me dead. And it's with life trapped in my lungs that I scrape the bowels of my soul for the strength to rasp, "Don't . . . hide it from me."

Something fractures in my brother's expression. "Don't hide?" Saxon echoes, almost inaudibly. "Damien, you've told me nothing for *months*."

Death suffers no prejudice.

It doesn't understand love or hope, greed or evil. No, it comes for us all, and when it does, there's no stopping the inevitable—but I tried. Whenever Matthews set down another bottle of pills before me, his dark eyes revealing not even the tiniest sliver of pity; whenever I reasoned with Guy, and failed, that I could hunt down Carrigan without dying or ending up imprisoned. Surviving became a mission that I undertook alone.

We are Godwins, and we're born to serve the Crown.

Our own wants and needs are hidden under a wash of conspiracy and murder. Pa died for not solving Princess Evangeline's assassination and we were exiled to Paris for no other reason than that we stood in the way of a man's ambition. And even after we returned to England, already hardened by life, there was no joy to be found. Every Godwin has put the success of Holyrood first.

Until Saxon chose Isla.

Clutching the fabric of his shirt, I give him a small shake. "It was—" My dry throat closes and panic drives a fist through my chest. *Easy, Godwin. Take it slow and take it easy.* I try again. "You were m-my . . . *my*—"

A clipboard appears between me and Saxon, and I turn to see that it's Guy holding it out for me. His expression remains inscrutable, that familiar mask of his already lowered into place.

"Write it down," he grunts.

Taking the clipboard, I balance it against my thigh. Fumbling for the pen that Guy tucked under the metal trapping, my hand trembles as the ball tip touches the paper. I grit my teeth. Regrip the pen. Then allow the ink to bleed life across the page in a shaky scrawl that proves that while the poison might be gone from my body, its aftereffects are currently here to stay.

With little fanfare, I shove the clipboard at Saxon.

His gaze falls.

A beat passes and then yet another, and then his shoulders rise while his Adam's apple bobs down the length of his throat. "You're not . . . Christ, Damien, you're not—"

His eyes squeeze shut, and he scrubs his hand over his scarred mouth. Saxon has always been the one person who I've never been able to predict, or read, but as he stands before me now, I watch him visibly crack.

The clipboard clatters against the bed's metal railing a second before he clasps the back of my neck to reel me in. We're forehead to forehead, the way Pa once did to us as children. And like Pa, Saxon's eyes glimmer an unholy green as he keeps me locked against him. "You're not responsible for the pain I've felt," he says roughly, "and it's not on you to protect me from suffering any more than I already have. We're *brothers*, Damien. Your pain is my own."

IVs tangle with my forearm as I lift my left hand to clamp it down on his nape. Only, as I stare at him, with our foreheads still pressed together, I think of him not as he is now but as he was after the butcher took the knife to his face.

I cried when I saw him.

Not out of fear but from an unparalleled rage that I couldn't control. Someone had hurt him, and I was powerless to do anything but watch shame and misery flicker over his young face. Saxon spent years covering his mouth whenever we stepped out in public—and I spent those same years slipping through the darkness to pummel anyone who dared look at him the wrong way.

The day he was scarred was the first time that I felt hate bloom in my heart for someone who wasn't Mum, and instead of ripping out the emotion by the roots, I nourished it. Thrived on it. The boy genius with a heart of gold who was always destined to become the Mad Priest.

"*Je t'aime, frére.*"

The same words that I whispered to him after the butcher's attack, and by the way his eyes widen, I know he recognizes their significance. When one bleeds, the other endures the same agony. Holyrood may have hardened us, but for the first time in years, Saxon wears his emotions on his sleeve. Squeezing the back of my neck, he rasps, "I love you, too, little brother."

He lets go, and I'm not surprised to see Guy and Matthews huddled in the corner of the room, giving us some privacy. Grabbing the clipboard, I scrawl a note below the last. *How many dead from the chambers?*

Saxon angles the clipboard so that he can see what I've written. "The commissioner," he answers, "along with Barker and Samuel. The big bastard—Gregory—made it back."

Guilt stabs me in the gut.

I asked for both men to be there, and while Samuel had volunteered, I'd dangled Barker's daughters before him like an enticing carrot. Those two girls are orphans now, and I make a mental note to find their closest kin. An anonymous deposit into a bank account won't bring their mum or dad back but the alternative is to leave them to the wolves. And I can't . . . Fucking hell, I won't let them struggle. Not after I've played a part in destroying their family.

Hugh Coney? I underline his name twice.

"Dead," Saxon says.

Good.

Without giving him the chance to walk away, I write my next question as fast as I can. *What did Rowena do for the antidote?*

Immediately my brother reaches up to thread his fingers through hair as dark as my own. "Not yet," he mutters, avoiding my gaze. "When you're better, we'll—"

"Tell me."

"Damien . . ."

"I choose h-her," I growl thickly, my voice so shaky that it audibly wavers. "Like you . . . chose I-Isla. Tell—" Swallowing, I dig deep to find the strength to fight even when exhaustion is a plague that slips over me like a shroud. "T-tell me. Because I love her and if someone hurt her, I'll make t-them wish they were never born."

CHAPTER 50

ROWENA

Hope has abandoned me.

After Mags and Isla shoo me away from the medical room with orders to sleep, I spend the midnight hours watching cars wind their way down Swain's Lane from my bedroom window. Not that long ago, I may have followed in their tracks, my feet eating up the short distance between Holly Village and Highgate Cemetery. But when dawn breaks over the horizon, I head for the old servant's stairwell instead.

The memory of Damien's voice chases me down the stone steps; the memory of his calloused hands on my skin propels me past the heavy oak doors and into the chapel.

The silence within is a stark contrast to my wild, turbulent thoughts.

Soft morning light spills in from the window, stretching brilliant fingers over dark-stained pews to cocoon the chapel in an ethereal glow. Tiny particles of dust dance in the sunrays, and when a shadowed streak slicks past, I accept it for the reminder that it is: I live and breathe when so many others do not.

When Damien might not.

Warmth dashes across my bare toes as I step toward the altar, and I wish . . . God, I wish that the sun might thaw the ice forming a cage around my dead, bleeding heart.

It's been four days since Dr. Matthews injected Damien with the antidote. And it's been four days since we almost buried him for good—heart rate spiking, then stopping, his body thrashing before going eerily still. Handsome face ashen, strong limbs unmoving as I held him, my head bent over his, and begged him to hold on.

The irony: I found him a cure and nearly managed to kill him instead.

He's not woken since.

Believe in him, Rowan. Just believe *in him.*

Trapping my lip under my teeth, I reach across the altar for a new candle. The marble is littered with them, the wrought-iron rack already full. I don't believe, and I pray. I'm without hope, and still I return. A woman, who has known only darkness, determined to hold onto the light, however she can. Muscle memory brings my fingers to the matchbox, and the hiss of the head striking to life is a balm to my ravaged soul.

Candle lit, my palms land firmly on the altar.

Here, in this chapel, with its thick walls that release no sound, there's no one to hear my sorrow. Here, in this place of peace, there's no one to bear witness to the strength that leaves me on a jagged sob. Shoulders shuddering, I sink down to my haunches with my hands clasped over my mouth.

The room spins with my blurring vision.

The sun feels like a mockery against my skin.

I'm in love with a dying man.

Our kiss down in the chambers will be our last, the night I slept cradled against his hard chest only a memory.

Dr. Matthews said that grief is a curse, and I feel damned by it. *Crushed* by it. Stricken, I lock my fingers in place, over my lips, in a pitiful attempt to leash my pain.

And I fail.

Tears fall and my grief expands with an unsteady breath, and I lean all my weight into the altar before slipping down onto my knees. Defeated. For the first time in thirty-three years, I am *defeated*. Dipping one hand into my pocket, I pull out the silver chain to smooth my thumb over the rounded links like a rosary. A lucky charm, Margaret called it, but luck turned its back on Damien a long time ago.

We were doomed from the start, destined to end before we'd even begun.

Give him up.

"I can't," I whisper raggedly, slamming my eyes shut. "Oh, God, I *can't*."

"Rowena."

The unfamiliar voice comes from behind me, hoarse and low. Not one of my men or any of Holyrood's spies. In the last four days, I've met them all. Learned their names and their backstories, all in a shoddy attempt to distract myself from the reality of Damien. Prepared to tell the intruder to leave me to my misery, I turn—and come face to face with a ghost.

Hot blue eyes ensnare me from across the chapel.

Calloused hands rest heavily on the door frame.

And then soft lips part and that foreign voice comes again: "Don't m-mourn me, love."

The sun burns hot through the window but my skin is cold like ice.

Clutching the silver chain, I shake my head fiercely. "*No.* No, you're not real."

"You ran." Throat working, he takes one step into the

chapel and then another. The once maddening, deadly stride is now uneven, his weight leaning heavily on his left leg, and he braces himself twice with a fist on a pew. But his gaze never leaves mine and his lips never stop moving, the words halted, the syllables shattered over a baritone so deep, so gritty, that it feels like a pulse beneath my skin. "You ran and I've c-chased you. Caught you. Wherever you are, however you got there, I will find you always, Rowena, until I'm b-buried and gone from this world for good."

A vow. A promise.

Tears burn the backs of my eyes.

I should leave my spot at the altar, should climb to my feet and meet him in the aisle, but I'm frozen in place, confronted with a hope that I don't dare believe. "You died." The chain threatens to draw blood, I clasp it so tight. "I've seen you die twice, and I—"

"L-look at me."

I tip my head back and let my eyes pass greedily over his long legs and the shirt that's plastered to his broad chest. His dark hair is damp, like he's recently showered, and his stubble is just as thick, just as rough, as it was last night when I brushed my mouth over his in a kiss that failed to wake him.

We are nothing if not a fairy tale steeped in tragedy.

With one hand balanced on the altar, Damien holds his other out to me in a wordless gesture. The same desperation that I feel crawling through my veins is mirrored in his expression. His lips part, his solemn gaze fastened on mine. As though he can already feel my hand against his, his fingers squeeze briefly into a fist before flexing back open.

He's no shade come to haunt me from the Underworld but neither is he the same infallible god who threw a grown man over one shoulder while ushering me to safety.

He grips the altar because he needs the support, and he rests his weight on his left leg because he clearly fears that his right might give out and send him sprawling to the floor. He was shot. Gunned down like prey, and in those flame-blue eyes, I see a silent plea for me to take his hand, along with the worry that if he lowers himself beside me, he may not rise again.

Vulnerable. Humbled.

Mine.

Choking on a small cry, I slip my hand into his, only to remember too late that I'm still holding the necklace. It dangles between us, a divider that I ignore because he's *alive.* Breathing, living, before me, and I don't know whether to throw my arms around his waist or bury my face in his chest. Or both.

"Damien, I—"

"Who gave this to you?" he asks, his velvet voice so raw that it's unrecognizable. When I look at him, questioning, he flips our hands over to reveal the necklace pooled in his palm.

I dance my fingers over the links. It may not be a lucky charm, but I can't deny that having it over these last few days has offered me comfort. Having something of Damien's was better than having none of him at all. "The queen. Your brother left it behind in Oxford, and she brought it with her to return to you."

Like fire trapped behind a pane of glass, the blue of Damien's stare is visceral. Haunted. Wanting to soothe him, I skim my hand up his corded forearm, then over the ball of his shoulder, until I'm framing his face, the thick stubble of his beard scraping my skin. His lids fall shut and a hard breath escapes him. When he angles his head to press his lips to the center of my palm, my toes curl into the stone floor.

I love you.

I'm yours, today and forevermore.

"No one comes into this world bearing h-hate," he utters roughly, before I can even open my mouth to confess. "It's something we're taught, something that shapes us. But in the b-beginning, before we're irrevocably hardened, we're born to *love*."

A shiver skates down my spine.

"I forgot what life could be without the rage." Interlacing our fingers, he brushes my knuckles against his cheek, back and forth. Gentle. Affectionate. But I feel their slight tremor and I hear his grim resolution, and the flutter of butterflies in my stomach falls eerily still. "For so many y-years, it lived right here"—he brings our clasped hands to his chest, where his heart beats a rapid tattoo beneath my palm—"and I thrived on it, *bled* for it. The anger. The pain. Until I learned that it was safer to hate than it ever was to love."

"Damien, were you . . ." My fingers grasp his shirt, holding on, and his hand follows to curl around mine, a shield even when all the world remains locked outside the chapel's thick walls. "Did someone—"

"No boy should endure what I did. No person should love as blindly, as wholly as I did, and be fed only hurt."

A boy.

He'd only been a *boy*.

Just as I'd once only been a girl.

"Your mum?" I manage hoarsely. At his curt nod, something inside me splinters. I feel the crack, hear the intangible snap, and register the break within me. A single tear falls, and Damien curses under his breath.

"Don't cry, love." He sinks his weight into the altar, the necklace going to the marble slab so that he can catch the teardrop's descent with the back of his forefinger. "Jesus.

Please don't c-cry for me. I'm not worth—"

I kiss him.

With one hand balanced on his chest, and the other sinking into his damp hair, I drag his head down close and kiss him with all the heartache and the love within me. He groans deep in his throat. Tentatively, as though unsure if his legs will support him, he presses one hand to the space between my shoulder blades and wraps the other around my waist. I'm tugged against him, our bodies flush, our mouths fused.

We are kindred souls bound by fate.

And I want . . . *I want*—

"There was a girl," I gasp, pulling away, "a long time ago, who felt both hope and disappointment. The hope soared with every promise made to her while the weight of disappointment brought her to her knees. But she rose again, and again, with hope always staggering to the forefront because one day, those promises would come true. One day, all the pain and misery she carried would be nothing but a long-forgotten memory."

"Rowena—"

My thumb grazes his bristled jaw, and the caress silences him. "Disappointment is a gift with no return label. It sits on your doorstep, day after day, waiting to be acknowledged. And when the girl stopped long enough to see the ruin of her life, she drowned. It broke her, Damien. The . . . past broke me. But I've never known defeat—never felt true hopelessness—until I held you in my arms and begged you to live, and you did not wake." The memory of him down on his knees is a plague, just as grief is a curse, and emotion cleaves my chest in two. "To me . . . to me, you are worth *everything*."

Damien jerks against me, his entire body tensing as

he hooks a finger under my chin. Blue eyes sweep over my face, missing nothing. With a low, pained noise, he kisses my cheek and then the corner of my mouth. His lips glisten with my tears as he drops his face into the crook of my neck. "I'm here," he husks, pressing another whisper-soft kiss to my skin, "I'm here, love, and you are not alone."

Those words.

Those same, gut-wrenching words that I've whispered to him, over and over again, since returning from the Bascule Chambers. "You heard me," I breathe, feeling unsteady on my feet. "Dr. Matthews wasn't sure if you would, but I couldn't . . . I *couldn't* leave you to the silence."

His slow inhale is ragged in my ear.

Vulnerable.

"Hate has always been my c-closest companion." When I peer up at him, it's to see that his lips are twisted in self-derision. "I've done things, Rowena . . . I've d-done things that will put horror in your heart when all I want is for you to always look at me the way you are right now."

My mouth turns dry. "And how is that?"

"Like I'm a man worth loving."

"*Damien—*"

"I'm owned by Death," he says, smoothing his hands up my sides until he's cradling the base of my skull in his palms with his lips hovering over mine, "and I did away with the key to Hell a long time ago. But you . . . it wasn't until y-you that I wanted to be good. Better. And when we were down in the chambers, I finally understood what my mum never did. Love is sacrifice, and even knowing what comes next, I'd do it all again." His breath is hot against my mouth, his gaze even hotter as he holds me captive in his embrace. "For you, Rowena, I would surrender my soul. I would take all of your pain and bear all your misery, and I would do it because I . . . because I *love* you."

The declaration falls at my feet, gritty and raw, and then he wrenches himself away.

Immediately, I feel bereft.

"You can't say that!" The words are hurled at his retreating back but they manage to stop him in his tracks all the same. "You can't say that you love me and then turn away as if I don't even exist."

"Don't exist?" Slowly, he looks back at me over one broad shoulder. His brows are knitted, his eyes narrowed. "Don't *exist?* R-Rowena, you stumbled into my life and the world stopped spinning. You speak, and I look for you. You smile, and I fucking ache. When I was d-dying, it was *you* who walked with me through the darkness. And all I wanted was to hold you just one m-more time, even when I knew it wouldn't be enough. For us, it will *n-never* be enough."

I don't dry the tears from my cheeks.

Don't stifle the anguished cry begging for escape.

"I want to live with you, away from the chaos and all the death. I want to be old and gray, and at your side. I want . . ." Sunlight casts golden warmth over his face, revealing the brilliance of his blue eyes just as it exposes the fatigue that's carved hollows of his cheeks. He puts a fist to his heart, as though the words are a new oath that he takes for me alone. "I want yours to be the last name I speak after I've spent an entire lifetime loving you."

"Then why do I feel like you're saying goodbye?" Frustration battles desperation, leaving me rattled and trembling as I close the distance between us to grasp him by the shirt. I'm on my toes, face thrust close to his, and still not close enough. "You have nothing to prove to me. I *see* you, all of you, and—"

"I dug her up."

My breath catches in my throat. "What?"

Shame flickers across his handsome face. "Under a starless sky in Paris," he confesses, his voice low, "I took a shovel and broke c-consecrated ground. The dirt went into a pile that rose and rose. I dug until I stood atop her. I d-dug until I cracked open the coffin. And twelve years after we buried her, I looked down at the woman who birthed me, and I *smiled*."

Thud-thud. Thud-thud. Thud-thud.

Madness.

"I did it all for this." He snatches the silver chain from the altar, holding it aloft between us. "Because it felt like k-karma, taking what she loved most when she loved me not at all. And you . . . *us* . . . I won't love you from the dark, Rowena, hiding what I've done. Not after the Bascule Chambers. Not after you risked your own life to save mine."

Baron Hastings.

The Reaper himself.

I swallow, painfully. "I did what needed to be done."

"You shouldn't have," he growls, slamming the necklace back on the altar. "You should have left Holyrood to d-deal with it—to deal with *me*—because the thought of you . . . Jesus, Rowena, you walked away from that life. You p-promised yourself that you'd never let someone take a piece of you again. And even though Saxon told me that you didn't promise your body to that bastard, I can't let you—"

"They gave up!"

At my outburst, he reels backward but I won't be deterred. "Dr. Matthews gave up," I bite off, wishing I could eviscerate that day from memory, "your *brother* gave up. You were as good as dead, they said. They'd already tried for *months*, they said." I jab the tip of my forefinger into my chest. "But I didn't give up on you. Not once. So, yes, one day Baron Hastings will knock on my door and, yes, he'll demand payment, but it'll be worth it, Damien. Whatever he asks for, however much it costs me, it will be worth it to have you."

"I'll fucking kill him."

"I won't let you."

"Listen to me—"

"A debt is a debt." Holding my head up high, I meet his furious stare. "Hastings fulfilled his half of the deal and I'll do my part when the time comes."

"Then when he comes knocking, it'll be *my* goddamned face he sees."

"The debt isn't yours to pay." The words sound strangled, even to my own ears. "You can't shield me from the dark, just like you can't protect me from what you've done. Did you think I wouldn't understand, about your mum? Did you think I'd turn my back on you when my own father wanted me dead?" An awful thought hits me, and air pumps hard and fast into my lungs. "Is the . . . Is the only reason you're telling me now because you want me to run?"

His jaw visibly tightens. "I'm giving you a choice. A chance to w-walk away, if that's what you want," he grits, stepping back. "I won't back you into a corner, not when you d-deserve everything that's good in this world."

"I deserve happiness."

He flinches as though I've physically struck him. "You do."

"I deserve love."

His voice is hoarse when he says, "You deserve nothing less."

"I deserve a man who will lay down his life for me—is that what you're saying?"

This time, his teeth audibly grind together. "Yes."

"And what do you deserve?"

When he stares at me in mute surprise, I know that I've caught him off guard. Then his gaze shifts to the altar, where he left his mum's necklace. A myriad of reactions flirts with his features but the one that takes hold, the one which furrows his brows and hastens his breathing, is a swift kick to the gut:

Wonder.

"I don't . . ." Shaking his head, he looks up at me from beneath thick, dark lashes. His cheeks are flushed, the blue of his irises glittering with suppressed emotion. "No one has ever asked me that, and I don't . . . Fucking hell, I don't know."

Oh, Damien.

"You deserve happiness," I say, softly, "and you deserve love."

"Rowena . . ."

"You deserve someone who will bleed with you and who will catch you when you fall." Gently, I push the silver chain out of reach. Nightmares have no place between us nor do the ghosts of the dead. "You deserve a love that lasts a lifetime—the kind that's captured with a shared glance from across a room and the brush of fingers when no one is looking. A love that burrows deep in your bones and gives you strength when all hope is lost."

Dragging in a deep breath, I whisper, "You deserve *me* because I will lay down my life for you, for as long as I live. I will never let you stand alone, not even when we're old and gray. But please don't walk away because you think it's best. Please don't play the hero when we both know that I'm already yours." Blinking rapidly to clear my vision, I clutch the altar and hold on for everything that I'm worth. "My heart beats only for you, Damien. And without you, I'm in hell."

CHAPTER 51

DAMIEN

I've died a thousand times over since that day behind Christ Church Spitalfields. I've chased vengeance with reckless abandon, and I've spent over two-hundred nights plotting the deaths of the two men who made me a prisoner in my own land.

The Mad Priest, Carrigan called me.

I hated him for it.

Because it was true.

Only a mad man unburies his dead mother. Only a mad man murders with little remorse, and only a mad man drags a good woman down into the depths of hell because he can't bear to let her go.

And drag her I did.

With dirty brick under my spine and damp air heavy in my lungs, I brought Rowena to the belly of London and nudged her right into a merciless cavern of nightmares. Her shattered cries will haunt me for the rest of my life. The memory of her tears will forever drive me to my knees. She stands before me now, backlit by the sun streaming in through the window, while I remain a fugitive in the eyes of the law.

Chained.

Collared.

Nothing has changed.

A good man would list out all the reasons why he'll bring danger to her front door. A better man would walk away and leave her to her life. But while Rowena may soften my rage and strip away my hate, even she can't turn me into someone I'm not. The angel is dead at my feet, the devil perched on my shoulder, and Rowena Carrigan is *mine*.

"You run now," I rasp, giving into sweet, fucking temptation by placing my hand next to hers on the altar, "and I'll let you go. I won't ever be the man who b-bends you to my will, and I promised that I'd have all of you or none of you at all."

Defiance lifts her chin. "And if I stay?"

Heat flares inside my veins. "Then I'll be yours from this day forward, until the air is gone from my lungs and the m-memory of us is forever tattooed on your soul." My hand slips over hers, temptation be damned, and I skim my palm over her forearm. Gooseflesh teases her skin and a shudder breaks past her lips when I bring my gaze to hers. "I'll love you, Rowena, like the monster I've always been, and I'll cherish you like the hero I'll never be to anyone but you."

"I don't need a hero," she whispers, her violet eyes luminous in her face, "I only need *you*."

Fucking hell.

My hands tremble as I round the curve of her waist to drag my palms up her spine, past her shoulders, until I'm cradling the base of her skull. Fire burns in my thigh. Sunlight slants across the bridge of Rowena's nose, the crest of her chin, and I feel its warmth against my throat as I urge her backward across the chapel.

She doesn't mention my broken gait.

She doesn't ask where I'm leading her.

The stone floor echoes hollowly under my boots. The pews mock me, taunting me with the promise of resting my aching body. But I've not come back from the dead to sit and let the world pass me by, and when Rowena's spine collides with the glass window, there's nothing but want and need tangled in my soul.

I lower one hand to the iron latch and push the window open. Dropping my head to hers, I brush my lips over the shell of her ear. "Go or I'll h-haul you out myself."

Her fingers dig into my sides, her entire body rising onto her toes. "Do I have a choice?"

"It's an ultimatum, Miss Carrigan, you're all out of choices."

The audible hitch of her breath stirs the want, fuels the need, and I feel her pull away to obey. With her head lowered to avoid the frame, she throws one leg over the windowsill and onto the grass. Does the same with the other, only to stop halfway, her bare foot poised on the sill. Violet eyes find me and, with the touch of her tongue to her bottom lip, she asks, "You plan to chase me?"

I plant one hand on the stone frame. Curl my body inward and let my mouth drift so close to hers that I can nearly fucking taste her. *Soon.* Feeling her hot breath on my lips, I give her a slow, ruthless smile. "*Run.*"

Her husky laughter is the sweetest sound I've ever heard.

Grasping my face, she stamps a hard kiss on my mouth, quipping, "I look forward to being caught, Mr. Godwin," and then she's off. The sun hugs her frame as she winds her way through the garden, her fingers flirting with the flowers that have already started to bloom in their beds. Then she throws me a glance over her shoulder and even from here, there's no mistaking her pure joy. Touching two fingers to her lips, she holds out that hand to me—

A vow, a promise, that together, we are not alone.

I follow her.

My leg throbs and my heart soars, and I may not be free of the chains that Carrigan and Guthram shackled around my wrists but every step through Holly Village's grounds is a gift that was almost ripped away from me for good. I push the sleeves of my jumper up to my elbows. Then strip it off completely, leaving me in a thin, short-sleeved shirt that allows the breeze to brush against my skin. My boots are abandoned by a small pond.

Bare feet sink into the grass.

Head tipped back, lids slammed closed, I allow sunshine free reign over my face.

And then I track the woman who's buried herself in my heart.

Listening for the sound of rustling movement, beyond the birds chirping in the trees, I watch for a glimpse of her amidst the ancient sycamores that follow the curve of Swain's Lane. Instinct drives me left, away from the main street and toward the heart of the estate.

Holly Village's Gothic façade slips from view. The clustered trees grow scattered as the ground gently slopes toward a stream. Up ahead, a Palladian building with a domed roof and ornate columns dominates the landscape. A flash of navy catches my eye, and I spot Rowena disappearing around the back end of the old temple.

There you are.

I chase her with slow, measured steps.

Stalk her with hope in my blood and love in my heart.

She, the she-wolf. She, the phoenix rising.

A woman no longer broken or ruined but still mine.

I find her tucked away behind the temple with one arm slung casually around a stone column, her body facing a thick grove of trees that separates Holly Village from its neighbors. She doesn't turn at the sound of my approach and I take full advantage, bringing my hands to her hips and my lips to the back of her neck.

An involuntary shiver ripples down her spine.

"Looks like you've nowhere to run," I murmur against her skin, my voice dredged in gravel, "and no one to come and s-save you."

Rowena's head falls forward with a small sigh, and the arm she's loosely wrapped around the column becomes a firm hand that she plants against its grooved surface. Then her ass thrusts backward, right into my groin, and a smothered hiss hits the back of my clenched teeth. That cunning smile flashes when she peers back at me over one shoulder. "I don't know, Damien, maybe I intend to let the world hear me scream."

My cock hardens.

Pulse races.

"Maybe," I allow, slipping my hand over her throat as I guide her backward to my chest, "I'll find a way to keep that pretty mouth of yours full."

Her hands clutch my forearm, nails unforgiving talons, even as her head tilts to the left in open invitation. "Back to being the B-grade villain again, are we?"

"Would you h-have it any other way?"

"No," she breathes, as my lips hit the slope of her shoulder, "no, I'll have you just as you are—oh, God, *Damien*."

I spin her around, clasping her wrists in one hand, and press them to the column above her head. Her back hits stone. My heart pounds ruthlessly against my rib cage, the sound so loud in my ears that it drowns out the birds and the quiet lapping of a nearby stream. In this tiny corner of London, there is no war or death or bloodshed.

There is only us.

Only this.

"A wish, love," I manage, fighting both the pain in my thigh and the grip on my vocal cords, "make a wish."

Understanding dawns in her expression. Her chest expands with a sharp, sudden inhale, and her hands strain against my inflexible grip. A moment later, she bites down on her bottom lip and I nearly come undone. The pressure leaves her mouth pink, swollen. Then, softly, "I want you to kiss me."

"Close your eyes."

Rowena's lids flutter shut obediently. Her chin notches north, lips pursed in expectation. But I don't submit to the request. Instead, I trace my fingers over the delicate lines of her face, the way she did to me at the Palace. She ruined me that night. Showed me all the ways a man harboring so much hate, so much rage, could bend to the will of a gentle touch.

I don't want her to bend. I only want her to feel as I did then.

Wanted. Craved. Treasured.

She squirms in my grip, her breath coming faster against my throat with every pass of my fingers over her soft skin. I dance them down over the slope of her nose, follow the natural hollow of her cheekbones. When I skim my fingers along her jawline, her lips part and her fragile eyelids tremble.

She's beautiful. Otherworldly.

A woman who has fought for life, both mine and her own, and survived to show the world that she will never kneel at their feet. A queen, even if she wears no crown. Awe for her gathers as a knot in my throat. Deliberately, I let my thumb pause over her full mouth. Deliberately, I tug down on the plump flesh.

Her breath catches.

Pupils remain dilated when her lids slide open, the violet irises nearly swallowed by black. She whispers my name, her voice low and husky, and a sweep of color stains her cheeks pink with lust, love, the same desperate, damnable need that's driven me to the brink of madness ever since she fell into my life.

"Tell me again."

"Kiss me," she begs, touching her tongue to the rough pad of my thumb, "please just kiss—"

I seal my mouth over hers.

Any hope I had of restraint, of maintaining some semblance of control, disintegrates the moment that she parts her lips and tangles her tongue with mine. She tastes like liquid silk, like happiness and dreams. With a low growl, I anchor one arm at the base of her spine and haul her up against me.

Our kiss is feverish.

Wild.

It's fucking *heartbreak*.

With every brush of her lips, I fight the nightmare of death and destruction. With every whimper that she feeds me, I taste her tears and terror. Her courage kept me alive, her fierce grit the only reason that she's even in my arms at all. Sunlight hits my back, warming my shoulders, but there's no turning away from Rowena.

I cup her face, my touch reverent, and angle her chin.

"I thought I'd never feel you again," I growl against her mouth, feeling anguish like a dagger to the chest. "I wanted to hold you. Needed to kiss you. And I couldn't move even a finger to reach for you." Desperation floods my broken body, and I feel no remorse when I nip at her bottom lip and she shudders against me. "It was a f-fate worse than death."

"Let me go," she breathes, jerking her wrists against the restraint of my hand, "and then make a wish."

Holding her gaze as I release her, my shoulders round forward when she presses her palm to my left clavicle. Her touch is a brand on my fucking soul. I feel her heat, the gentle pressure she exerts when she hooks a finger in the collar of my shirt to pull me down.

"Tell me your wish."

"Touch me," I rasp, brushing my lips over hers, "just touch me."

Agony pulses in my thigh but I barely notice when Rowena's hands are drifting down my chest to slip beneath the fabric of my shirt. Her palms are warm on my stomach, steady, and then she's guiding me backward. One step then two, until my spine hits rough stone and she's tugging on my shirt in a wordless order for me to strip.

I don't need to be told twice.

Clutching the fabric at the back of my neck, I pull the material over the top of my head and toss it aside. My body is bruised. Scarred permanently in ways that it wasn't a week ago. Dark lashes fan her cheeks as Rowena lowers her gaze to my chest. Gently, her fingers graze the tattoo of the raven before sweeping down to the Old Norse quote of Huginn and Muninn. With her palm laid flat over the script, she leans forward and presses her lips to the bruise dusting my collarbone.

My breath catches. "Fuck, Rowena . . ."

The breeze dances across my naked skin and Rowena's lips land a little lower with each and every kiss. I dig my fingers into the stone, praying for strength when she's clearly determined to send me up in flames. When she sinks to the ground, her fingers nimbly working the button of my trousers, I might as well be voiceless all over again.

Every word is jammed in my throat.

"If you're Death," she says softly, her lips briefly landing on my left thigh as she works my trousers down my legs, "then I'm the raven that you send to the slain."

"If I'm Death," I counter gruffly, locking my hands around her shoulders, "then you're the m-mercy in my bones that gives me hope."

And then I yank her up and slam my mouth back down on hers.

I devour her with possessive strokes of my tongue and swallow her mewls as I ease her against me, her spine to my chest. The stone wall offers support when I may not have managed otherwise, and I tip Rowena's head to the side to give me room to play. Grazing my teeth over her ear, I sink one hand down past her sternum and stomach to cup the apex of her thighs.

With a sharp cry, her hips roll restlessly against my palm.

I take pity on us both.

My fingers sink beneath the elastic waistband of her joggers, and I feel her strain onto the tips of her toes. Waiting. Hopeful. Her breathing grows ragged as I trace the seam of her knickers—but I never delve beneath the cotton. It's the anticipation of what's to come that heightens the need. The sweet, fucking temptation that pulls me closer to where she wants me most with every pass. She won't come until I'm buried inside her.

"Please," she begs, panting, "Damien, *please*."

I press a single finger over her center—and find her soaked. A guttural groan scrapes my raw throat. She arches in my embrace, the back of her head colliding with my chest. As if hoping I'll crack under the pressure, she slips her palm over the back of my hand, intent on bringing me back to her clit.

The frayed edges of my control hold strong.

With my left arm banded across her chest like a barbed-wire fence, I drag my teeth over the curve of her shoulder and shift my hand to grip the flesh of her inner thigh. "Another wish," I growl.

"To love," comes her husky voice, "and be loved."

Yes.

My body moves before my brain even registers the motion. Molars grinding against the pain, I lower us to the stone floor. My hands drag her shirt above her head, exposing the healing skin along her collarbone and stomach. Cheeks flushing, she lifts a hand to cover the blisters over her belly, but I intercept her quickly.

"You've lived when the w-world expected you to fail," I husk, sitting back on my heels to pull her joggers down the length of her legs. "You've stood tall when a weaker soul would have crept back into the shadows. Every scar you bear is a battle that you've fought and won. Wear them proudly and apologize for nothing."

"I choose you, Damien Godwin." Her smile is slow and sweet and so fucking beautiful that I feel it like a fist clamping tight around my heart. "I choose you today," she says, sitting up to help me ditch my trousers, "and I choose you tomorrow, and I choose you for all the days that come after."

Her vow is all I need to settle myself between her legs, bring my mouth down on hers, and thrust deep inside her.

We groan together.

Letting my head hang over hers, I move my hips in a slow and easy rhythm that drives her chin north as a breathy whimper crosses her lips. "I wanted to live," I rasp, fisting my hand above her head as I hold her gaze, "but never could I have predicted you."

"Damien—"

"I wanted happiness and you drove away the darkness."

With every forward drive, I angle my cock to glide against her clit. She cries out beneath me, her breasts brushing my bare chest, her lids fluttering shut at the sensation of me bare within her. Intent on fanning the flames that have turned her skin a rosy pink, I tilt my hips upward and thrust, hard.

Her nails claw ruthlessly down my spine.

Then she wraps a leg around my waist, securing me to her, and I fall even deeper.

I set the pace to the rhythm of her moans. With every rasped pant that leaves her, I grit my teeth and plunge forward like I'll never have her again. And when she sinks her nails into my ass, her lips parting on my name, I slow it all down to a sensual grind. I make her writhe beneath me and I make her cry out, and she is so fucking beautiful that it almost hurts to look at her. Only I do, letting my gaze mark the brightness in her gaze and the way she bites down on her lower lip to keep from screaming.

This woman owns me, heart and soul.

"*Please*," she begs, bowing her back and raking her foot down the length of my left calf, "give me another wish."

I shield her body with my own. "Tell me."

Her violet eyes are soft and hopeful and so damned perceptive that I feel stripped down. "Never let me go," she whispers, "please just never let me go."

"Love is carnage." The words are rasped against her lips but felt to the depth of my marrow. "Love is ruin. And I'm yours through the wreckage."

She gasps, nails digging into my sides, and I feel her tighten around my cock.

As I promised, I don't let go.

I hold her as she comes with a cry, and I drive in deep, head thrown back, as my own orgasm tears through me. I hold her as I draw her limp body over mine, the sunshine dancing across our naked skin. And I hold her as I bring my mouth to her ear and kiss the hollow of her throat.

Her fingers ease over Odin's raven with soft reverence. Then, quietly, "I love you forevermore."

I meet her gaze while I catch her wrist.

I give her a smile, one that's true and pure, when I press a kiss to the center of her palm.

And then I roll myself back on top of her, forehead to forehead, heart to heart, and I give her all of my soul: "I love you without mercy, Rowena, and I'll never let you go."

CHAPTER 52

DAMIEN

"We strike the day after tomorrow."

Stew spills over the side of my bowl when Guy drops into the chair opposite mine, his elbows landing hard on Holly Village's kitchen table. Cursing under my breath, I grab a paper napkin and run it over my laptop keyboard. Shoving the computer out of the way, before my brother can do more damage, I scrape together the strength to force the words from my tongue: "Strike *what* the day after tomorrow?"

"Westminster."

With the paper napkin still in hand, I jerk my gaze up to meet my brother's. The look on his face tells me he isn't taking the piss. *Jesus.* "You've lost your goddamned mind. Do you have any idea what they'll do to me if I walk into the Commons?"

"String you up by your bollocks, no doubt."

Shoulders tensing, I glance over to find Saxon hovering in the doorway. With his arms crossed over his chest and his shoulder propped up against the frame, his hard gaze never wavers from Guy when he adds, gruffly, "I told him it was a shit idea but here we are, *petit frére.*"

Fucking hell.

Scrubbing my hands over my face, I blow out a heavy breath and shove the stew away. Beneath the table, my leg is a jittery mess that jumps and twitches with absolutely no provocation. Matthews did his best but I won't be scaling roofs anytime soon. It's been a week since I was gunned down in the Bascule Chambers and I'm lucky if I can jog up the stairs without breaking into a clammy sweat. Rowena's taken to tagging along for my new nightly ritual, her lips my reward for every successful pass that I make up and down the old servant's stairwell—but still.

"The last time I walked into Westminster, I ended up with a bounty on my head." I grit my teeth. "Eight months, brother. Almost eight fucking *months* of house arrest and I'm no better off now than I was then. So, if I don't seem enthusiastic about tossing my ass into the ring for round number two then—"

"We didn't have the leverage eight months ago that we do now."

"*Leverage?*" I jab a finger toward the abandoned laptop. "I've just spent the last ten bloody hours backtracking through Marcus-fucking-Guthram's entire online blueprint. The whole goddamn city is searching for London's favorite police commissioner and you—"

"The bodies are gone," he counters, his voice low and curt, "and the place has been scrubbed. No Guthrams. No Coney. No Barker. Even if the Met is somehow tipped off to check the Bascule Chambers, they'll have no reason to pin it back on us."

I shake my head. "I'm the king of suicide missions, but this is . . ."

"Genius."

Genius is spending weeks at my desk, corroborating

on different reports and determining the right angle to dismantling a person before they even know that they're being hunted. This is just madness. "We all know that I want Carrigan's head on a goddamned platter," I mutter, resting my weight on my fists as I push up from the table, "but I won't have anyone else dead because of me. Enough is enough."

Samuel's body was retrieved from the chambers and laid to rest at Highgate Cemetery two nights past. He had no family that Rowena or I could find—no one but the people in this house—but that doesn't make his death any easier to swallow. He didn't deserve what Hugh Coney did to him, and the same goes for Alfie Barker, who may have tried to kill the queen, but his two little girls . . .

I squeeze my eyes shut.

They do not deserve to grow up fatherless because I made their old man a pawn in my quest for freedom. The guilt of that decision . . . the *ramifications* of making that judgment call will haunt me. And my conscience—once unburdened by all things even remotely emotional—can't handle the possibility of another person dying just to see my wrists unshackled.

It's a line that I won't cross. Not again.

I'm halfway to the door when Guy's cool baritone hits my back: "There are six-hundred-and-fifty seats in the Commons, and at least three-hundred are known anti-loyalists."

The soles of my boots grow bloody roots as I slam to a stop.

Slowly, I look back at him—only to find him unmoved from the table. "You want . . ." Mouth dry, I reach a hand for my trousers' pocket. Remember belatedly that my last pack of cigarettes went down in a blazing flame of glory along with the rest of me beneath Tower Bridge. "You want to stage a *coup*?"

Hands pressing flat on the table, Guy straightens to his full height. "You're not wrong—taking out Edward Carrigan is a suicide mission that'll get us all killed."

"Then what are you—"

"We need him ruined. Publicly. Politically." Exhaustion paints shadows under my brother's eyes and tension brackets his mouth, but his movements are smooth and precise as he rounds the head of the table. "What do you think those three-hundred anti-loyalists are going to do when they realize that their PM has been snatching their friends and family off the street?"

Awareness prickles my skin. "The patients from Broadmoor . . . *they're* your leverage?"

"Caren Fitz said he'd speak."

My gaze goes to Saxon, who's yet to move a muscle from his post at the door. "You already spoke with him?"

With a small, decisive dip of his head, Saxon passes a palm over his jaw. "We took an oath to protect the Crown, but we can't just . . . Christ, we spent ten years serving anti-loyalists at the pub. And The Bell & Hand may be gone but we know—we *know* that only a tiny fraction of those people ever made a move on the king. Most of them woke up and got pissed and went back to their homes. Carrigan doesn't deserve to walk free after what he's done to them."

I narrow my eyes on him. "You think Isla's parents might still be out there?"

"No." His scarred knuckles whiten where he grips his elbows. "No, her parents are dead. Long buried."

He's hiding something.

But when it comes to his relationship with Isla Quinn, it seems better to fake ignorance and carry on than pry for information. Whatever secrets my brother carries about Isla's parents, nothing they've done can be worse than killing the king. And Isla already unlocked that particular lifetime achievement award.

Ignoring the thudding pulse of my thigh, I turn back to Guy with a grimace. "You tell the world that the prime minister imprisoned innocent people and the world will come for blood. Chaos. Revolution. It'll be a plaster you can't ever stick back on, and we'll be locked and loaded in the middle of it all."

He doesn't answer, not right away.

Instead, his fingers skim over my open laptop. The expression on his face is inscrutable but the way his throat works tells me that whatever his thoughts are, they're lodged somewhere in the past. Paris, maybe. The tiny old flat in Whitechapel where we were born and raised. Pa's murder.

"There are three things we know," he finally says, using one finger to shut the laptop with a near-silent *click*, "and three things that we don't. We know that Carrigan was waiting for you at Westminster and we know that he's responsible for the death of Rowena's mum, along with what happened at Broadmoor with the anti-loyalists."

My throat is dry when I ask, "And the things we don't know?"

"His connection to Ian Coney. The bargain he offered Robert Guthram. And the hand he played on the night of the fire at Buckingham Palace." Guy leans against the table, one booted foot hiking up to rest on my abandoned chair. "But the first three are enough to nail his ass to the—"

"Four," I cut in.

Saxon's hard voice comes from behind: "For which side?"

"Clarke." The name falls from me, strangled and raw, even as I hold Guy's gaze. "He told the queen that Carrigan plans to see her dethroned on the grounds of her being mentally unfit to rule, remember?"

Blue eyes study me with laser-focused intensity. Then, "And you said that I'm the one who's lost my bloody mind. Half of Parliament wants her dead. Or did you forget that part?"

"And the other half wants her anointed like some god who can do no wrong." I let out a soft, dark laugh. "You want chaos and revolution, brother? Then long live the fucking queen."

CHAPTER 53

ROWENA

"You want *Margaret* to speak to the MPs?"

Damien sits on the edge of our bed. His shirt is gone, exposing his still-bruised clavicle and all the ridged muscles that ripple under the raven and the skull. With his hands propped behind him and his dark hair falling messily over his forehead, he appears more like a sullen Pagan god, come to collect the sacrifices owed to him, than a mere mortal who was only just resurrected from the dead. Especially as I sit on the floor between his spread legs, my hands moving carefully over the stiff muscles of his thigh.

Lips peeling back with a hiss when I hit a tender spot, he sits up to smooth a calloused hand over the crown of my head. Then, voice low and hoarse, he answers, "We're running out of options if we want . . ."

I tilt my head back to meet his gaze. "If we want what?"

"Your father in chains."

It's been years since I've thought of Edward Carrigan without tasting dread on the tip of my tongue. Maybe I would have felt a pang of remorse before Silas Hanover told me the truth about Mum and the fire in Golspie. Maybe, even a month ago, I would have made a scrambled, last-ditch effort to change Damien's mind and save the man who brought me into this world.

But Father made his bed a long time ago, and with it, he buried all my love for him.

"Chains?" I ask. "You don't want him dead?"

"Always." A thread of surprise winds through me when he continues roughly, "I want him dead for me but mostly I want him dead for *you*."

"Damien—"

"He chipped away at your fucking soul, Rowena." His fingers find my chin, his thumb gently brushing over my lips. "He stripped you of hope. Happiness. Your god-damned *life*. He hurt you, and for that I'd kill him a thousand times over."

Emotion lodges like a boulder in my throat.

This man . . . Shifting onto my knees, I frame Damien's face and pull him down for a kiss. It's soft, a communion of love. His palms find my nape, and a throaty groan escapes him when he touches his forehead to mine. "He deserves no better than death for what he's done."

I lick my lips. "But?"

"But I'd rather spend the next fifty years dancing with you in the sunshine than being locked away in the shad-ows." With a barely-there caress, he kisses my forehead. "If we back him into a corner, then we have a chance to finally move forward without needing to look over our shoulders all the time."

"And Margaret is the key?"

He leans back with a pained grunt, his eyes briefly slamming shut as he presses the heel of his hand into his wounded thigh. Sympathy spears me as I watch him push to his feet and take a hesitant step toward the wardrobe. When he pauses halfway, his features twisting with fatigue and unease, I give him the same reassurance that he gave me just days ago: "Every scar you bear is a battle fought and won."

"Jesus, it hurts," I hear him breathe, just before he swings his gaze back to meet mine. Vulnerable. Humbled. This is the side of the Mad Priest shown to no one but me, and I treasure him all the more for allowing me the chance to scale his fortressed walls and guard the gates to his heart. "When I'm finally free," he adds, his jaw cinched tight, "I'm going to take you far away from all of this. No more pain. No more wondering when the other shoe will drop. We deserve more than a life spent waiting to die, and we'll get nothing less than that in this goddamn city."

London has been my home for more than twenty years. I've inhaled its darkness and expelled none of its light, latching onto tiny moments of happiness that came my way as if they were all I'd ever be allowed. And I would leave it all behind—today, tomorrow, the moment he asked it of me—if I thought we'd get far enough before someone inevitably spotted Damien and turned him in to the authorities.

"I'd rather dance in the pits of Hell with you than go back to a life without you in it." Using the bed as leverage to stand, I offer him a soft smile over my shoulder. "I love you, you know."

Monster.

Villain.

The god who dons the crown of a hero for me alone.

On swift steps that I know will take their toll on him later, Damien catches me around the waist and crushes his mouth down over mine. He devours me, owns me. When my head falls back, he follows without missing a beat, nipping my bottom lip before claiming my mouth with a possessive sweep of his tongue. A moan vibrates in my chest.

I hold onto him, clutching his muscled arms. Then I lift onto my toes to battle his dominance with a will of my own. Strong fingers press into my flesh like he's physically torn between tossing me down on the mattress and throwing me over one shoulder to steal me away from London for good.

In the end, he tears his mouth away with a strangled grunt, his flame-blue eyes glittering with primitive hunger and something . . . sweet, tender. He is both the warrior who murdered all to find me at Broadmoor Hospital and the man who begged me to touch him when he thought that he'd never feel me again.

"I love you without mercy, Rowena Carrigan," he growls, lifting each finger from my skin with purposeful intent before stepping back, "and I want nothing more than to bury myself inside you and forget the world exists. Right now, though—"

"We need Margaret."

His nod is sharp. "Bring me to her."

We find Mags in the greenhouse.

With dirt dusting her knees and an assemblage of potted flowers scattered around her, she looks nothing like a queen and every bit the girl that I met at Dunrobin Castle years ago. Spotting us, she strips off her gloves and throws them down beside her. "I asked Gregory for one orchid and I'm pretty sure he cleared out every nursery in London."

That's Gregory, all right—always going above and beyond.

As if remembering all too well when Gregory shoved him from the Palace's roof, Damien brushes his hand over the small of my back. "I didn't realize that you garden, Your Majesty."

Margaret sits back on her heels and balances her hands on her upper thighs. "I kill things, Priest. Everything I touch, everything I've ever loved, will inevitably die by my hand."

Like Clarke.

Empathy is a vice-like grip around my heart, and Damien must sense the tension radiating from me because the hand on my lower spine smooths up and down over the scars from Buckingham Palace. There's no pain, not anymore, and I find sanctuary in the caress.

"And the orchids?" he asks the queen.

"Sometimes I like to pretend that I'm not a curse to all living things."

Bloody hell. "Mags, you're not—"

She cuts me off with a small jerk of her chin. Then, to Damien, she says, "I'm assuming you're here because you want help swaying over the MPs."

I blink, asking, "How did you know?" in the same breath that Damien deadpans, "You overheard me talking with my brothers."

"Three Priests frowning under one roof? Not at all suspicious." Her smile is stiff as she climbs to her feet and thwacks away some of the soil from her knees. "I may be sheltered but no one should ever call me naïve. No, all I needed was one look at the lot of you arguing to know that my fate was once again up for debate. And, as usual, I wasn't given a seat at the table to make my own voice heard."

"There's no way that you could have . . ." With narrowed eyes, Damien looks from the orchids to Holly Village. It takes me a full five seconds to realize that he's staring, hard, at the annex connecting the greenhouse to the house's kitchen. "You're more devious than I ever gave you credit for, ma'am."

"Devious . . ." A floater skates by, and I shake my head to clear my vision. "Wait. You sent Gregory to buy you orchids so that you could listen in on Damien and his brothers?"

"Not one of my finer moments," Margaret mutters, "but desperate times and all that."

I don't know whether to applaud her ingenuity or feel pity for the flowers in question. Margaret's thumb is decidedly black, and she's failed at gardening more times than she's ever succeeded.

"Then there's no point in rehashing everything you've already overheard." Damien's hand falls from my back as he steps forward, his brawny frame treading carefully on his weakened leg. "Confronting Carrigan in Westminster, of all places, is the very definition of insanity. We all know it. But this may be our only chance to—"

"I saw you at St. James's."

Damien's shoulders visibly tense. "Sorry?"

"You told my father that you suspected someone of wanting to murder me, the same as someone assassinated Evie." Her blue eyes slip my way, lingering briefly on my face, before returning to Damien. Her mouth firms into a thin line. "And he tossed you out on your arse for it."

The unexpected confession is a one-two punch to the gut.

One glance at Damien tells me he feels the blow, too. Though his expression barely twitches, he touches a palm to his left clavicle like he's reliving those final moments down in the Bascule Chambers when he was locked inside a body that would not obey him. Vulnerable. Paralyzed. His blue eyes gleam with suspicion when he lowers his arm. "Why are you telling me this now?"

"Because you've given your life to the protection of mine, and it's a debt that I . . ." Her eyes slam shut on a shuddering breath. With hands that visibly shake, she shoves her blond hair behind her ears. "I let you drown, didn't I? You've been treading waters for months, ever since that bounty ended up on your head, and I let you *drown*. However I look at it, I put you on that hospital bed."

"Your Majesty, it's not—"

"Father was paranoid," she interjects, pressing a hand to her abdomen, "and he was right to be paranoid. After twenty-five years of doing everything in his power to avoid the same fate as Evie, he was killed, too. Murdered. *Assassinated*. But he wasn't right to think that you would ever hurt me. If he'd just listened to you at St. James's . . . God, if he had just *listened* to what you had to say instead of spinning theories in his head, none of this would have happened and he'd still be alive."

The truth is insidious.

King John turned Damien away and then came to me to deliver the Priests their fall from grace. My mission brought Isla Quinn into direct contact with Ian, and then Hugh nearly killed us all in his grief for his brother. And my father, the greatest puppeteer of all time, made Silas Hanover jump through hoops for his freedom and started Damien down the road of vengeance months before we ever crossed paths.

Margaret may be the queen, the woman born to take the throne and reign over all of Britain, but she remains my oldest friend. She earned my loyalty the moment that she freed me from my bedroom in Golspie. Twenty years of friendship. Twenty years of sisterhood. She deserves the truth about Isla, but it won't . . . Oh, God, it won't come from me. My gaze moves to Damien, and all the air in the greenhouse feels like it's been eviscerated.

I can't breathe.

Turning in Isla means ending all chances of Damien walking free. Margaret will burn down all of Holyrood if she learns what we've kept from her, and I'll be the first to go for my betrayal. Treason. It would be *treason*. And I'll die knowing that I chose Damien Godwin above all else.

If war is hell, then love is carnage, and the blood that's spilled belongs to us both.

"If you agree to do this," Damien tells Mags, his voice gruff, "then there'll be no rewinding the clock. You'll back the anti-loyalists from Broadmoor in the same breath that you tell the MPs that Carrigan wants you stripped of your crown. Nothing will be left to chance, and we need every person in the Commons feeling like Carrigan is gunning for them personally."

Margaret's stare falls to the potted orchids.

The orchids sit, waiting to be placed in the soil and allowed time to flourish. In the months since Isla killed King John, Margaret has hidden herself from the world, same as the king once hid her away in the Highlands for safekeeping. She's become a monarch in name only, and a queen who refuses to rule will soon find herself without a throne.

"You want me to start a war," she says, softly.

"No." I swallow, hard, and feel Damien's gaze on me like I've spent hours bathing in the sun. It warms my soul and flames my courage. "No, Mags, my father started the war. We only need you to end it."

CHAPTER 54

ROWENA

Caren Fitz wears a mask of nausea.

In other words: he looks like absolute shite.

Dressed in a three-piece suit, the infamous London hotelier jerks hard on the lapels of his jacket as he stops in front of me. Against the backdrop of the Palace of Westminster, he looks rich and untouchable. Regal. Only the sunken hollows of his cheeks and the scar bisecting his left eyebrow tell the story of a man who was ripped away from his life and forced into a world of deceit and treason.

I lower my sunnies and tuck them into my handbag. "Mr. Fitz."

Carefully, he allows his gaze to roam the contours of my face. It's obvious from the way his brows lift that he misses nothing. Not the thin scar that winds itself around my head like a crown. Not the shiny blister that kisses my temple. He stares there the longest, and I'm tempted to quip that I would have been a feast for the eyes just weeks ago.

Biting my tongue has never felt like such an exercise in self-control.

"You were in the palace for the fire," he says, his voice whisky-smooth, "weren't you."

It's not phrased as a question, and since we both already know the answer, my welcoming smile veers straight into *mind-your-own-bloody-business* territory. I won't be bullied for supporting the Crown, just as I won't apologize if my appearance unnerves him. I refuse to feel ashamed for surviving. "I'm glad you could make it today, Mr. Fitz. And I'm grateful that the Priests were able to return you to your wife and children."

Embarrassment flickers in his expression. "I don't know how they managed it, but I always figured . . . Well, you know." When I raise a brow, he clears his throat. "They've always seemed a bit too *notorious*, if you catch my meaning. No pub owner can afford the toys the lot of them do. Not that I'm complaining, of course, because Broadmoor was . . ."

"Hell?"

This time, a genuine smile softens his austere features. "Hell is a good word, Miss Carrigan. Although I'll tell you— when Saxon Priest said that your father was the one responsible for our kidnappings, I didn't know what to believe. We never saw him there, not once. But I'll be . . . Well, I'll be glad to make a difference today, that's all."

With an apologetic murmur to Fitz, I step back and dig through my handbag for my new mobile. One glance at the home screen has my palms growing clammy, and I quickly open my last text thread.

Me: ETA for QM? Session starts in 15.

Damien's reply is immediate: Head in there now. Be strong. A moment later, a second text comes through: I love you without mercy.

Me: And I love you forevermore.

With sweaty hands, I dump the mobile back into my handbag and motion Gregory over with two fingers.

Stamping out a cigarette under his boot, he bypasses the equestrian statue of Richard the Lionheart and beelines straight for me. After a brief explanation to Caren Fitz about the role he's meant to play until we're seated in the Commons, I lead our trio toward Westminster's entrance.

The heels of my pumps clack loudly against the pavement.

My heart threatens to burst from my chest.

I don't allow us to be sidelined by security, instead smiling pleasantly at the guards as we put our electronics into proffered trays and step through the X-ray scanner with our arms lifted by our ears. To them, I'm just the prime minister's daughter visiting her father. To them, Gregory and Caren Fitz are nothing but members of my security team.

"Never can be too careful nowadays," I say with a trembling bottom lip.

As predicted, the flirty one working the scanner just grins. "Be safe now, Miss Carrigan. We hope you'll visit us again soon."

There's a good chance they'll want me dead within the hour.

Jerking my chin toward the nearest corridor, I make sure to keep my voice light and breezy. "Daddy will be down this way, lads! Follow me."

Gregory snickers under his breath.

Fitz's pallor whitens, and I have half a mind to ask if he'll be needing a vomit bag.

Knowing that they'll follow, I book it for the Commons Chamber. Ten minutes. We have exactly ten minutes to be situated in place or this will all come crashing down on our heads. I pick up the pace, spotting a few familiar faces along the way. None, however, seem to recognize me. My long hair was lost to the fire and my face is bare of makeup. No winged liner. No pop of blush. No bold red lip that was once my signature color.

I escaped death and lived to tell the tale.

And it'll be me who brings my father to his knees.

Slamming to a quick stop, I pull around and point a finger at the hotelier. "You'll speak when I tell you and not a moment before. Understood?"

Fitz blinks. "There's a protocol to the Commons, yeah? Ceremonial procedure? Will I know when I'm meant to—"

I shove him inside the chamber.

"'e looks like a bloody penguin in that getup," Gregory grunts, lowering his head so that his voice won't carry. "I thought Saxon told 'im to dress like me. Nondescript, yeah?"

Pressing a hand to my friend's shoulder, I murmur, "Trust me, no one will ever match you."

And then I turn around and collide with Quentin Keely.

Oh, fuck me.

"Running into you so soon," he says, his tone slick as he clasps my upper arms, "is beginning to feel like a brush with fate. First, my home and now Westminster." He bends at the waist to put us at eye level. "Did you miss me already, my girl?"

Bile swims in my gut.

I'm all too aware of the stares landing on me from all corners of the rapidly filling two-story chamber. Brows rising curiously. Rumors being traded from behind the fan of open hands. If I ask, Gregory will tear Keely's head clean from his body and punt it like a football. It'd sail over the Commons' infamous green benches and—

Be too much of a risk.

Sensing Gregory's bristling, bulldog energy, I touch a finger to his wrist to settle him down. Turning to Keely, I adopt a tone infused with saccharine sweetness even while my words spew poison: "Just imagine what Mr. Hastings will think when your little enterprise becomes the talk of Parliament."

Dark brows snap together over the bridge of his nose. "Don't you *dare*—"

"Then take your hands off my body," I seethe through a tight smile. "And if you so much as look at me again, Gregory here is going to enjoy severing your prick from the rest of you." Leaning forward, I allow my mouth to graze his ear. "There's not a single woman alive who'll shed a tear at your tragic loss."

With my head held high, I make sure to knock his elbow with mine as I skirt past him and lead Fitz to the long, wooden table sandwiched between the tiered benches dominating both halves of the Commons Chamber. Sweat coalesces on my spine as I push the hotelier into the chair meant for a Clerk of the House, then swat at his hand when he reaches for the antique copy of Erskine May. "Don't."

"But it's just a—"

"Touch nothing," I growl, "or we're going to have six-hundred MPs breathing down our necks for violating the ways of the land."

Then I spin around and claim the spot on the first bench that's reserved for the prime minister.

Ten years.

Ten years of silence and simmering hate, and it all comes full circle in the end. It would be poetic, maybe, if it weren't for the fact that I've done all that I can to avoid returning to Father's sphere. Politics. Mind games. Subterfuge. He used them against me, just as he used those same tactics against his peers.

One by one, those peers filter into the grand room with its wood-paneled walls and green-patterned benches. One by one, their whispers gain volume until Gregory's hand finds my shoulder in a silent squeeze of encouragement.

I am not alone.

Swallowing, hard, I set my handbag down beside me and fold my hands in my lap. Legs crossed at the ankle. Spine straight. Shoulders pressed back. Any minute now Father will walk into this room and the games will begin. Trial by fire. A battle with only one victor. The voices no longer carry on whispers:

What's she doing here?

Wait . . . is that Caren Fitz at the Table?

What the bloody hell is going on?

"Look sharp, Rowan," comes Gregory's gritty voice from my right, "Daddy's 'ere."

A shiver crawls down my spine.

Temptation begs me to watch my father enter the Chambers but that would give him the upper hand. After all that he's done, he deserves nothing but a space to rot behind a pair of bars for all eternity. I squeeze my linked fingers together to the point of pain.

A tangible hush sweeps over the room.

There's nothing but creaking benches, as people take their seats, and the heavy breathing of an elderly man behind me. One of my father's private secretaries, no doubt. He'd probably stab me with a pen, given the chance, and I resist the urge to clap a hand down on my nape like I'm swatting an obnoxious fly.

This was once my world.

The deceit. The power. The never-ending greed.

His approach is muffled by the rug beneath my feet, but I can *feel* his presence. Gregory is nothing but a shadow on my right-hand side. Before me, Fitz leans forward to touch one of the dispatch boxes and I pray for patience.

And then a lean body is cutting off my view of the hotelier and the Table and the opposition at large. The beat of my heart echoes in my ears. Nerves bundle into a tight knot in my belly. Every scar and fading blister from the fire at Buckingham Palace leaves me exposed and vulnerable.

If I am ruthless, it's because Father turned me cruel.

If I am cunning, it's because Father taught me all the ways that I'd be bested.

And if I show weakness, it's because a sliver of my soul will always be the little girl who beat her fists on a window, screaming to be saved from the fire that would swallow her whole.

Slowly, with methodical nonchalance, I allow my gaze to crawl over my father's body. His sleeves are rolled up to his forearms and his suit jacket buried under a stack of folders at his left elbow. His collar is undone, just one button, and his face is bristle-free. At the Jewel Tower, I'd stood back far enough that I missed the signs of age that have claimed him.

I see them all now.

The loose skin at his jowls and the gray peppered in with the black of his brows. His hair, thinner than it was a decade ago, is combed over to the right in the same style that he's worn for years. It hides a patch of baldness from when Mum tried to cut his hair and stabbed him with the shears instead.

Young Rowena cried over the spilled blood.

I wish that I still possessed even a quarter of her blissful innocence.

He killed that, too.

With the sly smile that was once my trademark, I lean back on the bench and spread my arms wide across the back—ownership, a line drawn in the sand from one opponent to another. And then my smile deepens, and I meet a pair of eyes as effervescently blue as my own, and *oh*, the satisfaction I feel at seeing all the rage locked behind a stare as sharp as his.

"Hello, Father. Have you missed me?"

CHAPTER 55

ROWENA

His reaction is instantaneous.

Gripping my arm, he shoves his face close to mine. "What the hell are you doing here?"

Pointedly, I look to the place where he's holding me. "Your hand."

"*What?*"

"Your hand," I repeat, emphasizing the statement with a kick of my chin toward our audience. "I'd hate for the world to realize that you aren't pleased to see me when it's been so long."

"I'm not—"

Only, he doesn't have the chance to finish that thought because Gregory has already pried him loose. Looking like a windup toy caught in a pair of big paws, Father's cheeks turn a blustery red as he grapples for control, never releasing his hold on the precious paperwork clutched in his arm. "What is the meaning of this?" he snarls, slapping one hand back at the man restraining him. "Release me!"

"Should I, Rowan?"

Instead of answering Gregory, my pumps sink into the soft rug as I stand. In every direction that I look, there are faces peering back. Puzzled. Uncomfortable. They stare as if I'm the shite beneath their shoe, that which they thought they'd already scraped off before stepping indoors. Unfortunately for them all, they've been harboring a cockroach in their midst. I'm nothing more than the trail of seed prepared to lead them down the path of no return.

"You all may be wondering what you've done to deserve my presence today," I say, raising my voice to ensure that every seat in the Commons will hear me, "and the answer is justice."

"*Rowan!*" Father hisses, wrenching his body fruitlessly against the restraint of Gregory's power. "Rowan, stop this bloody nonsense right now."

Too late, Father. You're years too late.

I turn my back on him, the same as he's always done to me.

"Today," I continue, flicking my gaze toward the Speaker, Belinda Bartholomew, who sits before the court on an ornate chair elevated above all the rest, "there will be no pomp or circumstance, and anyone who objects will learn that they'll be doing so against the well-being of the constituents who've elected you to the very bench your arse now warms."

There's a gasp, a grumbling, and then from above: "What gives *you* the right to tell us what to do? You, Rowena Carrigan, who are little more than a bloody hermit!"

"*Aye!*" shouts someone else and then another and then yet another, until the room is swallowed by a cacophony of aggrieved chanting that feels like knives being scraped against my bare flesh. "*Aye! Aye! Aye!*"

The nerves in my belly grow, the sweat in my palms turning slick with fear.

One glance over my shoulder reveals that Gregory has

proven resourceful yet again. He's managed to sneak a blade past security. A blade that he now holds to the underside of my father's chin. If he moves, he dies. If he speaks, he dies. I hold Father's stare for a prolonged moment, tasting his anger as if it were my own, before snapping my gaze away to give life to the sinister truth.

"Ten years ago, I was my father's pawn. And before you tell me that you're not here for a familial war, let me say this: I know your secrets." My smile is slow and merciless as I spin in a semi-circle, my gaze slipping from one troubled-looking MP to the next. "Oh, yes. Every smile that I gave you, every word of praise that I whispered in your ear, was the work of a woman who was told to bring you to your knees." I search out the first man who protested. "I'm a hermit, Mr. Willer, because I chose to walk away from the deceit—but the man who ordered me to act never left the public eye. No, he climbed the ranks of Parliament, knowing full well what he'd done to me and all of you."

A broken, defeated noise comes from behind me, and remorse . . . Remorse stiffens my shoulders. Bound by blood or not, Edward Carrigan will pay. I do not glance back at him. I do not allow myself to recall the few-and-far between memories of a man holding his daughter high up on his shoulders while hiking the land surrounding their Golspie cottage.

I do not.

I do not.

And yet, my body doesn't obey.

The heels of my pumps turn in place and my hands become trembling fists at my sides. With hate and disappointment flourishing in my veins, I meet my father's gaze. His blue eyes scream fury and a bead of blood trickles down the length of his neck.

"Here before you stands a man who murdered his wife." Silence reigns, not even a single gasp to be heard. "Here before you," I continue, hearing only the roar of blood in my ears, "stands a man who sentenced his thirteen-year-old daughter to die. Money. Greed. What forgiveness goes to a man willing to damn his own wife and child for a piece of property? In my heart, there is none."

Father's lids fall shut.

Look at me! I want to scream. *Look at what you've done!*

But he doesn't open them, and he doesn't acknowledge my pain. He doesn't even *acknowledge* me.

"For those of you who don't believe me, I have no living proof." Silas Hanover's body was dumped in the Channel six days back and he'll be halfway to Calais by now—if not lost to the sea forever. "And for those of you who are struggling to reconcile your knowledge of the prime minister with what I've told you, then I give to you Caren Fitz, a man who disappeared three years ago only to be found at Broadmoor Hospital last week . . . along with over a hundred other known anti-loyalists who have gone missing since the Westminster Riots. Mr. Fitz, if you would please—"

The far doors fling open.

And then, one by one, all begin to rise.

The Imperial State Crown adorning her head glitters under the Victorian chandeliers. An ivory satin gown clings to her frame, the collar high around her throat, the sleeves cinching neatly around her wrists. Matching gloves sheath her fingers and the heavy, ornamental Collar of Esses drapes her from throat to breastbone in a brocade of gold and gemstones.

Queen Margaret has arrived.

Flanked on either side of her are eight armored bodyguards, their black, glossy helmets shielding their identities—but one glimpse at the man standing at Margaret's right shoulder and I know him instantly.

The deadly, broken gait.

The breadth of his shoulders and the thickness of his thighs.

His helmet shifts, just a bit, and I feel the heat of his gaze even now.

I see you, Damien Godwin. I see all of you.

It's not the opening day of Parliament, and we aren't in the House of Lords, but as Margaret sweeps past me, there's no mistaking the crimson Robe of State that descends from an ermine cape at her shoulders to span the length of five meters behind her. Damien's gloved hand brushes my arm as he follows his queen to the Speaker's chair.

And then, in a haughty tone that would make King John proud, she says, "I'm in need of a throne, Mrs. Bartholomew."

The Speaker nearly trips in her haste to get out of Margaret's way. Feeling my pulse quicken, I watch Mags clutch the Robe of State in one hand. Holding the velvet train like she would a gown, she sits delicately in the spot that's always been reserved for the person responsible for maintaining order during parliamentary sessions. Today, like during her father's reign, that person wears a crown.

Her chin tilts upward.

Her blue eyes scan the room.

"Members of the House of Commons," she begins, her voice ringing throughout the chamber, "this moment has been four months in the making, since the king was killed outside St. Paul's Cathedral. The same way that I, too, almost died at the hands of an assassin only weeks ago."

Murmurings begin, gaining traction with alarming speed but with a raised hand, Margaret silences the chamber. Then she presses her gloved hands to the armrests, her body listing forward on her makeshift throne. "You saw a fire that ravaged a palace while I breathed smoke into my lungs. You felt fear like a finger trailing down your spine while I tasted blood on my lips. And you watched our history explode—our traditions go up in flames—while I crawled toward death on my hands and knees."

I'm pinned in place by the weight of her stare, and the guilt glittering in the blue nearly knocks me flat. "I was saved," she says, never allowing her gaze to waver from my face, "not by the guard assigned to protect me or the staffers who fled to save their own lives but by the woman who has been my best friend for twenty years—Rowena Carrigan."

Unshed tears clog my throat, and I feel myself stumble backward.

"We ought not to be punished for the sins of our fathers," Margaret says, cutting eye contact, "but by the misdeeds that we commit ourselves. We should be judged, right or wrong, for what good or evil we bring into this world—and today, I shall play your judge, jury, and executioner. Whatever grievances you held with the king will not be found with me. What say you?"

"Aye."

My head snaps toward the female voice, pinpointing her to the second tiered row on the opposition's side. I don't recognize her, but I watch with a small smile as she bows to Margaret and then lowers back down to the bench.

"Aye!" I discover the owner three rows behind where Gregory still holds Father. Like the woman who came before him, this man bows and then takes his seat.

"Aye," comes another voice.

An elderly woman sitting to the left of Margaret shouts, "Aye!"

If there are any nays, they're drowned out by the over-whelming support. I press a hand to my stomach, unable to breathe when the plan . . . Oh, God, the plan is *working*. Margaret turns to Caren Fitz and motions for him to step forward. When he stands before her, she asks, "Do you support the Crown, Mr. Fitz?"

His audible choking can be heard clear across the chamber. "Your Majesty, I don't . . . I mean, I—"

"An honest answer, please."

He throws a hasty glance in my direction.

Caren Fitz doesn't know me from a hole in the wall but whatever encouragement he sees in my expression must do the trick because he turns back to Margaret without further protest. "I didn't support your father, Your Majesty."

"Did you actively try to harm him?"

Fitz's shoulders draw up to his ears. "Ma'am, I manage hotels for a living—I'm no murderer."

"And yet . . ." Tapping her fingers on the armrests, Margaret purses her lips. "And *yet*, Mr. Fitz, you found yourself walking home three years ago when you suddenly vanished from thin air. Where were you brought?"

"I woke up in Broadmoor Hospital."

"Did you suspect my father of the crime?"

Head tilting, the hotelier peers up at the benches to the left of Margaret and then to the right, as if hedging his bets on whether he'll make it out of Westminster alive. In the end, though, he only runs a hand over the back of his neck. "In the beginning, it seemed like that was the case."

"But?" Margaret prompts.

"As often as I could, I'd sneak conversations with the other patients. Pretty soon it became obvious that we shared only one thing in common."

"Which is?"

"Well, the king couldn't have been responsible because we were asked if we would support an uprising *against* your father."

Boisterous shouting comes from all corners of the Commons, and I smother a small cry with the back of my hand. I knew, didn't I? From the moment Silas Hanover told me that Father promised to have him released from Broadmoor, I knew they'd both been wrapped up in something treasonous. But to hear it confirmed—to *know* that Father would happily start a war that's only outcome is death . . .

It makes me sick to my stomach.

"Those who agreed," Caren Fitz announces, raising his voice to be heard over the din, "weren't seen again. I have a wife, children. I didn't—I *don't*—support the monarchy, Your Majesty, but I don't want a war. So I said no to a revolution, and I sealed my fate."

"Until you were found by an unlikely ally." Margaret slips her hands forward so that her wrists dangle over the edge of the armrests. "Please, Mr. Fitz," she murmurs, "give us your hero's name."

My entire body jerks as if I've stuck my fingers into an electrical outlet, and I'm frozen, my feet rooted to the carpet and my arms hanging listlessly by my sides. This was not the plan. Fuck, *this was not the plan!* When I scan the guards for Damien's broad frame, I find him stepping backward.

Run.

Run!

Adrenaline hits my system the moment that Caren Fitz's tepid voice echoes in the chamber, and I'm not even aware of moving until Damien's body brushes up against my spine. A shield. A fortress. Until Margaret passes judgment, I remain the prime minister's daughter and no one will have access to him.

"The Mad Priest, Your Majesty," Fitz says, "it was Damien Priest who found me."

A gloved hand finds my waist, holding me tight, and I seal my palm over his.

All this work, all this preparation, only for Margaret to throw him to the wolves. I choke on fury when she actually has the gall to make eye contact with me from the Speaker's chair. The woman that I thought I knew . . .

We are *nothing*.

Not friends.

Not sisters.

Not even allies in this war.

"You were lucky to be rescued, Mr. Fitz. The irony, though, is that you were saved by the same man who committed such a treasonous act in this very building." The crown's gems gleam with retribution as Margaret pushes to her feet. "And don't we all feel lucky that we've been joined today by Mr. Fitz's hero? Mr. Priest, please remove your helmet."

I feel my heart cleave in two, feel what's left of my soul shatter and surrender.

Margaret is no better than her father who manipulated me for his own gain.

"Mr. Priest," she repeats firmly, "remove your helmet."

Damien's hand falls away from my hip, and with it, he takes the last of my hope.

Tears bleed to the surface.

We didn't have forevermore. We didn't even have days. I turn, in time, to see my panicked reflection in the dark glossiness of the visor. His calloused palms fit against the helmet. Then, in one sweep of motion, he tugs it off and all

I see are flame-blue eyes.

A collective gasp from the MPs floods my ears but I can't look away from Damien, who lowers his head and touches his lips to mine in a soft, devastating kiss. "Whether I'm in your arms or I'm buried in the ground, I love you with all my heart. And I'm happy . . ." He drags in a pained breath. "I'm *grateful* that I can call you mine. I only wish that I could be yours for just a little longer."

My hands catch only the ghost of him.

Benches whine as people leap to their feet, and the silence that previously owned the chamber is now decimated by screams:

Traitor!

Traitor!

Traitor!

Expression grim, Damien turns his back on the MPs and faces the queen. From the flash of satisfaction on her face, she feels no qualms about tearing down a man who's spent his entire life putting her survival first. "You may kneel, Mr. Priest."

My lips part. "*No!*"

Arms catch me from behind and a gruff voice hisses in my ear, "You attack her right now and none of us will get out of here alive."

Saxon.

"Let me go," I whisper, struggling against him, "please—I love him. *I love him.* Let me go, let me go!"

His arms are like iron shackles. "Guy's outside with the others. Anyone tries to leave with Damien, and they'll be dead. Do you hear me, Rowena? *No one will hurt him.*"

All of England has hurt Damien.

His bones bear the cracks of their rejection, his flesh the scars of their dismissal. As he lowers himself before

Margaret, with one hand pressed to his wounded thigh, his gaze flickers to me. I see pain. I see sorrow. Worst of all, I see defeat. Holyrood birthed him and Holyrood will be the death of him, too.

"I will walk through darkness with you," I rasp, my voice barely audible, "and I will dance in the pits of Hell at your side. I am here, and you are not alone."

His blue eyes slam shut, as if he's felt my vow like a brand on his skin. A visible shudder rolls over his frame as he slams the helmet down on the ground by his left foot.

He kneels, as told.

He bows his head, as told.

And the queen only smiles.

"All of England has searched for you, Mr. Priest. My father hunted you; Edward Carrigan hunted you—the Met, well, I'm sure they hunt you still." Her voice rises, every word feeling like a dagger to the gut. Hard. Unforgiving. Blue eyes roam the Commons. "Today, I give to you the country's number one fugitive. Today, I reveal the man behind the mask. Damien Priest, a man who kneels before his queen—my brother, the bastard prince."

CHAPTER 56

DAMIEN

Chaos erupts. War begins.

I kneel before a queen and hear nothing beyond Mum's whisper in my ear, just before she died: *You are a weapon, and you will be shown no mercy when they come to destroy you.*

Oh, hell.

Oh, *fucking hell.*

Air saws in and out of my chest, my gaze lifting past the red-velvet train to the white-satin dress, and then, finally, to the silver crown perched primly on the queen's blond head. Her mouth is flat, her gaze sweeping resolutely over the MPs at my back. She doesn't spare me a second glance.

What she said . . .

What she *implied*—

I must make a noise—ragged, choked—because her attention immediately shifts south and the blue eyes peering down at me are wholly unapologetic. The same callous shade of blue as King John's. The same merciless shade as my own. My stomach heaves. Hands turn sweaty. Jesus, I'm going to be sick.

Something hard strikes my spine.

Baring my teeth, I whip around to find an apple rolling to a stop near my boot. My assailant had the bollocks to pummel me but not the common sense to walk away. He stands, a lean streak of paleness, with his knees bobbing and his fists raised. "He's a bloody traitor and no prince of mine. He deserves to rot in prison for what he's done!"

I'm no traitor.

And neither am I a prince, bastard or otherwise.

"Throw one more thing at me," I growl tightly, "and I'll shove it so far up your ass, you'll know the taste of it for days."

The man blanches.

Then he jabs a finger at me like I'm a freak in a circus ring. "Did you hear him?" he crows. "He's an *animal*! To even suggest that King John would acknowledge his bastard from the grave—when he never did so while alive—makes a mockery of the entire monarchy. No illegitimate heir will ever stand in line for the throne."

"He's an anti-loyalist!"

"His brother killed the king!"

"He's a *criminal!*"

No mercy, Mum had said. The world would show me none, and it was best that I learned early. A warning. A prophecy. All of it my new fucking reality as MPs from across the aisle stand to get a good look at me. Their accusations are poison. And with every new object thrown at my broken body, the familiar rage that's always been my closest companion blooms, unfurls.

Dominates.

War beats in my blood and hate lives in my heart, and I snatch the queen by the arm to shove my face into hers. "What have you *done*?"

"I can pardon you."

Catching her crown to ensure that it doesn't fall from her head, she sends a hasty look toward the pandemonium. Anti-loyalists chant for usurpation; loyalists demand capital punishment. Hauled against me, the woman who claims to be my half-sister wears an expression of steely determination. "Dad changed the laws after the Riots," she says. "He may not have claimed you, but you have royal blood, Damien, which means that I can pardon—"

"Pardon me?" I shake my head, breathing heavily. "They want me *dead*."

"Authorities can't oppose, not if you're in line for the throne." She winces as something new hits my back, and I don't have it in me to turn around and see what it is. "Carrigan won't ever let you go free and we can't risk . . . Dammit, Damien, we can't risk a new PM hating you too. This is the way—the *only* way—you have to believe me."

"No, you've fucking damned me to—"

On my periphery, I spot Rowena springing free from Saxon's arms. Her face is ashen, her body twisting sideways to slide between two MPs gunning straight for me. Only, they turn for her instead, and I watch it all unfold with horror crashing through my system.

The pistol.

The wild glint of betrayal in their eyes.

"Rowena, get down!"

The fear in her gaze sends my pulse into a mad race. As humans, we promise to do better, *be* better, until those we love most are threatened. Then we become the wild beasts of mankind's worst nightmares.

The sound of my handgun discharging echoes with a resounding *crack!*

A scream follows and I feel its vibration in my bones.

Never stopping, I take down the second man. Pain pulses in my wounded thigh. I feel the heat, the silent demand of my body to sit and rest. Instead, I destroy the distance separating me from Rowena in seven quick strides. Sliding my free hand to the back of her neck, I press my mouth to her perspiring temple. "I'm here, love."

When I plant my body in front of hers, I feel her fingers sink into the back of my armored vest as we take in the sight before us. The Commons Chamber has devolved into Hell. Fists fly and blood spatters the Commons' green benches. There are no divides based on gender or age or wealth but solely on matters of the Crown.

Loyalists.

Anti-loyalists.

Madness.

"We have to go," I tell Rowena and Saxon, whose eye I struggle to meet after the queen's announcement. *The bastard prince*, she called me. Dread punctures my lungs. "We'll grab the queen and then get out of—"

"My father," Rowena gasps, pushing past my right arm to look at the front bench. "He was right there. Literally, *right there*." Her gaze turns to me, wide and frantic. "Damien, if he goes free, after what I told everyone today, he'll—"

Kill me.

She doesn't need to say the words.

Locking a hand around Gregory's arm, as he passes, I point to the queen. "Get her, do you hear me? You get her and take her out of here, and then you watch over her like it's the last thing you'll ever fucking do."

Without a spoken word, he turns on his heel and heads straight for where she stands by the Speaker's chair. Her crown is clutched in one hand, the Robe of State spun like a velvet noose around her legs. Good intentions or not, she began a war that we'd all hoped to see end today. And as Saxon and I follow Rowena out of the chamber, I throw one last glance at her over my shoulder.

Her blue eyes are locked on my face.

If what she says is true, I should feel kinship. Trust. But all I taste is a blinding fury that she revealed a secret that should have gone no further than the two of us—and she did so before all of Parliament in a move that now makes me the most hated man alive.

The Mad Priest.

The bastard prince.

Soft hands grasp my wrists, and a husky voice pulls me away from the edge of the proverbial cliff: "*Breathe, Damien. Please breathe for me.*"

Clarity hits as I realize, slowly, that I've thrown my back against the wall closest to the Commons Chamber. I'm breathing too hard, too loud. I'm . . . Oh, fuck, I'm *panicking.* "Rowena—"

She settles gentle hands over my heart.

As if she holds all the answers to my past, I meet her gaze and rasp, "I'm Henry Godwin's son." No mercy, no mercy, no mercy. It's an omen, a goddamned curse. Needing her warmth, I clutch Rowena's hands in mine. "I was born to take an oath to the Crown and I'm the fifth generation of Holyrood. I'm not . . . Fucking hell, I'm *not the son of—*"

John.

I can't say his name, not out loud, and Saxon saves me by jerking his head, still in the black helmet, toward the hallway. "We wait any longer and we're going to be ripe for the picking, brother." He says the word with purpose, conviction. "Move before I make you."

It's only when we're following Rowena down the hall,

toward her father's office, that my brother adds, "She could be lying."

"Margaret never lies." Rowena's mouth settles into a straight line. "It's her superpower. All the world could be crumbling down at her feet and she'll have not even the smallest false hope for a single soul."

I kill things, Priest.

Words that the queen gave me while surrounded by unpotted flowers.

Did she know about me then? Has she *always* known that I'm her half-brother? My gaze tracks the corridor for threats but the biggest danger of all seems to reside in my past with two dead parents who took the truth about my birth with them to the grave.

My heart pounds a quick, furious tattoo, and I stifle a rough grunt when I step on my leg at a bad angle.

Registering my broken stride, Rowena immediately slides her hand against mine. Calloused versus soft, large swallowing small. She squeezes, once, and whispers, "I have you, Damien. No matters what happens next, I *have you.*"

Her iron spine.

The courage in her bones.

Dragging her hand to my mouth, for a kiss to her palm, I growl, "I love—"

We spot Edward Carrigan at the same time.

With his head tucked down to his chest, he's hauling ass down the hallway. His right arm is heavy with a stack of papers that he tries to shuffle into an oversized leather bag—a sheaf slips away to drift lazily to the floor. Muttering a curse that echoes down the corridor, Carrigan twists and turns back around.

"You seem to be in a hurry, Father."

At Rowena's voice, the prime minister's entire body

goes perfectly still.

Stepping out from beside me, Rowena strolls down the hallway, hips swaying, her back ramrod straight. When she nears Carrigan, she makes a point to plant her foot down on the sheet of paper. "What? Nothing to say?" A serene, too pleasant smile spreads across her face. "And here I was thinking that you'd enjoy some time to reminisce with your daughter."

As though someone has taken a foot to his spine, Carrigan jerks upright. "There's already been enough reminiscing for one day."

He makes a move to sidestep her.

She follows with a quick shuffle to the right.

"How about you *look* at me, Father?" Though her voice is laced with steel, I sense the rage quivering beneath her skin when I stop behind her, Saxon on my right. "It's been at least ten years since you've actually acknowledged my existence."

"Rowan, I'm not in the mood."

"You never have been." Squaring off her shoulders, she intercepts his second attempt to escape their conversation. "Let me give you the quick rundown, shall I? Three weeks ago, I survived the fire at Buckingham Palace. There were complications. Then, a little over a week ago, I survived a madman trying to kill me at a psychiatric hospital. Ask me what both events had in common."

"After your little demonstration back there, I don't have the time—"

"You." Her arm slashes in a diagonal line to block Carrigan's access to the corridor. "*You* are the common link, Father."

"I have no idea what you're talking about."

"Of course, you don't." With her hands fisted down at her sides, she stands her ground. "Because there isn't a single thing that's off-limits to you when it comes to gaining more power. You are . . . you are—"

"Haven't I done enough for you?" Exasperation pulls Carrigan's eyes up to the ceiling for half a breath before he jabs a finger at his daughter. "You may not see me, Rowan, but every decision that I've made impacts you directly."

"I doubt that."

"I've let you keep Holly Village for all these years. I've left you alone even when you'd be more than welcomed back into the fold at Westminster. And when I saw you at the Jewel Tower, three months ago, I helped get rid of that low-brow professor hanging around you."

Rowena reels backward. "*Ian?* But he wasn't even there for the meeting. He met me—"

"It was pathetic," the prime minister grinds out, "how he followed you all around London like a lost little puppy. As if any daughter of mine would waste their breath on the likes of him." Nostrils flaring, Carrigan tightens his jaw. "You should be grateful that I stepped in. Not that he took the money that I offered him but after that, at least, he understood his boundaries when it came to his interactions with you."

The email.

The fifty-thousand pounds Carrigan promised Ian Coney if he would stay away from Rowena.

Jesus.

"Now," he says, his voice mocking, "if that's all you need from me, I'll be—"

"*I want you to care!*"

Hot air lodges in my throat at the desperation that I hear in those fragile words. I want to pull her close and dip my mouth down to hers in comfort. I want to shove Carrigan up against a wall and plow my fist into his face.

One glance at Saxon reveals that even my stoic brother is struggling to remain impartial.

But Rowena is no damsel in distress. So I force myself to stand sentry even though I'd love nothing more than to end Carrigan, and I remind myself that she's waited years to unburden her soul. My turn will come, and when it does, there won't be much of Edward Carrigan left to scrape together.

"You've left me to drown my entire life," she says, breathing hard. "And when I was no longer of value—when I chose to leave this world of ruin that you've created—you turned your back on me like I was *nothing*."

"It's politics, Rowan." He shakes his head with a dismissive grunt. "Sometimes bad deeds are the foundational blocks to all things good. And while I'd love to stand here and discuss the philosophies of moral decency with you, I'm reached my daily quota for—"

"Love is sacrifice."

"What?"

"Love is sacrifice," she repeats, lifting her chin with queenly defiance, "and *you*, Father, are the one to be sacrificed this time around." She sends me and Saxon a hard glance. "Take him."

We move in tandem.

The muzzle of Saxon's rifle is shoved against the prime minister's back. In the same breath, I reach for my wire coil and quickly tie Carrigan's wrists together. Loose sheafs of paper float to the floor like confetti caught in a cross-breeze and his leather bag hits the ground with a heavy *thud*.

"Rowan," he barks, thrashing wildly against me and Saxon. "You'll release me right now—do you hear me? You'll release me—"

"The same as you released me from my room twenty

years ago?" She snatches up the bag and pulls the strap over one shoulder. "Or maybe you mean the way your old mate Silas Hanover released me after you failed to rescue him from Broadmoor Hospital?"

"*Hanover?*" For the first time, the prime minister's voice carries a trace of unease. His gaze darts to me—and doesn't waver. "Is this a joke?" he demands. "Your way of striking back at me after what I did to you?"

I make a point to shove my face close to his when I growl, "You've played a fancy game of trickery all these months. Sending your men after me at The Bell & Hand, poisoning me, and then burning the place down just the other week. But—"

"I didn't burn down the pub."

Saxon releases a low chuckle. "You're a liar, Carrigan."

"*I'm* the liar? Your family is nothing but—"

"What deal did you offer Silas Hanover to get him out of Broadmoor?" Rowena asks, her eyes narrowing on her father. "Because we all know that you promised him something."

"I don't enjoy being played the fool, daughter."

I grit my teeth. "You may have been able to get away with what you've done to me, but the same can't be said for the hundreds of anti-loyalists that were held at Broadmoor Hospital. So, let me ask you this one more time—what were the terms for Hanover's release?"

"And what will you do for me in return?"

Saxon releases a tight growl. "Don't think that I won't pull the trigger."

"If you care at all about your life," Rowena bites off, "then tell us what we want to know."

"He agreed to do whatever I wanted for just the death of one man. I could have made it happen sometime in the last ten years, but Hanover proved more resourceful

in Broadmoor than he ever would have outside its walls."
The prime minister's laugh is low and rough. "Who could blame me for letting him rot away in there?"

It's an unexpected confession.

Even more unexpected is when he murmurs, "Take off the helmet."

"Why?" Saxon growls.

"Because, Mr. Priest, I prefer to look a man in the eye when I tell him a secret."

I shouldn't be surprised that Carrigan recognized Saxon. The man couldn't have climbed to the post of prime minister without a keen eye. With my jaw clenched, I gesture for Saxon to get on with it.

And he does.

The helmet comes off and Saxon's scarred mouth curves in a sneer. And then Carrigan gives us a slow, uneven smile. "And so here we are in the end, aren't we? The Priest who killed John. And the Priest who John apparently fathered." His smile turns lethal. "And, of course, we're missing one, aren't we? The third to our trio, and the particular Priest that I promised to an old—"

Footsteps come from behind us.

I turn, rifle raised, and come to a dead stop at the figure stumbling down the hallway. His hair is matted to his forehead and his trousers have been torn at the thigh and knee. His lips move, as if he's determined to pass us a message, but then his concentration diverts to the hand seeking support from the cream-colored wall.

Big shoulders tremble.

Another halted step in our direction.

Those strong legs go visibly weak, and he reaches out a hand to claim support again—only to find that none awaits him this time.

Gravity pulls him down and his knees hit the ground.

"Christ," whispers Saxon.

Rowena releases a short gasp. Skirting around my brother, she rushes forward to the man who shoved me from the Palace's roof just weeks ago. Her knees collapse to the space beside him, her hands already moving to keep his body upright. But when she presses a palm to his chest, her skin comes away with a print of blood. Slowly, with her hand raised, she turns back to me with horror glittering in her violet eyes. My name is a shuddered exhale off her lips.

Heart racing, I storm forward.

"Where is she?" Grasping him by the bloodied fabric of his shirt, I pull him back onto his knees. When he doesn't answer, I demand again, "Gregory, *where is she?*"

Blood beads from the corner of his mouth.

All the color leeches from his skin as the wristwatch I lent him slips from his grip to clatter onto the floor. His weight teeters backward and his hands go to his right side, fingers scraping at the fabric. It inches upward. My eyes snap down—and my stomach twists and grows heavy at the ravaged skin. A knife. He was meant to be watching Margaret, and Gregory—a bastard taller than even me—proved that he is not indestructible.

A single word leaves my tongue: "*Who?*"

And then, to the backdrop of Carrigan's low, maniacal laughter, Gregory lifts his gaze to mine and confesses on a hoarse whisper:

"'e took her, Priest. Your bastard brother kidnapped the queen."

TO BE CONTINUED…

A New King is coming Spring 2021!
Don't miss the epic conclusion to the Broken Crown series,
featuring Guy and Margaret.

Need to talk all things Sound of Madness?
Come find the Spoiler Group on Facebook or join my reader
group Book Boyfriends Anonymous.

And before you go!
Are you not ready to leave the *Broken Crown* world just yet?
I've written a short story prequel about the first Godwin who
saved Prince Robert, back in the Second Boer War. You can
find *An Oath To Take* on my website to download for free!

Dear Fabulous Reader

Hi there! I so hope you enjoyed *Sound of Madness*, and if you are new to my books, welcome to the family!

In the back of all my books, I love to include a Dear Fabulous Reader section that talks about which locations from the book can be visited in real life or what sparked my inspiration for a particular plot point. (I like to think of it as the Extras on DVD's, LOL).

As always, we'll hit it up bullet-point style—enjoy!

There are so many aspects of *Sound of Madness* captured from reality that it seems easier to start with something that is entirely fictional—Damien's poisoning! Alas, Baron Hastings does not exist and CL-152 can't be found in the world. Then again, this might be a good thing, LOL. Since I've always been fascinated with the sci-fi genre creating whole subplots around medicine impacting the life or death of a character (like in the *Matrix!*), I couldn't resist dipping my toes into the water, especially because . . .

- Rowena's experience with transient post-traumatic cortical blindness is very much based on a true case study—in fact, I used it in the book during that first scene with Dr. Matthews! Like Rowena, the patient's blindness occurred quite suddenly, after falling six stories. Also like Rowena, her vision returned entirely on its own days later. Unlike Rowena, however, the patient remained in critical care during her recovery so that she could be watched by doctors. For the sake of the plot, I sent Rowena out into the world. You can read the case study here, if you're interested.

- Did Damien's Old Norse tattoo catch your interest? I've always been a little obsessed with mythology, and when I saw the cover model's tattoos, I allowed my fantasies to spin to a very nerdy bent. While I used the English translation for Damien's ink about Odin's ravens, Huginn and Muninn, the *Anonymous Verse in the Third Grammatical Treatise* (Tarrin Wills) features the original version and discusses how the origin of the poem is unknown—though it began to appear around 1,000 A.D..

○ *Many* of the locations that I referenced in *Sound of Madness* can be visited. In no specific order, here are some of the lesser known places:

○ **Holly Village, North London:** Holly Village just may be my new favorite addition to the Broken Crown landscape. Completed in 1865, this Gothic-inspired estate actually boasts multiple properties for the Baroness Angela Burdett-Coutts, who was one of the richest women in England—second only to Queen Victoria! She was also good friends with Charles Dickens. While I took many liberties (the undercroft/chapel, medical room, and greenhouse), it seemed only fitting that Rowena make her home in a place that is both stately and regal. Today, these properties are leased to various tenants but you can still drive by Swain's Lane to catch a peek through the sycamore trees! P.S., there is no Palladian temple on site but hello creative liberties!

○ **The Jewel Tower, London:** Have I mentioned that I'm a total nerd? I loved the idea of Edward Carrigan being holed up in this building that *looks* like a fortress but was always just used for storage—jewelry, documents, the whole shebang. Architecturally, it's pretty fabulous. The iron door from the 17th century is real, as are the original vaulted ceilings. Plus, with its close proximity to Westminster, we know that the prime minister would be able to store his most valuable documents here without breaking too much of a sweat.

- **Broadmoor Hospital, Crowthorne, England:** When I first mentioned (in *Road To Fire)* that Robert Guthram had been stuck in an insane asylum for ten years, I never picked a location. And if I'm being *completely* honest, I chose Broadmoor—at first—because I used to live in New Orleans' Broadmoor neighborhood and it seemed like an ironic twist of fate. With that said, there's no better fit. Opened in 1863, Broadmoor Hospital has a storied past. It was used as a POW camp during World War I, has housed some of the country's most infamous serial killers over the years, and for many decades was particularly known for running a two-tone alarm system (inspired by the sirens during air raids) every Monday morning at 10 a.m. It was all too easy to allow my imagination to run wild while Damien & Rowena tried to save themselves.

- **The Bascule Chambers, London:** When sketching out this section of Damien & Rowena's journey, I really wanted to place the scene in a location that was as close to the "Underworld" as you might find in London. The air needed to be so damp that it felt oppressive while the darkness became a thick blanket that you had no hope of escaping. The Bascule Chambers are a functioning part of Tower Bridge—to me, it felt like the perfect spot for chaos to ensue. I highly recommend a tour on your next trip to London—you might even catch a concert there!

- **Honorable Mentions:** Dunrobin Castle, 3 Ryder Street, London (you can visit some beautiful galleries next door), Palace of Westminster, and the White Cliffs of Dover.

- **We'll Miss You Mentions:** Buckingham Palace, The Bell & Hand (aka The Bell In Hand, located in Boston,

Mass.), and Ightham Mote. Man, we had some major architectural casualties in this book! R.I.P.

As always, there are many more behind-the-scenes inspiration tidbits, but here is just a sampling! If you're thinking . . . that seems rather fascinating and I want to know more, you are always so welcome to reach out! Pretty much, nothing makes me happier =)

Much love,
Maria

ALSO BY MARIA LUIS

NOLA HEART
Say You'll Be Mine
Take A Chance On Me
Dare You To Love Me
Tempt Me With Forever

BLADES HOCKEY
Power Play
Sin Bin
Hat Trick
Body Check

BLOOD DUET
Sworn
Defied

PUT A RING ON IT
Hold Me Today
Kiss Me Tonight
Love Me Tomorrow

BROKEN CROWN
Road To Fire
Sound of Madness
A New King (coming Spring 2021)

FREEBIES
(AVAILABLE AT WWW.MARIALUIS.ORG)
Breathless (a Love Serial, #1)
Undeniable (a Love Serial, #2)
The First Fix
Kissing the Gentleman
(Put A Ring On It, #4: A Short Story)

MARIA LUIS is the author of sexy contemporary romances.

Historian by day and romance novelist by night, Maria lives in New Orleans, and loves bringing the city's cultural flair into her books. When Maria isn't frantically typing with coffee in hand, she can be found binging on reality TV, going on adventures with her other half and two pups, or plotting her next flirty romance.

STALK MARIA IN THE WILD
AT THE FOLLOWING!

Join Maria's Newsletter
Join Maria's Facebook Reader Group